WELCOME TO
HARROW HALL

A NOVEL BY

KEVIN FLANDERS

For Jaime,
Thanks so much
for your
support!

KEVIN FLANDERS

ACKNOWLEDGEMENTS

The tremendous efforts of the following individuals, as well as the constant support of readers, helped bring the magic – and the terror – to Harrow Hall.

Brian Allenberg
Michael Flanders
Susana Flanders
Ed Londergan
Cheryl Malandrinos
Brandi McCann
Kimmy Palmucci
Olivia Richman

ALSO FROM KEVIN FLANDERS

Please check out the following novels to be released by the author in 2016.

BURN, DO NOT READ!
Jan. 2016

INSIDE THE ORANGE GLOW
Feb. 2016

LASER TAG
Feb. 2016

THE INHABITANTS (trilogy)
Mar.-Apr. 2016

GRIDLOCKED
Apr. 2016

For more information about upcoming works, visit
www.kmflanders.wordpress.com.

WELCOME TO HARROW HALL

Prologue

He arrived at the bar beside Jerome Hudson with the swift, sinister silence of a wisp of smoke, his very presence telling of a recent fire.

A deadly fire.

Death radiated from the stranger, as easily detectable as his thick cologne. After four years in Vietnam, Jerome could identify the odious stench better than the Reaper – and this man was practically dripping with it, an ungodly depth of darkness lurking beyond two shifty coals that smoldered beneath the brim of a top hat.

It was getting late, and undoubtedly this man had come for deeds of malice.

Jerome, building with nausea and apprehension, wondered if his drunkenness was causing these impressions of evil and imminent death. He'd always been a speculative drunk, the world and its people seeming far different following a few sessions in the well, as if their masks and robes of pretense sloughed away to reveal the true compositions beneath.

But no, this couldn't be the whiskey talking. Whiskey had never before conjured the rotten stench of death.

The stranger who'd drifted beside Jerome, black-clad and enigmatic, ordered a bourbon, "straight up, good sir." Apropos, considering this was New Orleans and Friday night had finally slid over the Big Easy. Jerome was at his usual post at the end of the Canal Nine Tavern bar – scratching his jagged nails into the burnished wood and letting the whiskey and the music warm him – while old McGreevy, white apron bulging as though he were deeply pregnant, filled the magic potions and kept the patrons refreshed.

Bringing the bourbon to his lips, the man sniffed at the drink suspiciously. With a sidelong glance at Jerome, he set the drink down, removed a pipette from the pocket of his black vest, and dipped it into the glass, drawing a small amount of liquid and quickly pocketing the pipette. McGreevy, busy with another customer, didn't see this oddness, but Jerome watched with strengthening dread. This man was a fiend, he sensed. Undiluted evil. He gave Jerome the shivers – his softly glimmering eyes, his actions, his odor of death and devastation, even the way he spoke, gravelly and expectant.

Enough of this. Gulping down the last of his whiskey and then settling up for the night with McGreevy, leaving a generous tip as always, Jerome was about to find a new bar when the stranger very slowly turned in his direction. The brim of his hat had been nudged down even lower, shadowing his eyes. He was tall nearly to a daunting extent, with thick facial stubble and curls of long, scraggly black hair escaping his hat. He wasn't old but wasn't young, either, traveling the back roads of some intermediate and forgettable age. His face was scarred and sandpapery, worn by the years and now confined in shadows.

"Would you like to hear a story, lad?" the man said to Jerome in a new voice, as soft and foreboding as the headwinds of a storm. He removed his hat, grinning with unnaturally white, almost sparkling teeth, his hair tumbling free.

In that moment, half-paralyzed, Jerome feared this man was the Devil. At the very least, he was an inhabitant of Hell who'd risen for a brief sojourn, unleashed with orders of death and ruination. Even intoxicated, Jerome *knew* one of these alternatives to be true as instinctively as he knew rain would come when a certain scent swept in off the ocean and eased through his lonely bedroom window some nights.

"I ain't wanna hear nothin you gotta say, man," Jerome rebuffed, nodding goodnight to McGreevy and taking a moment to balance himself on wobbly legs. This was the weird time, as he called it, that dizzy, occasionally vertiginous moment that saw him stumbling and grasping for anything that might support him. Sometimes people asked if he'd like them to call a taxi, but he always waved them off, mumbling that he would walk.

Jerome Hudson always walked. He'd walked since he was a boy hiking fifteen blocks to school; he'd walked to the United States Army recruiting office as a teenager; he'd walked from the courtroom with tear-blurred eyes the day the drunk driver who'd killed his wife got off with a light sentence; and he'd walked from the hospital that rainy morning the doctors told him there was nothing they could do about his daughter's breast cancer, feeling very much like his legs would give out.

And walk he did right out of Canal Nine Tavern tonight, the earliest he'd left the place on a Friday night in years.

But the stranger followed him, the oppressive stench of death trailing Jerome through the doors and onto the sidewalk. "Don't you want to hear my story?" the man called from behind Jerome with that whispery, windy voice, the voice of the approaching storm, barely audible above the fine drumming of a sidewalk man.

Jerome said nothing. *Just keep walking. He's coming for you. That's the Devil back there, and he's coming for you,* he told himself, staring straight ahead, yes he did, straight ahead at the rain-slicked road and the sea of headlights and taillights, endless whites and reds, trying to ignore the Devil at his back, hollow, clunking footsteps creeping a little closer and a little closer still, carrying with them the faint screams of dying soldiers.

Beginning to panic, Jerome hurried down the sidewalk and stumbled past a young couple heading the other way, then a Hispanic man with a glowing iPod, then a man in a suit with a cell phone pressed against his ear, just a bunch of people in the night, unaware that they might be within arm's reach of Satan himself.

Still refusing to look back, growing obsessed that he was being targeted because of the many sins he'd accrued, Jerome ratcheted up his pace, darting across streets and ruining for himself what was usually a peaceful, contemplative walk. On summer nights like this, he would leisurely walk all the way back to his home in the Lower Ninth Ward, sometimes not reaching his stoop for hours, just walking off the whiskey and taking in the night. There was peace out here on the streets, with the sidewalk men playing their tunes and the streetcars clanging by and the college kids gamboling from bar to bar, fresh with the aspirations of youth. The streets were alive with color and spirit and music, infused with history, and graced by good people always willing to help a stranger – and not just during Mardi Gras. New Orleans was an ebullient town year-round, and if not for the energy its streets and neighborhoods inspired in him, Jerome knew he'd be six feet under by now.

Tonight, though, the streets were made menacing by those hollow footsteps that continued to pursue him. No matter how fast Jerome went, the Devil closed down the space, gaining and gaining and gaining, except the stranger's footsteps remained casual, unhurried.

Finally, Jerome told himself enough of all this. He wouldn't flee any longer. He was a United States soldier, proud and true. If the Devil had found him, he would answer for his sins right here this night. He'd known this meeting would eventually come – foreseeing it in his strangest nightmares – and perhaps now it was time to claim his deserved place in Hell, his number finally called at the deli line of eternal fire.

"Whatchou want, man?" Jerome said, spinning in confrontation, but although the footsteps had been directly behind him, the man responded from the other side of the street, waving to Jerome like an old friend from the opposite sidewalk.

"Come on now, mister, and hear my story!" he shouted.

Crumbling with fear, Jerome nonetheless found a space between the passing vehicles and crossed the street, knowing this marrow-chilling dance would last all night if he didn't face the darkness and embrace his fate.

Joining his pursuer on the suddenly empty sidewalk, Jerome said, "Why you botherin me, man?" He searched the stranger's face and found nothing but inscrutable shadows.

There was a dim alley behind them, the clattering of garbage cans storming up from its depths. Tipping his hat, the man pointed to the alley. "Let us find a quiet place, shall we?"

Jerome shook his head. "Hell, no, buddy! I ain't lettin you knife me in no alley. How dumb you think I am, boy?" He wanted to sprint away, but somehow he knew the man would find him anywhere. There'd be no sleep if he didn't end this right here, every predawn creaking floorboard to be construed as Death's approaching footsteps, every shadow cast on the walls and ceilings by passing headlights to be interpreted as Death's flapping cloak.

I have sinned. Time to pay up.

The man broke into a scratchy song, whispering more than singing the opening lyrics. "There is. A house. In New Or-lean-s." He waited, grinning at Jerome. Then: "They call the ri-sing sun," he said with little more enthusiasm than that of a gentle breeze.

Listening to the man's whisper-song, Jerome's legs might as well have been cemented in place. He felt heavy, lethargic, steadily mesmerized by each word. No one passed them, no people, no vehicles, nothing. If Jerome were to glance down the road at the traffic signals, they'd probably be frozen on their current color. It was as if the city stood still for them, suspended until the Devil's job was done.

By the time the man finished "House of the Rising Sun" – motioning for Jerome to enter the alley for much of the effort – they were indeed proceeding into the alley, Jerome's feet carried by an invisible conveyor. As if leading an orchestra, the man waved his hands above his head with a flourish and fluttered his fingers. Head tilted to the moon, eyes probably blazing with malevolent intentions, he slowly turned to Jerome.

"Ah, the Night Spirits have arrived," he said, inhaling deeply. "Can you feel them, mister?" A chilly wind whisked down the alley, far too cool for this time of year. Jerome shivered. In the distance, the loud clattering abruptly ceased, footsteps scampering off. "You know," the man said, "they're the ones who led me to you."

"Who led you?"

"The Night Spirits," he blurted impatiently. "Who else?"

"What's all this about me hearin your story?"

The man's lips curved into a smile. They were standing five feet apart, Jerome backed up against the side of a brick building. "It's actually your story that interests me," the man said. "My story, at least for this night, surrounds your story."

Lit by the emerging moon and the faint glow of lights from the street that seeped into the alley, the man's face took on a particularly spectral quality, his eyes still obscured by the low brim of his hat. Jerome knew he was toying with him, a cat playing with his mouse, but there was nothing he could do. Nowhere he could go. Above all else, a feeling of complete helplessness overcame him. He'd known this would happen, though, and now he would face the Devil's music, beginning with "House of the Rising Sun." He'd heard that song countless times, but never had it given him the shakes like tonight.

"If you're here to kill me, then just go on and get it done with already," Jerome challenged, eliciting a wheezing whisper of laughter from the man, who squatted down and pressed his palm against the wet blacktop. He waited, returning his gaze to the moon, then jolted up and licked his fingers.

"My story and your story are crossing, Jerome. Can't you feel it?" He regarded the buildings with outstretched arms, then extended a hand to Jerome. "The name's Harrow. Pleasure to make your acquaintance, sir."

Jerome kept his arm down. "How'd you know my name?"

"Hah!" The man waved a dismissive hand. "I know everything. The Night Spirits, they tell me all. Do you want to know what they told me when I stepped into that tavern?" He waited briefly for a response. When Jerome said nothing, listening to distant sirens and tooting horns, Harrow added, "The Spirits told me about that man you killed, Jerome. Not the ones in the war – the man upon American soil whose life you claimed."

There was a moment of breathlessness, as if Jerome had been punched hard in the gut. This was really happening. It wasn't the whiskey – the Devil had finally found him. He'd be dragged off to Hell tonight, subjected to the infernal fires Mama had always warned about. Tears stung his eyes, tears of guilt and sorrow and fear, for in the end his ardent repentance had carried the weight of feathers.

Only during the war had terror seized Jerome with such an iron fist. "What are you, some kind of…d…demon?" he sputtered.

Again Harrow laughed with the strained whispers of a dying man. His voice was smooth, but his laughter betrayed the festering abscess beneath. "I'm but a messenger of the night for now, Jerome, but I grow stronger by the hour. With you and others at my side, I will *rule* the night!" His eyes widened with ambitious fire.

Jerome shook his head violently. In his gut, the whiskey was roiling like an angry sea, the smell of death escaping this man almost too much to take. "No, sir, I will not stand by your side!" Jerome refused, shaking a finger. "If you ain't here to take me off this Earth, then I'll be on my way now."

Jerome started toward the street, but the man shouted, "Wait! Don't go so soon! You haven't even heard my offer, a very generous one at that."

"Whatchou talkin bout?"

The man going by Harrow stepped a little closer, moving with the hesitancy of someone hoping to pacify a furious dog. "I'm talking about *immortality*, Jerome." He removed his hat and spun it on a finger. "How would you like to live forever like me? It sure bests the torments that await you following the last breath. We both know what you've done, sir, and the Spirits say your day of reckoning's just over a month away."

A burst of cold finessed its way through Jerome, like a shot of something from the freezer. "Day of reckonin?"

Nodding solemnly, Harrow pulled a pack of cigarettes from his back pocket. "Spirits say a nasty gal named Kat's due to visit the Crescent City soon, and she'll take everything you've got and then take you."

He offered Jerome a cigarette. Jerome declined – he'd never been one for smoking, not when the drinks fulfilled just fine. Tonight, even the smell of smoke made him nauseous, especially when combined with the oppressively pungent odor of death.

Blowing out a thick puff, Harrow warned, "This is your only chance, Jerome. When Kat comes, there's nothing I can do for you. I'll be well north by then, assembling my army in every city along the mighty Mississippi. Join me, Jerome, and you won't regret it. Join my cause!" His tone had become overly beseeching, almost desperate. "With the strength I'm gaining, it won't be long before I own the night, but I need an army to stand with me. Those who dare to oppose us – we'll kill them, Jerome. You know what it's like to end lives. Together we'll end countless lives! We'll exist forever! Soon there'll only be night, Jerome!"

"Screw you, buddy!" Jerome shouted, and turned from the man – or the Devil, or whatever Harrow was – running back toward the street.

"You're making a terrible mistake!" Harrow called after him, his voice brimming with rage. "Don't you want to live forever? You'll be forsaken, boy! When your soul is burning, I'll send not a drop of rain to extinguish the flames!"

Jerome covered his ears, blocking out the madman and his own guilty thoughts alike, running, running, the lights and traffic blending together. Finally he stopped and puked on the sidewalk, his side aching sharply. With the darting eyes of a hunted animal, he searched the street, listening for the familiar hollow of Harrow's steps. But he was no longer being followed, no, not anymore. The Devil's offer had been made and turned down. Jerome had gotten out alive, and now he was left dazed and rattled and disoriented. The whiskey didn't help a touch. No, the turmoil in his gut only worsened matters in his head.

What was that? Who was that? How did he know my name? How did he find me? If he was the Devil, how am I still alive?

The questions were endless. What had begun as a chill down his chest was now a full-body freeze in the middle of summer! The things Harrow had said and the way he'd said them made Jerome long for the safety of home. Locked doors. A warm bed. A deep, leaden sleep devoid of dreams.

He resumed a staggering, nauseous run, glancing frequently over his shoulder. Streets that had always comforted him suddenly felt as threatening as the jungles of Nam. Every vehicle seemed suspicious, every passing person somehow dangerous. He knew he was being paranoid. He knew that alcohol was working dark magic on him. But he couldn't stop himself, couldn't turn off his mind.

Finally Jerome reached his front stoop, the evening rain having caused the street to glisten beneath orange lamps. Through the windows of houses down the line, colorful splashes poured out from televisions. A car passed slowly by, filling Jerome with dread. He half-expected Harrow to jump out and storm the house.

Shivering and shaky, he unlocked the front door and scrambled inside, securing both the deadbolt and the chain behind him. At last he was home, safe, alone.

Lying in bed that night, paying no attention to the muted late show, the faces of family peering down at him from pictures, Jerome thought hazily back to his exchange with Harrow. He'd suggested that a woman named Kat would take his life, but Jerome didn't know anyone by that name.

Who the hell is Kat?

Jerome searched his whiskey-fogged mind but found only the desire for sleep, his eyes growing too heavy to lift. Morning would come, he told himself, and the magic would wear off, and this nightmare would be just that, a thing that couldn't harm him anymore.

But when he woke with a start at seven a.m., emerging from an abstruse nightmare, he was shouting a single word, repeating it over and over and over. "Help!"

WELCOME TO HARROW HALL

Part I: A Building Storm

Chapter 1

His magic was no longer confined to the night bayou, its conquests seemingly unrelated. Even the most determined of investigators couldn't have traced its course, not a thread-thin tangential line of supposition to connect the ostensibly sleepwalking girl whose tongue dripped blood between her teeth and the teenager admitted to the hospital with a handful of spiders in his stomach and, many miles north, the beloved eighty-year-old woman who smilingly offered the neighborhood kids a plate of sprinkled chocolate cookies concealing shards of glass.

These were the snapshots that marked his journey – fine souvenirs of memory for him to savor as he followed the great river like many had done before him, pushing slowly northward and gathering assets he would need when he finally found a new home. His old home had served its purpose admirably, but there'd been no room for growth. Like a young soul graduating from a crib, he needed to embrace a new environment, one that would support his strengthening power. He didn't know where his new home would be, but the Spirits would undoubtedly guide him to it.

Until then, he tracked the river north, arriving in a new community each night and extracting from it specific supplies. Of late, he'd been collecting souls – the most important of supplies. Last night, in Memphis, outside a raucous biker bar pulsing with loud music and jollity, he'd discovered another useful soul, faithless and hopeless, easy to conscript into the night's army. Tonight he found himself in a new place, a small Tennessee town tucked quietly away in the broom closet of the country, its center comprised of a single row of buildings. There was a flashing yellow traffic signal a ways down the road, alerting drivers to an intersection with another sparsely traveled road – a pointless thing, really. Beyond the immediate hub of lights, darkness fanned out gloriously across a deeply wooded stretch.

Grinning, lighting a new cigarette, deciding after a brief contemplation to leave the old couple holding hands on the bench at peace, Harrow ambled into town along the crumbling, weedy sidewalk, just another nameless face in the night, passing Al's Antiques and Riverline Diner and House of Pizza, until he finally came to a cheerless three-story building at the corner of Main and River Streets. A mixed use property, the ground floor was occupied by multiple businesses – a barbershop, a sandwich shop, and a lawyer's office, among others – while the upper floors were rented out as apartment units.

Harrow was concerned with the residential facet of the building, specifically one of its tenants. He did not require the services of his army, not this time, and so his newly conscripted soldiers waited for him in the night woods.

Dimly lit, the third floor corridor was redolent with smoke. The air was hazy. Scanning each door as he passed, searching for a specific number, Harrow lit another cigarette and contributed to the ambience. Down the hall, a door clicked open, two grungy children spilling out, a boy and a girl dressed in shorts and T-shirts. They looked warily at Harrow as they scampered past him, a reaction to which he'd grown accustomed. Regardless of where he visited, people were always innately afraid of him. Perhaps they could sense his mastery of Maleficium. After nearly two hundred years of education, beginning with his first divination in the bayou with his father, he'd become an expert in necromancy and other specialties, the Spirits his faithful guides.

Tonight the Spirits told him to find apartment 322 at this address. There he would discover the next recruit, a faithless old woman with strong lines of magic in her family. Such was a commonality among each of Harrow's soldiers, their veins coursing with the blood of sorcerers and prophets and diviners. Together, with their combined powers and those of the Spirits, they would soon rule all, the most well-prepared, ruthless army ever known…with Harrow as its leader.

Finally it was time for darkness to dominate.

WELCOME TO HARROW HALL

At the end of the hall, Harrow arrived outside apartment 322, staring at the golden numbers for a few moments before rapping on the door. When no one answered, he spoke a few useful words, stepped shruggingly through the now inviting door, and familiarized himself with a snug, orderly interior. Candlelit, suffused with incense, flickering with shadows, it was like entering a place from the past. Harrow's father had taken him to countless similar venues for his lessons, each destination boasting its own unique charm. There was usually music – a maudlin instrumental, in most cases – though tonight there was silence but for the spattering of water beyond the closed bathroom door.

With a snap, Harrow commanded brighter lights and studied the three-room spread. In the bedroom, he found more candles upon a nightstand and bookshelf. On the shelves were several works from authors Harrow recognized – charlatans, all of them! They knew nothing of Maleficium, knew nothing of the endless preparations and sacrifices required to earn true power. To them, magic was learned deception, no more powerful than one's ability to distract and mislead. Cards up sleeves and trapdoors and secret compartments – that wasn't magic but foolishness. The real power they couldn't envisage in drunken dreams. They'd never raised a spirit. They'd never seen fog swirl from amorphousness to shape. They'd never heard the screams of souls relegated back to the depths of darkness. If they'd truly known the opportunities that existed, they wouldn't be writing books. No, Harrow could be certain of that.

The water ceased its fulsome spattering, and slowly the bathroom door came open. There were footsteps in the main room, then a toweled old woman in the bedroom, gasping in surprise, of course.

Harrow shook his head, still disappointed. "May I ask where within these walls the fine music hides, madame? A woman of your age, I was expecting a lovely record to be spinning at such an hour. Has all sense of refinement truly been lost?"

The woman brought an arm across her chest. "Who are you? Get out of my apartment! I'll call the police!"

Harrow sighed. "It's so hard these days to find someone with an appreciation for a good record. I must admit, I was hoping for Vivaldi or Bach tonight, though I would have settled for Mozart or Liszt, I suppose. My, how I love *The Four Seasons* – reminds me of the fine dances I used to attend in the French Quarter."

The woman's face had grown as white as her hair. "Get out!" she shrieked.

Harrow took a few steps toward her, the woman flinching. "Ah, but you see," he said, "a faithless woman has no power to make orders. You who believes in nothing – there is no hope of resistance for you. My army is waiting."

Desperation flashing in her eyes, the woman began reciting a few words of Maleficium, its language fluent to Harrow. His father had first introduced it to him in their bayou cabin centuries ago, and with his utterances the Night Spirits had risen like steam from the water and swept down from the Trees of Sagacity. Hissing like cornered cottonmouths, they'd circled themselves into form, surrounding Harrow and his father, invoked by an ancient recitation that included a few of the words this old woman now shouted in panic.

Harrow couldn't stifle a laugh. Of all the soldiers he'd recruited and the tremendous power of their ancestors, this woman was the first among them to possess even a cursory knowledge of Maleficium. These people had magic in their blood, all of them, but none knew how to properly harness it, much like the pathetic descendants of Samurai and Viking warriors who knew nothing of combat. Without the proper guidance and transference of tradition, even the most robust lineages were helpless against dilution.

Indeed, men once hunted and now shopped at grocery stores, the same gradual trend of destruction reserved for magic as well. Alas, blood cannot teach.

Harrow said, "You were introduced to the Night Conjuring many years ago, I see."

Backed against the far wall beside the bed, arms crossed over her chest, the woman knew escape was impossible. Like observing an object through a window, Harrow could see the hopelessness in her eyes. He'd seen these same sparks of dread last night, and the night before that, and so forth.

"Even if you'd remembered the correct sequence of words, you never would have been able to conjure the Night Spirits," Harrow continued, drifting a little closer with each word. "Only myself do the Spirits assist, madame, no one else. I've made the unbreakable covenant, you see. He has told me to raise an army, and so I follow the river, claiming new souls each night."

There was a brief twinkle of realization in the woman's eyes, as fleeting as a peripheral shadow.

"Mama said the Devil would find me," she whispered, her words not directed at Harrow but turned inward like an implement of suicide. Clearly she'd long doubted her mother's warnings – perhaps she'd even banished her mother from her life – but now the truth of prophecy had found her. In spite of her detachment from the power of her ancestors, she could still be trained to use the rusted tools within. As one of Harrow's soldiers, she would accept the gifts she'd either ignored or refused her entire life.

"You stay back!" she warned as Harrow drew nearer, eyeing the door.

But with a single word and a snap of his finger, every dancing flame in the room turned to smoke and her eyes lifted to his. "It is time, madame," he said, and extended his hand.

The woman's eyes glossed over, a routine sight. Conscription was involuntary for the faithless, their lives instantly torn from the light of normality and immersed in the darkness of slavery.

Suddenly Harrow knew this woman's story, words whispered in his ears by the Spirits.

"Such is the price of your ancestors' failure," Harrow explained. "You will pay for their weakness, I'm afraid. They thought they could shelter you by keeping you ignorant, but when destiny talks, we all must listen. A new day has finally come, madame, a day that will see you channel the powers previously kept from you. In time, your price will be recompensed in full."

Spellbound, the woman reached for Harrow's hand, another soldier conscripted. By this time tomorrow, the police would be investigating another missing person, the list steadily growing with Harrow's northward progression.

Chapter 2

Having resided in two houses for the majority of his life, both in the Lower Ninth Ward, Jerome had always thought he'd remain rooted in the neighborhood that defined him. During his service with the Army and subsequent travels throughout the country, he'd seen a lot of places and interacted with a lot of people, but in no place but the Lower Ninth did he experience an overwhelming sense of belonging. From Florida Avenue to Douglas Street, from Fats Domino House to Jackson Barracks (and every corner in between), the neighborhood and its residents embraced him like a brother. Hard-working, loyal, and dependable, Jerome's personality reflected that of his neighborhood, and he'd known he couldn't live anywhere else, even after personal tragedies had leveled him and a fresh start seemed inevitable.

The neighborhood had its problems, of course, but there were crimes and problems in every city in America. The people of the Lower Ninth weren't rich, but Jerome knew a few rich folks and he didn't like them very much. Far more important to Jerome than money was reliability, and he would entrust his friends and neighbors with his life. The neighborhood had his back, and vice versa. When he went to his good friend Calvin Baker's barbershop on Saturdays, the guys always seemed to pick up where the last story had left off. When Mrs. Dawson needed assistance with something across the street, Jerome was eager to help out and give her a few less items to worry about. And when someone in the neighborhood endured a tragedy as Jerome had, residents rallied together to offer support and comfort.

Outsiders would invariably focus on the negativity – crime, poverty, drug addiction – but they would never know the solidarity of this community. They would never feel the love that warmed its churches. They would never see the lifelong friendships built on a basketball court, friendships so strong that it didn't matter if you were gone ten days or ten years; everyone was welcomed back home. The Lower Ninth family would always be there for each other, inextricably connected, a blessing Jerome had known he could count on since walking these streets as a kid.

Most important, he'd discovered, when life hit people hard, the neighborhood grabbed them by the arms and pulled them up. Jerome had been helped back to his feet twice by the Lower Ninth family, relying heavily on his friends and neighbors following the deaths of his wife and daughter, which had occurred just over a year apart almost a decade earlier. Calvin Baker had been especially helpful, sometimes talking to Jerome for hours after closing up shop, his endless stories about Fats Domino and Little Richard dashing a few sprinkles of comfort into the depths of misery that ruled Jerome's heart.

That had been a dark time in his life destined to grow even darker three years later, impossibly dark, so disastrous that even Calvin hadn't been able to help him, exacerbated by the rumors of a rainy night. Jerome had been at Canal Nine, watching McGreevy slide drinks across the bar, when the rumors reached him. Half loaded with whiskey, a companion almost as comforting as Calvin, Jerome would never be able to recall the source of rumors accusing the drunk driver who'd killed Elise of continuing to drive under the influence, even after benefiting from a light sentence. With a clean record, a deep wallet, and a good lawyer, he'd only done two years and probation – and when the rumors were corroborated by another source later that month, Jerome had found himself compelled to confront...

...*Boy, seven years feels more like seven seconds.*

"Yo, Jerome, you sleepin on us or what?"

Torn from haunting memories, Jerome lifted his head and glanced at the mirror, meeting Calvin Baker's impatient stare.

"Sorry, Cal. Long night, that's all."

"You ain't too much for talk today, Jerry," piped Jackie Nelson from the corner of the shop, a newspaper folded across his lap. Since when had they all turned into old men, Jerome wondered.

"Why you gotta go to that stupid place all the time, anyway?" Calvin said, referring to Canal Nine as he evened Jerome's sideburns. "You know you ain't gonna find no positivity in a bar."

Jerome shrugged, trying to force the last remnants of recollection from his mind. If only Harrow had finished him last night, he might finally be free of the guilt that had laid eggs inside him the night he'd killed that drunk driver and kept on proliferating, every day, merciless, never relenting. There was no escape. Although Jerome had tried to ignore God these last ten years, he was still too spiritual to kill himself and too damn stubborn to die. His friends and neighbors and the city itself seemed to sustain him, but soon he would leave his home and the Lower Ninth Ward would be underwater.

Jerome did not know this as the sun shined without a cloud to block it on a hot Saturday afternoon in July, but somehow he sensed a major change coming, sensed it even as he sat in Calvin's chair, wrapped in a black apron, staring at the mirror while his friend shaved his sideburns to precise symmetry.

Jerome didn't know – couldn't have known – that Calvin Baker would be killed in just over a month, swept away when the levees failed and never seen again. He didn't know that Jackie Nelson would commit suicide following the storm, his life shattered by the deaths of his sons. He didn't know that another of his decades-long friends, Latroy James – currently relieving himself in the bathroom – would be left forgotten and destitute by the government he'd served for ten years, left to pick up the pieces of his life by himself, until he was eventually murdered outside a Houston, TX, homeless shelter many years later. He didn't know that the eyes of the nation would settle pityingly upon the Lower Ninth Ward, images of the streets he knew by heart flashed across every television as clueless reporters spewed out erroneous information.

Jerome knew none of the details. He only knew that dramatic change was coming – since last night, even the air had grown heavy with the promise of it. Now he became easily unsettled, goosebumps constantly rising on his arms. His shoulders tingled with something unpleasant. Harrow's words echoed in his head.

A nasty gal named Kat's due to visit the Crescent City soon, and she'll take everything you've got and then take you.

"You oughta resolve to steer right clear of that bar," Calvin insisted, checking the length of Jerome's sideburns with a comb. "Else you turn into one of those damn drunks you see pissin in the streets."

Jerome chuckled. "I think it's a few years too late for that." In the corner, Jackie let out a little laugh as well, shaking his head as he flipped through the newspaper. This was their time, their place, their tradition – a tradition soon to end, but they didn't know it.

"Never too late to change, man," Calvin said. "That's what my daddy always told my brothers and me." He was pointing the buzzer at the mirror and eyeing Jerome like a reproachful parent.

"I don't know if I wanna go back there for a while, anyhow, not after last night," Jerome said. He'd been contemplating telling his friends about Harrow all day, and finally the weight had grown too heavy to handle by himself. He had to get the ordeal off his chest.

By the time Jerome finished his story several minutes later, his friends shared an expression of bewilderment. Jackie, who'd gotten interested and wandered over from the corner, then grabbed a new seat two chairs down, was furrowing his white eyebrows and rubbing his chin. Latroy, who'd emerged from the bathroom halfway through the story, seemed eager to say something but remained silent.

"You should have beaten his freaky ass," Calvin finally said, the others nodding in assent. "You goin awfully soft on us these days, Jerry. The old boy I knew would've given him a poundin right quick."

Jerome shook his head. "Naw, not this guy. I didn't even want to touch him. I just got this bad vibe…a real bad vibe."

"Come on, he wasn't no devil or nothin," Latroy said. "That was just the whiskey, Jerry. You gotta take it easy on that stuff, man, or everyone's gonna start freakin yo ass out."

"What do you think he meant about Kat?" Jackie added. "Jerry don't know nobody named Kat, do you, Jerry?"

Jerome shook his head.

"Probably just messin with you, buddy," Latroy guessed, but Jerome couldn't resist thoughts that Harrow's words had somehow been prophetic. He remembered his father, a street magician for thirty years, and how he'd always spoken of prophecies.

Jerome Hudson, Sr., had made solid money working the streets and at local establishments – collecting upwards of fifty thousand dollars a year and earning a reputation as a legitimate "magic man" – but he'd refused to teach Jerome any tricks.

There's a dark side of magic you want no part of, Pops had always said. *It can bring much fun and joy, but the darkness is always around, waiting for someone to get greedy or misuse their powers.* He'd even likened magic to nuclear power, describing it as beneficial if used properly but potentially catastrophic if abused. *Some people use magic to do the Devil's work,* he'd said on more than a few occasions. *If one of them gets too strong, I fear the results.*

Thankfully, another patron walked into the shop, an oddball named Bradley who worked for an overhead door company. Jerome didn't know Bradley very well, but rumor had it there was a foot fetish ruling that boy. He seemed like a nice enough guy, though, and Jerome jumped at the opportunity to engage him in conversation. Anything to shift the subject from Harrow.

Still, no matter how hard he tried to distract himself with conversation, the presentiment stirring in his gut seemed to build and darken by the second. Something horrible was going to happen soon, he feared.

Harrow had spoken of knowledge and spirits, of creating an army and killing countless people. He'd seemed so confident and certain of success, almost as if...

Some people use magic to do the Devil's work.

No, it couldn't be! Spinning around in his swivel chair, staring at the wall opposite the chairs, Jerome's eyes leveled on a massive photo of Fats Domino at the piano, but even the warmth of the legend's ever-present smile did nothing to counteract the heavy chill that seemed to pervade the air. A ruthless storm was coming, Jerome sensed, but he could never imagine the extent of the suffering it would bring to the Lower Ninth Ward, devastating even the great Fats Domino himself. Domino would be rescued, as would many others, but thousands would die – and thousands more would be irreparably damaged.

Jerome would not die, at least not during the storm's wrath.

Chapter 3

At the confluence of the Mississippi and Ohio Rivers, the Spirits spoke to Harrow once more, whispering new instructions along a warm night wind. They told him to exchange rivers and proceed northeast. His new home was waiting in that direction, they said, waiting patiently for Harrow and his army to arrive and claim it.

Each with his or her own unique repertoire, the army was rounding into shape. Some had the gift of prophecy in their blood; others owned acute senses that could rival canines; a few possessed the power of telekinesis (a very handy trait, indeed); and, remarkably, one man gained insights through his communications with trees.

For a lucky few, their gifts had been carefully honed over an entire lifetime, while others remained completely oblivious to their latent talents. Life could often be cruelly ironic that way, Harrow had realized long ago. Most people spent decades practicing a skill and becoming only marginally better at it because that particular skill wasn't in their bloodline. Had they made a rapid shift to a craft that utilized their blood talents, they would have been far happier and, in many cases, wealthier.

In that sense, Harrow considered himself a mentor and guide for his soldiers. If he hadn't recruited them, they never would have learned what they were truly meant to do – what was in their blood. Now, under Harrow's command, these previously untapped resources hidden among the mire of society would be maximized.

Staring out at the dark waters, taking in the scent of imminent rain, Harrow paused for a moment of contemplation before leading his soldiers northeast. With tepid anticipation he considered the hours of training that would be required to transform this ragtag group into a smoothly functioning machine, but in the end it would all be worth it. Presently, the telekinetics couldn't lift a pebble with their minds; the prophets were limited to seeing that which inhabited their dreams; the witch could only remember a handful of incantations in the correct sequence; and the hybrid wizard, well…he could hardly get out of his own way, less a man, it seemed, than a cryptozoological translation from some dusty attic book about legends and folklore.

Soon, though, these rusty, eclectic parts would all come together in a vehicle of exceeding performance, a juggernaut of relentless power, a dynasty of dominance, with Harrow at the helm, not only commanding his resources but drawing from them to increase his own strength, always a tax to pay in the world between the seas.

Many hours later, in a tiny cardboard box of a town bordering the river, Harrow and his army came upon a dilapidated cabin in the middle of the woods. Windows cracked into spider webs, roof crumbling, walls rotting, it appeared to have been abandoned, soon to experience a full wilderness reclamation.

"What a fine, fine place," Harrow commented, yet he knew this cabin certainly was not his final destination; the Spirits hadn't graced it with a single word of acknowledgement.

Though he would have been wise to stay out of view, a heavyset man waddled through the cabin's front door, stepping onto the bowed porch and taking in the cool early morning air. The sun hadn't yet climbed very high into the sky, its light coruscating through the trees and bathing the cabin in splendorous glory.

Indeed, it would be a terrific day for death and tears. No one ever expected it to end on such a day, usually reserving the cold days and gloomy nights for disturbed absorption in dark thoughts.

Glancing to his left down the porch, the heavy man spotted Harrow and his army approaching. There was a brief moment of shock and perhaps some atavistic ingredient that saw the man go rigid, followed by a shadow of fear dancing in his eyes.

"Who are you people?" the man ventured, slowly retreating backward to the door, his morning peace disrupted by the unimaginable.

WELCOME TO HARROW HALL

Harrow stopped, tipped his hat. Behind him the soldiers halted. "Good morning, sir. How are we this fine day?"

The man, who was well into his middle years, with a thick salt-and-pepper beard and unkempt hair, could find no additional words beyond, "Fine."

"Glad to hear it," Harrow said, detecting the man's greatest weakness just then and debating between options of ruination. "We'll be on our way now. You have yourself a safe day, sir."

With these words the man produced a hunting knife and began in earnest a carving session upon his arm, then his face and neck, deeper and deeper, going fiercely at his task until there was scarcely enough blood left to sustain him.

Harrow, grinning, snacked on the man's tortured laughter. As the necromancer progressed, his footsteps made not a sound in the morning woods. His figure cast not a shadow – not even the anthracite-black top hat.

And when the birds and critters sensed him coming, their collective departure was without delay.

Late that afternoon, in northwestern Kentucky, Harrow's army reached the location of its next potential recruit. Young and pure of spirit, she was a practicing magician who knew nothing of the wonders of Maleficium. She knew deception and falsity, not magic. She knew inexpertly how to connive and swindle using the sleights of illusion, but the power of true magic eluded her, as foreign as Chinese hieroglyphics.

To most, magic was precisely how Victoria Eldridge perceived it – an art of misdirection and showmanship. In her unrefined way of thinking, the best magicians could show their guests what they wanted to show them, leading their helpless eyes astray from that which lurked right in front of them. With these clever, ingenious performers, audience members were nothing more than dogs on leashes, obeying the magician's every command. And there was absolutely nothing wrong with what these performers did. In fact, Harrow commended them for honing their crafts of illusion.

Where Harrow took objection, however – severe objection – was their insistence upon calling their performances acts of magic. Real magic does not require the slightest knowledge of deception, his father had told him long ago – it simply exists. If a magician wishes to make something disappear, he snaps his fingers and that object physically disappears, vanishing as graveyard revenants vanish at Harrow's command. As such, a true magician has no use for trapdoors and hidden compartments and gossamer strings and misdirection. With the proper mastery, the expert channels the magic, then becomes the magic, embodying it in every dimension of his soul, exuding it with every breath. Magic, his father had always said, is deeper than any ocean, higher than the sky itself, as mysterious as the origins of man. Therefore, to control magic is to control the world.

Maleficium – the apex of magic, governed by the Spirits, Harrow their new general.

Harrow smiled. Watching the young woman and how kindly the late light fell upon her face as she tended to her flowers and plants in the back yard garden, a feeling of deep comfort and poetry settled over him. She was the reflection of the flowers she nurtured, this girl, delicately exquisite and flourishing, with straw-blonde hair and eyes of evening cobalt. Her graceful, unhurried gait was like the moon's stroll across the sky, reminding Harrow very much of Her, the one he'd been meant for.

His smile quickly faded. Behind him, one of his soldiers coughed, drawing the girl's eyes to the woods. She couldn't see the soldiers, though, for they were hidden carefully behind the trees, watching the girl and patiently awaiting Harrow's instructions.

Not yet but soon – and Harrow knew they mustn't fail this time. They hadn't yet recruited a soldier in possession of faith and magic (the ultimate prize for the potion), not even Jerome Hudson back in New Orleans, a weary man of dim spirit who should have been easily manipulated. But he'd resisted, even when Harrow had told him of the power he could own.

Today, though, would yield a different result. In spite of the bright flame of faith in her heart, Harrow knew he could recruit this precious young Victoria if he flawlessly executed his plan, a new plan. She would never rival Her, not even close, but she would prove to be a major asset. Those with faith were far stronger than those without. They couldn't be taken involuntarily, either, just as magic could never be harnessed without consent.

Like the Spirits of Maleficium themselves, this girl would have to offer her gifts to Harrow. And he knew exactly how to go about coaxing her.

Chapter 4

The sound stole her attention again. Even in the absence of wind, the woods behind Victoria Eldridge's house were alive with occasional rustles and crunches.

Setting down her flower-patterned watering can, Vicky took a break and studied the shadowy, golden-lighted woods. There it was again, more rustling, and beyond a wide oak tree she thought she noticed gently shifting movement.

Was someone in the woods, watching her? She waited, looked closely, yet there was nothing more for the moment, the woods still and silent.

Unnerved, Vicky jogged back toward the house, following a walkway of brick pavers her father had installed during better financial times for the Eldridge family. Flanked by rows of lilies, roses, lilacs, hydrangeas, butterfly bushes, and daisies – her back yard sanctuary – Vicky looked once over her shoulder before reaching the back door. The woods remained quiet, and no masked intruders were upon her. She'd freaked herself out…again. Her nightmares were really starting to get to her, she realized, the ones in which she was stalked by an evil presence as ancient as civilization itself. Harassing Vicky for upwards of a week, these nightmares always ended with her on fire, flesh peeling and melting away until there was nothing but ashes – and even then the pain wouldn't relent. Even in the darkness of death she was in agony.

Then she would wake.

Vicky shut the back door behind her and locked it. Without removing her gardening gloves, she lingered briefly in the mudroom, staring through the window, irrationally afraid, not even sure what she expected to see. Still no one emerged from the woods. No phantoms, no nightmarish demons intending to set her ablaze, not even a stray dog.

Grabbing one of her father's dusty ping pong trophies from a shelf and clutching it as she would a baseball bat, she began to feel silly, childish, even idiotic. She was almost seventeen, soon to be a senior in high school, not a little girl who was frightened by her own shadow.

Yet here she was captivated by arcane fears, convinced that the evil from her nightmares was somehow real, that the dreams might be portentous.

The doorbell rang, a hollow, eerie sound that shattered the calm of a sunny evening. Vicky flinched.

Again the doorbell clanged its two-note call. A thought told Vicky to ignore the visitor. *What if it's...no, don't go there. Whoever it is will eventually give up and leave.*

Suddenly embarrassed by her childishness, Vicky forced herself through the house to the front door, where she straightened at the sight of a tall, wide-hatted silhouette beyond the frosted glass.

The visitor rang the doorbell a third time. Slipping into the adjoining living room and peering through the bay window curtains, Vicky took sight of the man and jolted back from the window, frightened beyond reason by his face. There'd been nothing gruesome about his features – no hideous deformities – but the cold expectancy in his eyes as he stared at the front door had terrified her.

She risked another peek through the curtains. Now the man's back was to the door, revealing shoulder-length curls and knots of unruly black hair. Although the summer heat was baking down on northwestern Kentucky, he wore a suit replete with black jacket and vest, as well as a top hat, its brim tilted downward.

Hide! Get out of view!

Trying her best to remain silent, Vicky scuttled up the stairs to her room and waited on her bed for two, five, ten minutes as the doorbell was pushed over and over and over, until finally she heard the man ambling down the porch. There was no sound of an engine starting up in the driveway, though, just silence and the TICK, TICK, TICK, TICKS of her Harry Houdini wall clock.

One of Dad's "friends" maybe? No, definitely not dressed like that.

Vicky didn't want to look out the window, too afraid that she would find the man peering up at her from the side yard. For several minutes she remained in her room behind the locked door, hugging her knees on the bed. Ready to call the police if needed, she kept expecting the door to be broken down or a window to smash somewhere on the first floor.

Stop being ridiculous. It's probably just a door-to-door salesman or someone from the Jehovah's Witnesses.

But Vicky couldn't recall the last time a salesman had come to her house, and the Jehovah's Witnesses usually left their pamphlets at the front door and hustled off to the next house in vans or station wagons crammed with their entire families, grandparents on down the line.

No, this man definitely hadn't been with the Jehovah's Witnesses. And why had he waited ten minutes, anyway, tapping the doorbell in persistent search of a response but saying nothing? Vicky remembered the expectancy she'd seen in the man's eyes; it had flashed like a shower of sparks in the night, impossible to miss. He'd clearly come to her house filled with intent, but his adamant behavior had only reinforced Vicky's fear of him.

Dredging up her sunken bravery, she forced herself into the hallway and down the stairs. She glanced out the bay window. No one there. She opened the front door and swept her gaze across the porch. No one there, no pamphlets left behind. The man was gone, and with this realization came a sigh of relief. He'd waited ten minutes for her to answer, seemingly knowing she was hiding inside, but now he was gone. She was safe.

But even though the man was gone, his dark eyes were imprinted in Vicky's mind. She feared she would see those eyes again soon. Very soon.

Later that evening, Vicky prepared two roast beef sandwiches, setting one plate at the dinner table for herself and neatly wrapping the other in tinfoil. The second sandwich, which she slid into the refrigerator, would be eaten much later by her father after he got home from gambling. If things didn't go his way, he would slouch in with the shuffling footsteps of an old woman, grab a few beers, fetch his sandwich from the fridge, and plop himself in front of the television for an hour of brain-drain shows on the History Channel or Discovery Channel, shows about dickering pawn shop owners and wilderness survivors and tow truck drivers and the world's dumbest this and the nation's stupidest that. Then he'd fall asleep on his recliner, sometimes with his crumb-filled plate rising on his belly with each inhalation, Vicky spreading a blanket across him and dutifully taking the plate and empty beer cans to the kitchen, where she would file another load into the dishwasher and hum her favorite country songs, wishing with every plate and glass that things would improve one day.

Vicky knew better than to wake her father after the bad gambling nights. He was usually angry after drinking his losses away, and an angry Pete Eldridge was a scary man, she'd come to learn. Just last night he'd shoved Vicky hard in the kitchen, a painful lump on the back of her head serving as a constant reminder of her collision with the wall. Alcohol leaping from his breath, her father had been furious that she'd forgotten his clothes in the dryer (laundry had become another chore she'd taken upon herself to complete, a list that seemed to grow by the day, each new task volunteered out of generosity soon becoming her father's expectation).

In the silent dining room, Vicky ate her sandwich and flipped through her most recently purchased book of magic tricks, a book dedicated to money and card magic, Vicky's favorites. She was getting pretty good after years of practice, but other than her flowers and close friends, no one had ever seen her perform. Her father had no interest in "that kid stuff", telling her to grow up and focus on "the real world." And Vicky was too nervous to demonstrate her abilities to large audiences, afraid that something would go wrong and people would laugh at her. Her friends always told her how great she was, but what if she messed up in public? What if she embarrassed herself? No, she preferred magic in the privacy of her own home, where no one would deride her for making a mistake.

Vicky practiced with a pair of coins for twenty minutes after dinner, trying to master the latest vanishing trick and pretending she possessed the deft hand of David Blaine. She would need to hide the new book in her room before her father came home; he'd thrown out her collection of magic books two years ago, describing magic as a waste of time. In the absence of books, Vicky had resorted to websites to assist her development, but there was nothing like the tangible process of thumbing through the pages of a book and becoming more familiar with a trick.

Vicky had always loved everything about magic. She loved where it took her and how it made her feel, elevating her to an even greater peace and joy than she found in the garden. With magic, she could turn ordinary things into objects of mystery and wonder, if only for a moment, dazzling herself along with her friends. Maybe her father was right – maybe it was just stupid kid stuff – but it made Vicky feel good, less alone. When her father was at work by day and gambling at night, Vicky could always keep herself busy with magic.

Finished practicing her tricks, Vicky decided to spend a few minutes gardening before she had to get ready for babysitting the neighbors' kids (she also worked down at the grocery store on weekends). Even with two jobs the money was next to nothing, but at least it allowed her to help her father out with some of his payments. On the nights when he "didn't do so hot" at gambling, he could sometimes find himself out thousands, which often required Vicky to pay for their groceries. But whenever Pete Eldridge "cleaned up" at the poker table, he would take Vicky out to dinner and tell her to order whatever she wanted, grinning proudly as if his wallet was limitless in its supply of cash.

This was the disastrous pattern, one that had consumed her father ever since her mother died in a car accident seven years ago. Her father never used to drink heavily and gamble. He never used to be angry all the time and hit Vicky. He never used to waste himself to sleep in front of the TV. He used to be a loving, active father who played games with her and read stories to her and took her out for ice cream on weeknights after helping her with homework. But Mom's death had changed him – darkened him – and he hadn't been the same since. He quit his full-time teaching position at the university a few years back and took "a less stressful" adjunct professor position (with considerably less pay). Last summer, he decided not to return to the adult league softball team he'd played on for fifteen years. A waste of time, he said. Vicky even overheard Uncle Dylan telling her father last Thanksgiving that his gambling was getting out of control. He warned Dad that his life would be ruined by gambling, but that was the last time her father attended a family event, instead choosing to shutter himself away at the bar and at his friends' houses. The only member of the family he saw with any regularity was his mother, Grandma Eldridge, who'd been diagnosed with chronic obstructive pulmonary disease three years ago and now required constant care. Nonetheless, Dad hadn't even made much time for Grandma lately, relying on a team of caretakers he paid for with the help of Uncle Dylan. "Your grandmother doesn't need me – she needs the nurses," he'd said a few days ago, and Vicky had driven to her grandmother's house and spent a night playing games and watching movies with her.

This was the pattern. And it was getting worse.

Stepping outside, Vicky surveyed the back yard and woods for a few moments before proceeding to her garden. The sun had dipped below the trees, previous flecks of shadow having expanded to drapes of infant dark spread thinly across the garden. Beyond the yard, ageless trees whispered conspiratorially as the slightest wind eased through. It was as if they knew secrets never to be told, withholding their knowledge from Vicky and keeping promises to ensure that she was left clueless. Something bad would happen soon, she feared, though she assumed her earlier visitor was fueling these thoughts. If only she could forget about the frightening man who'd come to her door and waited. If only she could just push an erase button and delete that tiny but somewhat harrowing portion of the day.

In spite of her own insistences that the man was gone and wouldn't return, Vicky couldn't complete a task tonight without glancing to the woods, then back toward the house to confirm no one was there. She knew she was being irrational again – perhaps even paranoid – but she realized it wasn't just the man who'd gotten her rattled. Her nightmares compounded the situation, the ones that always ended with her burning. Of all the times for an ominous man to appear at her doorstep, was it really a coincidence that he'd come today, at a time when she was already disturbed by recurring nightmares of death by fire?

A believer in spirits and angels and even witches, Vicky couldn't help but wonder if the nightmares had been warnings that danger was coming for her.

Rustling. Vicky's attention was drawn sharply to the woods. Gripping her pruning shears, she listened above the wind and stared into the woods, then heard it again. Fast-moving footsteps. Someone was approaching her, but she couldn't see anyone darting between the trees.

Just as Vicky was expecting someone to jump out at her, the footsteps abruptly stopped, Vicky not quite sure if she descried a swaying shadow amidst the deeper dark of the woods or if she was only imagining something inhabiting that slight hollow. It was still almost eighty degrees, but Vicky suddenly felt chilled, her hands sweating beneath her gloves.

Shakily, she pointed the shears at the woods, ready to use them if…if what? What would she really be able to do? She suddenly felt helpless – helpless and afraid in a place that had always brought her peace.

An animal. It was as if a flicker of rationality had penetrated the darkness of fear. The noises had to have been made by an animal, most likely a deer even more afraid of her than she was of it. Before reaching the back yard, it had stopped and was probably watching her with wary interest.

Lowering the shears to her side, Vicky let out a long sigh and turned to the house. And saw him – the man from this afternoon.

Arms folded across his chest, he was watching her from the back stoop. There was a moment of measured uncertainty – each person carefully studying the other from across the yard – before Vicky finally reached into her shorts pocket.

But her phone was gone! She was positive she'd stuffed it into her pocket before coming out here, but where was it?

Vicky turned to run, hoping to reach the familiar woods, but she was stopped by the man blocking her path, time and space defied. He tilted his head at her, flicked his tongue across his lips like a lizard. With self-conscious suddenness Vicky became aware of how exposed and vulnerable she appeared, dressed only in shorts and a loose tank top.

"Stay away from me!" she warned, pointing the shears at him, the ten feet separating them feeling but a pace away.

His gaze fell to her chest, forcing her to fold her other arm across it. Finally, he said, "How would you like to learn some *real* magic?"

Vicky managed a dry gulp. How long had this guy been following her?

"Just get out of here, or I'll call the cops!" she bluffed, knowing he'd never let her run inside. She was still trying to understand how he'd vanished from the stoop and appeared on the other side of the yard, a feat even the fastest sprinter wouldn't have been able to accomplish.

Her nightmares! Was he the thing from her nightmares?

The man frowned. He wore the same attire from before, the black suit and vest and hat. "We won't be requiring the police, Miss Victoria," he said, his voice like the lulling whisper of a night sea. Except Vicky did not find herself comforted but terrified by his words.

The man spread his arms wide, regarding her garden with an approving nod. "A lovely garden tended by a lovely young woman," he wheedled.

Vicky pressed her arm tighter against her chest, the shears starting to tremble in her left hand. "Just leave me alone!"

She began a slow backward retreat to the house, but the man matched each step. "There's no need for such hostility, Miss Victoria. I'm here to offer you the greatest opportunity of your life. You've always been interested in magic, have you not? Ever since you were a little girl and your parents bought you that first magic kit." Smiling eagerly, the man opened his jacket and retrieved a black top hat wrapped in a worn red band. He tossed it to Vicky, memories returning to her even before it fell to the grass beyond her sandals. This was not merely a hat – it was *her* hat, the one her mother had purchased for her along with that very first magic kit for her seventh birthday. She used to run around the house in that hat, waving her wand and pretending she was the great Harry Houdini himself.

"Your mother sent me here, Miss Victoria," the man said. Next, he pulled Vicky's childhood wand from his jacket and tossed it to her as he'd done with the hat. This time she caught it, tears pooling in her eyes as memories flooded back.

"Wh…who are you?" she said, wiping her eyes. A disbelieving, nearly breathless haze had come over her, as if she were stuck in a dream world where everything was distorted and illogical.

The man took a few short steps closer. Vicky remained where she stood, feeling numb and cold. Beneath the brim of his hat, the same dark expectancy from this afternoon still smoldered.

Is he…can he really be? No, he's the evil from my nightmares!

Vicky knew she should at least try to run back to the house and call the police, but something kept her there, wanting to know more even if it seemed senseless.

The man smiled again, but Vicky could detect something lurking behind that smile, something very dangerous yet oddly enticing. "My name is Harrow." He removed his hat and bowed, a mess of hair falling loose. "Like I said, I was sent here by your mother. You're destined for greater things in this life, Victoria." He closed his fists into tight balls, then held them straight out in front of him. "Look upon my hands, miss. Study them well."

Vicky blinked as if held in a stupor, watching as Harrow stared at his fists and muttered something unintelligible. Then, with an upward thrust of his arms reminiscent of a celebrating sports fan, he opened his fists and released two cooing doves into the sky.

Incapable of words, Vicky watched them fly above the house and disappear.

"There's far more whence that came," Harrow declared, drawing even closer. "You're destined for greatness, Miss Victoria."

"Stop calling me that!" she snapped, letting the wand fall to the grass beside the hat. She couldn't believe Harrow had returned her old possessions. How had he found them, anyway? She'd assumed her father had boxed them up or thrown them out after her mother's death, and in that time of stifling misery, she hadn't cared.

"How about you come with me? There's so much I have to show you." Harrow's eyes were wide and imploring. The contrast between his crisp suit and disheveled hair established an aura of insanity, not to mention his tongue incessantly flicking across his lips.

Still gripping the shears, Vicky folded both arms over her chest. In such minimal clothing, she felt like she was standing naked before him. She shook her head. "I'm not going anywhere with you. Just leave me alone, please!"

She turned toward the house but felt a quick tug on her hair that made her yelp. She spun around, ready to jab him with the shears, but Harrow was standing farther away now, maybe fifteen feet back from where he'd been, hands on his hips. He looked angry. "What would possess you to stay in such a foul place, Victoria? Do you enjoy babysitting your father when he's drunk? Do you enjoy it when he hits you and wastes your money?"

Vicky felt her face twisting with rage and perplexity and revulsion. How could this man possibly do these things and know these things?

Harrow's eyes narrowed, and Vicky was almost positive they darkened, too. "Your mother sent me to remove you from this cesspool and guide you to your new life, the one you were meant for."

Tears returned to Vicky's eyes. She felt overwhelmed and fraught with dread, like she was slowly slipping down into a place of black despair, helpless to climb back up to safety. She could scratch and grasp at the outcrops, but down she would continue to slide, down to her doom, to the fiery chamber of her nightmares. "My life is just fine," she blurted, nearly choking on her words.

Harrow shook his head pityingly. "You poor girl. You think you're going to college, don't you?" Vicky was about to respond, but Harrow kept going. "If only you knew your father already wasted your college savings at the poker table. And you can forget about poor grandmother receiving adequate care for much longer. Down the drain the money has swirled."

Vicky's jaw fell. "No," was all she could whisper.

"I'm afraid so, Miss Victoria. Used up every last cent of that college savings, he did. He was hoping to make it all back and then some with a stroke of luck, but believe me, beautiful child, when I tell you that I know the forces who bestow luck. We convene almost nightly, and they most certainly don't have anything in store for dearest daddy."

"No." Vicky shook her head repeatedly. "No, no, no…he wouldn't do that. He'd never do that. You're lying. He probably owes you money or something, right? That's why you came here, and you're lying!"

Harrow shrugged. Running a hand through his hair, he said, "You're free to find out the hard way, miss, but remember what I told you this fine evening when it's time to pay up the bursar and there's no wine in the chalice. And don't forget to ask grandmother why her caretakers can no longer be afforded."

Vicky gritted her teeth, furious with Harrow but even more livid with her father. Somehow she knew what Harrow said to be true. She felt it in her heart, a dreadful intuition that might as well have been a dagger to the back. Tears were streaming down her cheeks now, and Harrow was coming forward quickly, pulling her into a tight cologne-scented embrace and patting her on the back and then gently kissing the side of her neck…and suddenly everything felt too fast, way too fast, mesmerizingly fast. She knew things were all wrong – damaged beyond recognition – but in this quiet moment she could somehow take solace in the presence of a stranger. Insanely, she felt safe and balanced in his arms, his alleged connection to her mother suddenly providing a thin comfort.

"Did she really send you here?" Vicky said, looking up at Harrow, her voice sounding small and afraid like that of a child. She wished Harrow had indeed been dispatched by her mother, an angel, but *why*? Why had Vicky been so blessed?

"Of course." Harrow leaned in and kissed her neck again, his lips cold and stiff like steel. Vicky had never been kissed by anyone outside her family before, not even her one-month boyfriend sophomore year, a relationship that had ended because Vicky wasn't into parties and Friday night football games and drinking. She was different – "weird", according to her ex-boyfriend – and for some reason she could sense

Harrow knew she was different. In his arms she felt understood deeply and at a higher level; she felt…right.

But from the depths of her heart a thought broke through the barriers and rose. *Run*, it told her. *Run now! Don't look back!*

But Harrow held her close. He was humming strange words, his voice soft and soothing like a lullaby, his cologne oddly alluring. "Sweet, beautiful child," he said every so often, rocking her gently back and forth and stroking her hair, the experience so soporific as to be drug-induced. "Sweet little Victoria. How could he ever hurt you?"

Finally he pulled away, leaving her dazed and waiting for what might come next, like a dreamer soon to be transported to the next scene. The feeling reminded her of the only time she'd gotten drunk, a surreal October night at her friend's house, that dizzy, lost sensation taking over.

Harrow ran a hand across her cheek. "Let me show you the magic this world has reserved for you, sweet girl," he whispered.

Clouded with confusion, plagued by conflicting emotions, not knowing if she should run or stay, Vicky let him caress her face, let him trail a finger down her lips, let him hold her chin steady. His fingers smelled of smoke, his clothes of cologne, his breath of coolest mint. It was all so wrong yet indescribably right. As if spellbound, Vicky's fears and impulses to resist Harrow melted away. She knew she should be afraid of him, knew she shouldn't let him touch her – but something made her want to leave with Harrow. *You're going nowhere,* she thought. *Your life is so boring and worthless. You probably won't even be able to pay for college. Go with him! Get away from the abuse. Become a new person. See the world.*

Vicky searched his eyes, losing herself for a moment in the darkness, images of fireworks and brilliant skylines and applauding audiences filling her head, images of vanishing cards and soaring birds and smiling children, fantasies of all that might one day be hers.

Harrow reached for her hands, squeezing them in an icy grip. "Will you come with me, Miss Victoria?" he whispered.

Not wanting the fantasy to end, Vicky found herself nodding, but as she did the images dancing through her mind shifted, the fireworks and magic shows giving way to moonlit fields and hulking structures and flitting shadows. The shadows weren't limited to her mind, though. She was staring at them beyond Harrow, watching them come slowly into focus, dozens of people waiting in the woods.

"Let us go now," Harrow said, and Vicky felt her legs moving of their own accord, bringing her closer to the woods. Panic rushed over her but it was too late. Bewitched, she was going helplessly with Harrow, headed away from home, destined to arrive shortly at a new home.

Soon the Night Spirits would come, summoning Harrow and his army to the old institution, where darkness would rule.

Chapter 5

Beneath endlessly bleak and rainy skies, Harrow's army plodded on, stopping only for basic necessities and minimal rest. When his soldiers began demonstrating the inevitable signs of fatigue, the Spirits directed him to a muddy junkyard in northern Kentucky. Harrow knew not what he would find there, though he was confident the Spirits would never lead him astray. Something, or someone, was to be had at the One Stop Towing salvage yard.

For an ordinary man, entry to the yard would have been virtually impossible. Surrounded by barbed wire fences and patrolled by a pair of Rottweilers, the place was impenetrable to the masses. But Harrow, leaving his soldiers in the woods beyond the yard, sauntered to the nearest fence with confidence. A familiar recitation, followed by two snaps of his fingers, collapsed the chain-link sections before him, the fences bowing in as if backed into by an eighteen wheeler.

Passing the downed rolls of barbed wire, Harrow was immediately confronted by the two junkyard dogs, each snarling as though rabid. It was difficult to tell if they were normally this vicious, because every dog – from pit bulls to golden retrievers – reacted menacingly to Harrow. Dogs could always sense his mastery of Maleficium and behaved accordingly, but Harrow's father had long ago taught him how to handle the four-legged fiends.

Employing the old knowledge, Harrow spoke four very powerful words, then said, "Be calm now, slobbering creatures," and the dogs were at once silent and obedient. Tails wagging, they sat beside each other and allowed Harrow to pass without incident.

Whistling, Harrow ambled away from the beasts and proceeded through stacks of long forgotten vehicles, oblivious to the strengthening rain, his mind occupied by thoughts of his newest soldier, young Victoria Eldridge. She was a waif forsaken by the world, so light and airy and graceful – both in her movements and spirit – that she seemed to float from place to place. Forced to walk with her fellow soldiers, eyes confused and afraid, she reminded Harrow so very much of Her, their resemblance exceeding. Harrow had noticed it before, of course, but now it was much stronger. It was almost as if…no, the Spirits would not allow it. Harrow had been given great strength, but in exchange he'd consigned his love to the darkness.

The deal had been done, a bond of magic, and if given the chance, Harrow would not change a single thing.

Lifting his head to the sky, Harrow held out his tongue to collect a touch of rain. "Come forth, Spirits," he finally said. "Harrow awaits your next instruction."

Like the first time he'd ever seen them, the Night Spirits amazed Harrow with their rapid manifestations, seemingly poured from the rain itself, each drop adding another layer to their whirling forms. Linked by the dimensions of darkness, they spoke as one, telling Harrow to take a school bus out back. Once all of his soldiers boarded, he was to drive them to the highway and cross into Ohio, then proceed to their new home about an hour northeast.

Harrow strolled through the yard. In the back corner, a rusted school bus waited with its doors open. Most of the windows were blown out, including the windshield, but the tires were inflated and ready to roll. Harrow stepped aboard the bus, where he was greeted by the scent of ancient leather. The seats were torn open, the aisle cluttered with boxes and parts. Harrow had just begun the telekinetic process of clearing room for his soldiers, when a crabby voice snapped at him from the front of the bus. A little gray-haired head poked through the door.

"What do you think you're doing in my yard, buddy?" the old man demanded, bustling down the aisle toward Harrow and pumping his shotgun, CLACK-CLACK, CLACK-CLACK.

Harrow smiled. He always enjoyed it when people thought they were in control, unaware that their guns and knives were but harmless toys compared to the tools of Maleficium. "Good evening, sir," he said. "I mean you no trouble this rainy night. I'll simply be taking this bus and continuing my journey."

"Like hell you will!" the man growled, his rage-contorted face resembling those of his dogs. "Get off my property before I blow you away!"

For some reason Harrow was in an unusually generous mood tonight; he wouldn't force this man to slit his own throat with a butter knife, he decided, at least not yet. Like before, he uttered four words and snapped his fingers – and the gun was wrested away from the old man with such force that he fell onto his stomach in the aisle, watching helplessly as the gun floated to Harrow. Tossing it through a window, he said, "There's no need to be disagreeable, good fellow. For decades this bus has been sitting here unused. Surely you wouldn't mind if it was finally put to good use."

The man scrambled back to his feet, steadying himself by gripping the tops of seats. Dim light floating in from the yard revealed that he looked how people always do when they see the powers of Maleficium, his eyes wide and face pasty. His hands were shaking a little, too. "Good luck getting it to work," he sneered, still adversarial even when the ground of rationality was quaking beneath him. "The engine was stripped down years ago. Nothing but rats and spiders under the hood."

Harrow grinned, licking his lips. "Oh, lovely. I was just beginning to wonder where I'd find my next meal. Aren't spiders just delectable? The bigger the better, right? Plop 'em in a nice bowl of salad and top the whole thing off with rabbit blood, yes indeed. Healthiest snack you could eat, good sir."

"Who are you?" the man murmured.

Harrow waved a hand. "The less you know about me, the safer you and your family will be. Once I'm gone, it shall be as though I was never here…unless you'd prefer a souvenir, of course. Cancer? Blindness? What'll it be?"

WELCOME TO HARROW HALL

Harrow tilted his head at the man, and that slight movement alone was enough to send the codger bumbling off the bus like a panicked soul who'd upset a hornet's nest. Harrow kneeled on a seat and glanced through the window, watching the man limp hurriedly through the rain and disappear behind one of his junk heaps. Smiling at the thought of the pugnacious little man fleeing to his house like a treed squirrel, Harrow made his way to the driver's seat and cranked the doors shut. Should he kill the man for the fun of it, maybe leave him paralyzed? No, he supposed he'd abide by his generous mood and avoid stepping down on the angry ant.

"Congratulations. It's your lucky day, sir."

Humming quietly, Harrow took a moment to gather his strength and focus it, then waited as the bus coughed to life, powered by the night. When he jerked the bus into drive, the frame groaning and squeaking as it trundled out of its grave, the little ant-man was likely cowering in his home and peering out the window, shocked by the sight of an engineless bus rumbling through the junkyard, a story with which he'd probably fill every cop's ears for weeks. He could not begin to imagine the powers of Maleficium, dismissing it as society always does. But soon all would know who possessed the true power.

Tapping down on the brake, Harrow brought the bus to a shrill, screeching stop just before the gaping hole he'd made in the fence earlier. With four words and two snaps, the downed fence sections scattered away, lifting into the night like windblown leaves, the barbed rolls catching briefly on power lines and showering the road with sparks, the lines drooping in their wake, snakes of fire lashing from them as if insulted, a series of angry pops to follow, and then a snapping whip of flame ribboning across the road.

About this damage Harrow cared not, just another footprint in the sand. Whenever he came around, fires raged and vehicles crashed and people lost their lives; children's balloons popped and dogs barked and food suddenly tasted sour; the wind turned cold and luck turned bad and teeth ached and unexplainable impulses came into people's heads;

bulbs burned out and computers failed and the sick kept on getting sicker.

But these were all trivial matters compared to what was coming – hoaxes, really – his power still far from absolute. To rule the night, Harrow would require each of his soldiers to use his or her abilities to control the masses. Wherever they found a light, they would quickly and mercilessly extinguish it, returning the world to the order of darkness it had once known.

Chapter 6

Vicky followed the others aboard the bus and slid into the first row, another decision made for her. She wanted to run, wanted to sprint all the way home, but her legs were out of her control. Even her emotions were being partially dictated by Harrow. She could feel a strange uplifting warmth slithering around in her chest; Harrow wanted her to be happy and excited, but he couldn't completely stifle her fear and panic. She wished she could scream. She wished she could break out of her own body and tear off into the night.

But trapped she remained, a prisoner of herself. She'd tried countless times to shrink away from the group and slip into the woods, but her legs had carried their exhausted way onward, Harrow exhorting them to keep going. He called them his soldiers. He said they would soon know their true callings. But if this was Vicky's calling, advanced puppetry, she would sooner slit her wrists than embrace it. She couldn't believe she'd allowed Harrow to touch her and manipulate her, that dreamlike back yard encounter seeming to have occurred many years ago.

A pale old woman eased in beside Vicky. Her skin was wrinkly and flaccid, her eyes a dim blue that might have once been bright with youth. Wisps of thin white hair offered meager cover for patches of spotted skin beneath. "How are you holding up, sweetie?" she said, smiling at Vicky and taking her hand.

Vicky could feel tears pooling in her eyes. She tried to speak, but all that escaped her lips was a dry crackle. The last thing she'd had to drink was pond water, Harrow touting it as the purest form of hydration.

The old woman squeezed Vicky's hand. "Don't try to talk, sweetie. Just listen, okay?"

Vicky could hardly manage a nod, tears streaming down her cheeks. Wiping them away with her cold fingers, the woman said, "Soon you'll learn to master all kinds of magic. It'll get better – I promise. Right now the master needs to ensure that the group stays together. If we all go our separate ways now, we'll never be able to have a team."

"I don't want to be on a team," Vicky tried to say, but it came out as *Uh din wuh teeb inittim.*

The woman patted her thigh. "It's all right, dear. Everything will be just fine." Her tone was disquietingly robotic and cheerful, as if Harrow had programmed her to say these things, wound her up, and sent her to Vicky's row.

The doors creaked shut after the last people silently boarded. With a whoosh and a grunt, the bus jerked into motion, pulling away from the junkyard and onto a thin country road, curls of fire still lurking on the pavement from the earlier explosion. Rain was rat-a-tatting against the roof, its constant drumming making Vicky feel even more constricted and claustrophobic.

"Off to Ohio, everyone!" Harrow shouted from the driver's seat. He was leaning forward, both hands on the steering wheel, his wild hair flowing over his shoulders.

Vicky cringed, barely even capable of a scowl.

Patting Vicky's thigh again, the woman smiled and said, "You're his favorite, you know. Aren't you happy to be his favorite?"

Vicky tried to look away, but her eyes were glued to the woman's cracked lips. A foulness beyond decay suddenly emanated from her, as if she were dead inside and spreading her rotten, festering horrors outward.

"You're his favorite," she repeated, then rose from the seat and shuffled down the aisle to the back of the bus, leaving Vicky to her distressed imprisonment. She willed her body to move, straining and clenching her muscles to no avail. She imagined this was how it felt to be restrained by a straitjacket, or paralyzed.

WELCOME TO HARROW HALL

At the head of the bus, Harrow began whistling "House of the Rising Sun", the slow, ominous melody resonating in Vicky's soul, dragging along like the old rusted bus and transporting her to a baleful place. She couldn't possibly guess where she might end up, but regardless of the destination Harrow had in mind, Vicky knew it would reserve untold miseries for her and the others. What awaited her there would not be magic but something else entirely, something dark and dangerous, and oh God it was really real, all of it, but how could it be?

My nightmares! I knew something terrible would happen.

Her nightmares had indeed been premonitory, she feared. If she didn't find a way to wriggle free of Harrow's grasp, she would suffer the fires that had haunted her sleep – but this time the agony would be absolute. There was to be no magic or destiny, no fortunes, no improvement in her life, only the promise of a transformation from nightmare flames to real ones.

I should have run. I never should have let him touch me.

Vicky had been deceived for only a short time (just long enough for Harrow to take control), and now she would have to fight. You're his favorite, you know, echoed the old woman's words in her head, but Vicky forced them out, vowing in that moment – as she stared into darkness through the windowless frame and felt the wind in her face – to fight Harrow every inch of the way. If she would burn, it wouldn't be without a battle.

Hopefully there really was a little magic in her. To survive, she knew she'd need all the help she could get.

Chapter 7

Jerome Hudson was at his usual spot at the end of the Canal Nine bar, sipping his whiskey and watching old McGreevy towel the bar dry for the hundredth time, when the big man took a seat beside him.

Another Friday night had descended on the Big Easy – another workweek in the books – and Jerome wanted to be left alone. He wasn't in the mood for strangers, still reeling from the Harrow incident a few weeks back, his mind tormented by mostly shapeless fears during the day and nightmares after he tossed and turned his way to sleep. He sometimes awoke thinking about who Harrow would kill and how he'd go about doing it, convinced the madman hadn't been spewing a bunch of bull and bluster in that dark, dreary alley. Even though Jerome had been drunk, something in Harrow's eyes and voice had evinced what Jerome could only describe as a destiny to kill – and soon.

This new stranger, a big old boy who'd surely be excused from the roller coasters at Jazzland, ordered a rum and coke. He was vaguely familiar to Jerome, the two men about the same age – perhaps one of Calvin's customers at one point; or maybe he'd lived in the Lower Ninth Ward a few years back and moved. He certainly seemed to know Jerome, turning to him with a smile and saying, "Glad to find you here, man."

A shot of fear tore through Jerome's thin whiskey haze. A few drinks in, he was creeping steadily closer to that blissful state of detachment, where even his deepest worries weren't a bother. But this new boy's greeting brought along memories of Harrow.

"How are ya?" Jerome said absently, hoping for a quick exchange.

It wasn't to be.

"Good. Real good. New Orleans always gets me feeling all right," the man said, studying the bar with the wistful smile of a man returning to his boyhood home. Unlike Harrow, Jerome got good vibes from this stranger – no thoughts of the Devil tonight. No odors of death, either.

Jerome nodded. "I know just what you mean. Say, have we met someplace, maybe Calvin Baker's shop? You seem familiar."

With a fresh smile, the man said, "I reckon we might've met somewhere down the line. I grew up in this town, then moved around for a while." He extended a mammoth hand. "Name's Willy Thunder."

Jerome grinned at the name, though internally he was still on edge. "That's some name. You shoulda been a musician."

Willy laughed, an appropriately booming sound that seemed to fill up the room. "Damn right. Would've made things a lot easier." He consulted his rum and coke, sighing contentedly as the sweet stuff forged its downward path. For a moment he stared at the bar, watching McGreevy come by with the ever-present towel. "My parents and grandparents were all magicians," he offered. "The Thunder family's been cavorting in magic all the way back to the days before freedom, or at least that's what they told me. Extrasensory acumen, they say – runs in the blood."

The word *magic* made Jerome shudder. Here was another magician, he feared, who'd sought him out at Canal Nine, the second such happening in a few weeks. This was getting really spooky.

When Jerome said nothing, just blinked at his whiskey and tried to form a sentence, wondering if the Devil was messing with him, Willy continued, "I bet you're contemplating how it is I planted my fat ass beside you tonight. You're probably thinking it's just a coincidence, right?" Willy spoke like a man who'd paid attention in school, using words Jerome had never heard before, though one word he did understand disturbed him greatly.

"What do you mean, *coincidence*?"

Maybe it was a trick of the light, but Willy's face seemed to instantly darken, his eyes taking on a nervous, searching glint. He scratched his smooth scalp, made a little wince. "I shouldn't waste another second dancing around the subject," he said, the friendly smile gone from his face. "I'm tracking a man you came into contact with last month. I'm told he tried to persuade you to join his army."

Jerome was momentarily speechless, shaking a finger at Willy and waiting for the words to come. "How do you know that?" he finally said.

Amidst the distractions of carousing patrons and pulsing rock music, Jerome's voice was barely audible to himself. A little ways down the bar, a group of boisterous college kids was clinking their drinks together and hollering and threatening to drown out the thoughts in Jerome's head altogether, their colorful school sweatshirts – Loyola, Tulane, UNO – damp with the carelessness of revelry.

Willy took a moment to choose the right words, deliberating so earnestly that Jerome could practically see the mental gears spinning. "In truth, Harrow isn't a man at all," he said, glancing warily over his shoulder as if expecting to be accosted. When he turned to Jerome again, there was something very alarming in his eyes, not just fear but dread. "Harrow's been at it for centuries, growing stronger every year. He's a master of the dark occult, his necromancy more dangerous than that of any man before him. The dark spirits, usually fleeting in their favors, have become as loyal to him as dogs. That can only mean one thing."

"Whoa, hold up now. This all goin straight over my head, man," Jerome said, feeling as exposed as a deer in a field, disturbed by a dawning certainty that Willy was right about everything. He tried to remember precisely what Harrow had told him that night.

For some reason, though, the only memories that stepped immediately forth were those of killing the drunk driver who'd taken Elise from this world. Jerome had smelled the alcohol on his breath, had seen the glaze in his eyes, dark recollections seizing his soul – the call from the policeman saying there'd been an accident, his wife's funeral, the tireless court proceedings, every gruesome detail laid out for the jury – and very briefly now Jerome was staring not into Willy's eyes but those of Elise's killer. Raw and sharded, the claws of Jerome's rage from that night came at him again, but quickly they fell away, Willy's eyes his own again, not the eyes of a man falling down to his death, blood spilling from his head onto the pavement, spilling, spilling, spilling, Jerome turning away, panicking, telling himself the guy would be fine, just fine, a concussion maybe, but he got what he deserved. Some other guy's wife would live tonight, the would-be drunk driver denied access to the wheel…but then the awful stench arrived.

"If Harrow tried to recruit you, that must mean there's something he wants from you," Willy was saying, Jerome having blanked him out these last few moments. He hadn't experienced an incident of guilt this bad in months.

Willy continued, "He's got himself an army forming, a force that will cause unprecedented destruction if it isn't stopped."

"That's right, the army," Jerome remembered, shaking himself free of the past. "He said they'd kill everybody who opposed them, said he'd own the night." Now the haunting memories were trickling through his whiskey fog. "Damn, he even promised immortality! Said my day of reckonin's comin soon if I don't go with him."

Willy shook his head. "Sounds like just his style. He's used coercion, false promises, and a hell of a lotta dark poison to raise this army of his, and now he's got every kind of witch, wizard, sorcerer, conjurer, magician, and plain psycho you could imagine." He took a quick sip, then smoothed a palm across the bar. "And these people come from strong bloodlines, far as I can tell, only a few phonies among them – and those are his attack dogs. That means, if he made you an offer, there's gotta be some kind of magic twisting through your veins as well."

Jerome huffed. "Nah, man, I ain't done a trick of magic in my life. My daddy, though – he was a damn fine magician. Performed everywhere round here, from Pontchartrain to the neighborhood to tiny little bayou shacks out in Lord-knows-where."

Willy's eyes widened. "So there is magic in your blood."

"Whatever magic I was born with, it's long gone by now." Jerome wiped his lips. "Daddy never taught me nothin, too scared magic might lead the Devil to me. Looks like that happened anyway, don't it?" he said with a thin and troubled smile, wishing he could throw the brakes on this madness.

"Your father sounds like a smart man."

Jerome shrugged. "Yeah, he told me to get my ass into the service and make somethin of myself. He didn't want me strugglin for gigs like he did, but most of all, he didn't want me around magic. Always got this weird look in his eyes when I asked him to teach me, like it was a snake that might bite me. Said there's a dark side to magic I want no part of, and that some people use it to do the Devil's work."

"Harrow leading the way," Willy blurted. "He sold his own wife to the Devil for increased powers. She escaped, Lord willing, and came to our side. She died a while back, never got the revenge against Harrow she was seeking, but the crusade goes on." He leaned in even closer, jaw clenching, eyes locked upon Jerome. "Now the battle's reached a critical point. With Harrow building this army and heading north, there's no telling how many he'll kill. We need to track him and destroy him before it's too late. This is a matter of life or death for thousands, maybe even millions. If he gets too strong" – he looked around to ensure no one was listening – "this could be a catastrophe the likes of which we couldn't imagine."

Jerome remembered his father always spouting fears about a magician growing too strong, someone who used his gifts to ascend to power and strike down all who resisted him. "How come nobody offed this guy before he got so dangerous?" he said.

Willy waved McGreevy over and asked for another drink. "He's been hiding in the bayou for years, nearly impossible to track down there. We've got some new people on our side, though, people who are confident they can find him now that he's leading a group. We're hoping to get even more people." He was looking pointedly at Jerome now. "People who refused to join Harrow like you."

"Damn right I refused that shit." Jerome permitted himself a proud moment, then felt his pride shrivel away to nothingness. He was a murderer who hadn't answered for his crime, deserving of punishment, not praise.

Willy clasped his hands over a bulging gut. "What about our side?" He pulled a checkbook from his pocket and flipped it open. "Fifty thousand dollars if you help us take this bastard down. I'll write you a check right here."

"What? *Fifty* grand? Are you shittin me?"

Willy threw up his hands. "I won't lie to you about the risks. We all might get ourselves killed, but if we don't do something, a hell of a lot more people are gonna die. Nobody even knows Harrow's coming – they're all just sitting ducks, man, just sitting there unprepared and waiting to die."

Willy's hands were shaking. He hurried for his drink and raised it to his lips, taking a long swig and a deep breath. Meanwhile, Jerome's fear had been steadily building, the comfort of whiskey not nearly enough to melt down the latest upheaval. He couldn't believe he was having this conversation, talking with a stranger about a good versus evil battle with apparently prodigious implications.

Or was it all just the Devil's game, wagers from the underworld already ventured on Jerome's decision?

"What could I possibly do to help you?" Jerome said after Willy recovered himself a bit. "I ain't got no special powers or nothin. I'm just an old man, a tired old man."

"Everyone's got something to offer," Willy assured, tapping the checkbook against the bar. "You might not know what it is until the chaos arrives, but you'll be able to help us somehow. I can feel it."

Satisfied with his appeal, Willy scribbled out a check for fifty thousand dollars and handed it to Jerome.

"Come with us, Jerome. Whatever you've got to offer, it'll happen when the time is right. Remember, the dark spirits are on his side, but God's always been on ours. I'd take God over black magic any day."

Jerome stared at the check and downed his whiskey, thinking at length about whether he'd choose God over magic if a conjurer promised to bring his wife and daughter back to him and let them live forever. Would his faith that they'd all reunite one day in Heaven override, or would he take the deal knowing he wasn't destined for God's kingdom? Harrow had offered him immortality, citing Jerome's sins as evidence that all other roads led to Hell.

But he'd refused Harrow's offer. Why? Did a sliver of faith remain in his heart that he'd somehow see his loved ones again, that he'd make it to Heaven in spite of his sins? Or had he simply been a fool?

Watching McGreevy towel off the bar yet again, listening to the rowdy college boys to his left, and sensing the urgent anticipation exuding from Willy Thunder, time seemed for a moment to be suspended by the uncertainty of this unmistakable crossroads.

Again Jerome sensed a major change coming. If only it were all a trick, but no, the options were set starkly before him. To fight or to stay home – of all the decisions in his life, this one was of greatest consequence. Everything was riding, he sensed, on this one move, his choice to affect this life and the next.

WELCOME TO HARROW HALL

To fight or to stay home? At this late stage, the money didn't matter much to Jerome, no grandchildren to give it to. Anyway, this was much deeper than money – this was a defining decision, one that challenged him on multiple levels. His father had once said every man must make a handful of choices that stand out above all others, and Jerome knew this was one of those pivotal moments.

Willy sipped his second drink and drummed his fingers against the bar to the rhythm of the music, waiting patiently for Jerome's answer. It was a simple question, yes or no, but with it came a million possibilities.

Jerome glanced about the interior of Canal Nine, seeing what he always saw on Friday nights, feeling the same lousy emotions and the same throbbing desire to buy another whiskey. And another. Then he'd follow his normal route home, past the street musicians and through the boisterous intersections, until he finally reached his lonely stoop, a dark house waiting for him in the Lower Ninth Ward.

Now Harrow's words echoed in Jerome's head with perfect clarity: *With the strength I'm gaining, it won't be long before I own the night, but I need an army to stand with me.*

Suddenly the choice was clear. The storm was obviously strengthening fast, and even if Jerome did absolutely nothing to stop it, he felt he owed it to God to at least try. He knew one right could never undo the devastating failures of his life, but when it came down to this one decision between action and inaction – everything else torn away – Jerome relied on what he'd learned from living in the Lower Ninth for most of his life. No matter how stiff the challenge or how grim the circumstance, you can always try to leave things better than you'd found them. If a hungry child went to bed nourished, if a teen struggling with addiction received guidance, if an elderly woman's lawn was maintained, then the day would end better than it began. Such was the Lower Ninth way, to always strive to improve the lives of one's neighbors and thereby uplift the neighborhood, a giant family supporting its brothers and sisters in times of need. That infectious spirit of giving had been imbued in Jerome at an early age by his parents, may they rest in peace, and even as a defeated drunk his spirit was seeping through. He might fail gloriously, of course, might fall flat on his face and help no one, but the alternative – to do nothing when he thought there might be grave trouble – was unimaginable, unworthy of his upbringing, unworthy of the Lower Ninth Ward. He'd shamed himself and the neighborhood before God with his actions since the deaths of his wife and daughter, but this was his chance, he realized, his final chance to do something truly meaningful before his death. To go out the right way.

Jerome slid the check into his wallet. "I'll go with you," he heard himself say, Willy shooting a triumphant look at him.

With a toothy grin and a deep, hearty laugh, Willy said, "Then let's do this. Pack a few suitcases. We'll be on the road a while."

Chapter 8

Harrow did not require the Night Spirits to tell him he'd reached his new home. The place began calling to him a mile or two away, pulling him like a magnet in its direction, closer, closer, closer, until he finally saw the first building. Rising beyond a marsh across the road, sprouting from the shadows, it beckoned Harrow with warm enthusiasm.

Home! They'd finally made it home!

***

Cole Amos finished off another box of Kleenex and brought a steaming cup of coffee to his lips. It was August, damn it, why the hell was he sick again?

Maybe this job was making him sick, the sheer boredom slowly killing him. Every night was the same old routine: tour the creepy abandoned campus every hour, watch movies and play games on his laptop, and make small talk with his rotating set of overnight shift partners. Some of them watched movies with Cole. Others read novels and magazines. One man played chess against himself all night, blabbering "Check, Check, Check, Checkmate!" the whole damn shift, his constant fidgeting and shuffling of pieces like a metronome from Hell.

The job didn't even pay that well, but at least it put a little money in Cole's pocket. He never would have imagined he'd be working for Leach Security Group upon graduating from the police academy almost two years back, but landing a badge hadn't been as easy as he'd assumed. He didn't want to work far from his girlfriend in the city, and the smalltown positions seemed to get gobbled up faster than a Coney Island hot dog on the Fourth of July. Well, maybe not that fast, but they went pretty damn quick. Cole had gotten a few interviews that hadn't gone anywhere, and the opportunity with Leach had glimmered with the promise of an item to put on his resume.

But Cole had regretted taking the job since the very first night. He hadn't spent all that time and money at the academy to guard an abandoned property with a cast of clowns who'd have trouble chasing down a blind man with his hands tied behind his back. Most of them were out of shape and dim – and the only physically fit, intelligent one in the lot was the chessman, a seventy-five-year-old prune whose skin looked like it had been stewing underwater for a week.

Cole's interviewer at Leach's main office in Cincinnati, a schmuck who thought he was in the FBI, had said this job was "not just any security gig." Apparently state officials wanted to keep the six hundred-acre campus and all thirty of its buildings – a recently closed psychiatric facility – protected from vandals and thieves. The property would likely be purchased soon by a real estate developer for big money, and the state brass wanted everything in top shape for the renovations that would inevitably be made. Until then, the buildings would sit silent and ghostly, still displaying the remnants of their former purpose.

The buildings seem lonely tonight, so lonely, Ronny (the chessman) would always say. But tonight the buildings weren't lonely at all. Tonight they had a visitor. Both Cole and his current partner – Adam Brossard, a porky kid from Dayton – heard the rumbling engine at the same time. Peering through the front window of the security trailer, they watched a rusted, badly damaged school bus proceed down the lamplit entry road, passing the little parking lot outside Daly Hall where the trailer was set up, quickly accelerating toward the campus center.

There was a brief delay on the part of the two guards, a moment of wary incredulity. In order for that bus to pass the trailer, it would have needed to break through the gate that barred vehicular entry to the campus. In addition to the guards, only the town's fire and police departments had keys to the gate, and Cole had just confirmed it was locked during his latest rounds of the property twenty minutes earlier.

The wind picked up, buffeting the flimsy trailer.

Lightning flashed in the distance.

A bad feeling crept into Cole's gut, followed by an unpleasant tingling in the back of his neck.

"What the hell was that, man?" Adam said. He was about ten years older than Cole, in his early thirties, but he looked and acted like a high school freshman, skittish and uncertain and unconfident. Pathetic, really. He said he wanted to be a cop, but how could he wear a badge when he didn't even like to do the rounds here, always saying he heard something weird in one of the buildings and asking Cole to go with him next time?

This time, though, Cole could understand why Adam's eyes were wide with alarm. In almost a year of working here, Cole had never seen a suspicious vehicle breach one of the gates before. Occasionally some high school or college kids would come looking to party and he'd dismiss them, but whatever was going on at this strange hour was different, much different. He'd learned about the importance of trusting one's instincts at the academy, and his instincts were telling him this was a dangerous situation.

Another flash of lightning lit up the road. Across the street, three stories of Brookside Hall's white-trimmed windows flickered blue and then went black, thunder rumbling moments later.

"I'm reporting it to the cops," Cole replied. "They don't pay us enough to check that shit out alone, especially without a weapon."

Adam nodded rapidly. "That's a good idea. Did you see that thing? It was all rusted out and the windows were broken. And there were people on board, tons of them." He gulped loudly, looking like a spooked puppy. "I don't like this, man, not at all. It's almost two in the morning!"

"Just relax, bud. I'll get the cops on it," Cole said, crossing the trailer toward the phone on the desk. "You're sure you saw people? I didn't see anyone."

"Positive. This could be really serious. What if they have weapons?"

Cole called the police department and informed the dispatcher, who told him an officer would be there shortly.

Adam bit his fingernails. "How long till they get here?" He was standing immediately before the desk and glancing often at the door, which he'd locked when Cole had gone to the desk.

"Should be here in five." Cole shook his head, his initial apprehension having melted a little. Now he felt more curious about the bus than nervous; plus, when he eventually became a cop, he'd have to deal with far more dangerous situations than this. "You know what?" he said. "I'm gonna go check it out. That way, I'll be able to give the cop some info when he gets here."

Adam's jaw dropped. He looked at Cole as if he'd just announced he was planning to fly to Afghanistan for a weeklong vacation. "You want to check it out? Really? We're not even armed."

"Come on, let's go together," Cole urged impatiently. "At the very least, we need to see how badly the main gate was damaged."

Adam backed away, shaking his head and fiddling with the zipper of his navy blue Leach Security Group jacket. Maybe it was the air conditioning, but Cole was convinced he saw his partner shiver. "Nuh-uh, no way, man. We should wait for the cop to get here. Those people could have weapons."

"Fine, suit yourself." Cole started toward the door, Adam continuing to retreat from him. "I'll let you know what's happening on the radio."

Adam glanced down at his radio as though seeing it for the first time.

WELCOME TO HARROW HALL

Stepping through the door into the humid night (actually, it was early morning now), Cole wondered how his partner had ever passed a training exercise. Adam was liable to get spooked by his own shadow in that trailer and knock himself out – if only their boss knew Leach was wasting its money on a guy who was about as much of a guard as a hamster.

A new burst of lightning. The pine trees behind Brookside Hall swayed amidst a steady wind. Spatters of rain felt refreshing against Cole's face as he made his way to the parking lot, where a white 1998 Honda Civic waited for him. It was a clunky old thing, its sides emblazoned with the shield logo of Leach Security Group. It was actually a major company, renowned for its well-trained armed guards working in every city on the east coast. Some of them secured New York's corporate kings, collecting six-figure salaries for their work protecting Manhattan skyscrapers. But on every totem pole there is a low man (a low job, too), and for Leach, an abandoned property in a quiet country town in Ohio was fairly far down in the batting order. No one expected serious crime here. At worst, his boss had told him, you'll have to deal with some kids trying to vandalize the buildings.

Cole was not prepared for the approaching storm. No one was.

A resonant, rolling crack of thunder sent jolts of nervous energy skittering through Cole's bones. Before slipping into the crappy Civic, he lingered with his hand atop the door, staring down the lamp-lined road where the bus had gone and wondering if he should just wait for the cop.

But he was practically a cop himself. He'd gone to the academy to learn what it took to become a law enforcement officer, and soon he would hopefully earn a badge.

Get moving already!

Frustrated by his lack of decisiveness, Cole jerked the car into drive and took a left out of the parking lot. In a few moments he was studying the breached double barrier gate separating the institution's main entry road from North Ridge Street, a public way. The bus had indeed blown right through it, tearing one of the swinging gates completely off its hinge and trampling it twenty feet down the entry road.

"What the hell?" Cole muttered, dragging the mangled gate off the road.

He was about to return to his car when he spotted an unmarked town cruiser approaching on North Ridge Street. Without a gate to obstruct access, the officer coasted onto the entry road and pulled over beside Cole, who'd flagged him down with a flashlight.

"The bus blew out the main gate," Cole reported when the officer rolled down his window. He felt like an idiot for relaying obvious information that he'd already given the dispatcher, but at the moment it was all he had to go on.

The officer, a fiftyish man with gray hair and deep rings beneath his eyes, gave a quick nod. "Did you see which way he went?"

Now Cole felt even more useless. "My partner and I saw him pass the trailer, not sure where he went from there." He pointed down the road, which was evenly illuminated to its terminus a quarter of a mile away, where it intersected with Center Street (formerly Piggery Lane) at the campus center.

"All right, I'll check it out," the officer said tiredly. Cole was waiting for instructions, but the guy simply rolled up his window and drove off, leaving Cole to his miserable feeling of incompetence and worthlessness.

Screw this, he thought as the skies opened and the rain came cold and heavy. *Finally something's going down at this place, and I'm gonna be a part of it.*

Back in the car, he brushed water off his jacket and spoke into his radio. "Adam, I just updated the officer on the situation. The bus drove right through the main gate. We're gonna investigate now – I'll keep you posted."

"Be careful," his partner warned. "You never know what you might find."

Chapter 9

Harrow brought the bus to an abrupt, squealing stop and wrenched
open the doors. Grinning wildly, he scrambled down the stairs and
raced toward the front entrance of a large brick building.

"Home! We're home!" he shouted above the wind. If not for a flash of
lightning, Vicky wouldn't have seen him drop to his knees before the
front doors and flatten his palms against the glass. "Thank you! Thank
you! Finally has the master arrived!"

Vicky felt herself lurch to her feet, and suddenly she was shuffling
forward, then down the steps and off the bus, leading the others to
Harrow. She tried to resist, tried to break free, but it was like being
cemented to the base of a moving walkway, destined to go wherever it
took her.

Tonight, as lightning sizzled in the distance and thunder rumbled,
destiny would take her to the front entrance of the building, where
Harrow was still kneeling like a humble servant before his king.

Another flicker of lightning. This one drew Vicky's attention to large
white letters affixed to the brick facade: HARROW HALL.

Vicky felt a painful twitch in her chest, as if there'd been an awakening
of something deep within her at the sight of that name. Something
hostile and dangerously premonitory.

Is this the place where the fire will happen?

When Vicky's legs dragged her to Harrow at the front entrance, her
eyes fell upon a small cardboard sign leaning against the doors, a sign
smiling with two hand-drawn theater masks and a large arrow.
PERFORMANCE, it read, and now Vicky was shuddering in revulsion.
Through the doors she saw an auditorium bathed in lambent crimson,
one level down from the entrance.

The entire building suddenly seemed to radiate evil – the antechamber to Hell.

Standing again and slowly turning to Vicky, Harrow said, "Are you ready to learn some real magic, sweet Victoria?" He held his hands out to her. "With great honor, young girl, our new home I present to you."

Harrow's face was deeply shadowed below his hat, but by the brevity of lightning's next emergence Vicky glimpsed black holes where his eyes should have been. And though the wind was momentarily still, his hair began blowing chaotically as if he were on a roller coaster.

"Are you ready, Victoria?" His mouth expanded impossibly wide; from it swirls of mist came forth, rotating into shape.

Soon Vicky was surrounded by rapidly engendering forms. But she was no longer outside Harrow Hall looking in...she was on the slippery stage, scuffling beneath the heat of a spotlight, surrounded by flames dancing along the proscenium, gazing up to a balcony crammed with leering skeletons.

Outside, lightning flashed.

***

Just beyond the center of campus, Cole found the old school bus parked to the left of Harrow Hall. Its doors were open, the stop sign extended and flashing with oddly intermittent spurts of red. The police cruiser was parked behind it. The officer had already boarded the bus, his flashlight bouncing from row to row.

Cole wondered what he should do; the officer hadn't requested his help, and he didn't want to piss the guy off. Still, he felt obligated to impact the investigation somehow, especially since the intrusion had occurred in the middle of his shift. Yet it seemed there was nothing for him to accomplish here beyond the provision of annoyance, at least not yet.

Without leaving his car, Cole studied the bus carefully. Not a single window remained intact, and the paint – which had been bright yellow in another decade – was rusted away, the mud flaps gone, no license plate, either. Cole assumed someone had stolen the thing from a farm field or a scrap yard…but why?

Stepping off the bus, the officer summoned Cole with a wave of the flashlight. "You have keys to all of these buildings, kid?" he said when Cole walked over.

Cole nodded. "Yes, sir. We don't actually go inside the buildings, though. The state inspectors come by every month to take a look."

The officer pointed to Harrow Hall, one of the newest buildings on campus. According to Ronny, the chessman who claimed to know the complete history of the facility, Harrow Hall had been constructed in 1995 to accommodate everything from mental health lectures to theater activities for the patients. The main portion of the building was an auditorium, but nestled in the back were two stories of offices and conference rooms. Ronny claimed the place was haunted (apparently he'd heard rumors from former staff members about weird sightings), and Cole had always found the building a little unsettling himself. There was something distinctly unnerving about peering through the glass doors and looking down upon the empty stage and seats. Everything stood still and forgotten in Harrow Hall, yet the caged clock on the far wall ticked on and on, its battery never dying.

On and on, time pressing forward while all of these buildings withered away.

"Let's check all the doors," the officer said. "If there's no sign of forced entry, I don't see a point to going inside. I heard these damn buildings are filled with mold. My lungs are bad enough already."

Lightning pulsed when they reached the front doors, fooling Cole into thinking he saw a reflection of someone behind them. He spun around but found no one there, though a weird feeling clambered over him that someone was nearby, watching them.

Get over yourself. God, you're pathetic.

To Cole's right, the officer pressed his face against the glass and beamed his flashlight into the building, illuminating row after row of empty seats on the first floor, then the mezzanine and balcony. With each pass of the light, Cole half-expected a face to be revealed, though darkness was the prevailing tenant of this strange hour.

Thunder echoed against the brick facade. The wind picked up again, the rain coming down heavier. Cole didn't want to admit it, but he was glad the officer was here with him.

"What the hell was that?" Now it was the officer's turn to be startled. Whirling around, looking back toward the bus, he lowered a hand to his belt. "I heard voices," he said after a few moments of careful observation. "Multiple voices. I think they're in the woods."

The officer radioed for backup, then walked with Cole back to the bus. Shining his light into a shallow patch of woods opposite Harrow Hall, he shouted above the rain, "This is the police department – come out with your hands up! Don't make this any worse for yourself than it already is!"

Footsteps in the woods, beyond the flashlight's limit. *CRUNCH, CRUNCH, CRUNCH* went leaves and twigs beneath several footfalls – loud enough to be heard over the rain.

Dread slithered into Cole's stomach.

The officer drew his pistol. "Come out to the road! Do it now!"

The crunching tapered to a brushy sweep. The intruders were running away, scuttling up a slight wooded hill toward the east side of campus, where five former dormitory buildings overlooked the rest of the property.

The officer appeared for a moment as if he wanted to pursue the trespassers – even taking a few steps toward the woods – but he thought better of it and headed back to his cruiser.

"Damn kids. Usually it's quiet overnight, but tonight's been crazy," he said as they walked away from the bus, glancing occasionally back into the woods.

"What else happened?" Cole had to raise his voice over the building wind and rain. The breaks between lightning strikes were decreasing, the thunder growing sharper and more protracted.

"I just came from a bad wreck on South Main Street. Kid went off the road and smacked into a tree – lucky he didn't get himself killed." The officer gestured to the passenger side of his cruiser. "Hop in. Let's get out of the rain."

Cole pulled open the door and slid inside, the officer rounding the cruiser and settling into the driver's seat. He seemed to be warming up to Cole; maybe the guy could sense he was the real deal, not one of those jokers who couldn't detain a geriatric dog in a cattle corral.

"Was it a one-vehicle wreck?" Cole said.

The officer nodded. "Judging by the damage, it looks like he was in excess of sixty. That section of South Main – I've seen people close to one hundred. Might have been drag racing." He shook his head. "Last few summers we've seen an increase in guys thinking our town's a drag strip. Anyway, I should call for a tow. That bus isn't moving itself. Goddamn kids."

"Did you find anything inside that could tell us where it came from?"

"Nothing. No keys, no documentation. Thing was stripped." The officer took an extended look out the driver's window, flinching when thunder tore across the sky. Cole had been expecting it after the preceding bolt of jagged blue above the distant southern hills.

"I hate storms," the officer said. "Reminds me of the tornadoes in ninety-nine."

The officer went on to describe the tornado outbreak that almost killed his mother, but Cole's attention was fixed upon the woods. He kept expecting someone to attack them. It was a thought beyond irrational, but with each shot of lightning he imagined masked intruders charging at them from the woods.

Too many horror movies, he told himself, yet the fear remained.

Chapter 10

Hours later, after the cops had departed with the back seats of their cruisers empty and the tow truck had hauled the bus away with great difficulty, Cole made his final tour of the institution before the sun came up.

The strong overnight storm now just a memory, the sky was streaked with residual clouds, though it was clear off to the east, where bluish-orange light was beginning to corrode the darkness.

Cole didn't leave his car as he went from building to building, sweeping around semicircular driveways and slipping behind the forgotten brick monoliths. Usually he enjoyed a cigarette outside Hodskins or Wayside and glanced through the windows into sporadically illuminated rooms and hallways, imagining what these buildings had seen over the years. This time, though, he remained within the safety of his locked car.

It was hard for Cole to admit, but his nerves had been shaken by the weirdness of this shift. Where had the occupants of the bus gone? And why bring a bus here to begin with?

At the south end of the property – the very back – Cole looped around the crumbling driveway of Granite Hall, one of the oldest buildings on campus. According to Ronny, it had been closed due to safety concerns five years before the rest of the institution, but it still felt active and energized, the second floor windows glowing a sickly yellow as usual. Cole disliked the lights. They made these buildings seem alive somehow, as if people were still residing in them. No one was in there, of course. The state simply kept the buildings partially lit to discourage additional mold growth.

But that didn't make Cole's rounds less creepy. Every lighted window presented an opportunity for a flitting shadow to be glimpsed, or worse, an unmoving silhouette.

WELCOME TO HARROW HALL

Tonight, Cole tried not to look for very long at Granite Hall, its barred second floor windows providing his imagination with enough ammunition to load up a week's worth of nightmares. Between the second and third floors, a small tree protruded through the brick – a tree! – its tiny branches snaking out and casting eerie shadows upon the dilapidated awning below. The cracked windows were coated with moisture, portals to another time and place. The roof was like a row of sugar-rotted teeth.

Feeling goosebumps rise on his arms, Cole forced himself not to look back at the building as he pulled away, remembering the night he'd stared at Granite's circular attic window for so long that he thought he saw something moving in the darkness.

"This school bus thing's getting to you, man," he muttered. "At this rate you'll be a bigger pussy than Adam."

Cole finished up his rounds, thankful for each drop of light that bled into the day. When the sun was out and the institution was dappled by its light, the place was nothing more than a forgotten world that had once been bustling with purpose. But at night it was different, so much different with the lights on and the shadows and the strange noises.

The old asylum emitted more than a bad vibe.

At the conclusion of his rounds, when Cole swung back around Harrow Hall, another oddity awaited him. The building was dark as always (no mold problems in there, with its big glass doors ingesting plenty of sunlight by day).

But after a moment Cole realized the building's darkness had been broken. A bright light left him briefly breathless – a spotlight directed upon the center of the stage.

Chapter 11

Cursing each remaining drop of whiskey in his blood, Jerome checked the clock again – 9:21. He couldn't recall the last time he'd risen before noon on a Saturday. Usually he was snug beneath the covers at this hour, his head swimming even in sleep.

But this Saturday morning was different. Today's Jerome Hudson was nothing like the man he'd seen in the mirror yesterday, a new purpose having found him. He'd already cashed Willy Thunder's fifty thousand-dollar check (if only to confirm this was the real thing), then hurried back home to get everything in order, his body always a few steps behind his mind.

Working quickly, glancing often at the clock, Jerome stuffed a third suitcase full of belongings. Should he bring his photo albums? Yes, yes, he should, at least a few of them. Photos and memories were all he had left of Elise and Jennie, their faces confined to the past and the pages of albums, gone forever from this life.

Jerome wondered what else he should bring. Before departing Canal Nine last night, Willy had said he'd pick him up at ten o'clock sharp. "Have your things ready," he'd said. "And you'll want to bring plenty of clothes – this trip might take a while."

But how long did "a while" mean? How much should he pack? Jerome began tossing clothes into a fourth suitcase, then abruptly stopped. He rubbed his forehead, wondering if he would really pack up his things and pour himself into a stranger's car.

He shook his head, still unable to fathom the brewing cataclysm he'd stumbled upon, a storm of apparently unimaginable proportions. But what if he wasn't strong enough to handle it? For most of his life he'd been unimportant, living in the shadows and thriving on anonymity. He would always remember attending college basketball games as a kid, his father telling him he'd be there one day if he worked hard enough. But the dream had become increasingly distant, outrunning him as though he were trying to chase down a horse. The competition was too stiff, the other guys too fast and tall. No college scout ever looked at Jerome, but it wasn't the end of the world. He became a soldier. He served his country. He learned about America's true heroes, the ones who never sign a multi-million dollar deal or bloat their bank accounts with contractual incentives.

Jerome had rarely played basketball after returning home from Nam, but it hadn't mattered. He hadn't needed to be a star or balance the pressures and expectations of fame. To his daughter he'd always been a hero, a man as far from the spotlight as the neighborhood he called home yet irreplaceable to his loved ones.

But now, *now*, after all these years, when he was nothing but a withered old man, the big stage was calling, his advance payment already in the bank. Willy had said there was magic in him, that he could help the cause. But how? What made him so damn special? Why had Harrow come for him and now Willy? What made him worthy of fifty grand? He was just a drunk, a worn out lush with nothing left to give but the time of day.

Yet apparently he did have something to offer if these people kept gravitating toward him. Something big. A little paranoid because of the influx of oddities in his life, he couldn't help feeling like everyone was watching him and laughing at something beyond his grasp. Maybe he was just a joke. This entire thing – maybe it was all just an elaborate prank contrived not by the Devil but instead very rich and bored men.

But in his heart Jerome knew even the best actor couldn't have drawn the revulsion he'd felt for Harrow, strong enough to have led his first impression to Satan. And no actor could produce the smell of death, an ancient foulness that had arrived with Harrow at Canal Nine, Jerome detecting it right away. No, Harrow hadn't been part of a hoax. This was really happening, all of it.

The doorbell rang, sending fresh chirps of dread into Jerome's chest. What if Willy was working with Harrow, a man sent to try another angle of recruitment? *Damn, didn't even think of that.*

Jerome sighed; there were too many worries for such an early hour, too much paranoia. He wanted nothing more than to slide beneath the covers again, but obligation brought him down the stairs to the front door. Opening it, he was greeted by the warmth of Willy's smile, a thing that seemingly couldn't be fabricated.

"Good morning to you, Jerome!" the big man gleamed. "Are you all packed up and ready to roll?"

Jerome stared at Willy for a moment, measuring him. If that smile was fake, then this wasn't a world he wanted a thing to do with, he decided. Better to be someplace else if lies and malice lurked behind a smile brimming with such jollity.

"Almost done," Jerome said. He yawned, though it was less a tired product than an anxious one. "Just gimme five minutes."

Willy, dressed in a white T-shirt the size of a canopy tent and baggy black shorts, checked his watch with a hint of impatience. "We've got a little time, I guess. Just bring your suitcases to the door, and we'll take them out to the van."

The van, it turned out, was a blue Ford Windstar crammed with passengers, its roof practically caving in beneath the weight of suitcases, bags, and boxes. By the time Jerome reached the driveway with his last item, his other luggage had already been strapped atop the pile, forming a ridiculous looking pyramid that added five feet to the van's height.

Jerome turned to Willy, who was talking with a skinny thirtyish man wearing a Hawaiian shirt. The guy was standing on the roof of the van, securing Jerome's luggage with bungee cords.

"We better not have more people to pick up, or you won't be able to take this thing under bridges," Jerome said.

Willy chuckled deeply, again showing off that cheerful, somehow boyish smile. For a man of his size, it was odd to see such childlike qualities. Meantime, across the street, Mrs. Dawson was watching them from her porch swing, rocking back and forth and probably wondering what exactly these people were doing in Jerome's driveway. He never had visitors anymore, not since Elise and Jennie died. The house, once filled with joy and laughter, was now a bleak, lonely place, warmed only by fading memories. Jerome couldn't believe he'd stayed here this long. Looking back at the weathered house, with its crumbling shingles and overgrown bushes, he saw nothing that could hold him here anymore. The Lower Ninth Ward had always been his home, but it was time to move on, he realized, time to emerge from the shadows of defeat, time to make a meaningful impact elsewhere. He still didn't know how he'd go about making this impact, though, and along with unpreparedness came another wave of dread.

In a few moments, entering the van and sliding the door shut behind him and nodding uncomfortable greetings to a bunch of strangers, Jerome eased into the back seat beside an elderly Native American man with long white hair and a face as rough as granite.

"How y'all doin?" Jerome offered, breaking out in sweat despite the icy air-conditioned interior.

The Native American man, who'd been staring blankly out the window, slowly turned to Jerome with widening brown eyes. He flattened a shaky hand against Jerome's shoulder. "You very powerful man." Now he was nodding emphatically. "Very, very powerful. We good now that you here."

Jerome wanted to yank open the door and run back inside his house. He resisted the urge.

Poking her head out from the middle row of seats, a twentyish woman said in a dry voice, "Hey, buddy, I'm Sky. What's your name?"

Jerome stared for a moment at her short curls of blue hair. Upon entering the van, his attention had been drawn to her heavily tattooed arms and neck. "Jerome," he finally said. "Jerome Hudson."

Sky jolted up from her seat and shook Jerome's hand excitedly, her cargo pants jangling with chains. Her belt buckle was a grinning skeleton topped by a sombrero. Her black tank top, a skull and crossbones at its center, read, BLACK LIKE MY SOUL. A rainbow of words and images decorated her skin with the unsightliness of spray paint on a boxcar. Judging by appearance, she seemed a more suitable choice for Harrow's army.

"So what's your pitch?" Sky said, looking expectantly at Jerome.

"Whatchou talkin bout?" Still unsure if he was making the biggest mistake of his life, Jerome wanted to be left alone, not nattered at by Willy or the Native American or a morbid young gal exploding in color and noise.

But Sky wouldn't allow him the peace he desired. Giving her hazel eyes a dramatic roll, she said, "Your pitch, man. Come on, aren't you a baseball fan? Everyone's got an out pitch – slider, splitter, one hundred-mile-an-hour gas – what's yours?"

Jerome glanced at the old man, who shrugged and averted his eyes to the window.

"I ain't got a clue what you gettin at, girl," Jerome said.

With a weird undulating giggle, Sky said, "Life is like baseball, dude. We've all got an out pitch. For me, it's fire. I'm the fire girl. I'll light your ass up like it's Devil's Night in De-troit, so don't get me pissed." Extending both hands, she made a cryptic circling gesture and grinned at Jerome, then returned to her seat and buckled up.

Lifting himself with moderate difficulty into the driver's seat, Willy hollered, "Don't go scaring our new teammate, Sky! He don't wanna hear about all that fire stuff!"

Willy yanked the door shut and fired up the engine. This was it, Jerome's final chance to escape. As they backed out of the driveway, he took one last glance at the house he'd made his home. For nearly two decades before Jennie went to college, he'd looked forward to coming home after work and seeing his wife and daughter. Opening the front door during the early years, the smell of imminent dinner would greet him first, then little Jennie – usually toting her latest crayoned picture – and finally Elise, the warmth of her kiss melting away even the most stressful days. Nothing had been bad enough that it couldn't be cured by the sight of his two girls. They'd brought meaning to his life, defined him, made his little place of obscurity in the Lower Ninth Ward a kingdom of boundless wealth. On weekends there were cookouts and campouts in the back yard, church and football on Sundays, Jennie taking after her parents and cheering ardently for the Saints. On weeknights Jerome helped Jennie with math and social studies homework, Elise taking care of science and English. At night, switching off the local news and listening to the wind rattle the old house, Elise lying beside him in bed, Jerome always thanked God for blessing him with such a full and happy life. They were a team he'd thought would last forever.

Tears stung Jerome's eyes. The van was on the road now, accelerating, the house slipping away behind them. Beginning to panic, Jerome spun around and stared at his house through the back windshield. A smothering sensation took hold of him, starting at the shoulders and squeezing an upward path. Sweating profusely now, he wanted to scream at Willy to turn around and take him back, but the house was fading from view, receding into a place beyond recovery, his beautiful little nook in the world, the place he and Elise had bought all those years ago. As if it were yesterday, he could remember standing with his young wife on the sidewalk, holding her hand, their new home and a truckload of uncertainty before them. He'd promised her on that drizzly morning he would one day build her a mansion, but Elise had never wanted a mansion, only him and Jennie and a place to call their own.

They came to the stop sign at the end of the street. Jerome rubbed tears from his eyes, took a deep breath, and blew it out slowly, isolated in a moment of personal distress. He faced the back windshield again. Only his mailbox was in view now, a meaningless little notch in a lengthy timeline. In two weeks it would be underwater, his home destroyed, the possessions he left behind gone forever. He didn't know what was to come (he'd told his friends he was going to see the country for a while), but a new place awaited him. A new family. A new calling. Elise and Jennie and the Lower Ninth could never be replaced, but a new destination required skills he didn't know he possessed.

Still facing the back windshield, a soothing breeze suddenly swept over him, but the windows were closed. He felt a gentle touch on his shoulder and whirled around to find the Native American's gnarled hand upon him. "Let go of past now," he whispered, his eyes lifting to the roof. "Focus on future."

Chapter 12

Vicky awoke on the dusty stage of Harrow Hall. She was lying on her side, curled tightly as if she'd fallen asleep in defense mode. Slowly standing, her neck and back aching, she remembered everything that had transpired on this stage the previous night.

There was no spotlight today, only drafts of sunlight beaming down through the front doors. The auditorium was empty, the skeletons gone, their red balcony seats folded up. The place smelled old and musty and forgotten, but last night it had been alive with something awful. The misty snakelike creatures had slowly advanced toward her, stopping only at Harrow's command. He'd shouted at Vicky to abolish them, to reach into the depths of her soul and put an end to them. He'd given her full control of herself again, and when she'd failed her task, watching helplessly as the monsters drew steadily closer, he'd commanded them to disappear – and the things had vanished like smoke lifting away from a candle.

Now it was daytime, Vicky aware of footsteps issuing from somewhere behind the stage. She forced back her tears when Harrow slipped through the crimson curtains a few moments later, grinning at her like an old friend.

"Sweet Victoria!" he exclaimed. "How did you rest, angel child?"

Vicky started gingerly toward the staircase to her right, but Harrow trotted ahead of her and stood in her way. He wore the same clothes from last night, his wild black hair flowing out of his hat and down his back, much longer than she remembered it.

"You're always in such a hurry to leave, Victoria. What awaits you, pray tell, back in Kentucky? Why would you exchange a life of power and magic for mediocrity? What, young child, would possibly possess you to forsake your destiny?"

Vicky wanted to speak, but the words wouldn't form. She wanted to run, but her legs rebelled, holding their place on the stage. Again Harrow controlled her, his eyes wide and searching. Vicky remembered the ghoulish form his eyes had taken last night, when a flash of lightning had revealed two black, hollow holes. She felt tears in her own eyes as Harrow approached, arms outstretched.

Squeezing her hand in an icy grip, drawing her to the middle of the stage, he said, "It seems that some souls can be satisfied only by the comfort of promise. Do these words not carry truth, Victoria?"

He pulled away and began to pace the stage, gesturing emphatically at the empty seats as if communicating with an invisible audience. "Stay with me, Victoria, and I'll ensure your family is cared for always, in this life and the next."

With a snap of his finger, money began raining from the ceiling like confetti, thousands of bills showering the stage, all of them one hundreds. Then, with another snap, the money vanished. Vicky couldn't believe what she was seeing. Even if she'd been in control of her voice, she still might have been speechless.

Harrow adjusted his pacing to a wide circle, Vicky at its center, his eyes always upon her. "To your family all this money shall go, to be used to repay your father's debts and assist your grandmother. Doesn't she deserve the best medical care available?" His voice lowered to a whisper, incisive enough to be heard from the balcony. "I can shift dream to reality, young girl, for you and your family. Just stay with me. Stay and learn."

He came to Vicky again, taking both of her hands this time. "Please stay with me, child, in this lovely home we've found for ourselves. Whatever you desire shall be done. With a word, it exists."

His lips spread into a glinting smile of impossible white, Vicky feeling her head begin to nod even though she wanted to slap him.

But no longer did she want to run. What if Harrow really could help her family? Considering she was already ensnared in his web, there seemed to be no reason for him to make promises. Why was he doing this? Why did he want her to stay voluntarily when he could force her to stay? At this thought rose a trembling terror, strong and nauseating in her gut.

Harrow's eyes flashed with excitement. He had read something in her eyes just now, she was sure of it. "You want proof, of course," he gathered, a feat somehow more impressive than the manifestation of money – and far more frightening.

Vicky felt herself losing her balance, about to stumble backward, but Harrow reached out and pulled her into his chest, stroking her hair gently and saying, "It's all right, sweet child. You're safe here, beautiful angel. Upon me the burden of proof falls. He who arranges the show, expectation declares, should withhold no provision. I shall personally guide your family to health and fortune, and you shall claim this hall as your home."

Chapter 13

Brandon Joutel was sick of hockey. And the season hadn't even started yet.

The captains had demanded that everyone attend workouts each Tuesday, Thursday, and Saturday throughout the summer, a new initiative spearheaded by Eddy Englehart, last year's district leader in goals. According to Eddy, a lack of physical strength had cost their team the sectional championship the last two seasons.

"We need to be tougher," he always said, walking around with his hulking shoulders slumped forward. "We need to win the board battles this year, boys. We need to raise the compete level."

Brandon, the team's starting goaltender, and his older brother, Brady, a first-line winger heading into his senior season, spent most car rides to and from hockey practice laughing at something Eddy said or did. His pregame pump-up speeches often sounded like something out of a crusader movie. "This is a holy war, boys, a fucking holy war!" But although he always preached team, team, team, Eddy was really out there for himself, constantly ordering Brady and his other linemate to give him the puck, even when he was covered by two players and the passing option clearly wasn't there. Worse, after every game Eddy made sure to tell Coach Goderich how many points he recorded, just to be sure the coaches forwarded the correct info to the newspapers. And the coaches lapped up every sour drop of Englehart's Kool-aid, lauding him in the papers as a "once-a-decade type player" and "the heart and soul of the team." It was enough to make Brandon sick.

"Thank God Eddy's on vacation next week," Brady said, taking a bite of cheese pizza. "I can't stand it when he looms over people on bench press and says they need to do more."

"Tell that blockhead to get a life," said Brady's two-year girlfriend, Angie Prescott. They were tucked into a back booth at North Main Pizza, their frequent dinner hangout. The owner, Frankie Something-or-

Other, was chill, always giving them free bags of chips with their grinders and pizzas.

Brandon took a sip of Pepsi (soda was against Eddy's obsessive "nutrition guide", and so Brandon made sure to savor each can). He was seated opposite Brady and Angie, his sketchbook occupying the space his girlfriend would have taken if he'd had a girlfriend. He was an imminent junior and the hockey team's goalie – shouldn't he have a girlfriend?

"Sometimes I wish Eddy would just fail off the team," Brandon said. "He's such a puck hog douchebag – I honestly think we'd be better off without him."

"But he scores most of the goals," his brother said.

Brandon huffed. "Yeah, because you set him up all day. Without you doing the dirty work and getting him the puck, he's just a bum sitting in the slot."

Angie wrapped an arm around Brady's shoulders. "He has a point, you know. You're the one who fakes out the goalie and gives him lay-up opportunities. The passes are so good sometimes that my grandmother wouldn't miss."

Their laughter seemed to fill up the tiny restaurant. Aside from an old couple seated near the entrance, the place was empty, old Frankie What's-his-Name tinkering around behind the counter.

"So, Brandon, you want to come with us tonight?" Brady said, blotting his mouth with a napkin. "It took a lot of persuasion, but Cole said he'd take us through the institution."

Brandon shrugged. "I don't know, guys. It sounds kind of boring."

"Oh, come on, it'll be fun," Angie insisted. "You love horror movies – I heard this place is so creepy."

They were talking about the defunct mental hospital three towns over, where Brandon's and Brady's cousin Cole worked as a security guard. What a shitty, boring ass job that would be.

"Fine," Brandon sighed. He'd prefer to go home, jerk off, and play video games, but he figured he might as well see what the place was all about. Anyway, it was a summer night and he could always play video games later.

"Awesome," Brady said, and gave his little brother a fist bump.

Almost an hour later, Brady's virtually useless GPS finally brought them to the old hospital. First, it had decided to detour them to East Nowhere, USA, the robot woman's voice repeating, "When possible, make a legal U-turn. When possible, make a legal U-turn."

Piece of shit.

In the back seat, his sketchbook illuminated by the glow of his cell phone, Brandon was drawing another castle (he loved to draw school hallways and castles, over and over and over, a thing even *he* couldn't understand) when Brady brought the car to a stop outside a gate and said, "Here it is. We actually made it."

While his brother called Cole to let him know they'd arrived, Brandon looked past the gate down the entry road, which was flanked by brick buildings. One of them, immersed in moonlight and shadowed by branches, was particularly ominous. Maybe this would be kind of interesting, after all.

Cole rolled up a short time later in his little junker of a security car. Dressed in a dumbass uniform with a yellow shield patch on the shoulder, a cigarette between his lips, he came sauntering out of the car like he was legit or something. *Relax, dude, you're guarding a bunch of empty buildings*, Brandon thought.

~ 90 ~

Suddenly looking a little uneasy, Cole stamped out the cigarette and opened the gate for them. Earlier, Brady had said Cole was reluctant to have them come as previously planned because of what happened here last night, something about a bunch of sketchballs stealing a school bus, breaking through the gate, and driving onto the property. No one had been arrested. Weird.

Brady rolled down the passenger window. "Looks like they got the gate all fixed up, huh?" he said to Cole.

"Yeah, the maintenance guys came this afternoon." Cole glanced back toward his car. LEACH SECURITY GROUP, it read, the words confined within that stupid yellow shield logo. Brandon felt kind of bad for his cousin; all his life he'd wanted to be a cop. He'd busted nuts to get into the police academy and make good grades, only to be stuck with a gig that might earn a place on the top ten list of insufferably boring jobs. Oh well, at least it was a paying job, right? Brandon wasn't all that thrilled about his job, either (sharpening skates and stocking shelves at the local rink had its blah moments, especially when Mr. Plaskiewicz came around with his rancid breath).

Cole and Angie smiled and exchanged nice-to-see-you's. Then Cole shined his flashlight in Brandon's eyes and said, "Yo, what up, Brandy?"

Shielding his face with both hands, Brandon flicked out his middle fingers. Cole enjoyed messing with him, but it was all good. For cousins they were pretty close.

That Brandy shit had to go, though.

Later, when they all settled into chairs in the tiny security trailer – the air conditioner buzzing and rattling like it was dying – Cole grabbed them some sodas from the fridge. In the corner, Cole's old dude partner was playing chess against himself (if possible, he'd found a way to make the job even more boring). He was a friendly enough guy, though, hauling himself up from his chair and offering his wrinkly hand for shaking. Brandon would take him any day over his own grandfather, who literally answered his door with a shotgun in hand.

"Thanks again for having us, man," Brady said for the twenty-seventh time. "Tell us more about what happened last night."

Cracking open a soda, Cole took a seat before the cluttered desk, swung his legs up onto the paperwork, and shook his head at the memories. All around him, posted to the walls, were notices about state protocol and Leach Security this-and-that. Boring!

"Last night was the first real incident I've handled here," Cole said. "Last I heard, the police still haven't been able to determine where the bus came from."

"Whoever did it must have been destroyed on drugs," Brandon guessed.

Cole nodded. "Yeah, I keep wondering if they're still inside one of the buildings. The whole thing just didn't sit right with me."

"Check!" the old dude exclaimed from the corner. Really? Brandon couldn't stifle a chuckle. This was so whacked.

Cole, however, just kept on talking like he was used to the old guy's checky-check-checks. God, if Brandon had his job, he would bring beer every night.

"Do you think it was high school kids?" Angie said.

Cole shrugged. "Maybe, but you'd think we would've caught at least a few of them."

"Or maybe not, Barney Fife," Brandon said, and for a second, before he crumpled up a paper and tossed it at Brandon, Cole actually looked hurt. Brandon smirked. *I've only just started paying you back for the Superwedgie of 2001,* he thought.

"Anyway, the police said all sorts of weird stuff happened last night," Cole said. "There was a bad crash just before the bus incident here. Then, about an hour later, I guess there was another accident. Guy just randomly went off the road. He's still in critical condition."

"It must've been those storms," Brady said. "It was real bad overnight."

Angie brought a can of Sprite to her lips. "Yeah, the lightning was insane."

"Check!" the old man barked, squinting confusedly at the board. He wasn't even wearing a uniform, just a pair of khakis and a red and black plaid shirt. Was he really a security guard? Who could he possibly subdue, anyhow, an old lady in a wheelchair?

Brandon, feeling like he might lose it, pulled his phone from his pocket and texted the weirdness to his friend. He wished his friends could be here for this; it wouldn't be funny the next day, everyone telling him, *Yeah, real cool story, bro.*

"So, what do you say I give you guys that tour I promised?" Cole said.

"Sounds good, man." Standing, Brady reached for Angie's hand. Hopefully they wouldn't go all smoochy-smoochanovski like they always did, their tongues getting slobbery and making Brandon want to hurl.

Holding the door open for them, Cole said, "Maybe this isn't a good idea. I wouldn't want Brandy to get scared."

Brandon flipped him another bird. "You have to promise you'll protect me from the dreaded school bus driver," he said on his way down the steps.

Before the door clicked shut behind them, Brandon heard, "Checkmate!" What a strange night it was going to be.

Chapter 14

Leaving Jerome's house in the Lower Ninth Ward behind, Willy drove the blue Ford Windstar to the northern shore of Lake Pontchartrain. The six of them, even the old Native American, walked a short distance down to the water, everyone looking oddly serious. Jerome wondered what was happening. How would this eclectic group of strangers accomplish anything? They sure as hell wouldn't find Harrow here on the lake, at the edge of Fontainebleau State Park.

Although the others had already introduced themselves to Jerome during the ride, Willy insisted on another meet-and-greet session. "Form a circle, everybody. Come on now, let's bring it together," he said, waddling his way between Jerome and Sky.

As if praying before a meal, everyone extended arms and reached for the hands to their left and right. Uneasy, Jerome allowed Willy and the Native American, whose name was Ki, to squeeze his hands. He wondered if he was about to witness a séance.

Lifting his head to an overcast sky that darkened the lake, Willy closed his eyes and said, "Lord, I pray You'll guide us on our mission and give us strength. Our enemy possesses great power, to be sure, but by Your grace we too are empowered. It is not without risk that we accept the challenges and continue our quest, but this risk we embrace and cherish, for the mission is our call to serve You, Lord." He paused a moment, letting a cool breeze pour in off the water. It felt good against Jerome's face, a refreshing dose of normalcy. All around him the world appeared normal, but an unseen storm was gathering, a storm for which no one was prepared. Only this group of six could stop it, apparently, their mission to kill the storm before it could threaten anyone.

A mission from God? Jerome's father had always said there comes a day when every man will put his life on the line for the Lord, some in more obvious ways than others.

"Let us now officially welcome our newest member, Jerome Hudson," Willy said at the conclusion of his prayer. Chuckling, his eyes fell briefly to the ground, then returned to Jerome. "I'm still not sure what Jerome's abilities are, but do we not all feel the power emanating from this man?"

A collection of nods and murmurs. "Very powerful man," Ki agreed, repeating his first impression of Jerome.

Jerome shifted anxiously, gazing out to the lake and spotting a pair of sailboats. If only he could be on one of those boats now, away from these people and their mission. He didn't belong here. If they were to encounter Harrow, he'd have no idea what to do.

But something kept him there, a profound sense of purpose. The specifics of that purpose remained a mystery, but in the depths of his heart it seemed he'd been convinced by Willy that he had something to offer. Or maybe this was just desperation in action, a sinner's futile search for atonement, and he'd sell himself lies by the dozen if they were sugar-coated with promises.

"Welcome, Jerome," the others were saying, taking turns shaking hands with him. Sky's grip was firm and resolute. Oppositely, Ki had the handshake of a wraith, his brittle fingers sliding through Jerome's hand like sand.

The other two team members, both bespectacled – a thirtyish white man wearing a Hawaiian shirt and an elderly Hispanic woman in a flowery blouse – were named Buford Bancroft and Rosa Aylmer-Acosta. Buford, nicknamed Bu, was exceptionally skinny and unhealthy looking, with the gaunt face of a starving man and flamingo legs that somehow supported the rest of his body. Keeping a constant eye to the sky, he described himself as an aeromancer who could predict the future based on interpretations of clouds and rainbows and even wind currents.

Rosa had kind brown eyes and an inviting smile. She was heavyset in a well-distributed way, her black hair thick and sleek. Having practiced geomancy for more than fifty years, her head was often tilted to the ground in search of clues that might be provided by rocks and sand. According to Willy, she'd found over twenty dollars in change on the ground since they'd met, but this eighty-year-old lady's divinations weren't geared toward acquiring money but instead evidence of the man they pursued.

While the others spoke about their backgrounds and families, Sky – the pyromancer of the group – pulled away and began skimming rocks across the water. "Can we get the show on the road already?" she said impatiently, drawing a glare from Willy.

"We have to wait for Ki to get ready," Willy said, nodding toward the old man, who was staring raptly at the shallows, his eyes narrowed and searching. Earlier, on the way up here, the others had said Ki was a hydromancer. He saw imminent events in the ripples, they claimed, but Jerome couldn't fully believe it, nor could he believe that Sky saw things in fire and Bu saw things in the sky and Rosa saw things in the sand and Willy saw things in the lines of people's palms (big Willy was a proud chiromancer, said it was in his blood).

Yet a part of Jerome longed to learn his supposed skill. Another part of him wanted to call the police and report five likely escapees from a mental hospital. It was hard to admit life had led him here, to the shores of Lake Pontchartrain, a cast of "diviners" surrounding him. He should have been at home with Elise, preparing their Saturday brunch and then making plans with his daughter and her husband (at the time of her death, Jennie had been engaged to a boy she'd known since elementary school).

But now she was gone. Elise and Jennie were both gone, their time with Jerome cut far too short, like the warmth of a roaring fire extinguished to cold despair. His old life had been torn away and replaced by this inscrutable, irredeemable nightmare – it just wasn't fair.

Was this really God's plan for him? Or was it the work of the Devil, his hand behind each card? Considering what Jerome had done to Elise's killer, it wouldn't surprise him to find Satan lurking in every shadow of his fate.

"Quiet, everyone! Quiet! Give him some peace!" Willy barked. He was pointing at Ki, who'd knelt at the lake's edge and placed an ear to the lapping water, his ponytail dipping into Pontch's realm.

The group fell silent, everyone watching with heightened anticipation as if awaiting a jury's verdict. Rosa and Bu held hands, their eyes closed. Sky's arms were crossed, but her face had lost its impatient edge. These people legitimately believed in each other's divining abilities.

Ki plunked two rocks into the water, then pressed his face down again to mighty Pontch. With his palms he swished at the water, back and forth, as though he were trying to clear a car window of condensation. He chanted something unintelligible; it sounded to Jerome like *Ma-ha cheech kah! Uh-huh cheech mah! Ho bah bah bah!*

Jerome very nearly laughed, glad to keep it together.

After a few minutes of chanting and nodding and chopping at the water, Ki turned to the group and said, "I see a boy. Teenager. Harrow speaks to him tonight. I see buildings. Tall, old." He shook his head. "A theater, too. Big stage, yes. The place starts with O."

"Ohio!" Buford shouted. "I knew I saw Ohio in that vapor trail yesterday."

Jerome had to turn away so they wouldn't see his smile. These people were too much.

Now Willy was excited. He'd pulled a small notebook from his pocket and begun scribbling. "Sky, when you looked into the fire yesterday, you said you saw a bunch of old buildings burning, right?"

She nodded. "Yeah, really old brick pieces of shit. All of them ugly as fuck – they burnt up like toilet paper."

The others didn't seem bothered by Sky's choice of words, not even Rosa, who was studying the moist sand by the water. She scooped up a rock. "Here's another one, Willy," she said. "The guider rocks keep pointing north."

Willy nodded contemplatively, weighing all of the "clues" he'd been given. "It looks like we're off to Ohio, gang," he said with a shrug and a cautious smile.

Yet again Jerome suppressed a laugh. Just like that they were going to Ohio? Was this really how these people operated, determining a course of action based on recurring themes in their visions? What were they even seeing, anyway? Reflections of clouds in the water? Plumes of jet exhaust that just so happened to look like letters? Smoky shadows in a fire?

Or maybe they were on drugs.

Jerome forced himself to remember what had made him decide to join Willy. He'd wanted to help him, to leave life better than he'd found it, to act when inaction seemed inevitable. He truly believed there was a storm coming, in part because of what Willy had said but also because of how Jerome had felt in Harrow's presence. Thoughts of the Devil hadn't arisen purely from the whiskey.

But what could these people possibly do to stop Harrow? It was an enduring question. Even if they found him, how would they kill the guy?

Those who dare to oppose us – we'll kill them, Jerome, Harrow had said in the dark, dreary alley. *Soon there'll only be night, Jerome!*

A hand on his shoulder. "You coming or what, buddy?"

Separated from his thoughts, Jerome glanced to his left and saw Sky looking up at him. The others were heading back to the van, Willy leading the way.

"Yeah, let's go," Jerome said, and a smile spread across Sky's lips. She was happy he was coming, perhaps sensing he was an important part of their mission. All of them could sense his "power."

But Jerome remained in the dark, oblivious to his own gift. He didn't feel powerful. He felt useless and weak, a man without a family or even a home now, incapable of salvation. He belonged at Canal Nine, seated before the bar, sipping a glass of whiskey and waiting to die, yet these people seemed to think he belonged with them.

He would keep going, he told himself, if only to search his soul for that which Willy and the others could easily detect – that which the necromancer craved for his own purposes.

Chapter 15

Seated in the first row of the balcony, her hands clasped tightly together, Vicky looked down on the dark stage and waited for Harrow's show to begin. He'd restored her autonomy again, asking that in exchange for his generosity she join him in "spectatorship of a marvelous wonder."

Vicky glanced toward the side doors about one hundred feet to her left, wishing she could escape into the night. But Harrow, smelling strongly of cologne, sat beside her, his arm around her shoulders. He'd given her a fleece jacket to ensure she stayed warm, even though the theater was thick with August humidity.

Vicky had agreeably slid into the roomy jacket, wanting to keep as many layers between herself and Harrow as possible. Yet whenever he touched her, she found herself less and less repelled by his dark charisma, the soft, sinuous elegance of his voice bringing inexplicable hopes. It had to be the magic, she knew. He was manipulating her with sinister energies, but no matter how much she built up her guard, Harrow had his ways of slipping past it.

Eventually the lights clicked off and a spotlight fell upon the stage, then lifted to the crimson curtains which had been pulled shut.

"At last the show has begun!" Harrow exclaimed, clapping his gloved hands repeatedly. Earlier, he'd snapped on the white gloves and promised Vicky a pair of her own if she committed to the trade of magic.

As if they were in a movie theater, the spotlight yielded to motion pictures upon the curtains. Not a sound accompanied them, but there was no need for auditory enhancements. Vicky was awestruck by what she saw – her father standing between two suited men, a massive check before them. Plastered on the wall behind them were multiple Kentucky Lottery logos.

WELCOME TO HARROW HALL

Now the sound came crackling over the speakers, at first inaudible but then perfectly clear (after a few snaps from Harrow). Her father and the other men were being interviewed by a local news anchor. "Mr. Eldridge will take home five hundred thousand dollars," she said, eliciting additional applause from Harrow.

Turning to Vicky, he brushed a gloved hand through her hair, Vicky leaning away and grimacing in response. "Voila!" he whispered. "And this is only the beginning, my child. Just imagine the places magic will take you."

Vicky could only manage a befuddled stare, trying desperately to search his face. In the darkness of the auditorium, he was nothing more than a shifting shape, his voice like that of the darkness itself. "How are you doing all of this?" she said.

Harrow chuckled. "I already told you, I was sent by your mother. This is your gift, Victoria. You must embrace it. Why entrust your future to the whims of society when the occult holds your true destiny?"

Deeply shaken, Vicky stood and tried to get away. Whatever Harrow was doing, it was too powerful. Had her father even won the lottery, or had Harrow fabricated those images somehow, an elaborate trick of light? Vicky didn't know what to think. She couldn't tell what was real anymore, mistrustful of even her own emotions, desperate to get away from Harrow and his phantasmagoric theater and his promises, away from the others, who she hadn't seen since first arriving last night in the school bus, away from this nightmare.

But when Harrow restrained her by the wrist, a mesmerized peace came over her, as if she'd been sedated by his touch and brought instantly to a still and relaxed state. "Be calm now, child," he whispered. "With Harrow, healed will be all wounds. I shall never let a soul harm you, never, never, never shall that be." He leaned in and kissed her cheek. "Would you like a friend, sweet Victoria? I sense one approaching this moment, a charming lad to keep you company, a boy who knows nothing of his potential. Magic you both will learn, yes?"

Vicky felt like she was lifting upward, elevated by Harrow's words and his strange, soothing cadence. It was almost like being in a dream, surreal and safe, an inviolable place that – even if it became unexpectedly frightening – could never inflict physical harm.

Vicky closed her eyes, feeling very sleepy and calm, as comfortable as a child sliding beneath the covers of a freshly made bed.

"A friend," she murmured, falling away from life and letting the darkness take hold.

"A friend," Harrow said. "A kind, beautiful boy, his hand forever yours to guide."

The images went dark.

Harrow Hall was silent once more.

Chapter 16

The four of them climbed into the shitty little Leach Security Group car and hit the road, Cole driving granny-slow and showing them all the creepy buildings. The campus was a maze of moonlit brick, the buildings linked by dozens of access roads and driveways rising up hills and sweeping around corners.

The freakiest part, Brandon thought, were the sporadically illuminated windows, some of them on the top floors.

"Oh my God, that's so scary," Angie said from the back seat with Brady as they passed one of the buildings. "You can see into the rooms."

"Yeah, they keep different lights on each night to prevent mold from growing," Cole explained. "I heard the insides of a lot of these buildings are real nasty."

"What's with the exes on the buildings?" Brady said, referring to the reflective red lines and exes that marked each building near its front entrance.

"One line means the building will survive the first round of demolitions next spring," Cole said. "The buildings with exes are getting knocked down right away."

They drove around a while longer, everyone trying to get each other worked up by shouting stuff like, "I just saw someone in the window!" and "What's that in the road?" and "Who's that guy?"

Eventually Cole carried on about the history of the institution as they returned to the campus center, where a flagpole jutted into the night and a small pavilion lingered in shadowy decay. If it weren't for the lights spilling from a nearby building, the pavilion would have been completely hidden between a square of trees. This was one of many places where staff members used to gather for lunch during warm months, Cole announced tour guide-like. And sometimes special events were organized for patients in the pavilion – singing, dancing, games.

"One of my partners said he heard music and laughter one night. Some people say this place is haunted."

"That's bull. He was probably lit," Brandon said, staring out the passenger window.

Cole brought the car to a halt at the intersection with the road that would take them back to the little security trailer. "I'm telling you, he was legitimately scared. And this guy's never smoked a joint in his life."

Brandon shook his head. "Scared? Of this place? What a pussy."

"Being alone at night is tough. Sometimes you freak yourself out, you know?"

"Not really."

"You wouldn't last five minutes out here without pissing yourself," Brady said, Angie giggling beside him.

Smirking, Cole patted Brandon on the shoulder. "I have to agree with him, man. Even I get a little weirded out some nights."

"Are you kidding? I could spend a whole night out here."

"Yeah, prove it," Brady challenged. "Stay out here for five minutes. We'll loop around the buildings again and pick you up, but I bet you're too scared."

"I don't know," Angie said, sounding worried. "That's probably not a good idea. We should just go back to the trailer."

WELCOME TO HARROW HALL

A shot of adrenaline rushed through Brandon, the very same impetus that had caused him to jump off an old railroad trestle last summer, the first of his friends to leap into the lake below. He didn't like shying away from obstacles, and he absolutely hated it when people said he couldn't do something. All his life he'd been told he couldn't do things – a youth coach had once said he didn't have a quick enough glove to play goalie; a second grade reading teacher had told his mother he shouldn't be in the regular class because he wouldn't be able to keep up; during his first ever high school hockey practice, his goalie coach had said he'd need to be very patient, for he wouldn't likely ascend to the role of starter until junior year.

"Screw that," Brandon said, and yanked open the passenger door. "Go drive around for an hour if you want. Pick me up whenever. Maybe I'll even go inside one of the buildings."

Cole suddenly looked uncertain. After Brandon shut the door behind him, Cole rolled down the passenger window. "They're all locked, so just stay away from them. I'll meet you back here in five. Don't do anything stupid."

Brandon thought about flipping him off, but a better idea sparked into his head; he unbelted his shorts, bent down, and offered them a full moon. A collection of groans, Angie's the loudest, preceded the car tearing away and following a curve out of sight.

Now Brandon was completely alone, just him and the moonlit night, everything splashed in shadows. A slight breeze stirred the trees. The flagpole made a loud clanking noise that sent chills down Brandon's arms. Okay, so it was kind of freaky being out here alone, but he'd never admit it to Brady and Cole. They were always conspiring against him, as if *they* were brothers and Brandon was a little orphan boy to pick on. The Superwedgie of 2001, in fact, had been another of their team efforts, Brady holding his brother down while Cole delivered the pain.

That had been a bad Thanksgiving.

Clunking down the road – away from the campus center – with oddly hollow steps, Brandon walked toward a large building on the right side of the road. He didn't want Cole to return and find him in precisely the same spot where they'd left him (that would undoubtedly lead to a night of ribbing). No, he would explore this dark ass building – and if it happened to be unlocked, he would challenge himself to go inside.

Turning off the road and following a torn up walkway leading to the front entrance of the building, Brandon tried to think of some way to scare Brady and Cole. He wanted to get them really good, and this was the perfect opportunity. He just needed a plan, preferably something that would leave them fearing for his safety.

Brandon approached the building warily, not wanting to get too close for some reason. He wasn't afraid – there was just something off about the place, a weird vibe that made Brandon feel uneasy. Harrow Hall, the building was called, its white letters illuminated by the bright moon. Taped to the inside of the glass doors were NO TRESPASSING orders issued by the State of Ohio, Brandon shining his cell phone at them.

Violators may be subject to fine, arrest and or additional remedies prescribed by state law…

"Pfff." Brandon dismissed the threats and tried the doors.

Locked.

"As expected." He made his hands into blinders and tried to search the darkness inside. Not a single light outlined the interior.

"Would you like to go inside, boy?" came a voice from behind him.

Though he wouldn't confess to it unless tortured, Brandon let out an embarrassing gasp and whirled around. Standing in the road was a tall man, his arms crossed. *Oh, no*, Brandon thought. *A security guard's gonna bust me for trying to get into this place.*

But the man wasn't wearing a security uniform. Dressed in a trench coat and a tall hat, he looked like he belonged in another decade.

"Who are you?" Brandon strained his eyes to get a closer look, but suddenly a row of lampposts flanking the walkway came aglow, one after another, as though some prodigious happening was ready to unfurl itself.

Brandon's heart zipped into a higher gear, sweat spreading across his forehead. He felt that swimmy-slidy sensation in his gut that always arrived when hot girls spoke to him, except tonight he wasn't in the presence of a babe but a creepy dude.

The guy took a few steps closer. "I am Harrow."

Brandon wrinkled his forehead. "Harrow, like the building?"

The man's laughter rose like a released toxin. That Brandon couldn't see his eyes beneath the brim of the hat was unsettling. "Yes, like the building," he said. "My new home this place has become. Isn't it a grand place?"

"Wait, you live here?"

Drawing even closer along the walkway, Harrow said, "Yes, I have chosen this institution as my home. Or, more accurately, it has been chosen for me."

Brandon stuffed his hands into his shorts pockets. "So you're a drifter." He was no longer afraid; this guy was just like the bum who lived at the local rink, probably a drunk looking for a quiet place to throw back the bottle.

The man looked casually up to the moon. "Some would call me a magician, others a sorcerer. A few would choose soothsayer. You, young boy, may call me drifter if you prefer." He laughed again, pointing a finger at Brandon. "As long as you don't call me shaman, agreeable I'll remain."

Now it was Brandon who was laughing. This clown sounded like Johnny Depp from *Pirates of the Caribbean*. "Whatever you say, man. But you better not let my cousin see you when he gets back. He'll probably freak out and call the cops."

The man nodded understandingly. The closer he got, the easier it was to see his face, though his eyes remained a mystery. "To what name does your cousin answer?"

It took Brandon a moment to process the question. "Ah…Cole. He's one of the guards here."

"Oh, yes, the guards who patrol that which the state condemns." From his trench coat he pulled a pack of cigarettes. "Would you like a smoke, boy?" He inched a little closer, smiling invitingly at Brandon.

"No, thanks," Brandon said, watching as Harrow placed a finger against the tip of his cigarette and held it there a few seconds…and the thing ignited, the orange glow bringing a smile to Harrow's lips.

Brandon straightened. "Hold up. How'd you light that thing with your finger?"

Blowing out a puff of smoke, Harrow waved his hand and glanced up to the moon again. "Never does the power of magic cease to amaze, young boy. If you'd approve, perhaps a morsel or two of knowledge I might impart."

Harrow removed his hat. Beneath was a rag of long, messy black hair. When he turned briefly to the road, Brandon saw a trail of hair stretching past his shoulders.

"Such waste," Harrow said, locking his eyes upon Brandon once more. "The state justified the closure of this place as a cost-cutting initiative, yet it still pays thousands of dollars each month in electricity bills and security fees." He shook his head. "And these buildings rot while people go homeless. Is there not abject wrongness to such a notion?"

Brandon shot a look down the road, hoping to see the headlights of Cole's little car approaching. He was getting tired of this dude and his blah-blah-blah complaining – if he wasn't gonna do some magic, Brandon would peace out.

Almost as if Harrow had heard his thoughts, he said, "So, how about a touch of magic, boy?"

Nodding, Brandon wondered if this guy was on a sex offender list. "Show me a card trick or something. You do that stuff?"

"Hah!" the man shouted. "Why waste your time on the beach when the cool water beckons? Immerse yourself, lad. Feel the refreshing splendor within your soul."

Definitely a pervo. Brandon wanted to run, but something held him in place. Anticipation. He wanted to see what this guy could do.

Harrow tossed his cigarette away. Donning his hat again – and adjusting it several times – he said, "Pick a number, boy, and from your mind I shall extract it."

"Between one and ten?"

"Between zero and infinity. See the number in your mind. See it so clearly that it glows."

Brandon chuckled. Was this guy bullshitting? He decided on 739, a number Harrow would never be able to guess – but after only Brandon's second visualization of the number, Harrow shouted. "Seven! Three! Nine! Seven hundred and thirty-nine, Brandon."

Gasping, Brandon stumbled backward to the doors. Dry-mouthed and speechless, he stared agape at Harrow.

"How…how did you…how?"

Harrow jogged toward him. Brandon thought about running again but stayed put, not wanting to let Harrow think he'd intimidated him. "Relax, boy. Breathe in and out," Harrow said, placing a hand upon Brandon's shoulder, and he suddenly felt very lightheaded and tired. A faint smell of cologne came to him, barely registering above his drowsiness.

Behind them, one of the doors clicked open. Brandon was vaguely aware of walking into Harrow Hall – now dimly illuminated – with this stranger, but it was like he was navigating the lands of a dream, everything seeming to float and drift. It reminded Brandon of his tonsillectomy last year following complications with a peritonsillar abscess, particularly the moments before they anesthetized him.

The main room, a theater with a large stage, was swirling and spinning, Harrow's voice echoing from everywhere. When lucidity returned, Brandon was sitting in the first row, still lightheaded, the bright stage before him.

Seated beside Brandon was the most beautiful girl he'd ever seen.

Chapter 17

"I told you this was a bad idea," Angie grumbled.

Cole brought the car to a stop at the campus center, almost the exact spot where he'd let Brandon out five minutes ago. Now there was no sign of his cousin.

Cole rubbed his thin goatee in annoyance. "I'm gonna stuff that freaking kid in the trunk."

"He'll come any second," Brady assured. "He's just messing with us, that's all. Trying to get us back for saying he'd be too scared out there."

Cole silently cursed himself. He should have known Brandon would do something like this. He was just too damn smart for his own good, but he was also reckless and sophomoric (an appropriate description considering his age). From the night Brandon and his friends toilet-papered their entire neighborhood three Halloweens back to the winter afternoon last year he thought it would be a good idea to go skating on his family's frozen pool, the kid was always getting himself into trouble. Cole and Brady often tried to put him in his place, but it only seemed to spur Brandon to greater rebellion. Brady was afraid that next year, when he was away at college, his younger brother would fall victim to drugs and alcohol, a fear he'd occasionally expressed to Cole. Apparently Brandon had already taken to drinking at parties, and hopefully it wouldn't escalate. Several of Cole's high school friends who'd been early drinkers were now either full-blown alcoholics or shamelessly beer-gutted.

"What if he got lost?" Angie worried.

Brady sighed. "He didn't get lost. I'm telling you, it's just Brandon being Brandon."

They waited five minutes and tried Brandon's cell phone twice, both messages going straight to voicemail. Angie's apprehensiveness was becoming contagious; now even Cole found himself dreading an animal attack or a dark stumble down a staircase. Or, even worse, what if Brandon somehow snuck into one of the buildings and got injured? Although the other guards often invited friends and family members to check out the institution grounds during overnight shifts, Leach Security Group prohibited its staff from allowing any unapproved visitors onto the property. If Brandon was involved in some kind of incident and Cole's boss found out about it, he could lose his job…and then what? How would he ever get a job in law enforcement after being fired from his position as a security guard?

A minute or two later, Brady said, "How about we get out and wait here for him? Cole, you take another drive around the place – we'll call you if he comes back."

"Good idea. I'm gonna beat his ass when we find him."

"I don't like this, Brady," Angie said when they stepped out, her arms crossed and face twisted sourly. "Not at all. What if he's hurt?"

Cole sped off down the road, leaving them to their worries. "Damn it, Brandon!" he shouted, slamming a hand against the steering wheel.

Thoughts of last night's school bus got Cole driving even faster. The police hadn't caught the suspect(s). Whoever had brought that bus here might have…no, that was ridiculous. Or was it?

Cole circled the institution, roaring past Hodskins and Wayside and Longview and spooky old Granite, occasionally rolling down the window and shouting his cousin's name. This was getting too long for a prank – even Brandon wouldn't let it persist this long. What the hell was going on?

When Cole returned to the campus center, a bizarre sight stole his attention.

Harrow Hall was fully illuminated.

Chapter 18

Jerome finished off his roast beef po' boy and washed it down with a sip of beer. He'd worked up a mighty craving for whiskey, but he didn't want his new group thinking he was a lush; even two beers induced a trifle of guilt as their Pitch game continued.

"Winning time," Jerome said before lifting the cards and checking his hand. It was a pretty good one: ace, king, ten, and six of hearts. If he bid three and Sky delivered jack or low, they'd have a great shot to take command of the game.

"Two," Willy bid, smiling and nodding at his hand.

When Jerome, the dealer, announced his three bid, Sky rolled her eyes. "Whoa, bold move there, guy. Are you trying to get our asses set here?"

"Have a little faith, would ya?" Jerome chuckled. He couldn't believe he was actually having fun with these people, but they weren't a bad group.

After driving northeast toward Ohio for most of the day, they'd decided to stop at a hotel in Nashville, Willy paying for three rooms and a ton of food. He was obviously a wealthy man, refusing no request at the nearby grocery store before they got to the hotel, not even Sky's hoard of Sour Patch candies. At the rate she downed them, it was a wonder her teeth were still rooted to her gums.

After they'd all gotten settled into the hotel, Willy had ordered dinner for the group from an Italian place the clerk said was good. When he'd paid the delivery boy for all the food – a large pizza with everything on it, three po' boys, and an order of spaghetti – Jerome had pulled out his wallet and asked if he could help. It felt wrong to indulge on the house like this, their rooms and meals all taken care of (in addition to the fifty grand bonus), but Willy kept insisting they'd paid enough by simply agreeing to the mission. If that was the case, Jerome couldn't help wondering if these were their last meals.

Jerome won his bid with very little assistance from Sky. She provided a ten toward game, but Jerome had to do the hard work and capture low from Rosa, who'd only been playing Pitch for a few months.

The four of them were gathered around a small circular table by the window. At the desk, Ki was reading a *Harry Potter* book, squinting confusedly at the pages as though the book were written in Chinese. Bu was sitting against the backboard in bed, tapping away at his laptop. Everyone would have a roommate tonight, Willy had said, and this room would be shared by Bu and Ki.

When Jerome won another three bid – this one even riskier – Sky leaped up and began a celebratory dance, pointing at Willy and Rosa and shaking her hips and shoulders.

"Lucky game, all luck," Willy said, scooping up another slice of pizza from the box on the windowsill. "Sky, you're lucky to be playing with a pro here. If I'd known this guy was so good, I would have been partners with *him*."

"What a turncoat!" Rosa said. With an endearing giggle, she twirled a forkful of spaghetti in her tin container. At the grocery store, she'd selected a bag of apples and other healthy selections while Sky had been grabbing up all the sweets.

Willy glanced toward the door for what might have been the hundredth time. Jerome didn't like the look in his eyes – the look of paranoia. Jerome had seen that look in the mirror far too many times following the night he'd taken the life of Elise's killer. His eyes had been different thereafter, much darker, almost to the point of unfamiliarity. But with the help of the kind offerings at Canal Nine, Jerome had been able to endure his reflection for more than a few seconds at a time, whiskey mitigating the monster staring back at him.

You lost control. You let your grief take over. You're a murderer, his sober thoughts had condemned, but the whiskey had assured, *He had it coming. You saved lives, Jerry. He would have drove away and killed some other guy's wife.*

Jerome spent the next hour talking to Willy and Sky, the most talkative members of his new team. It was fascinating to hear their stories and how they'd wound up here. Willy, as Jerome already knew from their conversation at Canal Nine, had been tracking Harrow for years, inheriting the crusade from his father, who'd spent fifty years searching the bayous for the necromancer. But now Willy was plunging deeper into his father's story, delving down to the depths of misery and evil.

"Harrow raised spirits in the cemetery right next to our house one night," Willy said. "My father saw the whole thing, saw the tormented spirits torn from their places of rest." He clenched his fists, then released them slowly. "They floated and dragged their way through the fog to Harrow, obeying his every command, most awful thing my father ever saw. Then, just like that" – he snapped his fingers – "they were just gone, vanished. The next morning the coppers said half of the tombstones were destroyed, caskets blown open, bodies missing. My father never told them what he saw. Who would have believed him?"

Willy took a sip of water straight from the one-gallon jug he'd bought at the grocery store. "My father had heard plenty of rumors about what Harrow was doing in the area, but until that night he didn't believe them. That wasn't the worst of it, though. No, far from it." He shook his head, checking the door yet again. "About a month later, in St. Catherine's Cemetery across town, he raised the dead again. This time they looted Main Street, set buildings on fire, and sent five people to the hospital. Then it happened in another town. Everyone blamed it on kids, but my father knew what was going on, saw the patterns developing – but he still wasn't bent on chasing Harrow and exposing himself to the darkness. He had a good job and a family to look after, so he tried to put what he saw out of his head, tried to just keep on minding his business, but then Harrow approached him one day."

Sky pointed to her tank top (BLACK LIKE MY SOUL, it read). "His soul really is black."

"He has no soul," Willy murmured. "He wanted my father to help him, said he was raising an army."

"He tells that to everyone," Sky said. "He needs to come up with a new advertising campaign."

"Would you stop interrupting?" Willy snapped, and Sky stuck her tongue out at him.

"Anyway," Willy continued, "when my father refused him, Harrow said everything will burn and then set our house on fire, every room going up at once, floor to ceiling with flames. My father barely got me and my sister out alive, wrapped us up in blankets and burned himself real bad in the process. He was in the hospital for months, ended up losing his job. My mother had to take me and my sister to live with my grandmother in Biloxi. We didn't see Dad for almost a year, and when we finally did, he was a changed man. You could see the need for retribution in his eyes – it was all he ever talked about. I knew he wouldn't rest until he got his revenge against Harrow."

Willy shrugged. "Rest is pretty much history, I guess. I went my own way, made my money in New York, but I always had a sense I'd head back south one day and take up my father's cause. He died an alcoholic, you know, scarred and obsessed and ruined, and he never caught up with Harrow."

"Jesus Christ." It was all Jerome could say. Now he knew how lucky he'd been when Harrow simply let him stumble away that drizzly night. But why hadn't Harrow killed him? After Jerome refused to join his army, what value had he maintained?

"What about you, Sky?" Jerome said. "What made you want to team up with these guys against Harrow?"

She popped a few sour candies into her mouth. "I don't know," she shrugged between bites. "It's not nearly as dramatic as Willy's story. To be honest, I've got no personal beef with Harrow. Never even seen the guy anywhere but my visions." She nodded at Rosa to her right. "She recruited me."

"Recruited you?" Jerome said.

Sky emptied the bag of candies into her hand, then packed her cheeks with the sour-sugary cluster. Though her face didn't so much as twitch, Jerome was flinching vicariously across the table.

"Yeah, Rosa kept me straight when I was coming off the rails," Sky mumbled, chewing. "Used to live in Florida with my parents, two of the biggest losers you could imagine. My dad was a meth head who bailed when I was seven, and my mom drank all the time and watched TV religiously when she wasn't working at McDonald's. I was always on my own, which was how I liked it, but I couldn't stay out of trouble. Always lighting shit on fire."

"Is that because you wanted to see things in the fires?" Jerome guessed, remembering all that talk this afternoon about Sky being a skilled "pyromancer."

"Shit no," Sky said. "I just liked setting things on fire and seeing them burn. It was fun…until the night it got out of control. I must have been ten or eleven. Mom was passed out drunk in the house after dinner, and I had a nice little blaze going in the back yard pit I made. It was a windy night, though, and while I was looking for more shit to burn, my fire jumped the rocks and went wild."

Sky began gesturing excitedly, her eyes wide and expressive. As she continued her story, describing how her unruly back yard fire wound up burning her mother's shed to the ground and then spreading to an abandoned house on an adjacent street, Jerome stole glances at the tattoos on her chest. To do this he required furtive eye movements, for he didn't want Sky to misconstrue his intent. In spite of her curly blue hair, her multitude of tattoos, and her black fingernail polish – beneath all these distractions – she was a very pretty young woman, with slender cheekbones, a delicate nose, and enigmatic hazel eyes that seemed to constantly change color, ranging from a soft golden brown to a glittering green. Her chin was slight and angular, her skin darkened by a late summer's tan. Jerome wondered what color her hair really was; judging by her light eyebrows, it might well have been blonde.

Sky was smoothing the empty Sour Patch bag against the table. "After the debacle, they made me go to this dumbass fire safety program. Things got better for a little while, but then my mom got arrested for drunk driving when I was twelve. The courts said I had to live with my grandparents in New Orleans. Maybe I was rebelling or something, but I started lighting fires like crazy. I dug out this huge hole and surrounded it with rocks – The Incinerator, I called it, threw all sorts of stuff in there."

"But one of those fires went out of control," Rosa said with a thin smile.

Sky shrugged. "Maybe it was fate. The fire ended up burning my grandparents' house down – thank God they weren't home. Anyway, the courts forced me to do community service and attend behavioral therapy sessions, and guess who happened to be my therapist?"

Sky pushed her chair back and walked over to Rosa, wrapping her thin arms around the old woman and kissing her cheek. "Rosa helped me get my life together, showed me things I could do for fun other than setting fires."

Willy had tuned the conversation out. Now he was alternating glances between his cell phone and the door. He looked very tense, and he kept taking deep breaths, his actions making Jerome nervous but seeming to have no effect on the others.

"So when did you realize you could see stuff in the flames?" Jerome said.

Sky returned to her seat. "Not until I was sixteen. By that time Rosa and I had developed a close relationship. Even after the court-mandated appointments were over, I saw her almost every week for years. Neither of us knew about each other's talents, though, not until I told her I was seeing things in fires, even the flames of candles."

Yawning, Willy pocketed his phone and stood. "Well, I think I'll head to bed early, everyone. Y'all know how food gets me real sleepy."

Without being asked to do so, the others abruptly stopped what they were doing. Ki turned from the desk. Bu slid off the bed. Sky and Rosa popped up from the table. Everyone converged at the center of the room, forming the same circle they'd made at Pontchartrain, Willy and Ki leaving a space between them for Jerome.

When Jerome reluctantly entered the circle and everyone locked hands, they crouched down low and closed their eyes. Willy recited the Lord's Prayer, then asked God to spare them from evil through the night, and it was in that huddle that Jerome felt their sacred bond for the first time. A palpable, church-like solidarity had settled over the room, as intensely unseen as wind. When Willy fell silent, their hands remained connected, Willy and Ki almost simultaneously squeezing Jerome's hands even tighter.

Then Ki began to chant, fast-paced and unintelligible. Jerome had no idea what he was saying, but it sounded good, real good, practiced and inveterate, reminding him of the chants he'd learned while fighting in Vietnam. After a while they'd become second nature, those chants, representative of the iron bonds forged between warriors who'd lived and died by the same code – soldiers who'd fought the enemy and tried their best to avoid the scarcely less hateful racial war between men of the same flag, a war sometimes waged with the simple weaponry of an ill glance.

Now it was Rosa's turn. She spoke in Spanish, frequently saying Dios – another prayer. Later, Bu said a quick prayer, and then Sky, who simply said, "No matter what, this time tomorrow, we form another circle. Amen."

When Willy told Jerome it was his turn to say whatever he wanted, it seemed like everything had already been covered. However, their hands still linked, everyone was waiting for him to say something. Caught off guard, Jerome could only offer a chant from the darkest days of war, a time when the Viet Cong had sometimes felt like a lesser enemy than soldiers in his own infantry division. He would never forget those chilling glimpses into the eyes of fellow soldiers, nothing but malice searing back at him, deep with the desire to see him finished by the next day's violence. The race riots had been endless in the late sixties, the conflicts bitter, Jerome and his comrades fighting a ruthless war for their country in the jungles of Nam while, back home, racists declared war against his brothers in cities across the country.

"We fight for freedom," Jerome said quietly, remembering perfectly the chant that had originated as a poem written by a comrade in one of those too-short spaces between the killing. "We fight with grace. We fight for country, never for race. We come proudly. We come strong. With *You* in our hearts, Lord, we can't go wrong. Give us this night, we pray, O Lord, and another tomorrow, for it won't be long till we endure new sorrows. One day the war will end, but until then we fight. By Your endless strength, Lord, our hearts find light."

There lingered a screaming silence, wartime memories briefly ravaging Jerome, the sounds and sights and smells of death, scars reopened. Then, like a youth baseball team, everyone brought their hands to the middle and raised them, pointing up to God, who'd so often left Jerome devastated and defeated. For a moment he felt empty, but soon he found himself lifting his arm as well, warmed by some mysterious force – an expanding faith in himself and a group of strangers he'd only just met.

Yet he felt a familiar affection for them and a bolstered conviction in their purpose, the kind that spawns loyalty. If he stayed with them any longer, he feared he wouldn't be able to leave until their mission was complete.

Chapter 19

Within the crumbling shell of Granite Hall, seated upon a stool in the middle of a moldy, candlelit second floor room, Harrow sprinkled a pinch of conjuring dust upon his father's planchette, awakening the ancient piece for another assignment.

After receiving its instructions, the wooden planchette scraped its way to the Great Board, which Harrow had earlier unfolded in the far corner, assiduously preparing for another act of divination.

"A new time has arrived. Indeed, deepens does the darkness, its shores falling kindly away. Soon all must swim."

With a grin Harrow followed his little friend – a talisman long ago carved into the shape of a fleur-de-lis – to the Great Board, each square depicting in marvelous detail a scene of necromancy. Here, at the foremost section of the board, were stirred souls moving groggily about a moonlit graveyard, and in the center – beheld by the Wilderness Witch's violet eyes – were the Night Spirits, rising from the fog of a bayou and winding through the trees. At the right edge of the board, the sufferers grimaced in eternal torment beneath the blood-streaked pentagram, countless men and women who dared to stare into the flames and reject the existence of their Master. He who does not believe in magic shall fall to it, Harrow's father had always said, a message with which countless lessons had concluded.

Harrow watched the planchette begin its signature spin. It was harnessing the board's energies and measuring them against the energies of its assignment, essentially a magnet drawn to the point of greatest attraction. Soon it would ignite into a soft amber, then, gradually, shift into a magnificent orange, the color of oozing lava. At this stage, the pinnacle of intensity, the future would come to Harrow on the board, its squares and images replaced by events soon to transpire. On nights when the Spirits were occupied and a well-inhabited cemetery was not near (or whenever Harrow wished to see specific events in perfect clarity), he turned to the Great Board and his father's trusty planchette.

After killing his father countless decades ago, Harrow had ripped the beloved piece from the feeble man's necklace and claimed its glory as his own, its powers no longer sustaining stagnation but supporting a burgeoning supremacy. His father had often told him you must take by force that which is not willingly offered.

The planchette blazed orange, letting out a high vibrating whistle. Like a television being switched on, the colors and images burst forth. Harrow leaned over the board, arms outspread, carefully observing each face. He snapped his fingers, summoning four of his soldiers from the corner of the room, where they'd been sitting obediently as Harrow readied the planchette and the Great Board.

"Do not merely memorize these faces, lads," Harrow told them. "Emblazon these most hateful visages upon the fabric of your hearts and minds. Let their eyes guide you to them, and with the assistance of the Spirits, end swiftly their lives. Extinguished must be all who hold a light against the darkness!"

As Harrow had previously instructed, his soldiers joined hands and paid tribute to the Master, He who enabled the Spirits to rise, He who would forever darken the universe, He who – with Harrow as his worldly king – would wrest control from the oppressors.

When his soldiers were gone and Harrow was alone with the Great Board, the planchette still and cool in his palm, he returned to the stool and shook his head in fleeting disappointment.

"You could have joined my army, Jerome Hudson. I was hoping you'd make the proper decision, but now you must die. War you will never know until my soldiers' blades are upon your neck."

Deep within the infinite realm of the board, crackling laughter erupted from a world of fire, and Harrow was again reminded that, in order to achieve complete control, countless resources would need to burn.

Chapter 20

Brady and Angie were standing on the walkway leading to the front entrance of Harrow Hall. Stepping out of his car, Cole didn't notice them at first. He was too stunned by the brightly illuminated building; it seemed like every light in the auditorium had been turned on. The exterior lights had also been brought to life, including a row of lampposts delineating the walkway.

It wasn't until Brady shouted, "What the hell's going on?", that Cole spotted his cousin and Angie on the walkway. "This building just randomly lit up a few minutes ago. Does this happen every night?"

Cole shook his head. "No, usually Harrow Hall is dark. Come on, get in."

When they were back inside the car, Cole explained what he'd seen the previous night in Harrow Hall – a spotlight glaring down on center stage. "I wrote it up in my incident report, but I doubt anyone looked into it. Fixing the gate was their main priority."

"Well, maybe they *should* look into it." Angie let out a frustrated sigh. "Clearly whoever broke into this place last night is messing around in the buildings."

"Not necessarily," Cole said. "The maintenance guys might've decided to have the lights turn on and off every few hours to prevent mold from growing. Maybe it's a new directive from the state. Who knows – they might even be on a timer or something." Even Cole didn't believe that was the case, but what else could he tell them? The last thing he wanted was to worry them even more.

What if those people from last night really are still here? And what if Brandon came across them?

Cole considered contacting Ronny about the lights, then remembered that Ronny didn't care about anything beyond his chess games once he got started on them. He didn't even stop to look at the buildings during his rounds, just made a little circle of the institution, swiped his clearance card at the checkpoints to prove he actually toured the place, and hurriedly returned to his perpetual game against himself. He would probably die at the chess board, Cole figured, some unfortunate mortician forced to extract a pawn from his rigid fingers.

"What are we gonna do?" Brady said, panicked. "If Brandon's screwing with us, he can find his own ride home. You think *he* turned on the lights?"

Cole could use a cigarette – and a new job, too. Leave it to Brandon to make his lousy job even more miserable than it already was. He rubbed his goatee and took a deep breath. "Only one thing to do," he said, fidgeting with the set of keys on his belt. "I've gotta check out these buildings, one by one."

***

Brandon felt like he was in a dream. Nothing seemed real, especially not the gorgeous girl seated beside him. She was like an illusion, a dehydrating man's mirage, staring straight ahead at the dim, empty stage, her slender hands clasped across her lap, blue eyes vacant, a girl seemingly at peace within her own dream.

Brandon blinked in amazement, wondering at the sudden notion of an invisible wall standing between them. He wanted to say something, but to shatter her motionless trance felt not only wrong but criminal. She reminded him distinctly of a girl in a snow globe, unreachable beyond her glass enclosure, sheltered from life and not to be disturbed. Dressed in blue shorts and a black fleece jacket, her blonde hair straightened down her back, she could not have been more perfect, beyond description.

And then it was over, the seat suddenly unoccupied. The girl was gone.

***

Cole took a while to finally find the stupid master key to Harrow Hall. HH, it was labeled, one of twenty-plus keys on his chain.

"I'll go inside. You guys wait here to see if he comes back – maybe try his phone again," Cole told Brady and Angie before opening one of the glass doors. Leaves were piled up at the base of the other door, but not this one.

"Looks like someone's been in here," Brady said, but Angie guessed it was only the maintenance staff.

"It sure as hell wasn't security," Cole said, stepping inside.

A wave of humid air crashed against Cole when he passed through the interior entry doors, the auditorium visible one level below. Glancing up to the mezzanine and balcony, he detected a faded scent emanating from the depths of the building. Popcorn? Yes, Cole was almost sure he smelled popcorn.

Walking down a staircase to the first floor, the scent grew a little stronger. Unbelievable. Had someone snuck in here with a bag of popcorn? He told himself it had to be Brandon – it just had to be.

But where had he found popcorn?

Cole stopped at the base of the stairs, thinking he'd heard faint, shuffling footsteps behind him. He glanced over his shoulder – no one there – then passed through a pair of squeaky double-doors, their whines echoing throughout the building. Now he was in the auditorium, the spotlighted stage to his left, scarlet curtains drawn, the balcony forming a U of empty red seats above him. The building was silent, save for the clock mounted to the far wall.

TICK, TICK, TICK, TICK, each strike like the pounding of a hammer in a place of heightened acoustics.

Cole felt the hairs on his arms rising. He'd only been in this building once, and he hadn't liked it. The vast emptiness was oppressive. Auditoriums weren't supposed to be empty, their stages desolate. They were supposed to have performances and presentations of all kinds and booming applauses and intrigued people in the seats, but not Harrow Hall, at least not anymore. The stage lights, casting their blues and reds and yellows upon a forgotten space, had no performers to play up. The spotlight, though incredibly bright, accentuated nothing but an empty stage, its curtains seeming for a second to flap at the center, almost as if…

A draft, obviously a draft.

Cole exited the auditorium, turning right and following a silent hallway that reminded him of the halls at his old high school. A large dedication plaque still clung to the wall. In the hasty state-mandated closure of the institution, no one had even bothered to remove it.

WELCOME TO HARROW HALL

Our facility's brand new auditorium is dedicated this 10th day of April, 1995, to Dr. Robert Harrow. May every function within these walls honor the thirty-five years he committed to assisting those in his care.

The bronze plaque also featured a portrait of the bearded Dr. Harrow, as well as twelve additional names of honorees. Cole took a few seconds to read the list, absorbing each name with a dawning sadness. This place had been meant to serve a purpose, not to sit in silence, the time kept by its clock of consequence only to the ranks of empty seats. A sense of profound wrongness overcame Cole; what an awful waste all of this was, another state-initiated debacle. According to Ronny, whenever the property was eventually purchased, most of these buildings would be demolished.

Still facing the plaque, Cole glanced nervously to his right, again thinking he'd heard soft footsteps. He listened closely for a while, looking toward the staircase that had once brought guests from the front entrance to the auditorium. Now the building was empty and eerie, yet Cole still thought he heard a shuffling footstep or two as he continued to the rear of Harrow Hall, passing several offices and trying to push Ronny's words from his mind.

Ronny had often said these buildings were haunted.

Reaching the last door on the right before he came to a staircase and a service elevator entrance closed off with caution tape, Cole wondered what he was doing back here. He'd never been in this part of the building before, and though Brandon or last night's intruders almost certainly weren't hiding in any of these rooms, Cole nonetheless opened the door and entered a narrow hallway. Dimly lit by wall sconces, the corridor featured doors on both sides, each marked by golden numbers. Worried the lights would suddenly wink out and plunge him in darkness, Cole pulled his flashlight from his belt and thought about heading back. Brady and Angie were probably getting ready to call the cops.

But a senseless urge propelled Cole forward. He yanked open door number 105 on the right and found himself in a dressing room, lighted mirrors and makeup desks affixed to every wall. The frames of tiny light bulbs surrounding each mirror were particularly foreboding, some of them buzzing and flickering. Being in this room reminded Cole of his adolescent summers cleaning up the county fairgrounds after hours, that weird sense of anticipation trembling in his chest, as if something of great significance and excitement would happen. But there was also a profound aura of loss – empty finality – a tingling feeling that told him to get out and never come back, to leave this place to its memories and stop disrupting the solitude, for the show was over and now darkness loomed.

Cole tried not to look at the mirrors, knowing he'd probably imagine something creeping up on him as he'd so often done as a teenager in the late night funhouse–

Unmistakable! A single knock against the glass window of a door at the end of the room.

Cole lurched backward, away from the door, expecting another knock, or maybe the return of those footsteps. They would come, he feared, from the showers beyond a corner opening.

When silence persisted, Cole slowly approached the door, staring at the window that had just been rapped. He could not see through the window, a dark room lurking beyond.

"This is security!" he shouted, his words bouncing around the room. "You're trespassing on state property. If you come out now, I won't call the police. Brandon, if that's you I'm gonna call your parents…after I kick your ass."

No response. "Come out now. This is security!" he repeated, feeling outnumbered in the empty room, as though a thousand eyes were watching him from behind that door.

Again Cole thought about contacting Ronny on the radio, but it was no use. He would only get in the way.

No, dammit! No Ronny! You're gonna be a cop. Cops handle shit like this.

Emboldened by thoughts of his future, Cole tugged open the door and beamed his flashlight into a large storage room that extended one hundred feet back. Rows of industrial shelves climbed almost to the ceiling, each one stacked with boxes and bins and tools. Cole pulled a light string and studied the shelves. One was piled up with spare auditorium seats, another containing nothing but folded wheelchairs.

WELCOME TO HARROW HALL

Why hadn't all of this stuff been taken away?

Cole quickly checked the aisles between shelves, found no signs of trouble. The ceiling was an exposed mess of beams and pipes and torn up insulation. The far wall was unfinished, light from the next room spilling through a fairly large gap between the top of the wall and the ceiling. Perhaps a bat had flown into the door, then flitted away, Cole wondered. The thunking sound Cole had heard against the glass matched the intensity he'd expect from a bat striking it, yet his instincts told him something else had been responsible.

Giving up his useless search, Cole left the creepy lighted mirrors of the dressing room to their lonely reflections and hurried down the hall, taking a left and jogging back toward the staircase, past the plaque that read, WELCOME TO HARROW HALL, his sneakers squeaking on the tiles, the building still faintly redolent with popcorn.

If Cole hadn't glanced through the double-doors on his way up to the main entrance, he wouldn't have seen Brandon sitting in the first row of the auditorium.

***

"Brandon, what the hell are you doing in here?"

Cole's words yanked Brandon out of the near trancelike state. He felt dazed but no longer lightheaded and foggy in the lands of the surreal. He had no recollection of how he'd gotten in here, though, his last memory before seeing the striking girl that of walking toward Harrow Hall.

"There was a girl in here," he said, glancing to his right where the girl had been seated.

Crossing his arms, Cole looked at him disbelievingly, but Brandon was positive about what he'd seen.

"Cole, I swear to God, there was a girl right next to me."

Cole shot him a glare. "Gig's up, shithead. I'm gonna get you so bad for this – I could've been fired!"

Back in the car, as they drove off, everyone yelling at a silent Brandon, Harrow Hall went dark behind them.

Part II: The Dark Arts

Chapter 1

Jerome took a long shower before bed. One of the best parts about hotels was the hot, powerful showers, the water pressure offering a free massage to the neck and shoulders. It felt good to just stand there beneath the steaming jets of water and relax for a while, letting go of the day and its troubles. But the image of his house fading away down the street wouldn't leave him, the little place in the Lower Ninth Ward he'd found for his family gone forever, he feared.

But something told him this journey – whatever it was – with these people would transform him into a new man. A better man? Maybe not, but definitely a new man whose old life and home were drifting unalterably into the past. Could this be a good thing, God's intervening hand? Even so, he was reluctant to break the rituals that had grounded him following the deaths of Elise and Jennie… afternoons at the barbershop, chatting for hours with Calvin and his friends; nights at Canal Nine, sipping whiskey and watching McGreevy towel off the bar; unhurried walks around the city, taking in its infinite sights and sounds.

Now all of that was over – he could practically feel it.

But that wasn't necessarily an awful development, he figured. The rail he'd been riding before he met Willy was a fast track to death. He'd known that each time he went to Canal Nine, though, and he'd embraced it, a defeated man finishing out what were hopefully the final years of his life. Maybe he'd drink himself to death one night, he'd often thought. Or maybe he'd just pass out and die in the lonely house that had once been filled with joy.

Jerome sighed, the hot water beating down on him and burning a little.

"Why did I do this? Why did I come with these people?" he muttered, remembering his reasons and now finding them ridiculous. There would be no atonement for what he'd done, no forgiveness, no right way to go out for a murderer. He'd been forced to kill in the war, but that hadn't been the end of his killing. No, sir, it hadn't been. He'd gone to confront that drunk driver and found him ready to repeat the actions that took Elise from this world, another DUI in the making. There'd been a struggle, Jerome's rage seizing him. A single punch and the man had fallen, but he hadn't gotten back up. His head had struck the pavement, blood pooling around him.

Jerome had gone there that night to face down the man who'd killed his wife, not to murder him. But the man had died in the parking lot, no need to check for a pulse, his soul dragged away with the cold, hateful whispers Jerome knew from the war…along with the awful stench of fresh ruination. Jerome had seen enough death in Nam to be able to immediately detect the indelible evidence of a man's soul being whisked off to its next destination, often unwillingly, a fleeting experience that left him trembling each time and changed a little more for the worse.

When Jerome stepped out of the steam-clouded bathroom, Willy was already tucked into bed, reading glasses tilted over his nose like those of an English teacher. He was reading a hardcover, *An Examination of The Dark Arts*, reminding Jerome of his father and causing him to revisit consideration as to the abilities these people had sensed in him. He saw plenty of wild stuff when he was drunk – did that make him an alcomancer?

Jerome toweled himself off and threw on some clothes he'd stuffed into a bag that morning. It seemed like he'd left the Lower Ninth Ward a week ago.

"So how we gonna find this guy anyhow?" Jerome said, feeling briefly guilty about breaking the silence, his expression resembling that of the boy with the baseball bat after his homerun ball shatters the neighbor's window.

Willy slid a business card into the thick book and set it on the nightstand. He removed his glasses, rubbed his heavy eyes. He wore a red flannel pajama top with shiny gold buttons, looking to Jerome like a king ready for a long sleep.

Shrugging, Willy said, "I can't say for sure. We don't really operate on definitive plans and schedules – we go on visions and collective hunches. If our talents seem to be in agreement or build on someone else's divination, then we roll with it." He shifted with great difficulty to adjust the pillows. "Like this morning, for example, when Ki saw that O in the water. We were able to combine that with Bu seeing Ohio in the sky yesterday and Rosa's insistences that the rocks keep pointing north. For us, that's pretty solid evidence that Harrow's gone to Ohio."

"But where in Ohio? That's a pretty big ass state, man."

"We'll narrow it down," Willy said confidently. "Ki and Sky both saw tall, old buildings through their respective mediums. Ki saw a theater and a stage, too." A glimmer of excitement flashed into his eyes. "We'll get more information tomorrow. When they look into the fire and the water and the sky and the earth again, they'll receive more clues. It's almost like completing a huge puzzle, all of the pieces jumbled up in a big mess. But if you start by putting two of them together, the rest of it just sorts itself out."

Chuckling at some unexpressed thought, Willy took a long swig of water from the jug.

Jerome slid into his bed, tugging the sheets to his chest and pushing back the comforter (he'd heard plenty of nasty stories about comforters and their cleanliness, or lack thereof).

"What's so funny?" Jerome said, for Willy was still laughing a bit.

Willy shook his head. He was on his side now, facing Jerome. "I guess I shouldn't be talking like I'm sure all of this is gonna work out perfect. It almost definitely won't." His eyes seemed to shrink inward, then lifted to meet Jerome. "If we find Harrow, my fat ass might well get killed first. I don't have the heart to be so blunt in front of the others, but this is gonna be a war, man. I know it, they know it, but we try not to talk about it too much. Everyone here's prepared to…to make the ultimate sacrifice."

Now Willy's eyes were simmering, smoky with purpose and determination, eyes Jerome had seen a long time ago when his sergeants barked out orders. Some of them had been killed, shot by the Viet Cong in the relentlessly thick jungle or blown up in an ambush, little kids and women all over the place, and you couldn't trust anyone out there. But those guys weren't supposed to die. They were the leaders. They always knew what to say and how to keep morale up, even with the fires of racial strife often burning red hot, the tension as sharp and taut as razor wire – and yet somehow everyone came together to fight a common enemy, every sunrise a privilege, every sunset a cue to pray to God that you and your comrades survived the day.

Willy was pointing at him. "I know you're a veteran, Jerome. I felt it in your handshake. You're a survivor of war, a man who fought and lived." He nodded at length and gulped down another jug of spring water, Jerome wondering how he went five minutes without needing to piss.

"You, my friend, are a commendable man," Willy said. "I'm awful glad you're on our side."

"Nah, man, ain't nothin commendable about me. I just got lucky."

Again Jerome remembered the nightmare that was war, countless times navigating those hot, sticky, wet Godforsaken jungles with their venomous snakes and ticks and malarial mosquitoes. In the jungles of Hell the Vietnamese children had been used as shields, falling with the frailty of dolls in sprays of bloody mist, and all you could do was pretend it wasn't real and just keep going, even when the sickness roiled, *Keep going!!* And the sky – it had never been quite right beyond the trees, always something spurious and foreboding about it, as if the damn thing were an opaque window to a world you'd never see again.

Jerome recalled the constant nausea in his gut from war, the nightmares, the suffocating fears that were worst at the edges of sleep, the stench of death all around…the same stench Harrow had radiated at Canal Nine.

A new enemy. A new war.

"There's definitely a void of darkness in you, Jerome, but there's far more light," Willy assured. "Other people can see it, but you've denied yourself the opportunity."

"What are you, my damn shrink?" Jerome regretted lashing out at Willy, but the two beers at dinner hadn't been enough. He wanted more. Needed more, desperate to lose himself in the whiskey. Where was old McGreevy and his steady pouring hand when a man needed him most?

"You've got a gift somewhere in there," Willy insisted. "When you let the light in, maybe you'll see it."

Jerome leaped from the bed, pointing and gaping at the partly closed curtains, the lights of Music City flashing beyond the window, the hums of vehicles sweeping up through the vents.

"What is it, Jerome? What do you see?" Willy scrambled flailingly out of bed and joined Jerome in the corner where he huddled.

There was no way Jerome could explain everything he'd seen, the most vivid PTSD onslaught he'd experienced in decades. He couldn't even remember the last time he'd had one this bad, at least before Jennie was born. But this hallucination of the massacred children standing before the window had been accompanied by a voice in Jerome's head.

Harrow's voice: *Of the light you shall not avail yourself, Mr. Hudson.*

And then the second hallucination had come, swift and detailed, except this one had seemed to be more of a vision. "Men…in the hotel! They're in the elevator, comin up!" Jerome gasped. He was sweating heavily, barely able to breathe, his throat tight and achy.

Willy straightened with understanding. He hurried to his bed, reached beneath the pillow, and produced a silencer-equipped pistol.

"Jesus," Jerome murmured, but that was only the beginning.

From his travel bag Willy retrieved another pistol and handed it to Jerome, the steel feeling cold and hostile in his hand. He hadn't touched a gun since returning to U.S. soil.

"Follow me," Willy said. "Keep the gun out of sight."

Briefly immobile, Jerome gazed down upon his shaking hands. This was profoundly deranged, but the vision had been even more maddening. The men had been in this hotel, riding in the very elevator car Jerome had taken earlier, its mirrored walls and brass railings and diamond floor tiles offering incontrovertible proof.

"Get moving!" Willy ordered, awakening in Jerome the long-dormant immediacy of war, a weapon in his hand and a mission to be completed. For a time the hotel room became the jungle, pressing forward, swallowing down the fear, the door opening, into the hallway, farther, farther, around a corner, running toward the elevators, DING!, the noise like a grenade, the hotel in that moment a portal back to Hell.

The elevator doors opened, four big men stepping forth – the Viet Cong? – none of them prepared. Willy opened fire, silent death tearing into flesh, and it wasn't until all four men collapsed and a familiar stench rose up and those chilling whispers of departed souls slithered their way into Jerome's ears that realization set in.

The elevator car was painted with blood and brain matter, the doors closing on the deceased and bumping against their legs, as luridly irreverent as pink at a funeral.

"Damn mess," Jerome muttered, his war mode insulating him from horror's extent.

Willy let out a long exhalation of relief, checking the men's pockets and belts and finding four pistols.

"These guys were here for us." Willy glanced at Jerome with astonishment. He managed an incredulous half-grin, the stench of death just now beginning to subside, the whispering souls already gone to their next destination. They never stayed long, the vaporous orbs that sometimes joined them as difficult to discern as bats in the night. "I think you discovered your gift just in time, buddy boy!" Willy exclaimed. "Come on, now, we need to get the others and scoot. The police will–"

Jerome held up a hand to stop him. The bodies were gone, their blood vanished from the elevator. The doors closed, the whirring motor echoing down the shaft. In a few moments: DING! A young, giggling, drunken couple staggered out of the other elevator, and behind them, slumped in the corners, were two dead Vietnamese children, their clothes sodden with blood.

Jerome suddenly didn't know what was real, Harrow's voice returning crisply to his head: *You availed yourself of the light, Jerome. You chose your side. Now you must die along with your new friends. In the land of the dead Elise and Jennie await you, but you shall never see them again, fool, the fires of the damned to claim you!*

Harrow's laughter crackled fiercely, followed by the dying wails of a thousand soldiers.

Chapter 2

Vicky saw nothing, felt nothing, staring blankly ahead, immersed in the darkness, a prisoner of her own mind. Then, with two snaps, she was free, the darkness slowly corroded by a legion of lights, one after another flashing on. All around her the auditorium came into existence, with its dim balcony lights forming a ring and its massive spotlight burning down upon the stage.

There was a crisp flap on stage, Harrow stepping through the crimson curtains, dressed now in a tuxedo, his hair combed and shining. He held Vicky's magic wand, the one she'd waved about as a child, darting around the back yard and trying to transform dandelions to gold and ants to puppies. The magic hadn't come to her back then, but now she was caught in a world of mystery and fear, still unsure about what Harrow wanted from her.

Hopping off the stage and pacing over to Vicky in the front row, Harrow said, "Good morning, sweet girl. Sleep well did you last night?"

Vicky shook her head in disbelief. Morning? She glanced up to the main entrance and noticed sunlight beyond the doors – sunlight that surely hadn't been there a few seconds ago. "I…I can't remember anything."

"Of course, of course." Harrow touched the tip of Vicky's wand and produced a steaming plate of scrambled eggs and bacon. The meal had materialized in his hand – Vicky was positive he couldn't have hidden it within his garments.

Was he really…? No, he couldn't be. But, if not, how could he have done that?

Harrow handed the plate to Vicky. "You should eat, child," he said, but Vicky set the plate on the floor.

"I want to go home. Now," she demanded, hating the fragility in her voice.

Harrow nodded, taking a seat beside Vicky. "You're free to leave, Miss Victoria. But will you make me a promise?"

Vicky said nothing.

"Promise me, Victoria, that you'll return home and behold the blessings I have bestowed. Your father's wealth, your grandmother's health, your friends' fortunes – behind each gift is an angel sent from your mother. I'm here to lead you to your destiny, Victoria, but first you must extricate yourself from the burdens of your past."

"But I don't want to. This is my life – it's not a burden." Vicky stood, took a few tentative steps away from Harrow, who remained seated, twirling the wand. "I want to go home! Please let me go!" She forced back the tears, knowing she had to be strong. Whatever Harrow was doing to her, she had to fight it.

Yet when he stood the strange manipulations lorded again. Vicky suddenly wanted him to hold her, to tell her it would all be okay. Had he really been sent by her mother? She wanted so desperately to believe him, to embrace his magic as a gift from God.

"You're free, sweet bird, to sing your song." Harrow smiled warmly yet somewhat sadly at her, as if he were a father saying goodbye to his daughter departing for college.

Vicky managed a few more steps toward the door. On the other side, she could see the staircase that would take her up to the main entrance.

"Mary, it is time!" Harrow called, and through the curtains passed a waif of a woman, knots of dread tightening in Vicky's throat when she looked back and saw her. Perhaps thirty, the woman was short-haired and pale. Shuffling across the stage and stepping diffidently down the staircase, she looked up at Harrow like a dog awaiting a command.

"Mary, you will drive Miss Victoria back to her hometown in Kentucky. Allow her to take in the marvelous windfall without pressure." Harrow's eyes shifted to Vicky. "But do remember, Victoria, deprived can be these blessings just as easily as they were bestowed." His jaw seemed to momentarily clench. "Your calling is magic, child. If you do not embrace the calling, I'll be forced to find someone who rises when her name is announced. After you have seen the countless blessings in person, return to me with Mary and perfect your craft."

"Oh, and one more thing," Harrow said, pivoting on a heel and climbing up to the stage. "You mustn't make contact with any of your family members. This is an observational visit, not a return home. I've arranged things in such a way that they think you're safe, spending a few weeks with friends."

"But how–" Vicky started.

"About the details worry not, child. Just accept the opportunity to see all the good I've given your family." Pacing the stage, Harrow waved the wand with a flourish, and behind Vicky, up one level, the doors clicked open, sunlight waiting beyond.

Vicky moved uncertainly toward freedom, guessing at Harrow's intentions. But when she looked back, her captor was gone.

Wondering if it was all another trick, Vicky raced up the staircase toward the doors, through them, outside, the sun on her face.

Parked in front of the building was a small red sedan, the passenger door open. In the driver's seat was...but how could that be?

How could Mary have beaten her out here?

The mousy woman waved for Vicky to get inside. Both hands on the steering wheel, buckled up, it seemed as if she'd been waiting there for some time.

"No way," Vicky murmured, turning and sprinting down the sidewalk, away from Harrow Hall and its infinite deceptions.

When she reached the spray-painted stop sign at the end of the road, a collection of brick buildings around her, Vicky's stomach began to feel mildly unsettled. The farther she walked the worse the discomfort became, quickly escalating into a rising, dizzying, nauseous pain that brought an urge to vomit.

Vicky stumbled across a worn brick walkway onto the dewy grass and collapsed to her knees, resisting the pulses of nausea. Birds were chirping happily from the trees. A plane soared high above, leaving foamy whitecaps in its wake. Behind her a vehicle was creeping down the road. The red sedan, Mary calling to her through the window.

"Come with me, Victoria!" she shouted. "You'll feel better if you come with me!"

The pain worsened, less nauseous and more acute, wrapping around Vicky's stomach like an elastic band and stretching across her back. It throbbed. Tears stung her eyes.

Appendicitis? No, Harrow had done this to her. He was responsible. How else could Mary know she was hurting?

"Just stay away from me!" Vicky rolled onto her back and rubbed her stomach, the cool grass no longer a comfort but a cloying annoyance.

In the hollow distance, the shutting of a door echoed like a voice in an empty museum. Footsteps. Vicky began to feel a little better, the spasms of agony less intense.

A shadow looming over her. Mary's shadow. "It'll only get worse if you stay," she said, her tone carrying a grimness that scared Vicky. Again she felt trapped and alone. Out of options.

I let this happen to me, she thought, remembering the expectancy in Harrow's eyes when she'd first seen him knocking on her door. *I let him into my life and now he won't leave.*

Thinking only of the pain, imagining how bad it might get if she didn't go with Mary, Vicky allowed the woman to pull her up by the arm. Walking back with her to the car, the pain rapidly diminishing, relief swept triumphantly over her.

"What did he do to me?" Vicky demanded, but Mary kept her eyes on the car, looking wary and wan, her complexion that of a terminally ill patient waiting for the merciful hand of death.

"Don't you want to see everything he's done?" Mary said, and it was then that Vicky finally understood the extent of Harrow's power. Even after the magical bewilderments she'd seen from him – producing items out of nothingness – she hadn't truly comprehended his strength. Here was a man who could seemingly manipulate the color of the sky, controlling everyone he came across. Once you let him in as Vicky had, you were his to dictate upon the stage of deceit, where he spoke in that sinister yet assuring and eloquent way, conjuring up happy things from the past and making promises of a bright future. He kept telling Vicky about her calling, kept saying her mother had sent him, kept trying to persuade her to stay – but why would he go to such lengths if he could control her as easily as a puppet? Why make her *want* to stay?

Resigning herself to Harrow's will, at least for the moment, Vicky surveyed her surroundings before getting in the car. All of these buildings were empty, she concluded, most likely part of some closed down school, though not merely for the summer. The property was too dilapidated and overgrown, a forgotten facility discovered by a man with immense power. And now he controlled it as he controlled Vicky and Mary and the others he'd bused here, everyone playing a role upon his stage.

A director handing out the lines.

Both hands tightly gripping the wheel, Mary followed a series of potholed roads, the crumbling pavement displaying several painted markings (SLOW, ONE WAY, 25 MPH), brick buildings on either side of them, not a person in sight. Some of the buildings had names. Others stood anonymous and abandoned, ranging in their state of disrepair. Most of them seemed fairly modern, but a few were on the verge of caving in. Driving past them was like rolling through an apocalyptic town, a profound sense of wrongness flexing in Vicky's heart. Wherever there were roads and sidewalks and buildings, there were supposed to be people, lots of them.

"What is this place?" Vicky said, her stomach having returned almost to normal now that she'd been brought into compliance.

"It's home." Mary nodded repeatedly, stopping fully at each desolate intersection and flipping on her turn signals, even though no other vehicles were around. This place was huge…and completely empty.

At last they came to a locked barrier gate, a flimsy thing that could be driven through if needed. Mary stopped, waited a few seconds, hands still clenching the wheel, and very slowly the gate eased open.

"Just like Harrow said." Grinning, Mary turned left onto a freshly paved road, leaving isolation and rejoining society, two cars passing in the opposite direction.

Vicky smiled, a thought and a prayer fluttering into her head. If she got far enough away from Harrow, perhaps his grip on her would weaken – and then she would be free of the trap she'd allowed herself to fall in.

"Time for you to see his glory," Mary whispered, and Vicky's warm thoughts suddenly iced away, replaced by frigid dread.

Chapter 3

The ride home was like a bad hangover. Brandon's head ached, and Brady wouldn't stop chewing him out, and Angie wouldn't stop bitching, her voice like a fucking hammer to his skull. He'd sooner chew on glass shards than listen to any more of their shit about *You're too immature* and *You could have gotten Cole fired* and *Why did we even bring you?*

Passing headlights were the worst, searing straight into Brandon's brain. He felt like his head and body were in two different hemispheres. If only he could get a minute of silence, but his brother and Angie kept going on and on about *That stunt you pulled* and *You're lucky Cole didn't call the cops* and *You need to learn respect, kid.*

Brandon had once suffered a mild concussion after being sideswiped in a game, but that was nothing compared to this. His head started to throb halfway home, and he felt sick to his stomach. Was he coming down with something, maybe?

The girl. Aside from that beautiful girl sitting beside him, everything between walking to Harrow Hall and leaving the building with Cole yapping at him was a blank. He couldn't recall going inside. Cole had grilled him about it, saying the doors were locked, always locked, impossible to open, *did you break a window somewhere*? But Brandon couldn't remember. Only her face remained in his head, the face of an untouchable girl in a snow globe. Watching her stare at the stage, his whole body had fluttered with excitement, yet he hadn't wanted to disturb her. She was like the ocean at dawn, or the skating pond at Heritage Park before everyone went out for a day of hockey, fresh and stunning in her solitude.

Brandon smiled in spite of the pain, his head pressed against the window. He knew he had to see her again.

But how?

WELCOME TO HARROW HALL

At home, Brandon popped two Advils, trudged up the stairs, and limped into the shower. He felt only marginally better than before, too weak to stand. Instead, he kneeled in the tub, indifferent to the world. His fading hockey bruises from camp last week – the ones on his chest and arms and knees produced by slapshots penetrating his equipment – were particularly sore tonight. At least he hadn't taken a shot to the balls lately – those made him want to quit hockey until the earth-shattering pain eventually subsided. Then he went back out the next day and took more shots.

Some people said he'd seen too much rubber to the head. Maybe they were right.

Brandon toweled off and gingerly put on some clothes for bed. He felt stiff and brittle, like he might break if he bent his knees. He'd trained hard to improve his flexibility over the last year, and now he could almost do the splits, his teammates always giving him shit about it and saying only chicks could spread their legs that far.

But tonight Brandon could hardly even walk without hurting.

"I'm screwed," he muttered, climbing into bed. It wasn't fair to feel like he had a hangover without at least having enjoyed the beers to warrant it. This was just bullshit, plain and simple.

At least tomorrow was Sunday and he could sleep in. His mother no longer nagged him and Brady about going to church and sitting through those dumbass sermons, people always coming up and shaking your hand and saying, *Peace be with you.* What a farce. According to Brandon's father, a police sergeant, at least three people in their church had been arrested within the last five years: one for OUI, one for A&B, and the other for disorderly conduct at a bar. And who knew what those other creepers did when they weren't stuffing their heads in bibles and singing Blah, Blah, Blah, Almighty Blah, Peace be with you.

Brandon had almost reached the sweet oblivion of sleep when it all came surging back to him like a mini throw-up. Harrow. Fucking freak. He'd lit a cigarette with his finger and guessed Brandon's number. 739.

Between zero and infinity. And he'd known his name, too.

How the hell had he done that? He was a magician, he'd said. That's how. But magicians were just phonies who hid cards up their sleeves and slid coins off tables while they distracted you by waving their hands around. But Harrow – he wasn't a fake. The dude was legit, an actual magician; he'd asked if Brandon wanted to go inside the building – and then he *had* gone inside somehow.

The girl had been there.

Beautiful Snow Globe Girl.

But where had Harrow gone?

Some would call me a magician, others a sorcerer. A few would choose soothsayer. You, young boy, may call me drifter if you prefer. As long as you don't call me shaman, agreeable I'll remain.

Johnny Depp weirdo.

Rubbing his head, Brandon navigated the darkness of his bedroom and flipped open his laptop. He went to Google and searched for Harrow and Harrow Hall. The building he'd just visited came up among the results, featured in a bunch of articles about mental health and loony bins. But nothing on the man he'd met.

My new home this place has become. Isn't it a grand place?

The words rang back perfectly to Brandon, almost as if they were being spoken again in his head. Suddenly feeling cold, he grabbed a sweatshirt from the closet and returned to bed. Not good enough, his legs still cold. Back to the closet, where he dug up a pair of sweatpants beneath his messy floor pile of shorts and T-shirts, a few socks and boxers intermingled.

A sweatshirt and sweatpants to bed in August? He really was screwed.

Brandon lifted himself back into bed, feeling like he'd just faced a fifty-shot game. He kept rolling and groaning and trying to find a comfortable position. *Fucking Advil, are you wearing off already?*

Finally he stumbled into sleep, dreams about the girl and nightmares about Harrow carrying him to morning's light.

Chapter 4

Early on Sunday morning, Cole omitted from his report the little detail about his cousin sneaking into Harrow Hall, instead focusing on the building's lights going on and off without explanation.

I strongly recommend the maintenance crews check out the building from top to bottom, he wrote, wondering as he did so if anyone even read his reports. He was supposed to keep a detailed record of suspicious activities during the night, in addition to providing a list of recommended actions to "ensure the property receives the appropriate maintenance procedures and remains safe and secure." He always received mass emails from his boss describing the guards' duties in grandiose terms – at times making it seem like they were defending the White House – but when it got right down to it, how much did his boss really care? He hadn't even questioned Cole at length after the school bus incident, dismissing it as the work of "juvenile delinquents."

Cole had his very own juvenile delinquent for a cousin.

When his report was finished, before heading home to sleep, Cole asked Ronny to tell him more about the supposed haunting of Harrow Hall. He couldn't get the building out of his head, especially with the lights illuminating at random following the bus incident. Still no arrests had been made in connection with that debacle, at least not that Cole was aware of; and there was nothing online or in the news about a stolen bus barging into the old institution.

Looking up from the chess board, Ronny grabbed a spare pawn and fiddled with it. His eyes shifted about the trailer with contemplative intensity. "Those lights gotcha a little spooked, huh?"

Cole shrugged. "I wouldn't say spooked, more like vigilant. Mostly I want to make sure no one's getting a free hotel." Yet there were additional fears left unspoken, Cole not quite ready to paint the entire apprehensive picture for his partner just yet.

Ronny nodded, twirling the pawn in his fingers, thoughts dashing into Cole's head that there was at least a little symbolism to be derived. Here they were, a couple of pawns in life's game, twirled about in God's hand, unable to see the greater happenings beyond the next congested rank.

"Can't say for sure the place is haunted," Ronny said after a while, running a hand through his snowy hair. "But I *think* it might be haunted cuz of what I heard. Maybe there's something to the stories, and maybe there's not."

Cole could sense this would be another arduous conversation with Ronny; he felt as if he were trying to coax a stubborn horse into a trailer. "What kind of stories have you heard?"

"I know a couple people used to work here. One of 'em's a doctor – good man who found himself out of a job when the state closed this place." Ronny bit his lower lip, shook his head. "Anyway, this doc told me he always used to hear weird sounds in Harrow Hall. And he swore he saw things through the windows at night – strange shadows and shit."

"Another guy I knew, Davy Bielmeister," Ronny continued, "worked maintenance here for a decade. He spent so much time here he could probably draw ya a perfect floor map of each building, and Lord knows dodging them crazies all the time wasn't easy, with their grunting and shouting and trying to hug ya all the time." A broken, wheezy laugh escaped him. "Davy's a real good guy, great dad, always taking his kids to sporting events and doing volunteer projects at the boys and girls club." There was a moment's pause, Ronny reminiscing. "He's an alcoholic, though, but a good kind of drunk, you know? Keeps himself together enough to be functional. Ain't nothing wrong with being a drunk – you just gotta know how to manage yourself and keep the wife happy. Give her some flowers on occasion, right? And chocolates, them too. Flowers and chocolates'll tame even the angriest lady."

Ronny shot him a very discomforting wink. "That's a big life secret I just told ya there, son."

"Did he see and hear stuff, too, the maintenance guy, I mean?" Cole asked.

Glancing to the ceiling as if trying to remember, Ronny finally said, "Yeah, he claimed to see all kinds of crazy stuff in Harrow Hall. I guess one day he was on the stage fixing something and he saw a little girl sitting in the balcony, all done up in a pink dress and ribbons in her hair. Davy tried to talk to her, but she took off through the doors and never came back, at least that's what he said." Ronny wagged a finger at Cole. "But remember, Davy was a drunk, said he routinely consulted the flask on the job. He might have been three sheets to the wind that day. Who really knows?"

"So his stories basically have no credibility."

"I didn't say that." Ronny set down the pawn and crossed his arms over his chest, looking like a grumpy grandfather in a hurry to leave a family get-together. "There could be merit to Davy's stories. Never seen nothing out of the ordinary up there myself, but all of these buildings are no doubt spooky. Man could drive himself a little nuts circling these empty shells all day. Start to see shadows around every corner, you know what I'm saying?" He regarded the cluttered chess board with a confused look. "Take it from me, kid, you gotta find something that grounds you on this job – something that keeps the mind from wandering too much. For me it's chess. Ain't no demons on a chess board, 'cept them pesky knights sneaking up on ya just when ya least expect it. Never trust a knight, kid. Bastards'll pop out and bite you every time."

Cole looked over his report, Ronny resuming his game and announcing, "Check!", to himself almost immediately. Time to get home and grab some sleep, Cole figured. Maybe, just maybe, he could find a way to put the job out of his mind, especially Harrow Hall, a building that had always been ordinary. The whole facility had been ordinary, at times deliriously boring.

But now things were different. The bus had changed everything, and Cole feared the weirdness had only just begun, that great, incomprehensible chess game of life only a few moves deep.

Chapter 5

"Like I said last night, we all have to be more vigilant. Everyone's gotta look out for each other."

One hand resting atop the steering wheel, a pink-frosted doughnut in the other, a cup of Dunkin' Donuts coffee on standby in the cup holder, Willy Thunder drove the Windstar slowly north. They were on I-65, approaching the Kentucky border, a van full of tired and apprehensive people. Last night, after killing Harrow's men in the elevator, Willy had woken everyone and told them to leave the hotel. Guests who'd heard the gunshots had called the police, several officers racing into the lobby just after Jerome and his crew left. They'd spent the rest of the night sleeping in the Windstar.

No one had been shocked by news of Harrow sending hitmen for them, but that had done nothing to lessen the impact of fear upon their hearts. Harrow knew what they were doing, knew their location, and now he'd sent men to erase them. For Jerome, that was the exclamation point. He was in a brand new war, a war with a man who wasn't a man at all – a thing that craved more power, growing stronger by the day. If Harrow wasn't stopped, there was no estimating the extent of the damage he would cause.

It was officially on now, Jerome eager to hunt down their target, a new enemy to overcome, Willy his commander. Jerome would remain steadfast in this mission, unwavering in his loyalty, until either Harrow was dead or he, himself, was felled. The implications were clear now, and though his own life mattered very little to him, Jerome wanted long, prosperous lives for his friends and relatives, for the people of the Lower Ninth Ward, for the people in this van, for all of the children out there whose futures might be damaged in some way by Harrow's continued rise. No one knew about the threat he posed, no one but them. Possessing the power to make corpses disappear, it seemed Harrow loomed larger than a full moon above an open road.

As he'd done last night, Jerome studied the others, trying to read their faces. How heavily was the burden of all this falling on them? Having survived the jungles of Nam, Jerome knew he was receiving this challenge from a different angle – from a dark, desensitized corner into which no man should find himself thrust, the corner of the war veteran, as lonely and despairing a place as any in the universe.

But what about the others, a group of everyday people? They'd no doubt faced their demons, but nothing could have prepared them for hunting Harrow the way war had prepared Jerome. He'd lived combat for four years, becoming acclimated to an environment of death. No, that wasn't the right word. A man can never fully adjust to the gruesomeness of war, can never adapt to the inundating horrors. He changes and shatters his former self but never completely adapts. He must survive each mission, and so his brain shrinks back into a simple, visceral mode of act and react, of command and obey, of orders and responses, of live or die. At the end of the day, he must try his best to let go of everything – the good, the bad, the lucky, the unthinkable – and wake up ready for a new day. Survival mode. Find it quickly or be killed. Push back your fear and revulsion, or find yourself expelling your final breaths.

Expect anything from war, one of his sergeants had said a long time ago. *Just when it seems bad, it'll only get worse.*

The van was unusually quiet. No one seemed to want to talk about Harrow's preemptive strike last night. Jerome glanced at Ki, who was watching vehicles on the other side of the highway, a half-eaten apple in hand, his head rocking gently back and forth. In the next row up, Sky and Rosa were silently eating their treats from Dunkin' Donuts, a jelly-filled powdered doughnut and a blueberry muffin, respectively. In the passenger seat, Bu was going to town on a ham and egg sandwich, munching it down like he had to be somewhere.

Jerome hadn't wanted anything to eat, the cup of coffee in his hand more than sufficient to wake him up. He wasn't a breakfast person, not anymore. Back when he'd been a husband and a father, breakfast had been his favorite meal, especially on weekends, Elise and Jennie always looking forward to his Saturday brunches and early Sunday breakfasts before church. In those days he used to love getting up early and preparing the eggs and bacon and pancakes, sometimes introducing omelets and blueberry waffles and French toast to the equation. He was a good cook, but he didn't have much use for the kitchen anymore. It was just too hard to take in those smells in an empty house. Alone and broken, meal time was not a pleasure but a daily chore he completed before heading into town and keeping old McGreevy busy.

"Let's not all interrupt each other now," Willy said, taking a bite of his doughnut from the driver's seat. "Everyone will get a turn."

Nervous laughter, the others focusing on their food.

"I think he's getting desperate," Bu finally said. "He obviously fears us – that's why he sent those thugs. But with Jerome's visions" – he said this with a backward glance – "we've got a major advantage over him."

"Saved our asses, dude," Sky said. Last night, when the hitmen were dead and everyone was frazzled, she'd engaged Jerome in a ridiculous series of high-low handshakes, then leaped against him for a congratulatory "belly bump."

Kids these days, bunch of knuckleheads.

"Hold up a second now," Jerome said. "Those visions could have been a one-time deal. Maybe I just got lucky, who knows?"

He was met with objections, everyone shaking their heads in disagreement, even Ki.

"Sorry, dude, but you've found your calling," Sky said. "Don't resist it. Just let it take control, and pretty soon you'll be able to call the Super Bowl. But whatever you make on bets, I get half for coming up with the idea."

"She's right, Jerome. You gotta embrace your gift." Willy finished off his doughnut and licked his fingertips. He was a painfully slow driver, creeping along in the right lane behind a big rig. At this rate, Harrow wouldn't have to worry about them getting to Ohio for a week.

Jerome thought again about last night's visions. He was reluctant to tell these people about the other absurdities he'd experienced. Through some cosmic wormhole Harrow could communicate with him, his voice as clear in Jerome's ears last night as if the necromancer had been standing right behind him. But revealing this to the others, he feared, would only create undue panic. Worst of all, it might require him to talk about the war and his PTSD attacks, which he preferred to keep buried in the recesses of his mind, forced as far from consciousness as possible. If Harrow spoke to him again, though, he knew he'd be obligated to tell the others about everything and how it might be affecting his present ordeal. That was only fair, it seemed.

For now, wanting to change the subject, Jerome said, "So how'd you people all come together, anyhow?"

"Ki and I have been together the longest," Willy said. "He's the only man left from my old group, the one that included Harrow's wife."

"The chick he sold to the Devil?" Sky interrupted.

Willy scowled at her in the rearview mirror. "Would you let me finish already? Jeez! Anyway, people in certain circles knew I'd taken up the pursuit of Harrow after my father passed. The group was disorganized back then, real tough for us to find new members. But Harrow's wife found us one night, tracked us down like a bloodhound. Nicest lady you could ever imagine, and a brilliant sorceress – Amelie was her name."

"The broad who escaped the Devil," Sky said incredulously.

"It's true," Willy assured. "Amelie told us the whole story. No one wanted Harrow dead worse than her, but he went deep into the bayou during that time. All of our powers combined couldn't bring him into focus, and Amelie's powers were badly diminished. It took everything she had to escape the caverns of Hell."

Sky poked her head past the seat to whisper to Jerome. "I wonder if she took any pictures while she was there, maybe bought a souvenir or two."

"I heard that!" Willy snapped. "You shouldn't joke around about her suffering. That poor lady had to endure worse horrors than any of us. She was lucky to save her soul, so damn lucky it ain't even funny. *No one can imagine what she went through.*"

The way Willy spoke about this woman, Jerome wondered if they'd shared something more than hatred of Harrow during their hunt.

"Amelie insane," Ki said, still looking out the window, and the van's attention was his. He hadn't ordered anything from Dunk's, eating only an apple he'd purchased at the supermarket last night, along with other healthy choices. Without another word, he bit into his apple and continued his observation of southbound traffic.

"Dude, you can't just say something like that and then go all mysterious on us again," Sky said.

Ki's lips parted into the slightest smile imaginable. He slowly nibbled his apple, Jerome assuming he'd clam up. But when the others nagged at him to elaborate, he said, "Amelie no good, insane magic. Killing things, living creatures, use blood for potions. Bad, real bad."

"Those were all rituals she'd learned from her mother and grandmother," Willy defended. "Rituals that go back for centuries, tried and true. It's not like she enjoyed killing. Like a hunter or a fisherman, she used each of her kills for a useful purpose."

Ki held up a finger. "Her rituals bullshit," and that got everyone laughing, even Rosa, who slapped her thighs in delight.

"Don't tell me she was a cat killer," Sky said. "No, wait, it was probably goats, right? And sheep, too, definitely sheep."

Willy sighed, rubbed his forehead. "It was cats," he admitted, the van erupting in expressions of disgust.

"I would have sold her to the Devil, too," Sky hollered, and Rosa kept saying, "Dios Mio, Dios Mio." Bu was shaking his head.

Damn sick lady, Jerome thought.

"Wait, I think we should all be straight about this. None of us kills animals, right?" Bu said, peering quizzically back at the others.

Everyone shook their heads, but Jerome wouldn't settle for that. "Hell, no, I don't kill no animals, man!" he exclaimed. "Where'd all this go now, people? I asked how y'all got together, and we talkin bout cat killin now."

Ki broke into fleeting laughter, then coughed a little.

Bu looked relieved. Facing forward again, he said, "Good, very good. I think it's important we hold ourselves to a certain standard, right folks? Animal sacrifices definitely aren't cool with us, that's good."

"How'd that dumbass cat killer die, anyway?" Sky said. Clearly she wasn't planning to let this one go.

"Old age," Willy said. "Died peacefully in her sleep. She really was a good person, you know."

"Except for the times she rescued kittens from the shelter so she could kill them," Sky countered.

A momentary silence was eventually broken by Willy. "Back in those days, I was in desperate need of trackers. We were planning to track Harrow through every single alligator-infested swamp on the Gulf

Coast till we had his head." Bravely, Willy blinkered and shifted into the left lane to pass a fifty-mile-per-hour truck. "Couple of people I found turned out to be conmen – I even brought one guy out on my airboat. He kept telling me to turn this way and that, saying he was losing the scent and shit. After a while I knew he was bullshitting me."

Willy took a sip of coffee. "Just when I was about to give up, thinking I wouldn't find a guy who could track a fire from its smoke, someone told me about this Indian guy out in Texas who helped the police track drug dealers on occasion after their dogs lost a trail. Said he'd helped arrest twenty or so guys, so I figured I'd check him out. At first he told me to get lost, and understandably so, but after I described who we were after, we grabbed his interest, didn't we, big man?"

Ki offered a quick, resolute nod. "Harrow must be stopped."

"Indeed he does," Willy said. "But I wanted to make sure Ki was legit before I brought him on board. I arranged a little test for him to complete, but it wasn't until later I learned he doesn't track through conventional means." Willy chuckled. "When he told me he saw the future in water, I thought he was crazy. Turns out I was the crazy one for not believing."

"Water much better than palm reading," Ki said with another nod.

"Yeah, but fire's the best of all," Sky snapped.

Ki shook his head. "Water put out fire."

"Not if the fire's big enough."

Willy cleared his throat, a deep rumbling sound like thunder rolling across a mountain. "*Anyway*," he enunciated, "Ki was part of the group five years before I met Rosa. By that time everyone was getting tired of hunting Harrow. We were always a few steps behind, like climbing a staircase that never ends. We tracked him through countless swamps, but we never so much as saw him. Always too late."

WELCOME TO HARROW HALL

After another sip of coffee, Willy continued, "It was tough to keep morale up with the constant disappointments. Like me, most of the people in our original group had it out for Harrow due to personal reasons, but they all eventually quit on us. Some people got sick of living for the hunt. Others got too old. One got pregnant. One guy had his sorry butt hauled off to jail on a warrant. The rest just gave up, leaving myself, Ki, and Amelie. After she died, I knew it was time to do some serious recruiting, but this time I took a different route. I wasn't interested in bringing people on board who hated Harrow but couldn't offer very much. I wanted a group of specialists, diviners like me and Ki, people with talent who could put their skills together to reach a common goal."

"Through a mutual friend," Willy said, "I had the good fortune of meeting Rosa. Once she was on board a few years, she introduced me to Sky, who was living at Rosa's house at the time, I believe. Last year I took Bu on after meeting him at a precognition seminar in Baton Rouge. The team was looking strong, but we knew we could use another asset, one that would put us over the top. We didn't try to force it, though. We stayed focused and kept tracking Harrow, keeping on him every day. We pooled our resources, using every vision the earth, water, fire, sky, and palm lines had to offer – and the trail led to you, Jerome. Now look, the very first day you join up, Harrow makes his first attempt to take us out! We've finally earned his fear, ladies and gentlemen."

Jerome tried to take everything in. "So you were only able to find me because Harrow found me first?"

"Duh," Sky said, and proceeded to uncoil her iPod earphones from the device, no longer interested in the history lesson.

They talked a while longer about days and years past, but inevitably the conversation wound its way back to the elephant everyone was trying to ignore.

"Harrow will send more men for us," Willy said. "He senses we're right on his heels, and y'all know what they say about offense being the best defense. He's not gonna wait for us to reach him. The closer we get, the more resistance we can expect to encounter."

"We should always stay near the van, maybe buy some camping gear and put up tents at night," Bu suggested. "No more hotels. He's hoping we'll get separated."

"That's a good idea," Willy said. "We've got enough ammo to defend a small space. We'll take turns keeping watch when we need to stop. Until we get a bead on Harrow's location, we'll try to stay in motion as much as possible."

"How are we supposed to kill this guy if he's supposedly lived hundreds of years?" Jerome was stunned the question hadn't come to him earlier.

"Kill isn't the right word," Willy said. "We'll destroy him. And there's only one way to fight fire."

A nervous silence spread through the van. Back in the right lane, a pair of buses blowing past them to the left, it felt to Jerome like they were stuck in the breakdown lane, a feeling that applied both to their progress on the highway and their pursuit of Harrow. When, and if, they reached Harrow, what exactly would these people do to "destroy" him? They had pistols, but how effective would bullets be against a supposed immortal?

Harrow's words snarled in Jerome's head. *You chose your side. Now you must die along with your new friends. In the land of the dead Elise and Jennie await you, but you shall never see them again, fool, the fires of the damned to claim you!*

Jerome felt as if a layer of ice clung to his skin. He tried to summon his courage from Nam, tried to force back his fears, but frigid instinct told him to return to the Lower Ninth Ward before it was too late. This wasn't a war but suicide, he suspected, their enemy far more daunting than the Viet Cong. When Jerome had shot enemy soldiers, they'd fallen, but this guy was different, verging on insuperable. Combating him would be like combating the wind, or the sky...but if Harrow had sent men to kill them, then clearly he wasn't invincible. A man of truly limitless power wouldn't have cared if the entire human population came at him.

Harrow indeed had weaknesses, Jerome realized, and before long the battle mode slid over him again, his dark thoughts finally receding to their compartments. He could do this. *They* could do this. As individuals they were nothing, but together they could make a stand. He had no idea how they'd confront Harrow – perhaps even Willy didn't know – but as an old drunk at the twilight of his life, it seemed Jerome might as well complete the circle and follow the same calling which had brought him to that Army recruiting center all those years ago. He'd wanted to serve his country, to be a part of something bigger than himself, and to defend the freedoms he enjoyed every day...but none of the sacrifices he and his comrades made in Nam had been appreciated. People had jeered them upon returning home. Racial insults had abounded. After everything they'd endured, to come home to hatred and violence was like a knife to the back.

Jerome could still remember the disillusioned emptiness that had haunted his first weeks back on U.S. soil. His life would never be the same, and no one beyond his Lower Ninth community had cared. Back then, they didn't have veterans support programs all over the place like nowadays, no fancy reintegration assistance initiatives and corporate emphasis on hiring wounded veterans. After seeing and hearing about the way some vets were treated, even in New Orleans, Jerome had decided to keep his mouth shut about his service. It had been hard enough dealing with racial tensions, never mind withstanding another channel of hatred.

But now, riding in the back seat of a slow-moving van with an odd assemblage of people, Jerome sensed a passion of rebirth and repurpose coming over him. Few people had given a damn about his service in

Nam because most Americans had opposed the war from the start; regardless of what had happened in the wretched jungles thousands of miles away, life in New York and L.A. and New Orleans hadn't been threatened by the Viet Cong.

But decades later, everything was different. An insidious storm was sneaking up on the good ole U.S. of A., and no one outside this van knew about it.

This really is redemption, Jerome suddenly understood. Even if he didn't receive a sliver of recognition, even if no one knew what he and the others did, he vowed to make a difference in keeping his country safe.

He vowed to destroy Harrow.

Chapter 6

When the roads became familiar again and the hills of northern Kentucky came into view, Vicky swelled with nervous anticipation. As the miles had stretched along, Mary maintaining her tight, two-handed grip on the wheel, Vicky had formulated a plan.

It was a simple but highly risky plan, her best shot at survival. She knew she couldn't let herself be taken back to Harrow. With each passing mile the bewitching fog he'd used to ensnare her had slowly lifted away. She still couldn't believe she'd allowed herself to be abducted, Harrow's will imposed on her with the ease of a child manipulating Play-Doh.

But now she was free of him. Only Mary separated her from escape, a thin, pale young woman who looked like she'd been locked away in a prison camp and deprived of food. Vicky knew she could overwhelm her – as soon as the car stopped, she kept telling herself, but suddenly the plan eluded her, a helpless feeling of emptiness taking control, as if her brain were a sifter and her thoughts were grains of sand, all but one remaining, a vivid image…

…a vaguely familiar boy about her age. Only his face was visible amidst a sea of black. Handsome, with green eyes and wavy hair, his features twisted into an unruly scowl, he looked like the kind of kid who belonged in detention, a high school outlaw who partied all the time, ambitious only in his pursuit of girls and fun. Certainly not Vicky's type.

Yet excitement coiled through her with the sustained image of this stranger in her mind. Then he was gone, Vicky delivered back to her previous thoughts, the ones of freedom, the outline of the boy's face limned weakly in her head like faded chalk on a rain-slicked sidewalk.

I know him from somewhere, she thought, feeling dazed yet again.

Harrow. He was doing this.

No, I won't let him! She willed herself to stay focused. They were five minutes from her house, almost there, so close, but in her heart she wondered if this was all…no it couldn't be. But what if it was?

Her world suddenly feeling as untenable as a sandcastle at high tide, Vicky closed her eyes and prayed.

***

Brandon awoke sweating and panting, so thirsty that he could gulp down an entire bottle of water. He tore off the sweatshirt and sweatpants he'd found necessary to ward off the cold last night. Sitting in his boxers, legs dangling over the side of the bed, he strained his mind to remember something just out of reach. A dream? It felt so close, mere inches beyond his grasp, as if he'd been dreaming about it right up until the time of his awakening.

He suddenly remembered, his lips spreading into a smile. He'd been dreaming of her, the girl from last night in the auditorium. Snow Globe Girl. God, that sounded fucking stupid. She'd been so mysterious and stunning in the dark auditorium, but now, with sunlight spilling into the room and chasing out the shadows of secrecy, the whole thing seemed like an extension of his dreams. If Brandon ever revealed any of this to his teammates, he'd get relentlessly razzed the entire hockey season – and deservedly so. Even Cole, Brady, and Angie hadn't believed him about the girl, but she'd definitely been there, and Harrow, too, easily the most bizarre night of Brandon's life (and that was saying something considering his liberal alcohol consumption).

Brandon brushed his teeth and splashed cold water against his face. Not bothering to get dressed, he dragged himself downstairs in his boxers and T-shirt, slogging without purpose through the empty house and eventually collapsing on the couch. His head ached mildly, though not nearly as badly as last night. The rest of him felt fine, except he had zero energy. Toasting a few slices of bread and slapping peanut butter on them seemed like an exerting act.

Instead, Brandon reclined on the couch and watched TV, wishing someone was there to make him breakfast. No such luck. His parents would be churching it up until mid-afternoon – they always helped with auctions and bake sales and brunches and other boring shit after church with the Peace-Be-With-You creepers, LAME! – and Brady had sent a text saying he and Angie would be waterskiing all day.

Great. Guess I'll just watch TV.

But TV didn't prove to be much of a distraction from his thoughts about Harrow and that girl. Last night had been way too weird, and quickly Brandon's lethargy was replaced by an uncomfortable edginess. Unable to keep still, drawn into a pace of the first floor, he kept thinking about everything Harrow had said and how he'd picked his number.

Between zero and infinity.

739. Brandon had thought it, and Harrow had reached into his mind. How? *How the hell did he do that?*

Later, circling the kitchen, waiting for his toast to spring up, a glass of orange juice in hand, Brandon felt perplexed almost to the point of distress, like a frustrated little kid who cries because he can't figure something out. Other than Harrow being an actual magician, there seemed to be no other way the guy could have identified 739. A guess was out of the question – Harrow had announced the number with confidence, as if Brandon had held up a card for him to read with 739 written on it. And then there was the cigarette Harrow had lit with his finger!

Brandon still couldn't even remember how he'd gotten into the auditorium, which bothered him immensely. It was almost like he'd gone through a time warp and found himself inside the building, sitting beside the girl. But how? The little patch of time remained a dark, unreachable void in Brandon's mind, frightening in its inaccessibility.

The toast popped up, but Brandon ignored it, a vivid image flashing into his head and then appearing steadily before him, as if he could reach out and…

…It was her, Snow Globe Girl! Brandon could see her in a car, so beautiful and elusive, but she looked scared, her eyes betraying a deep and ruthless fear…

…but too soon she was gone, Brandon left a little short of breath by what could only be described as a vision. He'd once smoked pot allegedly laced with PCP, his friend promising him wild hallucinations, but he'd seen nothing that night like what he'd just glimpsed this morning. Her face had been so clear, as if a photograph had been implanted in his mind (he couldn't even picture his parents' faces in that much detail).

Brandon blinked, and it was like waking up from a dream. He was in the kitchen, of course he was, his toast ready to be Jiffed up. But he wasn't very hungry anymore, his thoughts dominated by that enigmatic girl.

"I have to go back there," he murmured, nodding at the countertop, his instincts speaking to him. But also clamoring to be heard were apprehensive thoughts that told him to stay away from that place, the same type of cautionary thoughts Brandon always ignored before visiting new porn sites potentially rigged with viruses. The risks were undeniable, but they were nothing compared to the rewards.

There was no further debate. Brandon Joutel's mind was made up.

***

That Sunday afternoon, Patrick Bay reviewed a report written by one of the overnight guards who described the lights inexplicably coming on last night in Harrow Hall.

Patrick, whose nearly flawless memory served him well in all three of his jobs – this being the tertiary position, a weekend security gig working for Leach – furrowed his eyebrows in confusion when he neared the end of Cole Joutel's report.

"Dressing rooms?" he mumbled, rereading Cole's description: *Even the lights in the dressing rooms came on...*

But there weren't any dressing rooms in Harrow Hall. Patrick had gone through that building with state inspectors during his first week on the job, and he remembered the layout perfectly – there was an auditorium and conference rooms and plenty of offices, but definitely no dressing rooms.

So what the heck was Cole talking about?

Patrick wondered if he'd missed something. No, he never missed anything. His primary occupation was insurance inspector; banks paid him to go through houses and record in painstaking detail every possible safety violation. Over the years Patrick had toured hundreds of houses, observing and documenting the potential hazards within every room. And he never forgot a house. In fact, he could probably return to a house he'd entered two years ago and rattle off the locations of every bathroom. His wife called his memory superhuman. His two teenage sons called it freakish. Regardless of whether Patrick was Superman or Freakman, his memory never failed him.

Harrow Hall didn't have dressing rooms.

Chapter 7

They decided to linger in northern Tennessee for a while, keeping the state of Kentucky as a sort of no man's land between them and Harrow. Willy had said they shouldn't venture any farther north until they knew exactly where to find the necromancer and could subsequently "call in some muscle", a suggestion none of them had disputed.

Sticking with the moving target strategy, they exited the highway and drove around for several monotonous hours, stopping only when it was time to gas up, buy additional groceries, and seek out opportunities for divination. If they went about an hour west, Bu had a good friend willing to let them stay, but Sky quickly reminded him that stopping there would take away the "moving" aspect of moving targets.

Later, having switched positions with Ki, who was now sleeping, Jerome stared out the window at a seemingly endless forest. The evening sun was angling golden through the trees, the gently undulating road ahead shining brilliantly like a sea of brass plates. Soon the curtains of clouds would be edged with color, and then the night would come, sliding over these unfamiliar roads and bringing with it the possibility of new threats.

Jerome let out a deep breath. It felt weird to be absorbed in this silent yet prodigious war, society oblivious to Harrow's intentions. It was on them to stop him, six people in a van, each with his or her own unique gift. Jerome didn't even know how to summon his gift – the visions had come to him impeccably at the hotel, just before the men had arrived. Was that the extent of his offerings, he wondered, relying on the luck of visions? In the Army he'd received countless hours of training to prepare him for combat, but now there seemed to be nothing he could do to hone his "skills." It bothered him, not just his own unpreparedness but that of the group. How could Rosa, Sky, Ki, and Bu be expected to fight Harrow and his goons? They'd admitted to never having physically fought anyone (outside of Bu's fourth-grade scuffle with a bully).

Apparently Willy didn't share Jerome's fears. "We've got plenty of weapons and people on standby," he'd assured a little earlier, referencing a flamethrower that could reach up to one hundred feet and a team of tactical experts who owed him a favor or two. "I've been training our group with the weapons, and you should practice up, too, Jerome. We'll find a place for you to get acquainted with the heavy stuff."

Still, Jerome felt about as confident as an occupant of a tube raft in stormy, shark-infested waters. Yet he didn't worry about his own death as much as those of the others. Bu still had a long way to go, and Sky was just a kid, her whole life ahead of her. But if they didn't stop Harrow, who would? The police? The National Guard? No, certainly not the authorities – and they couldn't expect this infection to go away on its own. It was gradually worsening, with or without them. As surreal and implausible as it sounded, as much as Jerome wished he could deny it, Harrow really was forming an army intent on genocide, proof of his dark ambitions supplied by the four soldiers who'd come to kill them last night.

Jerome craved a glass of whiskey. All this thinking and brooding and driving was enough to give a man quite a whopper of a headache. He wondered how the others had tolerated it this long. In Nam there'd been orders and missions and objectives – some of them seemingly impossible to achieve against an enemy that had often felt more like a ghost, but at least there'd been objectives.

But now, many years later, the spontaneity of this group was mindboggling. How did they manage to keep it together driving around from place to place and searching for signs in lakes and flames? Divinations, they called them, everything ending in "mancer."

Currently the divining was taking a break. Even Buford, whose eyes were always drawn to the sky, was reading a paperback, the passenger side sun visor pulled down to block the assault of blinding gold. Willy was driving even slower than usual with the sun in their faces, his orange-tinted sunglasses creating an undeniable CeeLo Green resemblance. Jerome and Sky had both offered to drive, but Willy was adamantly resistant to anyone touching "his baby."

A row ahead of Jerome, the ladies were keeping themselves busy as the miles rolled along, Rosa crocheting a blanket and Sky clicking through her iPod, loud music escaping the earphones (she'd probably be deaf by the time she turned fifty, Jerome assumed). Meanwhile, Ki had dozed off beside Jerome, his head slumped forward and hands folded across his lap.

These people were all voluntary or involuntary outcasts, Jerome had come to realize after hearing more stories during the trip – a motley selection of souls who'd banded together against the elusive darkness. Rosa's husband had died of a stroke; Bu's fiancée had broken things off just days after he popped the question; and Sky, she was just a blue-haired rebel who liked setting fires. None of them had regular jobs or careers, at least not anymore, but they all had plenty of stories.

Their current collective story was playing out in a slow-moving van, with late sunlight streaking in from the west and Harrow's soldiers tracking them from Lord knew where. For Willy, this was a story of retribution. For Jerome and the others, it was a tale of reclamation and rediscovery and renewal. Regardless of how they'd come together, they were all ready to challenge Harrow, no one turning away. Though the van was moving slowly, it was nonetheless moving steadily closer to an inevitable clash.

There was no going back now. The scene had been established, the characters defined, and soon the thunderheads of war would clout.

After the sun fell beyond the hills and the temperature dropped off, they stopped at a diner in the middle of a small railroad town. Sky didn't like the idea, insisting that they keep moving, but the rest of them were hungry and desperate to get out of the van for a few minutes.

"It'll only take half an hour," Willy said. "Plus, me and Jerome will be armed in case something goes wrong."

This information seemed to appease Sky, at least for the moment, and she gave them a little shrug of approval. They slid open the door and stepped out of the van into the uninviting night, which, even with the decreased temperature, felt sticky after leaving the air-conditioned Windstar.

A few people congregating on the sidewalk outside the diner looked at them suspiciously as they walked up, and Jerome realized how odd they must have seemed, six people of varying age and ethnicity stumbling out of a van in the middle of Smalltown, Tennessee, the roof loaded with a mountain of luggage.

Entering Dee's Diner, a cozy little place ensconced within a brick storefront on Main Street, was like going back to the fifties. With black and white floor tiles, red barstools and booths, photos of old cars on the walls, and a Wurlitzer in the corner, Jerome wouldn't have been surprised to glance into a mirror and see the face of a child, a milkshake in his hand and a smile on his face, Fats Domino's voice soon to be filling the room. There was comfort of reunion to be found in such an experience, like bumping into a childhood friend and striking up a conversation. As the years went by and the kids kept getting younger and the gadgets kept getting smaller, it was reassuring to realize certain things didn't change – that only a portion of the carpet beneath you had been tugged away and not the whole damn floor. Old age was a lot like the highway, Jerome thought. You just keep moving further and further out of people's way over the years, steadily slowing down, newer models passing you by, until finally you're in the breakdown lane, forgotten, all of the love and joy in the world now belonging to other men. Younger men.

But maybe that was just *his* way of thinking, a product of his wife's and daughter's deaths. Maybe if they'd still been alive, he would have felt like his life had meaning, like he was still flying in the express lane, not just another faltering clunker in the breakdown lane waiting to be towed off, each day the same empty show, whiskey the only thing that kept him feeling okay on the worst days…and the Lower Ninth family, they never passed you up and forgot you, but outside in SOCIETY he was swallowed up, washed over by the seas of change, his time to serve his country having come and gone, his family and his home gone, too – and with the admission of such truths came heavy, sullen nights where every thought gravitated to his losses and his demons and what could have been, nights best spent at Canal Nine watching McGreevy wipe down the bar.

"Shit, I'm getting the biggest ass hamburger this place has!" Sky announced, tearing Jerome from his thoughts.

A few patrons, including a cop, eyed them as they filed into booths, three people per table, Willy instructing everyone to keep their wallets in their pockets. Like everything else, he would pay.

Jerome sat with Sky and Ki, the ultimate contrast of dining company. When the waitress came by with the menus and a wooden smile, Sky ordered enough for three people, telling the waitress twice to include extra fries. Ki ordered only a bowl of vegetable soup and a glass of water, even after Sky's insistences to, "Go crazy, dude. It's on Willy!"

Jerome settled on a steak burger and fries, telling himself he would at least leave a tip. Willy was a generous host, but this was getting to be too much – a man needs to pay his way in life.

"I'm stoked for the fiesta tonight," Sky said after the waitress left. She was referring to what they'd planned before arriving in town, a little gathering near a lake during which each of their specialties of "mancy" would unfold. They'd light a small fire for Sky. Bu would stare at the stars, Ki the night waters. And Rosa would observe the sand and rocks, Willy perhaps to find a camper or vagrant whose palm he could read.

When it was all wrapped up, maybe, *maybe* they would have a better idea of where Harrow had set up shop. Jerome smiled at the idea of it. This was how these people operated, riding around in Willy's Windstar and waiting for the cosmos to offer clues. It was comical but effective, and now Jerome could better appreciate their extrasensory talents. At least they'd honed their skills to a practicable degree, unlike Jerome, who could only pray another vision would get around to reaching him soon, preferably without Harrow's voice to accompany it. He still hadn't told his new mates about that wrinkle in the fabric.

When the food arrived, Sky launched ravenously into her double cheeseburger, biting deeply into it like a starving person and squirting half a bottle of ketchup onto her plate. Most of the burger's contents – tomatoes, lettuce, onions – spilled onto the plate and table, but she scooped them up and shoved them into her mouth. "Damn good stuff," she said with quick nods, swallowing everything down with a gulp of Pepsi.

Seated beside Jerome, opposite Sky, Ki blew on his soup and swirled it delicately with a spoon, then gazed intently into the broth. Apparently there was something of interest in there, for he retrieved his glasses from his shirt pocket and continued the examination.

Jerome salted his fries and cut his burger in half. "You see somethin in there, big man?"

Ki nodded, pressing his lips together and squinting. "Thought I saw face."

"Get used to it – he always sees faces in soup," Sky said between bites. "The key to finding Harrow will probably be some dumbass shit like Ki seeing something in his soup."

Even Ki couldn't force back a smile. Sky, with her blue hair and tattoos and profanities, could take over a room in a hurry, the other diners sneaking glances at her, including the little kid a few booths down, who Sky spooked into turning around by making contorted faces. Self-consciousness and Sky would never be spoken in the same sentence.

Eventually Ki gave up on whatever he thought he'd seen, digging into his soup and seeming to enjoy it. He was the only person in the group whose past largely eluded Jerome, and there seemed to be no way to coax the goods out of him. Jerome wished Ki would speak a little more – even with extremely limited words, he'd already conveyed superior intelligence and humor. Hell, he was probably smarter than all of them combined, but there lurked a deep sadness in him, locked far beneath the surface. Jerome could sometimes catch it in his eyes, but only because he'd seen that same glinting grief in his own eyes.

Such grief, Jerome knew well, was best kept buried inside. He, himself, hadn't spoken the names of his wife and daughter to these people, and though he sometimes felt inclined to tell them about the amazing ladies who'd once illuminated his life, it just seemed like too long a trek out from the dark, overgrown wilderness his heart had become. Plus, when it came down to it, these people weren't his family; officially, by decree of the fifty thousand dollars in his bank account, they were coworkers. Anyway, even if he opened up to them, there was nothing they could do to melt the ice of sorrow. They held a small place in his life, a tiny yet crucial chapter, but he wouldn't let them in, nor would Ki shine a light for them into the tenebrous chambers of his heart.

There was no room for all that baggage, certainly not now. This wasn't a psychiatry session or a senior home – their focus needed to remain exclusively on Harrow. No complications.

Chapter 8

Vicky kept trying to engage Mary in conversation. It was as much an effort to distract Mary as it was to distract herself, especially now that she was resolute about her escape plan. But Mary, eyes fixed on the road and hands glued to the wheel, ignored her constant questioning, repeating the lines, "Almost there now" and "Just a few more minutes."

Soon there would be no further need for questions.

I'd rather die than go back to that place.

Vicky tensed up as they rounded a corner, the center of her town coming into view. "Almost there," Mary said again, but Vicky was focused on a traffic signal in the distance, yellow giving way to red, a small line of vehicles ahead of them coasting to a stop.

This was it. Finally they would be forced to stop, pedestrians all around to see them, the storefront busy with shoppers bustling in and out of Bluegrass Antiques and Countyline Hardware and Sheila's Coffee House. The police station, a squat brick building at the corner, was two hundred feet ahead.

Closer to the intersection, closer…they were slowing, almost stopped. Hope sprouted wings in Vicky's heart, and now it was lifting her into adrenalized action, her fingers finding the door handle and tugging. It flew open, Vicky dashing out and screaming, "Help! Help me!"

But the people kept on walking, oblivious to her screams, the wings of hope failing, sending her crashing down, down, down, plummeting inexorably. She knew what was happening without understanding it, a dreadful instinct that came devoid of explanation, tears pooling in her eyes. Here she was in the middle of her town, but it was like she was invisible, a ghost on the sidewalk outside Countyline Hardware, life rambling on without her. The fear was immense, robbing her of breath. Her screams degraded to rasping wheezes – the frantic sounds of nightmares. Everything seemed to slow and shift away from the order of the world, not only the vehicles and pedestrians but the noises. Even people's voices sounded distorted and deep – drawn out with incomprehensible rhymes that went: Oh, lo, oh, mo, lo, doh, bo – senseless babble that crushed down on Vicky with a steely hand.

She made a helpless little circle, feeling completely adrift on a sidewalk she'd followed countless times. Gray skies crept overhead, but there wasn't a cloud in sight, everything darkened as if sunglasses had been forced over Vicky's eyes, renegade shadows spilling everywhere, free of ruthless masters, colliding into shallow, inky pools that lapped against the curbs. Slowly the vehicles disappeared, evaporating one by one, and the people departed, too, leaving only the black rising liquid, Harrow's voice conquering the chorus of: *Lo, bo, so, mo, doh, ho, ro, bo.*

"The storm cannot be stopped, Victoria. Removed is the privilege of choice when destiny calls. Whereupon I snap my fingers, you will return," and SNAP, Vicky was back in the dim emptiness of Harrow Hall, chained to a seat in the first row.

The scarlet curtains trembled, sliding soundlessly open moments later. Vicky screamed and strained against the chains until her voice cracked like a dropped egg, her chest and arms hurting from repeated wrenching.

Eventually Harrow came through the eldritch curtains, his form at first a blur of movement because of Vicky's watery, stinging eyes. Dressed in plaid shorts and a T-shirt, he emerged from the backstage shadows and stepped into the spotlight – except it wasn't Harrow, no, it was him, the handsome green-eyed boy she'd seen before in a vision!

He leaped off the stage and came to her, kneeled down, hands extended, and wiped a tear from her cheek…

…and now, inexplicably, she knew him, his shrouding veil of mystery removed. He'd been taken by Harrow as well, his presence offering Vicky a flicker of hope to light the way. A thin warmth spread through her, scarce and tepid but brimming with reassuring truth. It made her feel less alone. The darkness was all around them, but at least they wouldn't have to navigate it alone.

Without moving his lips, the boy told her, *There's a way out. I'll help you find it.*

***

Brandon knew his brother would never drive him back to the institution, not after everything that went down last night.

That's where Vinny Stettler and his driver's license came in. Heading into his senior season, Vinny was the hockey team's backup goalie, a relegation he'd accepted gracefully when Brandon came in two years ago as a freshman, flashing his glove around and showing off the skills he'd developed from a lifetime in net. With only his incumbency to stand on, Vinny had gotten the nod in goal for the first month of Brandon's freshman season – but after a disastrous handful of games the coach had given Brandon his first start in January. He'd shut that game out and then the next one, taking the team all the way to the championship game, and now Vinny knew his spot well on the bench.

But he was a pretty cool guy, opening the doors dutifully for line changes and filling up water bottles when asked and offering Brandon support. He was a fat kid, easily in excess of two-fifty, and he had no qualms about admitting how he'd come to playing goal. ("They put the fattest kid in net to take up space.") Rest was history, Vinny eating a double-whopper and extra fries from Burger King every day between the last bell at school and the first whistle at practice. Just the thought was enough to make Brandon hurl.

"Yo, Vinny, you wanna check out this old mental hospital with me tonight?" Brandon was playing a video game in the living room, his cell phone tucked between his cheek and his shoulder. "I know you're into all that ghost hunting stuff, so I thought maybe you'd wanna go with me. I went there last night with Brady – place is mad dope. Real fucking creepy."

"You want to go *tonight*?" There was crunch-munching on the other end – Vinny undoubtedly eating Doritos, his favorite snack – then the gross telltale sound of finger-sucking.

Brandon cringed. "Yeah, we could go early if you want, like around sunset maybe, keep the Rents happy. We'll tell them we're going to work out for a few hours. You drive and dinner's on me, okay?"

"But my mom knows I don't work out." It was true. Vinny wasn't even required to take part in the team's summer exercises. No one cared if he got stronger or faster – and he definitely didn't need flexibility to sit on the bench.

"Well…I don't know," Brandon said, "just tell her Coach wants you to push me to do better. Say I'm a slacker and need your guidance."

A munch-crunch chuckle exploded over the line. "Yeah, right, Brad, like you ever need me for anything. I was supplanted the day you showed up at freshmen orientation."

"You'll think of something," Brandon insisted. "Come on, dude. If you drive me, I'll buy you all the BK you want, even those little Hershey pies you like so much."

There was a silent moment of contemplation. Then: "You'll have to do better than that. How about dinner at North Main Pizza? I could really go for chicken parm tonight, with lots of cheese sticks."

"Sounds good to me. I'll get you an extra side of cheese sticks."

"Wow, Brad, you must really want to go to this place. Why don't you get Brady to take you some other time?"

"He's doing something with Angie. I want to go tonight."

WELCOME TO HARROW HALL

"Operative word's *doing*, right?"

"Wait, what?" Vinny being an AP English word master, Brandon didn't understand half of the shit the guy said.

A series of munches from Vinny's end. "Never mind, kid. It's not far, right?"

"Not really. We made it there in like half an hour, I think."

"Okay. I'll pick you up at eight?"

"Yeah, meet me at the end of my street at eight. I'll tell the Rents something believable."

Just as Brandon was finishing up his convo with Vinny, his video game avatar was shot and killed by a sniper, GAME OVER flashing tauntingly across the screen. *A bad omen?* he thought. *Nah, don't be a dumbass.*

But apprehensions about his return to the old asylum stayed with him throughout the afternoon. He couldn't shake that anxious, night-before-the-big-game feeling, his stomach feeling heavy and crawly. He kept wondering if this was a huge mistake, but then he thought of her – and Snow Globe Girl made his stomach twist for a different reason.

"We're home, Brandon!" his mother shouted just after four o'clock. "Get down here and help me put the groceries away!"

Brandon looked up from his sketchbook. He'd just finished an outline of her face, as well as a stage in the background and a few rows of seats. God, if only he could see her again. What had she been doing there, anyway? The whole experience was surreally mystifying, almost as if the girl had been a hallucination. Harrow had somehow gotten Brandon inside the building – *hypnotism*??? – and suddenly Brandon had found himself sitting beside her. But why? How? And what had happened to him during those few minutes he couldn't remember?

These were the questions that had nagged him all afternoon, questions that made him fearful about returning. A part of him wanted to put the whole weird night in the rearview mirror, but a larger part of him desired to confront the unexplained and gain deeper insights into that which eluded him. A magician and a beautiful girl – who the hell were they and why had they shown themselves to Brandon the one night he was there? Maybe they were connected to the bus incident from the previous night; Brandon had mentioned the girl to Cole and Brady, but they'd only assumed he was bullshitting them.

Maybe she really had been a hallucination.

But no, NO, she was real, she *felt* real, and Brandon needed answers. If Harrow hadn't tried to hurt him last night, then he was harmless – right? If he was a serial killer, wouldn't he have offed Brandon at first chance? No, he was a magician, he'd said.

Some would call me a magician, others a sorcerer. A few would choose soothsayer. You, young boy, may call me drifter if you prefer. As long as you don't call me shaman, agreeable I'll remain.

Harrow's words echoed in Brandon's mind long after he finished with the groceries, replaying over and over as he added layers of definition to Snow Globe Girl's face. But even a talented artist couldn't have captured the mesmerizing delicacy of her features, never mind the restless renderings of a teenager. A picture! Brandon hadn't even thought to take a picture of her with his cell phone last night, nearly too transfixed to breathe.

Tonight he would do it – if she was there, of course. But what if she wasn't? What if the asylum had announced the presence of this intriguing obfuscation only for a night?

A sustained line of thoughts kept warning Brandon to stay away tonight, but he would go, damn it. He had to go. Who in their sane mind would see a girl like that and not go back? If he didn't return, maybe *he* should be in the loony bin – and permanently. Whatever the risk, Snow Globe Girl was worth it; this much Brandon knew, even without a word having passed between them.

Aching with anticipation, Brandon checked the clock often, willing it to click faster toward eight o'clock.

Chapter 9

On the way to the lake for the "fiesta", nourished by the offerings of a smalltown, fifties-themed diner, their conversation turned to a man everyone referred to as, "The Ghost."

It all started with some gentle ribbing courtesy of Sky. "So, Willy," she said, "when's The Ghost coming down to help us out?"

The van broke into laughter, even Ki, and Jerome knew he was being exposed to an inside joke. Luckily, Sky filled him in after Willy adamantly defended himself.

"Willy's been talking about this guy ever since I met him," she said. "He's this French weapons specialist-slash-mercenary with a really long, dumb name."

"Jean-Sylvain Paradis," Bu said with a mocking French accent, pronouncing it, John Syl-*VEHN* Para-*DEE*.

"You wouldn't be making fun of him if you could see the weapons he has," Willy said.

Sky groaned. "Yeah, yeah, yeah – his weapons don't do us any good if he isn't here." She turned back to Jerome. "Willy keeps saying this Para-dee joker owes him a favor, always talking about the crazy weapons he could bring."

"He owns more guns than some countries. That's what I heard a few weeks back," Rosa said, and they all fell into laughter at Willy's expense.

"He's coming!" Willy insisted. "You all mark my words, he and his team are coming to meet us whenever we're ready. We just need to get our work done first and give him Harrow's location."

"Bull. Shit," Sky countered. "Why don't you face the facts, man? The guy's a pipe dream." Again she glanced at Jerome. "Supposedly he has two houses, one in New Orleans and one in Quebec. I guess he's absolutely loaded."

"Literally and figuratively," Bu said. "At this point, we could really use someone with heavy weapons. I'm not feeling particularly secure after last night."

"This Paradis guy have any special talents…you know, magical?" Jerome asked.

"Not that I'm aware of," Willy said, "but he's got enough weapons to host his own gun show. J.S. was in the Army Special Forces for twenty years."

"And he won't come till you tell him Harrow's exact location?"

"He's got other business on his plate, really big stuff." Willy was about to go on, but Sky interrupted.

"He's a hitman," she said.

Willy let out a growling sigh. "More of a garbage collector than a hitman. He only takes out criminals and terrorists – no telling how many lives he's saved."

"Regardless, the man's an assassin," Rosa said.

Sky huffed. "I'd take a hitman over a cat killer. Willy really knows how to find the gems, doesn't he?"

Willy smoothed a hand across his scalp. "Trust me, you'll be thanking him after he finishes Harrow."

The remainder of the short trip to the lake brimmed with badinage, Willy at the wrong end of the teasing. Even Ki and Rosa got in a few good shots, taking steady aim at the man known as, "The Ghost." But when Willy parked outside a closed gate securing a boat launch and they exited the van, moonlit waters in the distance, the mood instantly became serious, everyone preparing for their respective duties.

Ki, not wanting to waste a minute, jogged with surprising speed around the gate toward the lake, a flashlight guiding the way. Standing outside the van, Rosa shared insect repellant with Sky while Willy and Buford shoved batteries into two additional flashlights.

Jerome smiled, thinking back to this ragtag group spilling out of the overloaded van outside the diner; the people who'd seen them would have all kinds of stories to share with their families tonight.

"All right, let's get down there," Willy said when the flashlights were ready, waddling past the gate and getting himself caught up in a thicket. "Damn pricker bushes," he snarled, waving his arms and inciting Sky to laughter.

Jerome wasn't laughing. He'd suddenly developed a bad feeling about this, and for once it had nothing to do with Harrow. What if some cop found them out here and gave them a hard time? The red and white sign on the locked gate said NO TRESSPASSING AFTER HOURS – VIOLATORS WILL BE PROSECUTED.

Jerome decided not to communicate his worries to the others. Considering their silent war, the police would be the least of their problems.

Later, after a failed fiesta during which no one garnered anything useful (other than a few rocks Rosa identified as "good omens"), they trudged back up to the van, Jerome leading the way. He wished they'd all hurry up so they could get out of here, his bad feeling having blossomed into a bad vibe. A gentle wind rustled the trees as they reached the van, Ki glancing often back to the dark waters. Luckily traffic was sparse on the road.

"Give it up, Ki," Sky said. "It was a bad night. We'll do better tomorrow."

They slid open the door and filed into the van. *A bad night* – what did that mean? It wasn't like they'd missed free throws all night or committed too many fouls. They simply hadn't seen anything in the night firmament or the water or the fire, Sky complaining about the fire being too small. "Can't see shit in that tiny thing," she'd said, but there was no way they could have lit a bonfire on the boat launch beach, not without attracting unwanted attention, Willy promising a bigger fire tomorrow morning.

Jerome sighed when they pulled onto the road and headed east again. In the silence of disappointment it was easy to slip into sleep, his head supported by a pillow Rosa had given him. But sleep was unfriendly and fitful, the thin kind of sleep that made him vaguely aware of the van's light bumps and the occasional whispers of others. There must have been at least a few deeper pockets, though, allowing a vicious nightmare to cut through the peace and slash Jerome.

It transported him back to his home in the Lower Ninth Ward, a place of countless Christmases and birthday parties and barbecues, its walls witnesses to much love and laughter. At first the nightmare was wrapped in decorative paper and topped with a bow, Jerome delivered to better times with Elise and Jennie – a dinner at the table, Elise serving chicken and young Jennie making "train tracks" with her fork in the mashed potatoes. It was a good dinner, with stories and laughter and Jerome embracing the warmth of his home. He was safe here with his family, insulated from harm within his little house in the LNW.

Then came the water.

It started out as a trickling nuisance that seeped through Jerome's socks. Elise noticed it, too, a tiny stream of water tracking into the dining room from the front of the house. They followed the water to its point of entry, the front door, but soon it was coming with greater strength, leaking beneath the door and eventually spilling through the sides, then the windows, an inexplicable thing, just a few inches of water in the house quickly rising to a foot.

Jerome looked through the windows and saw that the street had turned into a river, vehicles and people carried away by the freak flood.

"Go upstairs!" Jerome shouted to his wife and daughter, but the water kept rising and rising and rising, breaking down the door with a roar that sounded like a waterfall.

His girls scrambled upstairs, Jerome right behind them, but the torrents chased them into Jennie's room, busted down her door, surging at them voraciously and forcing them onto the bed. For a moment the water seemed to cease its relentless climb, sloshing with great violence as if something were churning it from beneath. They clung to each other on the bed, listening to screams and sirens down the street.

There was a period of eerie silence, interrupted only by a windy whisper Jerome had heard somewhere before. "Storm's coming, Jerome. Storm's coming. One, two, voila!"

The explosion thundered with the sounds of war – a wave twenty feet high – and Jerome was thrust into the chaos, no longer in his house but drowning in a sea that engulfed his neighborhood, rooftops sliding past, Elise and Jennie torn from his arms. They'd been taken under, he assumed, but he couldn't see them in the dark waters, couldn't hear them over the endless screams and gunfire and wailing soldiers, for now they were in the flooded jungle, the smell of death all around.

Jerome dove beneath the water, tried to search for his wife and daughter, but he couldn't see. He couldn't see anything but darkness, the salt stinging his eyes. He had to come up. The sky peeled with violet lightning, thunder ripping the night, Jerome swept along the weltering current. He jarred into something submerged, a vehicle maybe, then went completely under the water again, couldn't get back up, couldn't breathe, pinned down, dying, the eyes of dead soldiers blinking at him from the depths, eyes never to see their wives and children again, so many men never to come home.

"You made your choice, Jerome!" the storm shouted from above and below. "Do you see the dead? I know the dead well, Jerome. They've come all the way from Vietnam to see me. And soon they will speak to me from the sea grave of the Lower Ninth Ward. I will take all you've ever loved!"

Jerome woke with a strained, choking gasp, faces peering at him from every direction, the faces of children in the jungle. "Elise! Jennie! Where are you?" he shouted, then realized where he was.

A hand upon his shoulder. The old guy, what was his name? Ki, that was it. "Ki, thank God it's you! It wasn't real!"

A light came on. "What in the hell's going on back there?" Willy said.

"Just a nightmare, big guy," Sky said, looking worriedly at Jerome over the seat, her chin resting on her hands.

Ki patted his shoulder. "You safe now," and he started into some Native American sounding song that almost brought Jerome to tears, the flood and the Vietnamese children's faces slowly receding from his mind, relief spreading over him.

"Sorry bout that," Jerome said with a sheepish half-grin. He'd never thought he would be this relieved to see a group of virtual strangers. Even his friends from the Lower Ninth Ward might not have provided him with such comfort – there was something about these damn people that dug into you and wouldn't let go.

Rosa turned back and handed him a bottle of water. "We all have our nightmares," she said.

"Hell yeah we do," Sky added. "Everyone except Mr. Para-DEE. He's probably got a gun to shoot his nightmares away."

Chapter 10

A new mandate awaited Cole Amos's next shift. His superiors at Leach Security had determined that, due to the suspicious events of the last two nights, an extra guard would be indefinitely added to the overnight shift. Until further notice, guards were expected to take paired tours of the asylum grounds every half hour.

Cole wondered what would become of the report he'd filed that morning. Would Harrow Hall get a thorough review? Since it was Sunday night, he didn't expect anything to be done until at least tomorrow in terms of maintenance visits, which might translate into another strange night if the lights stayed on the fritz.

But a grinding, grating feeling in Cole's gut told him the problems were entirely manmade.

When Cole entered the little security trailer at a quarter to nine, ready for whatever oddities the shift had to offer, Ronny was already in his favorite corner, a cup of coffee in hand as he studied the chess board.

"Hey, Cole," he muttered. "How goes it?"

Cole turned down the rattling air conditioner, which had practically transformed the place into an igloo. "Not bad, Ronny. Tired as hell but glad this is the last night for me till Thursday. How's the chess game?"

"Pretty challenging, actually. One side's got the damn bishop fianchettoed on G2; the other's activating with the knights." He spoke in an almost exasperated tone. "If these pawns keep pushing and the bishops don't sacrifice, we're looking at another draw."

"It's gotta be tough playing against yourself all the time. You always know what's coming next, right?"

Rubbing his chin, Ronny scanned the board. "It's a real pain in the neck sometimes. Defensive quality has been real strong lately, lot of blocks, not much opening up in the middle." Finally he took a moment to look up from the board. "You hear about this new three-man crap they want us to do?" He checked his watch. "Where's the new guy, anyhow. We're supposed to get some kid transferring out of Cleveland. He better not listen to rap music. Can't stand that damn stuff."

Cole logged onto his email account and checked the schedule. "Yeah, the boss called me this afternoon about the changes. I guess we're supposed to have two-man tours now."

Waving a hand, Ronny said, "Absolutely ridiculous. If it weren't for those damn kids and that bus, we wouldn't be dealing with all of this crap."

Tuning Ronny out, Cole read through the report left by the day shift guards. Nothing of interest had taken place – nothing ever happened during the daytime, it seemed. Only during the last two overnight shifts had things gotten weird.

And Cole sensed an imminent trifecta.

***

Vinny picked Brandon up right on time at the end of his street. It had been a chore for Brandon to get out of the house, his mother all crazy about making sure he didn't go to parties. "Back by eleven," she'd ordered. "Not a minute later."

Brandon had fought an urge to complain about Brady never being given the third degree when he took Angie out. There were never any *back-by-elevens* for Brady. Bullshit. But parents always had to be right, so there'd been no sense in fighting the uphill battle, not when his mother was already permitting him to leave the house, even if it was for only a few hours.

They made it to the defunct institution in good time, back roads darkening before them as the cloud-streaked sky shifted from pinkish orange to a placid night blue. Brandon told Vinny to pass the main gate and park on the shoulder up the road; the last thing they wanted was to attract the attention of Cole and his partner. This would need to be a stealthy operation, especially after what had happened last night. Cole would never ask him back now, not after the whole *You're irresponsible, You need to Grow Up* shit.

Stealth was the key to seeing her again, if she was still around.

They were parked on the wide shoulder, gathering their things, when Vinny started going soft. "Maybe this isn't such a good idea. What if they bust us for trespassing?" He was holding his camcorder, eager to film the old buildings, but fear was creeping into his eyes.

"No one's gonna see us," Brandon said. "They do their rounds like twice an hour, and the rest of the time they sit in their stupid trailer. Come on, don't you want to check this place out? It's really creepy."

Vinny winced, similar to the expression that sprawled across his face before sprints at the end of practice. "I don't know, Brad, maybe–"

Irritated, Brandon yanked open the passenger door. "We drove all this way, dude. Don't puss out on me now."

With a deep breath, Vinny reluctantly followed Brandon down the road toward the main gate at the intersection with the entry road. When they were sure no one was around, the security car parked in the illuminated lot beside the trailer about three hundred feet away, they jumped a guardrail well ahead of the gate and followed a wooded slope down to the entry road, their cell phones lighting the way. The place wasn't fenced off over here, the abandoned institution theirs to explore (they'd avoided the triangle containing the security trailer and main gate by sidling in obliquely from the road).

"Wow, this place is huge!" Vinny said, his confidence starting to build. Now that they were past the security trailer, the open road ahead, he was realizing the risks of getting caught were slim. It was almost fully dark now, making it virtually impossible for anyone to spot them. Their biggest worry, Brandon decided, was the police discovering their abandoned vehicle back on the road and requesting a tow.

No risk, no reward, right?

Vinny turned on his camcorder when they left the road and slipped behind Brookside Hall, a three-story building with snarls of ivy crawling up the brick walls. Its white-trimmed windows reflected the bright moon, though a few of them glowed with dull interior lights, shadows of branches sweeping across every wall.

To their left, down a steep embankment, water burbled through the asylum, journeying beneath a bridge and eventually winding behind Harrow Hall on the next road – the building that dominated Brandon's mind. While Vinny pointed his camcorder up at Brookside Hall and narrated cheesily like those jokers on the ghost hunting shows, Brandon grew increasingly restless. He couldn't wait to get to Harrow Hall. Luckily he hadn't told Vinny about Harrow and Snow Globe Girl – otherwise his friend would have gone soft on him for sure.

"Come on, there's tons of other buildings here," Brandon said when it looked like Vinny might never leave the shadows of Brookside.

They returned to the road, crossing the little bridge over the brook and passing short brick buildings on both sides of the road, a few of them encumbered with awkward scaffolding and bowing canvas awnings, everything dappled in moonlight and shadows. Brandon kept thinking he saw movement at the edges of buildings, where overgrown bushes crowded the walls.

But they were alone, at least for now, followed only by the soughing wind as they reached the first intersection.

WELCOME TO HARROW HALL

"Let's go this way," Brandon said, turning right toward Harrow Hall and hoping to sound spontaneous.

Vinny had no qualms. Grinning into his camcorder, practically salivating over the creepy footage he was getting, he followed Brandon up the sidewalk, Harrow Hall looming into view in the baleful distance. With each step Brandon felt nervous excitement rising higher in his chest, bolstered by the inherent risks, the least fearful of which was getting snagged by Cole. There was a mysterious energy about this place that whispered to him with every gust of wind, manifesting in the shadows and up in the lighted windows, a life force that shouldn't have existed in an abandoned institution, as if blood bubbled beneath the crumbling roads and sidewalks, sustaining the heart of the asylum.

Closer to Harrow Hall. Closer, the building seeming to enlarge with every step. But Vinny was crossing the road toward the campus center, where the flagpole clanged like a night ship's bell.

"Wow, check this out!" Vinny exclaimed, hurrying past the pavilion to an unstill set of swings, the wind having taken repeated indulgences – and yet the creaking remnants of the swings' lifts and falls displayed a momentum seemingly beyond the wind's capability to muster.

Vinny set his camcorder down on the grass and pulled himself onto one of the wooden seats, the chains groaning and jangling.

"Be careful, or you might bring the whole thing down," Brandon said, looking frustratedly back toward Harrow Hall. The building was completely dark tonight, no signs of activity.

Vinny was starting to achieve some height, thrusting his legs with every push. *God, if he fell now it might trigger an earthquake.*

"Come on, Brad, try it. This is awesome!"

"I think I'll pass, man. Wasn't planning to go to the hospital tonight."

Headlights down the road! Vinny spotted them first and leaped off the swing, landing with surprising grace and grabbing his camcorder. "Security car's coming. Where should we hide?"

Brandon pointed to the pavilion. "In there," and they scuttled inside, hunkering below the leaf-filled benches as the car slid by, stopping outside Harrow Hall and then moving on.

"See that, easy as hell to avoid them," Brandon said. "They just stay in their car and drive around."

Vinny was smiling like a kid who's finally reached the head of the roller coaster line. "I can't wait to see more of this place. This is sweet, Brad!"

You haven't seen anything yet, Brandon thought.

They waited a few minutes in the pavilion to make sure the car didn't double back, then crossed the street and approached Harrow Hall, Brandon retracing his steps from last night until he reached the front doors. Locked.

Taped to one of the doors was a small cardboard sign featuring two masks and an arrow, the masks caricaturing tragedy and comedy through exaggerated expressions of laughter and sorrow. The sign announced PERFORMANCE! in red, squiggly letters, but even with its artistic frivolity, the piece of cardboard carried an imposing weight, Brandon assuming Harrow was behind it.

Of course it was him!

Brandon spun around, no one there, then tried the doors again. Locked, all of them, and Brandon was almost certain the sign hadn't been there last night.

"We shouldn't go in. They might have alarms," Vinny worried.

WELCOME TO HARROW HALL

Brandon searched the shadowy trees opposite the road, convinced Harrow would come if he waited long enough. He would let them into the building – and then they would see her, the girl Brandon had taken all of these risks for.

Done filming Harrow Hall, Vinny started toward the road a few minutes later.

"Wait up!" Brandon called, hoping to invent an excuse to stall his friend. He looked up to the moon, wondering if this had all been a waste of time. What if Harrow didn't come? What if he'd moved on to the next town? What if…?

A surge of wind rattled the front doors. Brandon expected them to open a few inches, perhaps a gift of magic or maybe just a stroke of luck. But the doors remained closed.

Vinny, meanwhile, was jogging back toward the campus center, leaving Brandon in a daze of disbelief. He'd been so excited, so inexplicably positive that he would encounter Harrow and the girl again – even a little scared – but now he was deflated, Harrow Hall reduced from a mystifying place of promise to a simple building. A dark, abandoned building, the hope drained away.

Reluctantly, very reluctantly, Brandon moved on, following Vinny to the next attraction.

***

"Whatcha think they're gonna do with this place?" Ronny said.

Cole gazed up at the barred windows of Granite Hall and then the red X near the entrance foretelling the building's demolition. He tossed his cigarette out the window. "Who knows? By the time they decide what they want to do, none of these buildings will be usable."

"Weather'll get to 'em quick without daily maintenance. Heavy snow on these flat roofs – you've got yourself a disaster waiting to happen."

They completed their tour of the asylum and returned to the trailer, where the new guy from Cleveland, Barry Hoffman, was still on edge about what he'd allegedly seen during his tour with Ronny half an hour ago – two people walking behind one of the buildings. Having been told about the school bus incident from Friday night, the poor guy seemed convinced that something unpleasant would happen. Not that Cole could blame him; he himself remained uneasy about an overnight shift that, until two nights ago, had been nothing but boring. Now the empty, moonlit roads reached out into the unknown with troubling possibilities, every shadow a menace.

Barry, a nervous, fidgety man in his thirties, had just made a career change to security. He used to be an accountant but claimed the tedium of the job had made him long for something different and exciting. But perhaps this job was a little too exciting – the guy could barely sit still for a minute.

"If you see people on the grounds, aren't you supposed to call the cops?" he said.

"Check," Ronny said from the chess table, then: "I'm sure it was just a couple deer, man. We was a long ways off."

"No, these were two *people*," Barry insisted. "I'm positive."

"Tell you what, if you see them again, we'll call the cops," Cole said, assuming that Barry had gotten himself a little too wound up on his first night. "By the time they get here, though, the trespassers will probably be long gone."

Ronny looked up from the board. "This place gets tons of trespassers. People who want to smoke pot, people who want to find somewhere private for the birds and the bees, people who just want to look at the buildings and get themselves spooked. As long as they don't deface the property, it don't much matter to me."

Barry looked at Ronny disapprovingly, as if to suggest he wasn't taking the job seriously enough. The wind brushed against the trailer, causing Barry to flinch. Yes, this security gig was definitely too much excitement for the former accountant.

Cole sighed, wondering if what Barry had seen would give them problems. Either way, it would be a long night, he assumed.

***

As they walked all the way to the opposite end of the asylum, Brandon resigned himself to the reality that Snow Globe Girl had been a blip on life's radar, appearing for a night and then submerging into the depths of obscurity. Harrow, too, the magician confounding Brandon and leaving him with a load of questions.

Perhaps Brandon hadn't come here entirely for the girl, he realized, his questions demanding answers in the wake of the minutes lost.

Brandon checked his watch – half past nine. "We better get back to the car. My mom's gonna kill me if I'm not home by eleven."

"You better not forget about that dinner you owe me. We don't have time tonight, but I'm gona hold you to it."

"Name the night, and it's on me."

Satisfied with the footage he'd collected, Vinny switched off his camcorder. To their right was Wayside Hall, a decidedly more Gothic building than the others, with its rows of arched windows and two towers at either end, a massive structure that likely housed hundreds of patients when this place was operational. Fascinated with architecture styles, Brandon knew the Gothic elements well and could easily identify them (most, if not all, of the castles in his sketchbook were

Gothic-inspired creations, though he had no idea what possessed him to constantly draw castles). Maybe he really had taken too many pucks to the head.

They dodged the security car once more on their way back to the campus center. When its taillights disappeared from view and the road was empty again, they both saw the person at the same time. Maybe two hundred feet away, he or she was wide-stanced in the middle of the moonlit road near Harrow Hall, coat flapping in a stiff breeze, impossible to tell which way he/she was facing.

A flurry of thoughts raced into Brandon's head, the first of which warned him that this individual was dangerous. *Run! Hide!*

They stopped walking. "Who the hell is that?" Vinny murmured, the chill of fear audible in his voice.

"I...I don't know. Maybe we should–"

The person shouted Brandon's name. Waved for them to come closer.

Harrow.

Chapter 11

They couldn't stay at another hotel, not after the close call last night. But the ideas of sleeping in the van or camping had lost their appeal somewhere along the way, especially for Rosa and Ki. Jerome didn't mind these prospects – Lord knew he'd slept in plenty of worse places – but poor Rosa didn't need to be subjected to a camping expedition. She would probably have a stiff back for a month.

Again Jerome dreaded how this would all play out. The more time he spent with his new teammates, the stronger his fear became that the continued mingling of their "mancies" would lead them straight to their graves. So what if they had pistols and a flamethrower if half of them wouldn't be able to use these weapons effectively under pressure? How would Rosa and Ki and Sky and Bu possibly hold up in a war? They weren't soldiers. They were civilians with special gifts but not fighters, and no matter how often Jerome tried to tell himself that reinforcements would assist them, his belief that they would all be killed kept gnawing at him. Personally, he was ready to do what it took to destroy Harrow, but he'd been trained in combat. He'd survived war. The others…

… You chose your side. Now you must die along with your new friends. In the land of the dead Elise and Jennie await you, but you shall never see them again, fool, the fires of the damned to claim you!

Jerome remembered every word Harrow had spoken to him last night. And the nightmare tonight – had Harrow foisted that upon him as well? It remained inexplicable why the necromancer would go to such lengths when he could have killed Jerome back in New Orleans. Why communicate with him now and try to scare him? Was Harrow a legitimately powerful force, or was he simply an instrument of deception, perhaps dictated by an even greater force?

Jerome sat quietly for many minutes, deep with fear for these people who had taken him in. He was starting to come around to them, all of them, a bunch of strangers who'd turned into…well, they'd turned into friends. There was no other way to describe them. Sky, with her blue hair and constant sass; Ki and his pithy wisdom; Rosa's warmth and generosity; Bu's overanalyzing and quiet humor; and Willy, whose slow driving and determined spirit kept the van moving forward.

When this had all started out, it had at times seemed to Jerome like a surreal adventure – no more threatening than a video game in terms of bodily harm – but now their lives were in immediate danger. Yet Jerome knew he couldn't ask them to walk away from this; they'd made their decisions after assessing the risks. They all knew how dangerous Harrow was, especially after last night, but they continued to make Willy's war their own, just as Jerome did (and he knew it had nothing to do with the fifty grand in their bank accounts).

No, this was far more important than money – this was about keeping people safe.

And with the unification of unique talents came the formation of a team possessing a single goal, everyone willing to sacrifice themselves for the achievement of that goal. As Jerome had seen in war, the goal of the group inevitably takes eminence over the needs of individuals, and when that mindset is embraced by everyone in the unit – each person prepared to die for the next – it's impossible to just walk away.

Jerome understood this was the situation for the six people riding in Willy's van. They were in a war, and, terrified or not, you can't quit when it's fighting time.

"Let's just get a room at a Motel 6," Sky suggested. "We'll take turns keeping watch."

"Sounds like a good plan to me," Bu said.

Rosa let out a relieved sigh. "If I get one of the beds, I'm all for it."

They laughed and joked about the seniority among the group, but Jerome's attention was inwardly fixed. Another vision had just come to him, flashing through his head like a vivid memory. A black SUV.

Bright headlights. Approaching fast. He hadn't seen any other details –
nothing about the road, no landmarks, just the fast-moving SUV, its
windshield tinted black…

…Another vision. This one revealed a motel room, two beds with beige
blankets. An orange wall. A lamp lit in the corner. The curtains were
partly drawn, but he could still see headlights out there. Bright
headlights. The same SUV, it was parked outside!

"We can't go to a motel," Jerome blurted, eliciting a sudden silence. "I
just had another vision – more guys are coming for us. Willy, you're
gonna need to drive faster, a hell of a lot faster."

Chapter 12

The wind ratcheted up as they approached Harrow along the moonlit road, the flagpole clanging at the campus center. Nestled in ghostly shadows, the pavilion sat empty but for the rustling chorus of leaves. To their left, Harrow Hall was dark and foreboding.

Straight ahead, trench coat flapping, top hat reaching into the blackness, Harrow was a shadow brought to life, seemingly in full command of the institution and the night itself. Eagerly, he waved them closer, and it felt to Brandon like there was little choice in the matter.

Run! Run now!

Instead, they kept walking, Brandon unable to distinguish Harrow's facial features until they were within a few feet.

"Brandon, child, so good to see you again. To what name does your friend answer? No, wait, don't tell me." Harrow made a little circle, unruly hair dancing in the wind as he stared up at the moon. He raised his hands, spaced his fingers apart. "If you'll spare a few seconds, his name the Spirits will disclose."

Vinny shoved Brandon's shoulder. "You know this guy? What's going–?"

"Vincent Stettler!" Harrow proclaimed, searching them intently.

Again Brandon was stripped of words, Vinny reduced to a stuttering idiot.

"H-how? How d-d-did you know my name?"

Harrow lifted a hand in acknowledgement of something unseen. "The Night Spirits, of course. The name's Harrow. Pleased to meet you, boy," and they shook hands, Vinny quickly retracting his hand as if he'd been scorched.

WELCOME TO HARROW HALL

"Who's that girl I saw last night? And how did I get into the building?" Brandon said, staring dully at Harrow in spite of the adrenaline flooding his veins. His vision went a little blurry, and he couldn't seem to focus on Harrow's face. He rubbed his eyes but achieved no relief.

Harrow pulled his hat a little lower, further shadowing his eyes. "Just a touch of magic, Brandon. To the wondrous realm I exposed you, my boy. I hope you enjoyed it."

"Seriously, who's that girl – the one in the auditorium last night?"

Harrow shrugged. "I'm aware of no girl sharing my home."

"Hold up, who *are* you?" Vinny said, his eyes glassy with fear. "Brad, what the hell is going on?"

"I am a humble magic man, a sorcerer of the centuries," Harrow announced, his eyes splitting time between Brandon and Vinny. "The birth of this country I have witnessed, a curious thing, indeed. I have seen the witches burn, the battles of the voodoo queens, and the forgotten quests of midnight diviners. I have beheld unendingly the two sorts of people this world contrives – the admittedly unimportant and the misguidedly self-important. None could accomplish what I accomplished, the sacred covenant."

Vinny had backed away. "Come on, Brad, this guy's crazy."

But Brandon remained rooted to the pavement before Harrow. "Who was that girl?" he said in a low voice, ignoring Vinny's continued pleas, suddenly aching desperately to have the mystery revealed for him. "Please tell me. I just want to see her again."

A hand on his arm, tugging him. Vinny's hand. "Brad, let's go!"

Harrow tilted his head, studying Vinny with unnerving intensity. "How impertinent of you to disrespect the magic, boy."

"There is no magic!" Vinny snapped, still dragging Brandon along by the arm. One hundred pounds lighter than his friend, Brandon didn't have much of a choice, but somehow Harrow got ahead of them, blocking their way.

And he was holding Vinny's camcorder!

"I'm told you weren't the initial owner of this fine device," Harrow said, repeatedly stroking the camcorder with his index finger. Again he glanced to the moon, and Brandon's legs went tired and rubbery, his eyes still freaking out a little. He could focus better than before, but his vision was far from perfect.

"I b-b-bought it from a friend," Vinny stammered. "What's it to you?"

Harrow tossed the camcorder to Vinny, who managed to make a one-handed catch with only the moon to assist him, probably the best save he'd ever authored.

"To nonbelievers magic must offer proof," Harrow said, sounding mildly displeased. He pointed at Vinny's camcorder. "A rough senior year I predict for the boy who bestowed that gift upon you," he said with a rasping laugh. Before sauntering off to the shadows of the campus center, he added, "See you soon, Brandon."

Even the coldest of winter nights couldn't have made Brandon feel as mortally frigid with fear as he did in that moment, an awful, crushing, panic-inducing weight coming down on him, impossible to outrun. He was convinced something horrible would happen – he could feel the itching crawl of it on his skin – and whatever the disaster was, it would happen soon.

"Who was that freak?" Vinny shouted, looking back often as they sprinted toward the main gate. "What the fuck did you get yourself into, man?"

Soon Vinny was out of breath, forcing Brandon to slow down and then stop. "I met him here last night. I'll tell you everything later. Let's just peace, okay?"

Vinny nodded, his eyes smoking with rage. Again Brandon was departing this place as the villain, due for another verbal lashing, the guilt intolerable this time. At least his vision had returned to normal operating conditions, but his mind was in a knot of panic and dread and regret. He imagined himself as a fly stuck in a web, desperate for an escape, twisting helplessly as the spider closed in.

Someone's gonna die. Jesus, someone's gonna die, and it's all my fault.

They didn't bother to sneak back through the woods. In their frightened haste, they ran straight past the security trailer, shouting voices and footsteps pursuing them, including Cole's voice.

"Hey, get back here! This is security! Stop! Security!"

They kept running, Vinny moving faster than Brandon had ever believed possible. They made it to the guardrail, Brandon hurdling it and then watching as Vinny struggled over it, their pursuers gaining on them. The road was devoid of traffic, moonlit and ominous, Vinny's car a shadow waiting for them in the distance.

"Just a little farther," Brandon urged.

The voices and footsteps fell silent behind them. A look over the shoulder proved they were no longer being chased, Cole and his partner remaining near the gate.

"I'm calling the cops!" Cole finally shouted.

Back in the car, Vinny downed the remaining water from a bottle in the cup holder. Brandon, gathering his breath, checked the passenger side mirror – no approaching headlights. "I think we're good," he said.

"We'll be long gone by the time the cops get here, and I don't think the guards are allowed to leave the grounds."

Vinny's lip had curled into what might've been a permanent snarl. "Absolutely ridiculous," he growled. "You didn't tell me we'd be meeting some junkie psycho. Is that guy giving you drugs, Brad?"

"No, of course not. Look, I'm sorry, okay? I should have told you about him, but he's not a junkie. Honestly, I don't know what he is." Brandon braced for the onslaught, but there was only silence, Vinny shaking his head.

It would be another miserable trip home.

Chapter 13

They stood by the gate in a triangle of futility, Cole feeling dumb and disillusioned. Was he really cut out to be a cop? He hadn't even been able to catch a fat kid and his friend.

Barry was doubled over, wheezing and gagging, a strand of spit stretching down nearly to the pavement. Apparently he hadn't done much exercise in his former career as an accountant.

"I should have had them," Barry complained when he regained control of himself. It was true. Barry had been going out to the car when the kids had run by, giving him the best shot of apprehension. Cole had been around back, smoking a cigarette, when he'd heard Barry shouting. To Ronny's credit, he'd been in the trailer playing chess; plus, he was old (he'd wound up taking the car and joining them).

"Dammit," Cole growled, angry at himself for not having caught those kids before they reached the guardrail. Cole had passed Barry and advanced quickly on the fat kid, who'd climbed over the guardrail fifty feet ahead and escaped the jurisdiction of Leach's security guards. Once you were on public roads, you were the problem of the town police department, which Cole had notified via cell phone.

Another trespassing report. More paperwork. All he'd wanted to do was have a nice cigarette. Was that too much to ask? Maybe this was God's way of telling him to quit.

"Ya get a look at their faces, kid?" Ronny said.

Barry shook his head. "Not really. It's dark, and I just kind of went into pursuit mode, you know?" He nodded proudly, as if deserving of respect for his efforts. "They were definitely young – high school age for sure."

"You guys wait for the cops," Cole instructed. "Barry, since you saw the trespassers first, I think you earned the honor of filling out the report, don't you, Ronny?"

"Oh, absolutely." Ronny patted Barry on the back, a hint of a smile spreading across his lips. "Report's all yours, kid. Shift report, too, don't you think, Cole?"

"I'd say that's a good idea," Cole replied, and finally a glimmer of doubt came into Barry's eyes. Soon he would dislike the reports as much as everyone, especially if trouble kept targeting the overnight shift.

Time to find a new job, Cole thought. *Better paying and less drama.* If he couldn't be a cop just yet, he certainly didn't want to perform the duties of an officer without the commensurate pay.

***

Brandon and Vinny never made it home. There was a rested, completely sober driver navigating that moonlit road, a man whose hands declared sudden autonomy by jerking the steering wheel to the left. He was a man without faith, an empty vessel waiting to be filled, the Spirits guiding Harrow's searching hand of Maleficium to him along the Great Board of life.

Brandon knew none of this when the headlights came careening at them.

He only saw the headlights and felt the pain, a hot, sizzling white flash enveloping him. Sharp ringing filled his ears, the same sound he occasionally heard after getting hit in the mask by a heavy slapshot at practice. Sometimes the ringing of a puck to the head didn't fade for a few seconds, rendering Brandon nearly deaf as coaches and players asked, *Are you all right? Are you good?* Their lips moved but only the thinnest of sounds escaped, a trace of burnt rubber to be detected if it was a particularly hard rip.

The ringing didn't fade this time, nor did the hot, blinding white. Brandon was still conscious, or at least he thought he was conscious, flailing his arms helplessly about and calling out to Vinny.

Fear menaced him. He tried to breathe through the pain, tried to ignore the panic of thinking he would die, his chest feeling like it had been impaled by a flaming rod, his knees shooting with bursts of agony. He could feel the blood hot on his face, could smell it, too, slick iron and creeping death.

"Help us! Help!" he managed. "Vinny, are you okay?"

The panic worsened the pain, but then the white wall dimmed slightly and took on a vaporous consistency, revealing shadows on the other side.

Brandon tried to free himself from the seatbelt again, but suddenly there was no seatbelt. He was able to stand without incident, the pain abating substantially and then disappearing altogether. No more dripping blood, no more agony in his knees, a sense of relief sweeping over him...but then came dark speculations as to Harrow's role in the wreck.

"Hello?" Brandon called out, his voice echoing as he moved gingerly through the cool fog, no longer in Vinny's car but...somewhere else. Heaven? There were no sounds in this place, only the hollows of his unsteady footsteps. He briefly wondered if he was in Hell, but eventually the fog yielded to a dark, narrow corridor, bright lights visible in the distance.

A hospital? No, he would have remembered being taken there in the ambulance.

He kept going, dread encasing his heart in a steel cage as he followed the lights and observed rows of seats in the distance. The corridor widened to a stage, the curtains pulled open straight ahead of him.

Additional lights snapped on, a colorful overhead panel–

"How?" It was all Brandon could say, his thoughts stopped by the sight of her.

Snow Globe Girl. She was sitting in the front row again, possibly in the same seat as last night, but this time she was wrapped in chains.

Brandon moved cautiously toward her, crossed the stage, passed beneath a spotlight beaming hot from the ceiling, and jumped down. The girl was crying, her eyes streaked red. Brandon didn't know what to do, nor could he find anything to say – he just wanted to tell her everything would be all right, that he'd help her find a way out, but he couldn't even convince himself of that. Would they be trapped here forever? Were they dead? How had Harrow done this to them? The questions were endless but Brandon couldn't answer them, powerless but for a single act.

He brought his finger to the girl's icy cheek and wiped a tear away. She smiled almost imperceptibly, her eyes briefly fluttering…

…and in that moment he knew this girl, her name no longer Snow Globe Girl but Victoria Eldridge. She didn't need to say a word to communicate with him, and he could sense it worked both ways. He'd never felt this connected to anyone before. It was like he'd known her all his life, perhaps even in his previous life.

He sat beside her, cupped a hand over hers. She looked dazed and concussed; Brandon had seen the signs before, seen them in the mirror.

Brandon squeezed her hand, suddenly filled with an inexplicable need to protect Victoria Eldridge, even if it meant giving his life. "I'm gonna get you out of here, I promise."

***

"You're Brandon, right?" Vicky said, stunned that the boy from her vision had become real. How could Harrow do all of this? There was magic and then there was impossibility – this crossed the line. Harrow was not a magician but a demon, released from Hell to cause mayhem. And Vicky had wandered right into his snare, believing every word about Harrow being sent by her mother.

The boy nodded. His rebellious scowl from her vision was absent now, his green eyes soft with fear. "And you're Victoria?"

She smiled, happy to not be alone but terrified nonetheless. "How do we know each other's names? It must be him, right?"

He glanced behind him to the stage, his expression dark with urgency. "Did Harrow do this to you?"

"Yeah, and I take it he brought you here, too."

He jostled with the chains securing her to the armrests and seat, tugging desperately without success. "I have no idea how!" he exclaimed. "Last thing I remember was a fucking car hitting us!" He looked up at her, embarrassed by the outburst. "Sorry."

Vicky couldn't believe she was laughing. Unable to trust her perceptions of reality anymore – unsure if any of this was really happening or if it was all part of a sinister trick – laughter shouldn't have held a place in her heart.

But Brandon, with his impetuous charm, had brought a life into this darkness, not only his reaction a moment ago but everything about him. When he'd touched her cheek and then her hand, little pieces of him had come to her somehow and she'd *known* him.

Harrow! He was tormenting her again, intent on breaking her.

Maybe Brandon wasn't even real.

More tears slid down her cheeks, Brandon insisting that he wouldn't leave her.

"If I'm not dead already, my parents are gonna kill me," he eventually said, and that elicited another rogue laugh.

After a while Brandon sat beside her, staring out at the stage with a hopeless expression. "Should I even try the doors?"

"He won't let us out that easily," she said, remembering a recently completed summer reading assignment for her upcoming AP English course. Of all the works to choose from, why had her teacher selected *The Divine Comedy*? Surely their present circumstance would qualify as a circle of Hell.

Brandon stood, then returned to the seat. "I don't want to leave you. I'm afraid you won't be here when I get back." He shook his head. "This is all so screwed up. Why is he doing this to us?"

"Don't leave," Vicky said, wishing she could take his hand. "Just stay with me, please."

He eyed the balcony warily, then looked across to the main entrance. "When did he take you here, anyway?"

"I don't know, a few days ago. He messes with your mind – I don't know what's real anymore."

"Me neither. My cousin Cole works here. I came last night with my brother – that's when I first saw Harrow. He did all this crazy magic stuff, lighting a cigarette with his finger, asking me to pick a number and then guessing it. I can't believe this is happening." He threw his hands up in exasperation. "I never should have come back here, never!"

Vicky, feeling shaky and shivery with dark anticipation, searched the stage for movement. Now that Harrow had trapped them, it seemed obvious that he would make another appearance.

"He took a huge group of people," she said. "He forced us to get on a bus and come out here. No one could do anything to stop him – our bodies were moving against our will."

"Hypnotism, I bet…drugs, too," he muttered, following her stare across the stage. Most of the auxiliary and effect lights had been switched off, but the spotlight continued to sear down upon center stage.

An eerie flicker of expectancy crawled into Vicky's consciousness, like they were waiting for a performance to begin, the stage calm and vacant before a storm of activity. The audience would soon arrive, she sensed – dead and demanding of souls to join them – and then the show would commence with a slow fade to black.

Brandon went earnestly back to work on the chains that forced Vicky's arms down, grappling with the tightly wrapped silver links. He didn't make any progress, but failure only seemed to increase his determination. The tip of his tongue escaping his lips, he stopped for a moment and regarded the chains analytically, as if their removal was a math equation he could figure out through dogged, diligent work. Earlier, when he'd touched her hand, she'd been able to feel his persistence. Brandon Joutel never gave up when his mind was set to something.

Minutes passed. Surprisingly, Harrow didn't appear; maybe he was watching them from the backstage shadows, allowing his captives a bonding experience. This whole thing felt contrived, as if they were characters in a play, doomed to follow the script of a madman.

Again Vicky wondered if Brandon was even real, or if he was simply part of the carefully detailed performance.

Deep in brooding thought, Vicky didn't realize what was happening until Brandon erupted with excitement. "I'm getting it!" he triumphed, and Vicky felt the chains on her left arm loosening, Brandon unspooling them like yarn.

"How did you do that?" Vicky wanted to hug him, wanted to run her hands through his hair and–

Harrow's voice boomed down from the balcony behind them. "Brandon, child, if it's assistance you request, just ask."

Vicky was sharp with nausea, Brandon whirling around in search of their enemy.

But Harrow was on the stage, standing in the spotlight and twirling his hat, shadows flitting through the air around him. One by one, a perimeter of candles burst to life, outlining the stage.

Clearing his throat, Harrow waved Vicky's childhood wand and bowed. "Are you ready, my young magicians, for our show to begin?"

Chapter 14

The gas gauge needle was kissing **E**, the night getting late. Everyone but Willy and Jerome was asleep when the headlights appeared fast and bright behind them.

Jerome spun around and saw through the back windshield much of what he'd seen in his vision almost an hour earlier, except this time there were even fewer details, only the blinding headlights closing in rapidly.

"That's them!" Jerome shouted. "Harrow's goons! Gun it, Willy!"

Rosa screamed as Willy tore through an intersection, the others jarred from sleep and submerged in cold fear. Even with the traffic light switching to red, the SUV stayed right on them, the lights of a quiet town center revealing it as the same vehicle Jerome had seen in his vision.

"Get down!" Jerome warned, preceding by mere seconds the sounds of gunfire and shattering glass, Rosa's screaming accompanied by that of Sky and Bu.

Reaching for the pistol Willy had given him, now tucked away in his belt, Jerome was about to raise it above the seat and shoot at the pursuing vehicle, but they were rammed hard from behind, sending Jerome and Ki sprawling forward like spilled groceries.

Willy stomped on the accelerator, but his increased speed was matched easily by the SUV. They were struck again, the contact ricocheting pinball-style in Jerome's old bones.

"Damn bastards!" Willy shouted as he hooked a sharp right, the van feeling like it was leaning on two wheels, tires screeching and skidding.

But the headlights followed them, spreading through the van like searchlights.

More gunfire, *TINK, TINK, TINK, TINK, TINK*, rattled off the frame, and then a third collision. This time the SUV lodged into the van, pushing it along sideways, tires locking and dragging…and then they were rolling with the clouting clatters of an unbalanced washer load, glass smashing, screams piercing the night, Jerome's breath vacuumed clean out of his chest.

The tumbling chaos was punctuated with eerie silence, interrupted only by the groaning, leaking aftermath of the wreck. Jerome, flat on his back, was at first oblivious to the pain, adrenaline having taken control.

"Sumbitches ran us off the road," Jerome muttered, half-dazed and hoping for a response.

The pain beginning to sharpen in his back and shoulders, Jerome crawled through the dark wreckage, realizing the van had come to rest on its roof. The others – they weren't moving but they'd be okay, he told himself…but then the stench of death wafted its way into the van and Jerome went rigid, no longer wanting to move because he knew absolutely that one or more of them was gone.

But who? All of them? Half of them?

Gunfire! *TINK, TINK, TINK, TINK, TINK, TINK.*

Jerome dragged himself out of the van through a jagged opening that had once been the windshield, too panicked to check on his friends, desperate to get outside and take out the gunmen before they reached the van.

The gunfire ceased. There were approaching footsteps coming from behind the van, crunching rapidly over leaves and twigs.

Jerome grabbed the pistol from his belt and readied himself, taking a knee and leveling the weapon straight ahead, his body shielded by the front of the van. He was vaguely aware now of suffering moans coming from inside the vehicle, but he didn't allow himself to be distracted.

He waited, waited, his enemy appearing…*CRACK!*

The thundering reverberations of the gunshot brought Jerome back to the jungles of Nam, his enemy collapsing before him. The tormented whisper-screams of a soul being dragged violently away from this world rose up above the wind, followed by a fresh odor of repulsive death.

Movement behind him. Jerome whirled around, ready to shoot, but it was Sky crawling out of the van, her face bloody. "I think they're all dead," she murmured in the stolid voice of shock.

Jerome had heard that voice often in the war, twice before suicides. War can break the mind and spirit – you fight the darkness down, day after day, but sometimes it just eats you up and you need to find a way out of the dark, so many doors to choose from. Several guys had turned to drugs to get them through the war. Some hadn't been able to endure it anymore and killed themselves, their deaths probably reported as combat-related. A few had simply set down their weapons and receded quietly into the jungle, occasionally in the middle of battle, never to be seen again.

The worst of the war-poisoned minds had turned against their own government, killing their superior officers with grenades. Fragging, it was called, not the sort of stuff they like to glorify in the movies and history books but the truth, the God's honest truth of the awfulness war had thrust upon everyone involved, the Viet Cong scuttling beneath them in secret tunnels and appearing with the ubiquity of mist. If only they'd known the goddamn rats had been right there, scurrying under their feet, ready to set the next booby traps – and if you'd found yourself caught and screaming in a punji trap, the protocol was to stay very still, for the worst damage came when you tried to pull out.

"Stay down and be quiet. There could be more coming," Jerome instructed, and Sky remained on her knees, staring blankly up at the wooded hillside.

Jerome listened for a few minutes. No further footsteps, only the
persistent wind and the incessant chirping of crickets, drafts of
moonlight spilling through the trees.

Eventually another sound broke through – flapping. It came from up
the hill, at first sounding like a few birds taking flight but quickly
blossoming into a fury of wings, branches shaking with activity.
Jerome could see hundreds of flitting movements between the trees;
bats, he assumed, tons of them.

"What's going on?" Sky whimpered.

"Shh. Just stay here," he whispered, straining to achieve greater clarity.

As he glanced up the hill again, his search stumbled upon a pair of
phantasms huddled beside a tree – two Vietnamese children, one of
them missing an arm, the other with a black, eyeless socket.

Jerome forced himself to look away, and when he hazarded his gaze in
their direction again the children were gone. Had they even been there
to begin with? Of course they hadn't.

Jerome kneeled beside Sky. "Are you okay?" He reached for her hand.
"Where does it hurt?"

She wiped blood from her forehead, revealing a thin gash. "Where
doesn't it hurt?"

Another survivor wriggled free of the wreckage. Ki. His face was
bloody as well, a few of his front teeth missing. He glanced behind
him, into the van. "Good driving."

"Like I had a choice," came Willy's voice, and Jerome could feel the
warmth spreading through him as he and Ki assisted Willy; more were
alive than dead.

"I'll kill those assholes! Every last one!" Willy growled once he'd gotten to his feet, waving a pistol around.

"Where's Rosa and Bu?" Jerome said, but the others weren't paying attention to him. They were staring up the hill, their eyes wide.

Jerome suddenly – violently – plunged into future sight, the images coming at him with such momentum that his head throbbed and he seemed to step outside himself. The woods were alive with fleeing wildlife, mostly birds lifting into the air and squawking maniacally as trees came down, snapped and uprooted by a force of exceptional strength. The trees up by the road looked like bowling pins, tumbling down the hill with a furious roar.

The vision lasted only a few more seconds, though long enough for Jerome to partially glimpse what was coming for them.

"Get back in the van!" he shouted. "Back in the van now!"

***

Harrow traced his fingers across the Great Board, following the precise route his father's planchette had taken. It was glowing orange now, like an ember in a hearth, soon to reveal to Harrow the Whammy's carnage.

Waiting patiently for the Great Board to display live images, Harrow thought back to the first time he'd seen the Whammy in action.

"Many years ago, indeed," he grinned. "Time, it has been kind."

His father's friend, a great necromancer, had summoned the Whammy that night centuries ago in Alabama, the foggy cemetery soon dominated by the most formidable beast Harrow had ever seen. A collection of doomed souls briefly released from captivity, the Whammy had growled at Harrow, then a boy, with dozens of teeth-baring faces. Harrow had cried at the sight of such a monstrosity, countless snarling, slimy faces sprouting from its shoulders and elbows and hands. Looming ten feet tall, maybe taller, the thing had balanced upon legs as thick as tree trunks – and even smaller heads had yapped out from these lower regions.

The Whammy, though owning an utterly abhorrent moniker, possessed inimitable strength among conjured fiends. The beast had razed an entire town that night Harrow was first introduced to it, officials inevitably blaming the Indians upon inspection of the devastation. Indians had always been the scapegoats in those days, mankind in constant search over the centuries for anything to blame for magic's wrath. It seemed humanity would sooner embrace mass psychosis than accept the existence of diviners, the reason quite simple. People don't like to admit that they aren't in control.

But now, finally, it was time for a new power to rise, its storm to ravage the masses. Those who refused to embrace Harrow as their leader would be burned or drowned, the last hours of their entitled existences fading steadily away. *Dear Children*, Harrow's Lord would soon whisper to the sleeping youths, and new soldiers would rise to the call of their names.

First, however, the army needed to be fully trained, a force that – through its combined powers – would be able to suppress every opponent. But if the army didn't reach its optimal strength, if its members didn't properly mature, then light could still prevail.

We must expedite the process. All flames of faith must be doused.

Harrow resolved to accelerate the destruction of the remaining elusive souls. He would show them Maleficium. And from their wellspring he would drink, every gift his to draw from, every sacrifice to strengthen a bond forged in blackness.

***

Jerome brought his hands to his ears, desperate to silence Harrow's sudden taunting words in his head.

WELCOME TO HARROW HALL

The ground quaked beneath a massive approaching force, as if Sasquatch were thundering toward them.

"Jesus, what in the hell is that?" Willy whispered.

Jerome, huddled tightly together with the others in the van, shuddered when the night echoed with an enraged, unearthly roar. He could feel Sky shaking beside him. Ki whispered something in his native tongue, Willy pointing his gun through an exposed side window. Jerome, whose gun was at his side, feared firearms would do them no good against whatever was coming for them.

"Everybody stay quiet," he said, searching the ruined interior for Rosa and Bu – but it was too dark. They'd been thrown from the van, Jerome feared. They were out there somewhere, exposed to their hunter if not dead already.

The thing took comparatively lighter footsteps now, creeping closer to them with all the stealth of coupling freight cars, its movements jolting vibrations down Jerome's spine. He thought of Elise and Jennie, tried to put himself in a peaceful place if these were indeed his final moments. If it'd been just him, he might've gone out there and challenged the thing – dying a soldier's death, firing on the enemy – but the hand of responsibility held him back. He knew he needed to protect these people at all costs, because if they died society would apparently know the horrors of war. Harrow's rise to dangerous levels of power was undeniable, this…creature further proof of his dominance.

A strange bluish glow rained down. With legs as wide as industrial drain pipes, the thing pounded its way past the van. There were countless lumps attached; wait, were those *heads* stuck to that thing's legs? Jesus, they were!

Growling and hissing, eyes darting about, dozens of brownish-orange heads oozed from the flesh, each one roughly the size of a softball.

One of the searching pairs of eyes glanced into the van and locked onto Jerome, the accompanying tongue flashing and curling. A strident scream wailed out, and the beast stopped, sniffed with the whoosh of airbrakes, and bent low, its head not a singular entity but a jumble of wobbly heads forming a hideous pyramid.

Roaring, the thing reached forward with a hand the size of a chair, about to pick up the van like a toy.

"Shoot it!" Willy ordered, and without hesitation Jerome dove left and joined him in splattering face after face after face, the beast shrieking volcanically and stumbling backward. But it wouldn't go down. Staying on its feet, it staggered toward the van again.

"Everyone out!" Jerome shouted, still firing at the thing. Just as it was about to reach down again, Jerome lunged through the window and shot upward into its many faces, Willy crawling through the front windshield and doing the same.

They kept shooting, putting the thing back on its heels. It stomped and swiped wildly – heads snarling and spitting – nearly crushing Jerome, but still they unloaded their magazines into its viscous flesh.

Finally Jerome made it around the van, where Sky and Ki were cowering. "Go! Find somewhere to hide!"

Willy was reloading, Jerome warning him that they couldn't hold the thing back for long. Before disappearing into the woods, Sky stopped and looked over her shoulder, her eyes remaining fearfully on Jerome for a few moments – and then they were gone, filling Jerome with temporary relief.

As if emanating from a helicopter searchlight, the bluish glow poured in through the trees. "We gotta go, man! This thing's too big!" Jerome shouted as he reloaded, but Willy couldn't hear him beyond his determined barrage.

Reluctantly, Jerome rejoined the fusillade, driving the roaring menace steadily backward up the hill, but it seemed a counterstrike was imminent, perhaps a surge of fire from its mouth or a bolt of lightning shot out from one of those grizzly little heads.

What Jerome didn't expect was the heads themselves to be the weapons. Like arrows launched from a bow, they flew out of the thing's legs and arms, cracking open upon contact with the wrecked van that shielded Jerome. The result was a repeated splatter of green, gooey, incandescent fluid, several projectile heads narrowly missing Jerome, bursting like water balloons against the van and on the ground before him.

Willy, off to the right and unprotected, didn't share Jerome's luck. One head smacked hard into his chest, knocking him off balance, accompanied by a fierce sizzling sound. "Goddamn it!" Willy howled, still shooting at the thing, but then another head torpedoed into him, and another after that, his face and chest glowing green.

"Come on! We gotta go!" Jerome called, keeping the beast at bay as he receded slowly from the van.

But Willy refused to follow him. Dripping with green glop, he kept shooting blindly, wiping his face and firing, ignoring the pain, another round of heads surging at him. The ones that didn't break rolled themselves up Willy's sneakers and nipped frenetically at the laces until he kicked them away.

More projectiles – they were like miniature cannonballs, no longer targeting Jerome, every single one coming at Willy. Clearly sensing a weakening opponent, they sent him sprawling to his back, and then – *Jesus Christ!!!* – the beast lashed forward and scooped him up.

Clutched him in a massive fist.

Lifted him screaming into the air!

CLICK, CLICK, CLICK! Jerome ran out of ammo, reloaded, but the thing was coming at him fast–

A hissing roar behind him, heat singeing his right arm. Spinning around, Jerome saw Sky approaching off to his right, a wave of fire exploding from a flamethrower.

"Get out of the way, Jerry!" she hollered, spraying the fire toward the beast. It tapered well short of her target, but with a terrified shriek the thing dashed back up the hill, crushing trees and creating a new path, then taking flight, soaring off into the night with Willy still trapped in its fist and screaming.

Jerome kept shooting and shooting, even after the thing was gone, the moonlit woods transformed briefly into a thick jungle. The image of Willy being carried away sent flashbacks blitzing into Jerome's head, one memory more prominent than the rest – the first time he'd seen one of his sergeants killed. The man had always known what to say to fire up the troops. He'd seemed invincible in battle – his equanimity unshakeable – but one day he'd gone down amidst heavy fire, as vulnerable to bullets as anyone else. Jerome had somehow managed to carry him out of there, expecting a bullet with every step, his sergeant coughing up blood. By the time they'd gotten him to the medics, his eyes were vacant with death, Jerome left with the same empty disbelief that ravaged him now.

Willy was gone.

For a long while Jerome pointed his weapon to the dismal night sky, expecting a resurgence. But the thing never came back, the bluish light gone as well.

"What the hell was that thing?" Jerome murmured, but Sky drew his attention to music. Tinkling music. A muffled song. It sounded like, "When the Saints Go Marching In."

"It's coming from the van," she said, removing her backpack-style canisters that supplied the fuel for the fire.

Sky was right. The van. Jerome burrowed his way through the wreckage, eventually finding the source of the music: Willy's glowing cell phone. There was a name on the screen. Paradis. At first Jerome didn't make the connection, but quickly he realized who was calling. Paradis was Para-DEE, the Special Forces assassin or whatever.

Too little, too late, Jerome thought, but still he decided to call Paradis when he knew it was safe, not because he thought the guy would help them but instead because Willy would have wanted him to do everything he could to keep the mission going.

Though the war appeared to be lost with a single battle, they weren't dead yet.

Chapter 15

"I'm not a fucking magician!" Brandon repeated, but Harrow ignored him.

Twirling a plastic stick, Harrow looked them over patronizingly.

"The obvious you children refuse to acknowledge." He shook his head, remaining in the spotlight on the stage. "Brandon, child, the magic I thought you would have seen by now. Do you not witness it with each sketch?" He pointed the stick at Brandon. "Your art is your magic, child. There's a reason why you feel compelled to draw certain things and little else – you're resisting the calling."

"What are you talking about? And stop calling me child!" Brandon stepped in front of Vicky, wanting to protect her but feeling weak. Compared to Harrow he was nothing, just a teenager incapable of saving himself, never mind Vicky. He didn't even have a weapon, and his phone had somehow left him during the chaos of the accident.

Harrow tossed the stick to Brandon, but when he caught it the thing had transformed. In his left hand he was holding his sketchbook, gripping it loosely with shaky fingers. For a few moments he was rapt with disbelief, as if he were watching the sky melt away like candle wax, revealing a black, menacing firmament that had been there all along.

How could this be happening? How could Harrow do these things?

"What do you want from us?" Vicky said, jerking violently against the chains still securing her torso to the seat, her words articulating Brandon's trapped thoughts. Again they seemed to be connected somehow, surfing the same extrasensory wavelength.

Harrow paced the stage. Surrounded by hundreds of red and white candles, the spotlight now following his every movement, he waved his hands in acknowledgement of an invisible audience. But Brandon intuited that they weren't alone. The auditorium suddenly seemed abuzz with energy, no longer hollow and vacant but pulsing with excitement, like the bristling electrical expectancy that precedes a thunderstorm.

"Ladies and gentlemen!" Harrow shouted, walking the stage from end to end with the ebullient flash of a showman. "Welcome to Harrow Hall, a theater commanded by the finest talents this land has to offer. Within these walls we invite you to indulge in the madness, to embrace the unimaginable, to witness the impossible. A new order will soon arrive, and earnestly we must celebrate!" He removed his hat, tossed it into the air – and it exploded into a cluster of black birds flocking to the ceiling.

Harrow came to the edge of the stage, hands clasped behind his back. Now he seemed to be staring at one front-row seat in particular, his gaze intently fixed on a single point in space. "Prepare, ladies and gentlemen, boys and girls, to see logic defied this fine evening. Prepare to see time and space redefined. To discover Harrow Hall is to achieve understanding, to see through the opaque window and glimpse the true nature of things, to resist the stifling structure of society and proclaim to the world, *I believe in change*!"

Returning to motion, dashing down the stage, he announced, "It is my great pleasure to present tonight's first performer – master of rapid death, ruler of Piggery Lane, necromancy's good son, the one and only…Slaughterhouse Jones!"

At once the theater was dark, a rich red light slowly suffusing the stage. Dropping his sketchbook, Brandon scrambled back into the seat beside Vicky and reached for her arm, held on tightly, expecting them to be pulled apart. He couldn't see her face at first, but eventually the red glow crept across the first few rows, lighting her face dimly, dismally, the stage filling with fog.

In the distance rose a slight clanking, building steadily, the sound of chains rattling together. There was dripping in every corner, discordant with uneven pace and volume, some drips resembling spatters against a tin roof and others sounding like a steady dribble muffled by a saturated rug, all while the tide of crimson fog thickened, cool condensation clinging to Brandon's face.

Vicky squinted against the fog. "Don't leave me, Brandon, please don't leave me," she whispered.

"It's okay, I'm right here," he said over the strengthening clashes of metal, but Vicky's gaze had returned to the stage, where hundreds of lowering hooks and chains were gently swaying into each other, the entire auditorium clinking and clanking with metal, it seemed, the *DRIP, DRIP, DRIP, DRIPS* growing steadier, centralizing.

Something warm and wet slithered down Brandon's back, then his face. Bringing a hand to his forehead, he came away with a bloody palm, the fresh scent of iron fluttering over him.

Vicky screamed, a sound to dominate all others, and Brandon saw the splash of blood upon her face as well.

In a moment the dripping bloomed into a downpour, Vicky's screaming unbroken as her face was drenched in blood.

Brandon forced his lips tightly shut, squeezed his eyes, but still the blood slipped inside his mouth, iron acrid on his tongue. He flung his T-shirt off, tried his best to cover Vicky's face, but it was just a T-shirt, not an umbrella, and the bloody deluge wouldn't relent, chains and hooks swinging energetically above the stage, coarse laughter cavorting about the auditorium.

When the cascade of blood finally ceased, a new voice boomed from the stage, its master a tall, hulking figure emerging from the fog.

"Wanna play, kids?" came his rumbling voice.

Vicky's screaming dimmed to terrified whimpers, Brandon leveling a hand across her stomach as if to protect an unbelted passenger from a quick stop.

The massive man came to the edge of the stage. Raised a colossal hand upward. Took hold of a hook. "How bout I hang you kids up and skin ya?" he laughed, a stentorian sound like boulders crashing down a hill.

Brandon was confined to his seat, not by chains but the force of fear. It pressed against him like a lap bar, keeping him there as the giant leaped off the stage, his black beard thick and wild.

The man produced a cattle prod and a knife – *This is Hell, we're in Hell*, Brandon thought, bile rising to his throat – and now the man was creeping closer with leaden bootsteps.

"First the sweet little sow," he growled, dark holes for eyes fixed on Vicky.

Brandon fought his way forward, standing on wobbly legs between Vicky and their tormenter. "Stay away," he warned, but his voice conveyed the confidence of a withdrawn turtle.

Laughing at him, the man pointed his weapons and took a few steps toward him. "Run while you've got the chance, boy, or I'll skin ya alive."

Torrents of abrasive laughter flowed forth, but Brandon stood his ground. Every atom in his being told him to run, run, run, get the hell out, but he knew he would stay. He wouldn't leave Vicky, and he wouldn't back down. He'd never backed down – not when coaches told him he was too small to make this team and that team; not when he gave up fifteen goals in a peewee game and kept on going, telling opposing players to quit passing the puck around with that mercy bullshit and keep shooting; not even when a thug on his bantam travel team held him down in the locker room after practice one night, threatening to break his finger if he didn't call himself a pussy.

Brandon had been the newest kid on the team, but when he'd refused to give in to the asshole's demands, risking a broken finger or worse, respect had swiftly followed. Some people called him a psycho for never giving in; others suggested he'd taken too many pucks to the head; no one ever called him a pussy.

Yet tonight's standoff transcended pride and bravado. Tonight, facing death, Brandon did not challenge this devil of a man out of stubbornness or desire for respect. Tonight he thought only about Vicky, felt only a sickened desperation to protect her, the girl he barely knew but somehow knew completely. She was helpless, chained to the seat behind him, and the man was wielding his weapons, close enough for Brandon to observe that the knife was streaked red.

"Last chance, boy." His rough, rocky words made Brandon recoil slightly, but worst of all was his eyes, or rather the absence thereof. They were just craters beneath his soaked cap, his clothes nothing more than tattered rags.

Brandon swallowed hard but held firm, briefly and senselessly aware of the auditorium's clock ticking in the darkness – and then the man was lunging at him with the cattle prod.

Brandon dove low at him beneath the weapon, trying to take out his knees, but it was like diving into a concrete wall. Brandon went down hard, his bones compressing with a gruesome crunch, the air rushing out of him.

The man hauled him up by the belt of his shorts and dragged him onto the stage. Brandon flailed and kicked with helpless panic, but he wasn't without relief that the guy was focusing on him and giving Vicky extra time to free herself. Brandon had already gotten one of her arms loose – maybe, *maybe* she could find a way to liberate herself from the other restraints.

It was the only hope Brandon could cling to as the chain came down with a villainous crank, the hook forced through his belt, the chain lurching upward, pulling him ten feet off the ground and jerking to a stop, his body a slave to the loops of metal. He was tilting forward toward the seats, suspended above the stage like a stuffed animal in a crane game, the psycho looking up at him from the edge of the stage and grinning.

Brandon glanced at the front row, but Vicky's seat was occupied only by chains!

Her voice came from below, and there she was on the stage, immediately beneath him.

"Brandon, catch!" she shouted, and hurled his sketchbook up to him with both hands. The throw was wide, but Brandon's glove hand had always been his signature. Arching his back against the waves of pain, he shot his left hand out and windmilled the book into his grasp, his shoulder burning in protest.

The book was his again. But now what?

"You bitch!" the bearded hulk bellowed, firing his knife at Vicky but missing high, the clank of metal against the stage making Brandon flinch.

Vicky ran backstage, the psycho going after her, and suddenly Brandon knew what he had to do, remembering Harrow's words. It seemed impossible, absurd, but here he was hanging on a hook, trapped in a magician's theater. This whole thing was impossible, and so he opened his sketchbook, retrieved his pencil from the inner pocket, flipped to a clean page, and rendered the quickest sketch of his life, the image seemingly drawing itself into form.

When he was done, he closed the book and listened to the ticking clock and remnant drips, waiting for…for what?

The weight of failure added a few extra pounds to his strain, the pain worst at his bent back. In spite of the clock, time seemed nonexistent.

Brandon shouted Vicky's name, answered only by metronomic clicks and drips. He felt like he'd be sick, bile burning into his throat again.

But then the lights came on. A vigorous applause from the audience, every seat now filled. Blinking in shock, Brandon scanned the crowd of cheering men and women for Vicky. But she wasn't there. What the fuck was going on?

"Help me!" he screamed. "Help me!" and this time Harrow answered him.

Brandon glanced down to the stage, where Harrow stood beside Vicky, holding her hand up as the crowd roared into a standing ovation. But they were getting farther and farther away, Brandon fraught with icy dread at the realization that he was being pulled up to the ceiling, the chains grating against the rusted railing of a catwalk, where two men grabbed his arms and lifted him over the railing to safety.

He collapsed to his knees on the rubber tread, unable to catch his breath, feeling like he'd just sprinted a mile. Dizzy, he looked up to find the men gone, replaced by Harrow, who lightly patted Brandon's bare shoulder.

"My child, you did it!" he exclaimed, smiling as if he'd won the lottery. "A performance it required, but finally the magic you discovered. Now you can do anything, your hand more powerful than a thousand soldiers."

Brandon forced himself up. "Don't hurt her! If you hurt her–"

Harrow held up a hand. "Worry not, child, she's safe. As long as that beautiful hand of yours converts my words to images, safe she'll remain."

Chapter 16

Vinny agreed to speak to Brandon's parents in his hospital room the morning after the accident. Vinny had suffered a concussion and a broken arm, but that was it, luck finding him but not Brandon, who might not wake up from a coma.

"Please make it quick. He needs to rest," the nurse ordered, but Vinny wanted the Joutels to stay as long as possible, wanted to tell them he wished he could trade places with his friend. The accident hadn't been Vinny's fault, but he still felt responsible. If Brandon died, it would be on him. *He'd* been the one who'd agreed to take Brandon to that stupid place. If only he'd just stayed home.

"What were you guys doing out there?" Mr. Joutel said quietly, and Vinny gave the condensed version of the night's unfoldings, leaving out the part about the psycho "magic man" who'd said all of those bizarre things.

When Vinny finished his explanation, Brandon's parents were shaking their heads and staring at him like he was a criminal. Vinny hated seeing them like this. Their son might die, and they couldn't do anything to help him, his fate in God's hands.

Eyes glistening at the thought of his friend, all Vinny could do to assist Brandon was to pray. "He's my best friend on the team," he managed, choking back the tears.

It wasn't a lie to make them feel better, either. Brandon was not only his goalie partner but one of his greatest friends in the school. Constantly striving to exude a tough exterior but failing to hide his gentle nature, Brandon was one of those kids who would always have your back. He'd often helped the team equipment manager pick up pucks after practices when everyone else peaced out; he and Brady had even fulfilled Coach Goderich's request for members of the team to serve as volunteers for a local learn-to-skate program.

In spite of his pretenses, Brandon was a good kid, not someone who required shouting and threatening to treat people right. If he'd been so inclined, he easily could have used his popularity as the team's goalie to take advantage of girls like many of their teammates did. But Brandon wasn't like that – sure, he drank and smoked pot and swore too much, but his good qualities far outweighed the bad ones.

Vinny could no longer hold back his tears. He imagined a casket and a hearse and a throng of black-clad funeralgoers – his teammates among them – all of it beneath a miserably gray sky.

"I'm sorry, I'm so sorry," Vinny sputtered before breaking down.

***

Cole didn't find out about Brandon's accident until the next afternoon.

His aunt was frantic. "He's in a coma! They don't know if he'll live! It happened a mile from the institution. He and his friend snuck in. Did you know anything about this?"

There was a tearfully accusatory bite to her voice that caused Cole to delay his response. "No, not last night. He and Brady came out Saturday night."

Cole's mind was trampolining with awful thoughts. He remembered the pursuit last night and the two kids who'd run away toward North Ridge Street – had that been Brandon and his friend? But why had Brandon gone back to the asylum?

"They went there *Saturday*?" his aunt exploded. "How could you allow that without telling me? Were they drinking?" In the background, Cole could hear his uncle telling her to calm down.

"Everything was under control," Cole lied. "My partner and I gave them a guided tour of the place. There was no drinking, no drugs – I had no idea he went back there last night. He probably just wanted to show the place to his friend."

Cole's aunt declined into hysteria, her husband taking the phone.

"Fucking idiot driver swerved into them," he said, his voice shaking with hatred. "I could kill him!"

Cole sat down in the middle of his kitchen, literally floored by the news. Brandon had returned to the institution, probably to try to find that girl he'd rambled on about Saturday night, insisting that he'd seen her inside Harrow Hall.

And now he might die for his curiosity.

Chapter 17

"Who is this? Where's Willy?" Paradis spoke with a noticeable French accent, pronouncing *this* as *dis*.

"This is Jerome Hudson, from N'Orleans. I'm with Willy's group, but we were just run off the road and attacked by Harrow's guys. Willy…he didn't make it, man, I'm so sorry."

"Willy's *dead*?"

"Yeah, him and two others. I should be dead, too. Barely got out alive."

Jerome was sitting on a log behind the wrecked van, staring dazedly at Rosa's crushed, lifeless body, half-believing she would rise. She'd been such a tough, determined woman – but now she was dead, her pursuit of Harrow paid for with her life. Jerome and Sky had discovered Bu's body a few minutes earlier, a sight that had brought Jerome back to Nam. Buford had gone through the windshield, but only by observing his clothes had they been able to identify him.

Unable to keep her food down, Sky had turned from the gruesome finality and collapsed in a fury of tears, later telling Jerome she would keep watch on the other side of the van while he spoke to Paradis. Jerome wished he'd been able to spare Sky from the sight of violent death, but she'd immersed herself in war and was now enduring its inevitable horrors.

"Hey, you still there, guy?" Paradis said. He'd been talking fast about one of his recent jobs, but Jerome's attention had fallen off, commanded by Rosa's somehow peaceful looking face.

"Still here," Jerome mumbled, his voice scarcely exceeding a whisper. He was still trying to put all of it together – the visions, the accident, the monster that had torn down the hillside, snatched Willy, and flown into the night. It was all too much. At least in war there were limitations. Enemies couldn't withstand dozens of bullets and shoot little snarling faces at you from their legs and then take flight. But this war was psychosis, like something out of a warped comic book, their enemy seemingly restricted by no limitations.

Some people use magic to do the Devil's work, his father's voice echoed from years long past.

"Where are you?" Paradis said. "This guy takes out old Willy – he just moved up to number one on the kill list."

For a moment Jerome couldn't even remember where he was. "Tennessee," he finally said. "Northern Tennessee. Some small town, don't quite know where."

Jerome descended into the traumatic story, which felt strangely fictional as he described it, a nightmarish tale that could never be real. The first few weeks at war had been the same way, Jerome at times questioning whether killing was really his reality, or if he'd just wake up in his bed back home one morning and find shafts of sunlight spreading across his sheets, a new day his to claim. It must have been even worse for the draftees, he'd assumed. At least Jerome had signed up voluntarily. He'd wanted to serve and had prepared himself to serve, but he couldn't imagine being torn away from his home and family by the government and thrust into madness.

Thrust into madness. Jerome had found war again; either that, or war had found him. He heard himself rolling out the deranged story for Paradis at breakneck speed, concentrating on the human attackers and leaving out the part that would make him sound insane.

Even so, Paradis managed a few words (*Jesus! Holy fuck!*) of astonishment. Jerome wondered if the guy would still want to help them by the time the story was over, or if he'd get on a plane back to Canada or France or wherever he'd originally come from.

When Jerome finally mentioned calling the cops, Paradis interrupted him.

"No, no cops! This is well beyond cops," he said emphatically. There was a moment of muffled words, Paradis talking to someone else. "Tell you what, just keep everyone in your group together. If they're not hurt too bad, stay in the woods out of sight. And keep that cell phone on – we'll track you using the phone."

"Okay, yeah, I guess that could work." Jerome wondered how they'd go about tracking the phone. Weren't cops the only ones who could do that? Hell, maybe one of them was a cop. "What about Harrow?" he said. "You think he's been tracking the phone, too? Maybe I should get rid of it."

"Just make sure everyone stays together," Paradis repeated. "You'll have to take a chance and keep the phone on – it's the only way we can find you. How much battery is left?"

"Almost full."

"Good. We'll be there as soon as we can, and then we're gonna go after this bastard together."

"Yes, sir, betcho ass we'll go after him."

Jerome pocketed the phone. Kneeling beside Rosa and then Bu, he recited twice The Lord's Prayer, then recovered two sleeping bags from the wreckage and sealed their bodies. After easing them down beside the van, Jerome called Sky over and together they salvaged what they could from the crunched soda can Willy's Windstar had become.

"What now?" Sky said, plucking her iPod from the ruins, the screen dutifully lighting up when she turned the device on.

"Gotta find Ki. Where'd he go?"

She shrugged. "I told him to wait for me up by the road. Hopefully that, that...thing didn't get him, too," and the tears cut off whatever was coming next.

Jerome put an arm around her shoulders. "You saved my life. I would've been taken…"

He couldn't finish. Instead he led her through the moonlit woods and up the hill toward the road. He knew they had to find a safer place, for Harrow would be sending reinforcements soon.

At least there were no further visions, not yet, though Harrow's previous words sent Jerome into a run when the woods thinned out and they came to the road.

You chose your side. Now you must die along with your new friends.

Chapter 18

Vicky forced herself to stop crying. Even if her life was in shambles, even if the shattered glass of normalcy was glittering around her feet, even if she'd lost all perception of reality, she told herself to be strong. Her mother was no doubt watching, and she would want Vicky to be brave.

For a thinly peaceful moment, standing on the empty stage – the applauding crowd and Harrow having disappeared – Vicky could hear her mother's voice. "Don't give in, baby," she urged. "Don't give in, and don't give up."

Vicky glanced about the shadowy auditorium, briefly certain she would see her mother in one of the seats. Her voice had sung out with such clarity and strength – she had to be here, if not in visible form then in spirit. But regardless of whether her words of encouragement had been real or imagined, Vicky embraced them like a war cry.

Don't give in. Don't give up.

There were clunking footsteps behind her, Vicky whirling around to find Brandon surfacing from the backstage depths. Still shirtless, soaked with blood from the earlier drenching, wearing only his plaid shorts, Vicky's eyes were drawn to his torso of burgeoning strength. The definition of his stomach suggested regular exercise, his shoulder muscles robust but not yet bulky.

Now running toward her, Brandon didn't allow for an extended inspection. When he got to Vicky, he pulled her into a tight hug and lifted her off the ground. "You saved my life! How did you get free?"

Vicky, overwhelmed by the stench of blood, intercepted a few more of Brandon's thoughts/emotions that hadn't been brought to life with words, somehow hearing what was in his head as clearly as she'd just heard her mother's voice.

WELCOME TO HARROW HALL

Thank God she's alive, he was thinking. *What if he comes back? We have to get out of here.*

They both scanned the auditorium.

"It was him – Harrow. He unchained me," she said, taking his hand. It inspired confidence to touch him; with Brandon at her side she felt hopeful, like they'd somehow find a way out. Of course, he might get beaten up like before, but at least she knew he wouldn't leave her.

For a moment Vicky wondered if traces of a deeper enchantment were nestling in her heart…

…but she knew for certain what was in Brandon's heart and mind, his fears still coming to her in fear-driven fragments. On the outside, though, he presented an air of relative calm.

"*Harrow* unchained you?" he said.

"Yeah, he gave me the book and told me to throw it to you."

Brandon scooped up his sketchbook. He'd dropped it before hugging her, and now he flipped through its pages, searching for a specific one.

"Here it is! I just drew this!" He handed her the book, Vicky's eyes widening in shock when she saw the image, a fairly detailed sketch of the thing that had just attacked them, right down to the black, gaping maws that had constituted its eyes.

Vicky studied the eyes carefully; they'd been darkened by repeated circles of the pencil, reminding her of exam bubble sheets. But Brandon hadn't simply scribbled circles – he'd actually rendered the shape of the eye, even in his panicked haste, suggesting that the drawing of facial features had become second nature to him.

Yet the eyes were far from the most captivating aspect of Brandon's drawing. Slaughterhouse Jones's head was separated from his body, spurts of what could only be interpreted as blood spraying emphatically from the fatal wound.

Suddenly Vicky remembered what Harrow had said…

…Your art is your magic, child. There's a reason why you feel compelled to draw certain things…

…and now she *knew* Brandon's gift, knew it as unmistakably as she knew other things about him, their connection still strong. But was it truly their connection, or had Harrow established it for them? Vicky understood that nothing could be trusted in this place, not even her own impulses, yet she desperately wanted to rely on her bond with Brandon.

"Whatever you draw becomes real," she whispered.

Brandon blinked in disbelief. "I think that's what Harrow wants us to think, but it's really just him doing all of this. He said you'd be safe if I draw what he wants, but why does he need us if he has all the power? Maybe he's just screwing with us before he kills us, if we're not already, you know…"

With the emergence of an idea Vicky felt her hopes building, as if she'd spent hours of toiling and finally figured out how to untie the undefeatable knot. "You should try drawing Harrow's death, just like you did with that slaughterhouse creep."

"But it's not my power, it's *his*," Brandon insisted, sounding frustrated and petulant. "He's the magician, not me. He'd never let me have the book back if I could hurt him with it. He probably even hypnotized me up there and made me draw what I did."

Instinct told Vicky different, but perhaps her instincts were corrupted. She found herself flipping through his sketchbook, her eyes sliding across some of the images she'd previously seen, just a few of the little pieces of Brandon she'd somehow received before. Most of the sketches were of…

…"Castles and hallways," he said. "I don't know why I'm so obsessed with drawing them – I'm kind of OCD, I guess."

Vicky glanced behind her at the empty seats. Save for the echoing strikes of the clock and the drips of blood from the ceiling, the auditorium was silent.

"Harrow said you're resisting the calling. What do you think he meant?" Vicky said, marveling at the intricate details in each hallway sketch, the symmetry achieved with painstaking care. The castles were no different, every window straight and symmetrical.

Brandon shrugged. "No clue, but I'm pretty sure he was bullshitting me."

Now it was Brandon's turn to survey the auditorium, the crimson curtains seeming to tremble ever so faintly. He bit his lower lip, shook his head. "This is all just crap. Harrow's controlling it the same way he's allowing us to know about each other. It must be drugs, drugs and mindfuckery." He paused, looked at Vicky searchingly. "Or do you think we're in Hell?"

Ignoring the question, she said, "Draw an apple."

He sighed. "Come on, we should be looking for a way out."

Vicky clapped the book shut and handed it to him. "Just try it."

"Fine," he said miserably, opening the book and extracting the pencil, a cursory apple drawn a moment later. "This is completely insane."

Vicky searched the auditorium expectantly.

"See," Brandon said when nothing happened.

"Maybe it takes a few minutes."

"What do you think he wants from us?" he said, returning to his earlier question. "I mean, why waste time on us? Maybe he just wants to put us in some messed up play or something."

"Whatever it is, I want no part of it." The tears were making a new push. "I just want to go home, Brandon."

His hands were surprising at her hips now, shining a needed light through the black of fear. *I promise I won't leave you*, he said, though he didn't utter a word.

Vicky thought hard, trying to carefully form the words and send them to him. At first she didn't know if it worked, but then he pulled her in close, embraced her, seemingly ready to kiss her, his green eyes speaking to her yet again. *I really like you, Vicky.*

She flattened a palm against his chest, her breaths escaping in short, shallow, surreal bursts of not quite full terror. *I really like you, too.* She looked up at him wonderingly, anticipating his kiss, but his attention was now fixed on the seats, his eyes dilated with dread.

Vicky wheeled around. There, in the first row, a lush apple in hand, sat the menace, this time wearing a burgundy top hat and suit.

"Time for the next show, my children."

Vicky stared intently at Brandon, willing her words into his head. *Draw him dead, Brandon, a stick figure if you have to! Now!*

Chapter 19

Two bags slung over his shoulder, Jerome followed the moonlit road with Sky, listening to the crickets chirp noisily in the grass and the occasional calls of an owl, their footsteps thudding heavily against the blacktop. They kept shouting out to Ki, but gradually their voices lost energy and volume. Jerome's body felt like it had been wrenched around on a rickety old roller coaster, punished by every dive and curve.

"Better not go too far, or we'll lose him for good," Jerome muttered.

"Yeah, you're right," she agreed, her face a mess of dried blood. "Wish I'd brought the flamethrower."

"Nah, too bulky to carry around all over the place," he said, maintaining his earlier reasoning for leaving the weapon behind. "Plus, you'd eventually run out of fuel. Our best bet if that thing comes back is to run like hell."

They eventually slogged off the road and sat beside a speed limit sign, realization finally catching up to Jerome. It had been that way in war, too, the blurs of chaos never to be fully remembered, their consequences tracking him down much later.

What was that thing? Jerome wondered. *How could it have…?*

A distant voice. Footsteps. Jerome glanced down the road, noticing an approaching shadow.

"Jerome!" Ki shouted, and they tore away from the sign, Jerome stumbling over a rock as they returned to the road.

Sky, sprinting with youthful legs, was hugging Ki before Jerome could get halfway there.

"Where's others?" Ki said when Jerome reached him, looking around as if expecting Willy and Rosa and Bu to emerge from the woods.

Jerome let out a long exhalation. "They didn't make it. That…that thing was just too strong. Willy and me shot the shit out of it, but the thing just reached down and took him. Took him away, gone, just like that." Jerome stooped down, new with tears. "If it wasn't for Sky comin back to save my ass with that flamethrower, I'd be gone too."

Jerome still had trouble believing what he'd witnessed. *Some people use magic to do the Devil's work.*

"Rosa and Bu – they were killed in the accident," Sky reported, barely able to project the words.

"Yeah, died in the wreck. I'm so sorry, Ki – I know you were really close to them." For some reason Jerome had felt obligated to confirm that Rosa and Bu hadn't been gotten by the monster, as if that made their deaths any easier to take. "I'm really sorry," he repeated, and then his words died out.

Jerome had never been any good at condolences, though not for lack of practice. He'd consoled his comrades' widows after returning home from Nam – and they'd probably wondered why Jerome had been spared while their husbands were killed. A few feet here or a different move there and those guys might have come back safely to their wives, but that was war and what man had the right to question it? Once you signed up or found yourself conscripted, you were a slave to the fickle hand of death. If it picked you out of the crowd, away you went to the next place – no choices, no bargains – the final whispers of your soul perhaps to be heard by those around you.

Sobbing furiously, Sky embraced Ki again. After a long while he said, "No war won without sacrifice," and that might have been the truest, most candid thing Jerome had heard in his life.

WELCOME TO HARROW HALL

There was an extended period of roadside grieving, the three of them trying to process everything that had happened back in the woods and salvage something from their losses. It was like studying a thousand broken pieces and attempting to work them into a halfway recognizable version of the former whole.

But all Jerome could see was damage. At least in war you relied on superiors to get you through the worst days – they'd always known what to do and say when things had gone bad and men had died. They'd known how to inspire you to keep fighting, saying things like, *Don't let those guys die in vain* and, later, when their prospects had been far bleaker, *They gave their lives for their country – we owe it to them to keep going.*

Jerome wished he knew what to say to Sky and Ki, who sat huddled together at the side of the road, Sky crying intermittently and Ki mostly just staring up at the moon, perhaps searching for some sort of sign. Wait, that was Bu's job to derive meaning from the clouds and stars, but Bu was gone, as were Rosa and Willy. Their leader was gone, snatched up by that devilish thing and flown off into the night, leaving their little army of six cut in half, their van ruined, most of their possessions scrapped, only a few rounds remaining of a once impressive ammo supply.

Jerome said nothing. He was no leader, and so he kept his mouth shut. Instead, he reached into one of the bags and retrieved Sky's iPod charger, which he'd found beside the van while trying to recover what he could. He handed it to her, drawing the faintest of smiles.

She stood and hugged him. "We're gonna kill that psycho for Willy and Rosa and Bu," she said. The quiet determination in her voice sent Jerome stepping backward, a little unnerved but mostly shocked.

Just moments ago she'd been racked by sorrow, seemingly broken beyond recovery, surely in no shape to continue their quest. But now, wiping her eyes dry, she told Ki and Jerome to hold her hands. "We stay together," she said. "We keep fighting."

Jerome wanted to interrupt, wanted to tell her that there was no shame in backing out now, but he kept quiet, watching as Sky's resolve spread to Ki, his slumping shoulders rising, his eyes brightening.

We're all gonna get ourselves killed long before we even find Harrow, Jerome thought, but his mind was quickly overlaid by a vision of war, not a scene from Nam but that of a new war, a future war, Sky and Ki at its center, joined by a man who could only be…what was his name again? Something French.

Headlights in the distance, and now Jerome remembered the name of the man who would hopefully come to help them. Paradis.

Chapter 20

Zach Markham hefted his bulky camcorder through the woods, wishing he hadn't smoked two joints before coming here. Usually pot made him feel light and carefree, but tonight it had strained his stomach. He felt uneasy and cold, the way he sometimes felt after certain nightmares or at the conclusions of certain movies, when his apartment was dark and silent, whispers of wind rising up outside, the shadows around him seeming to develop mass and texture. This was how he felt upon entering a hospital or viewing a car accident or contemplating death and its infinite possibilities. This was not how he wanted to feel tonight.

They broke free of the woods, came to an abandoned road. Up a slight hill the heart of the institution was waiting for them, dozens of brick buildings they would spend hours shooting for a film.

Toughen up, Zach told himself. This was no time to be feeling crappy. This was shoot time, another opportunity for them to hone their skills. Spielberg and Tarantino and Welles had all started somewhere, and for Zach Markham and Clay Barrie, future fans would track them back to vacant houses, hotels, churches, and mental hospitals in Ohio. Last week they'd gotten great footage at a burnt out hotel, its exposed sides revealing curtains that flapped in the wind like hangmen's clothes. Two summers ago they'd traveled to the House of Nightmares and The Columbus School for the Blind, but nothing much had piqued their interest in those places. They were still looking for something to wholly inspire them, a thirst that could only be sated if they kept at it, exploring new buildings until one finally called out to them.

"Which way, droog?" Clay said, fetching a joint from his pocket. An avid reader, Clay was in the midst of another literary hangover during which he borrowed language from his most recent read. This time it was *A Clockwork Orange*.

Zach pointed straight ahead to a two-story building up the rise. They followed the quiet road littered with leaves, the sun departing beyond western hills, cloaking the forgotten asylum in hazy orange. Soon it would be easier to see, but for now the glare was nasty, reflecting off windows and painting a broad and blinding sheen across the pavement.

They kept looking behind them for police or security. Only once had they been escorted off a property; since then they'd learned to be more careful, for no one wanted college kids filming their property.

College kids meant trouble.

"This place is real horrorshow!" Clay praised, keeping with his Anthony Burgess craze. Zach couldn't wait till he moved on to something else. All of this droogy, horrorshow, viddying stuff was getting awfully annoying.

Clay was right about the institution being awesome, though. It wasn't merely one or two buildings but multiple sentinels of forgotten brick, windows and doors all boarded up, signs posted everywhere warning trespassers to stay away. For Zach and Clay, such signs were evidence that they'd found a good place to film.

They crested the hill, Zach surprised by the level of deterioration this nearest building had endured. LONGVIEW, a green and white sign affixed to the side of the building read.

"I can't believe they just packed everything up and left this place," Zach said, but there was no response from Clay.

His friend was staring down the road, and that's when Zach saw him, a tall man looming on the shadowy road maybe two hundred feet away, his legs spaced widely apart, his coat flapping in a sudden breeze. A coat in August? There was a hat involved as well, tall and black.

"Who the hell is that?" Zach said, but Clay was silent, perhaps feeling the same dread that had invaded Zach's heart upon seeing the unmoving man, who remained where he stood in the middle of the road, coat flapping as he watched them approach.

They couldn't see the man's face from this distance, but something about him conveyed hatred, as if the wind had transported his fierce loathing across the space between them and deposited it.

Even worse, the way the man stood – arms at his side, legs wide and firm, head lowered slightly – made Zach feel threatened.

"Maybe we should get out of here," he said.

"No, dude, are you kidding?" Clay looked at him like he was nuts. "Why aren't you filming this guy?"

Zach hadn't even considered the camcorder. In fact, he hadn't filmed anything yet – what was wrong with him? But in the few seconds it took to turn on the camcorder, the man disappeared.

"Where'd he go?"

Clay looked stunned. "I…I don't know. I was looking at you."

A queasy insistence took hold in Zach's gut. It told him to leave immediately, that something was very wrong about this place and the man they'd just seen, but he found himself following Clay and filming more buildings and narrating. He felt inspired yet terrified, wanting to keep going but all too aware of that cold, creeping feeling, the one that had been with him since first arriving here, worsened by seeing the man.

The feeling made Zach twist with discomfort – the way he felt when ASPCA commercials showed sad, lonely dogs and cats, the way he felt when he saw kids with cancer lining up to be honored at sporting events – and it only got worse as they ventured farther into the institution, accompanied by dark thoughts seemingly forced into his head by some external source.

When they came to Valleyview Park, a grassy space of dusk shadows nestled between buildings – with its netless basketball hoop and its

rusted swingset and its small pavilion festooned with wind chimes –
Zach read the names on a sign titled, VALLEYVIEW PARK, WHERE
EVERYONE HAS FUN, and felt an immense sadness come over him at
the thought of doctors and staff telling their patients that they would
have to live somewhere else now. No more fun at Valleyview Park, no
more gatherings in the pavilion or shots through the basket or rises on
the swingset.

To their left, the screened porch of Valleyview Hall, once likely used
for crafts sessions, rattled solemnly in the evening wind, telling of
better times before the roof partially collapsed beneath the weight of
snow. To their right, Baypath Hall was a ghost, its second floor rooms
lit a pale yellow.

Zach and Clay had toured many abandoned complexes together, but
unlike past adventures, the history of this place compelled Zach. He
tried to imagine what it had been like for the patients to be shipped
away to some other institution. And what about the staff? They hadn't
merely worked here and collected their paychecks, but had gone to
great lengths to make a home for their patients – erecting swingsets and
pavilions, maintaining little parks here and there, and transcending the
place from a state facility to a sanctuary. This hadn't been a typical
lock-you-up, forget-you-were-there mental hospital, Zach sensed, but
maybe that was just the pot talking.

Still, no complex had ever spoken to him this passionately before.

Zach's cold disquiet gradually subsided as they crisscrossed roads and
parking lots, taking turns filming the silent, deteriorating buildings,
narrating on occasion based on their prior research. The facility was
nothing short of sprawling, brick structures springing up from hillsides
in every direction, some of them in far better shape than others. The
sidewalks were crumbling, the roads buckled from untreated potholes
and frost heaves. Most of the signs stood at slants of varying degrees, a
few flattened or bent beyond repair. Zach kept imagining the institution
at its height of glory, hundreds of patients with access to the various
activities the place had to offer, doctors and nurses filing down the

corridors, everything neat and orderly, an utter antithesis of what lay before them.

"What was that?" Clay said, searching the woods to their left.

Zach shifted his camcorder from the building he was filming (Harrow Hall) to the opposite woods. He thought he heard footsteps, but the gathering wind muddled everything together.

"There it is again!" Clay was smiling absently, his eyes glassy.

"I think it's just the wind, man. Take it easy on those joints."

Zach went back to filming Harrow Hall, but he was distracted a moment later by an unmistakable noise, a loud crunching sound in the woods. An animal? The guy from before?

Going rigid with worry, Zach studied the woods for movement and listened closely. Nothing, only the building wind. But the woods, rising up along a steep hill, suddenly seemed like a living, menacing presence, an army of trees ready to crush them.

"We should get out of here," Zach said, frightened now of far more ridiculous things than man and beast. "We've got enough footage."

Zach turned back toward Harrow Hall, his heart beating the rapid tune of urgency, but he was met by a wall of a man, the man from the road!

For a moment Zach couldn't breathe, the air squeezed out of him by the sheerness of shock; not merely shock, though, complete dread.

The man, unspeaking, looked down on Zach with a portentous grin, and somehow, perhaps insinuated by the wind, Zach knew–

No, please, NOOO!–

Yes, he knew the end was near. This man would kill them. They shouldn't have come.

They never should have come!

***

Harrow examined the intruders carefully, just as he'd inspected young Brandon Joutel Saturday night and discovered something stunning in his soul, a gift of untold power, a diamond glinting in the sand, unknown even to the boy himself.

But these two trespassers were devoid of talent, the latest additions to society's trash heap, soon to be buried beneath more wasted lives. A brief analysis yielded nothing of importance, not a sliver of magic in their bones – only an unpleasant stench – and as such they were expendable.

Harrow could let them live, of course. He could allow them to finish up their frivolities and be on their way, but tonight he was in no mood for generosity. He was frustrated by the lack of progress of his army (it was taking an unexpectedly long time to mold the faithful into mastery of their gifts). A few of them were fully conditioned, ready for battle, but the majority was still deficient in some way. A handful even held out hope of escape, refusing to submit and accept magic's role for them. They remained under Harrow's control, but to achieve true power they would need to thrive on their own strength, prepared to die for their leader, prepared to offer their gifts to Harrow, prepared to do whatever it took to seize authority of the masses, a machine operating seamlessly, flawlessly.

"Unwise was your decision to come here, children," Harrow said, and the pair staggered backward, their eyes like great big windows, revealing the mounting terror on the other side.

WELCOME TO HARROW HALL

One man was far more afraid than the other, Harrow recognized. Clearly he was the perceptive one, sensing swiftest death, and death he would receive, though not of an overly swift nature.

Harrow summoned two of his soldiers from the woods. "Take them!" he ordered, pointing to Harrow Hall, his new home. "Bring them to the stage. There is much work to be done."

Chapter 21

When Brandon awoke, he was shivering in the middle of a snowy field, naked but for a pair of oversized boots. It was dark, snowing heavily, the wind driving at his exposed skin and forcing him into motion.

He stumbled into a panicked run, tried to move in the same direction as the wind, but it stung him no matter which way he ran, his massive boots sinking a little with every step. The boots, extending to his knees, were intolerably rough on the inside, as if the lining were made of sandpaper and pumice – and Brandon's feet kept sliding around in the expansive depths, feeling like they'd pull clean out.

Disoriented, shivering, his face going numb, the tips of his fingers aching sharply, Brandon tried to think, but voices piped into his head – quick, grating, vibrating voices.

You're gonna die, Brandy. You're gonna die, Brandy, they chanted, the wind assailing him without mercy, piling snow into his face.

Shaking violently, his teeth clacking together, the voices unrelenting in his head, Brandon persisted through the field, twice sinking so deep that he lost his balance and fell, snow clinging to him like sprinkles on ice cream.

Finally he made it to a road rough with rock salt, crossed it, spotted a yellow light burning within a gray shadow of a building not far away. But he was tired and freezing. He wouldn't make it, he feared, willing his muscles to keep functioning. If he locked up now and collapsed, he'd be dead, the snow ready to swallow him.

He tried to remember how he'd gotten here. Where had he been before? Nothing came to him, though, only the voices in his head growing louder, wilder.

You're gonna die, Brandy! You're gonna die, Brandy! You're shutting down from within, boy! You're gonna die out here!

Coughing and shivering and panting, Brandon concentrated on each step, forcing himself toward the building, very close now, even closer, the wind shrieking in his face, so strong that it pushed him backward, knocked him over, the snow burying his chest as if ten men with shovels had been directed to pile it on, each snowflake as big as a dinner plate.

Now it was the voice of Eddy Englehart, the team captain, in Brandon's head.

You need to bulk up, kid! What do you weigh, one hundred-fifty soaking wet? You gotta get stronger in case they crash the crease. Get out of that snow, kid!

Splayed out on his back, agony radiating through him, Brandon began to convulse…and through the slow fade from reality he managed to remember everything Harrow had said. He'd ordered Brandon to draw the deaths of two men in his sketchbook.

"Draw them hanging from a tree and write the following names, Brandon," he'd commanded. "Do it, or you and Victoria will die."

Brandon had refused, assuming Harrow would eventually kill him and Vicky regardless of what he did. Apparently Vicky had sensed it, too; if they were destined to sink, they wouldn't drag others down with them.

"Don't draw it!" Vicky had urged, and Brandon had tossed the sketchbook away. Then he'd awakened to the wind and snow, death ready to…

…not yet, though, for something coiled around his right ankle with vicious speed, making a whistling-snapping sound as it latched onto the boot. Brandon, briefly freed from his convulsions, tried to sit up – but someone yanked a rope and tugged him toward the building, his backside burning across the crunchy snow, the pain conquering fear.

Brandon screamed, his eardrums shattering with anguish but also with deafening waves of laughter. It sounded like a laugh track, occasionally interspersed with, *You're gonna die, Brandy! You're gonna die, Brandy!*

Resisting the rope's tug, Brandon flashed out his left leg and tried to dig the heel of his boot into the snow, his legs momentarily spreading into a near full splits, his adductors/hamstrings screaming at him to go no further, as tight as rubber bands stretched at arm's length.

Over the shredding sound of his body towed across the snow, Brandon heard a door fling open, felt the warmth of the building as he was dragged in and released.

The door snapped shut behind him. If not for his towering pain, Brandon would have been relieved by the wall of heat that enveloped him – and overwhelmed by the intolerable smell of the place.

Shaking and suffering, feeling like he was on fire, Brandon rolled onto his stomach and gritted his teeth against the pain. There he remained for a long time, oblivious to the putrescent stench and the sound of clanking chains, his cheek pressed flat against the concrete floor, warmth spreading over him like a blanket. He didn't want to move, didn't even want to look up and acknowledge his next horror.

Eventually, after the pain downgraded from an inferno to a bonfire, Brandon reluctantly inventoried his "shelter", the smell coming at him with unendurable velocity. He'd never in his young life been nearly floored by an odor, but this, whatever it was, made him want to return outside to the snow. It smelled like a thousand unflushed toilets in a sealed room, not simply filled with feces but vomit and…something else, something beyond definition.

And what were those massive sacks hanging in the shadows at the far end of the room, pinkish and torn open?

WELCOME TO HARROW HALL

From the unseen depths of the building, a piercing shriek bounced off the walls like a racquetball. The shrill, penetrating sound jolted its way into Brandon's bones, momentarily making his injuries worse, and he suddenly knew what was hanging from those hooks along the far wall. Mutilated pig carcasses. They formed a twenty-foot line, dangling from their hind legs, heads lopped off, the floor painted with blood. Brandon twitched with the need to vomit. He wobbled to his feet, studying his immediate surroundings: hooks, conveyor belts, machinery, bins nearly as large as dumpsters, countertops scattered with sharp objects.

Brandon grabbed a cleaver from the nearest counter; then, not feeling protected enough, he swiped a knife, his still numb hands barely managing to clutch each utensil. His face remained numb as well, as if a dentist had just jabbed him all over with Novocaine needles. His fingers were alarmingly red at the tips, and he feared what they'd look like in days, weeks, months (if he somehow escaped this purgatory and made it back to his old existence, the one in which he was about to be a junior in high school).

His thoughts turned to Vicky, all alone now against Harrow. He had to get back to her – if he could save her, it'd be worth every injury.

Brandon tried to steady his grip on the newly acquired weapons, but he felt like he was attempting to write with oven mitts on. He lurched backward when another stabbing shriek erupted from the bowels of the building, this one gurgling and messy and protracted, forcing Brandon to cover his ears.

He hobbled to the near door (the one he'd been dragged through) and tugged the handle. Locked. "Fuck you!" he shouted, repeatedly kicking the door. "Stupid fucking fuck!"

When he turned exasperatedly from the door, the big man was closing on him quickly – the guy from Harrow Hall who'd hung him on the hook.

The man lunged with a crowbar, Brandon narrowly ducking a wild swing, the weapon lodging in the door.

You're gonna die, Brandy! came the vexing voices in his head. *Slaughterhouse Jones will finish you, Brandy!*

With a deep, rumbling laugh, Jones extracted the crowbar from the now splintered door and faced Brandon. Brown overalls stained red, black beard foresting his face, crater eyes showing the fastest way to Hell, he looked like a prop that belonged in a haunted hayride.

"Stay the fuck back!" Brandon slashed the air with the knife, hoping and failing to seem threatening.

Jones laughed at him, allowing Brandon to slowly recede. The psycho crossed his arms, seeming oddly patient, and Brandon couldn't escape a fear that Jones would eventually kill him – it was just a matter of how long he'd wait.

Finally Jones took a step forward. "I can smell the terror on ya, boy," he growled. "You smell just like all the little piggies come through here. They all got souls just like people, ya know, same fear-a-death. Man, pig, kid, don't matter to me – flesh cuts the same, blood flows nice and red. Finer than wine."

Brandon turned, sprinted to the back of the room, where the carcasses hung one after another, Jones's laughter pursuing him. But by the time he reached the far wall, his boots sliding on a fresh layer of blood, Jones was right behind him.

"Ya know what I'll do first, boy?" Jones feinted a strike with the crowbar. "I'll cut off that little pecker and let you bleed out. If ya don't die from that, I'm gonna lop off those acorns you got for nuts and mix 'em in my sandwich tonight. You ain't lived till you eaten a man's nuts...or his heart."

Gulping down hot, moist air, gagging on the smell of blood and guts and death, Brandon searched for a new weapon, but there was nothing back here but hooks and carcasses.

Slowly approaching, Jones's lips curved into a gruesome, toothless rictus. "Cut off your pecker, boy, thas' what I'll do. Then I'm gonna feed it to that sweet sow-a-yours. Stuff it in her little mouth and make her choke on it."

"Fuck you!" Brandon shouted, straining to breathe. The room began to blur, the voices in his head sounding crackly and distorted. Suddenly dizzy, he knew he had to do something immediately, Jones's hazy form creeping closer.

Desperation dominating, Brandon flung the cleaver at Jones. Missed, the stupid thing rattling uselessly away, Jones laughing at him again, coming closer, one last chance. Brandon held up the knife, tried to aim, but it was like he was wearing those drunk simulation goggles the cops forced on you during dumbass DUI awareness exercises each year. He could hardly see anything now, only lights and shadows, Jones's shadow the most prominent.

Additional laughter boomed directly in front of Brandon, a long, thunderous sound, and then there was an arm reaching for him. Brandon thrust the knife forward, waved it ineffectually, slicing only the air. More laughter, straight ahead, louder, louder, louder, and Brandon hurled the knife, his throw met by a glorious squishing-howling-thudding and then silence.

The voices were gone. Brandon's vision was quickly restored, but he was no longer in the slaughterhouse.

Please, God, no. I'll go to church every Sunday for the rest of my life and say PEACE BE WITH YOU to every fucking old person. NOOOO, God, please…

…Suddenly he was back on the stage of Harrow Hall, a heartily applauding audience before him, everyone standing and cheering.

Collapsing to his knees, Brandon noticed that he was fully dressed again, even his T-shirt, the one he'd given to Vicky to protect her from the raining blood – but his clothes were no longer bloody, as if none of it had happened.

A voice projected over the speakers. Harrow's voice. "Ladies and gentlemen, with that riveting scene we bring you to intermission. A fifteen-minute recess we shall entertain for snacks and smokes and a consultation of the restrooms, which you will find on the auditorium floor, just beyond the stairwell."

The balcony lights flashed on. Tranquil music played, light and instrumental, audience members yawning and conversing, a few men checking their watches.

Brandon glanced down at his hands, which had returned to normalcy as well. His backside no longer hurt. Everything was an illusion, Harrow's illusion.

But where was Vicky?

Part III: Supremacy

Chapter 1

Throughout Brandon's ordeal Vicky found herself confined to a small backstage room, imprisoned along with the two men Harrow had recently captured, Zach and Clay.

In the mirror that was Zach's and Clay's misfortune, Vicky saw her own reflection. They'd all encountered the wrong man/place, just as Brandon had, the brutal randomness of the nightmare seizing Vicky like a hand around her throat.

She tried talking with Zach and Clay, tried asking them questions, but she couldn't sit still, could hardly even think…

…for she could feel Brandon's terror and just a fraction of his pain, strong enough to cause her own muscles to ache. But in spite of the titanic suffering he endured, Brandon was worried mostly about *her*, desperate to keep her safe, his thoughts at times blossoming to whispers in her head.

"You sure you're okay?" said the taller man, Zach Markham. He was seated on a bench opposite Vicky, looking worriedly at her, the little square of a room bordered by rough oak benches.

Vicky nodded. Though she'd already told Zach the blood soaking her clothes had been rained on her from the rafters much earlier, he kept asking if she was hurt.

Vicky tried to push back tears for Brandon, convinced there was still a chance for them. Whatever Brandon was facing, Harrow had forced it upon him because he'd refused to draw the deaths of Zach and Clay. But he would survive – he had to survive.

Don't give in. Don't give up. Brandon will find a way to get us out of this.

Yet Brandon's gift still didn't sink into full acceptance for Vicky; just the idea of such power frightened her, though it was entirely possible he possessed no preternatural abilities whatsoever. As Brandon had assumed, this whole thing might be Harrow's doing, an elaborate act to coerce them to…to what? If they held no legitimate power to rival his own, what could he possibly want from them?

"Jesus, this is bad, real bad," Clay said for maybe the hundredth time, lying on the floor and blinking rapidly at the ceiling. "What if he's a cannibal or something, man?"

"Clay, this isn't helping." Zach came beside Vicky, wrapping an arm around her shoulders, but she only wanted Brandon's arm around her.

She stood, trying to keep Brandon's thoughts close. His energy (that was the best way she could describe it) had trailed off these last few seconds, his thoughts muted. She sensed he was concentrating intently on something, devoting every drop of adrenaline to it.

Over the next several minutes Vicky felt hardly anything from Brandon, receiving little more than a faint ping of fear from his corner of their ordeal. She paced the room, her body tense and achy. The longer the nothingness persisted, the more convinced of his death she became…

…A strong series of jolts hammered into her head, Brandon's thoughts. He was searching for her, mildly relieved by…

…Oh, Jesus, she could see part of what he'd just endured, and she momentarily felt guilty for receiving these images, like she was violating Brandon by seeing them – but this was no time to hold anything back or turn from what she'd seen. If they were to maximize their benefits from this connection, they would have to share everything.

A hopeful smile stretched thinly along Vicky's lips. *I don't think Harrow's doing this. It really is our thing!*

WELCOME TO HARROW HALL

Brandon's relief continued to pour forth, but it was tempered with dread; Vicky could feel it crawling in him, crawling and scraping and jostling him because he couldn't find her. No matter where he looked, she wasn't there.

Vicky took a deep breath, trying to gather her thoughts and consolidate them into something direct and powerful, something she could transmit. It helped to close her eyes, everything else eliminated from her head but a single thought. Then, once it was confidently secured, she wished-begged-prayed it to Brandon, reminding her of the days she used to choose a card and tell her friends to read it in her eyes – FOUR OF HEARTS!!!! – but they'd rarely even guessed the right suit.

Brandon, however, was different, much different, unlike anyone she'd ever known. Less than a minute later, there was a clattering storm against the door, sending Zach and Clay scurrying to the back of the room.

But Vicky hurried to the door, knowing who would enter. It swung open, Brandon lifting her off her feet and hugging her. He was fully dressed again, all traces of blood effaced from his clothes, and when he set her down he kissed her lips for a frenetic brevity, Vicky holding him close.

Thank God you're okay, she thought, words far more powerful felt than spoken, even if he couldn't hear them.

But Brandon stepped backward with understanding. Lips slightly parted, he turned his attention inward for a moment before replying, *I got you, Vicky. We'll get through this together.* He was efforting a smile but his eyes were haunted, his fear only marginally less than it had been a few minutes ago, his words never clearer in her head.

This is how we have to beat him, Brandon said after a transcendent moment of gathered thoughts, both of them held in thrall of the miracle that had invented itself at Harrow Hall.

Yes, she agreed, *we have to use this gift. Whatever this is, I don't think Harrow knows about it.*

To Zach and Clay, not a word was uttered between Vicky and Brandon.

Chapter 2

Vinny Stettler was released from the hospital early Monday afternoon, his right arm in a cast. He asked if he could visit Brandon in the ICU, wanting to hold his friend's hand and tell him to get better, but the staff said it was family only. Anyway, Vinny was probably the last person Brad's parents wished to see right now.

It began to rain on the ride home, Vinny unable to force the guilt from his heart. It kept clawing and clawing, like a dog repeatedly scratching on a screen door, insisting to be let in. Eventually, he feared, it would consume him. If Brad didn't wake up, everything would go to a very dark place, and Vinny wasn't without a realization that the unexpectedness of life was finally being revealed to him. Until now his life had been easy – two loving parents, good health, food always on the table, success in the classroom, a spot on the hockey team. There hadn't been much venturing into the realm of adversity, except for the death of a grandmother he'd rarely seen. But that had been it, Vinny coasting all the way to adulthood.

But now the darkness had found him. And it wasn't done with him just yet.

Hours later, at the dinner table, Vinny's father relayed news that nearly made Vinny choke on his mashed potatoes.

"This day keeps on getting worse," his father said. "I just talked to Marty. I guess Eddy had a bad waterskiing accident, nearly tore his hamstring straight off the bone."

Vinny's mother shot his father a glare. "Do we really need to hear about this at dinner?"

"Sorry," Dad said. "But Eddy's done for the year – I just thought Vinny should know."

Vinny couldn't believe this was happening. Eddy had been badly injured, and upon hearing the news Vinny's memories had instantly catapulted back to the previous night. The magician freak! He'd said something about a rough senior year for the person who'd given the camcorder to Vinny.

That person was Eddy Englehart, who just so happened to be heading into his senior year. Eddy had sold the camcorder to Vinny last year, but how could the magician have possibly known that?

Brandon's accident. Did that guy have something to do with it?

Even though the doctors had advised Vinny to get as much rest as possible, he called Brady Joutel immediately after dinner and proceeded to tell him everything.

Chapter 3

Jerome, Sky, and Ki had patiently waited over a day for backup, sheltering beside a boulder in the woods and finding a stream to sustain themselves. Ki had even snagged a few fish the Native American way (or perhaps just his own way), snapping a hand into the water and coming away almost every time with a victim. Following Ki's impressive display, they'd cooked the fish with a modest fire (which was started by rubbing sticks, Ki effective yet again) and had themselves a miserable outing devoid of divinations.

Then they'd taken turns sleeping throughout the night, but no one had slept well.

Now the earliest light was beginning to seep into a fresh morning. Last night, they'd decided to get moving at daybreak, convinced that Paradis and his crew weren't coming. Perhaps Paradis had gone against his word, or maybe they hadn't been able to track Willy's cell phone. Regardless, it seemed like they were on their own.

But shortly after they awakened, an SUV came to a brisk stop in the breakdown lane. The sky was tinted blue at its eastern edge, darkness soon to be chased off again, the same old cycle repeating as it always did. But the sunrise was pretty much the only predictable element of this morning.

"You think that's them? Let's go see," Sky said, desperate for the SUV to belong to Paradis and his men. It was towing a small cargo trailer, perfect for transporting the weapons for which Paradis was allegedly famous.

But was it really them, or were these Harrow's next soldiers?

"No, wait here," Jerome warned. They were just inside the woods, staring out from behind a massive hemlock tree, maybe two miles down the road from where they'd reunited following the wreck.

"Yes, wait, could be trap," Ki said.

Sky, sandwiched between Jerome and Ki, sighed in frustration as the SUV's doors flew open, three men spilling out. They were big. They moved authoritatively. And they all had weapons. One of them was checking a gadget that looked like a GPS device, his face lit a dim white by the screen. "We're close," he told the others. "Within a hundred feet, south-southwest."

Fear sprang into Jerome's heart when one of the other men called his name. Could they really trust these people? At the moment they seemed to be fresh out of better options.

"Stay here," Jerome whispered to Ki and Sky, then emerged from the woods and announced his presence.

The men moved quickly – tactically – in Jerome's direction.

The man who'd called Jerome's name extended his hand. "Jean-Sylvain Paradis, pleasure to meet you," he said with the same French accent Jerome had heard on the phone.

Jerome offered his hand for the obligatory shake. "Jerome Hudson. Just startin to think you boys weren't comin."

Paradis nodded understandingly. "Sorry to keep you waiting. We had some unexpected…circumstances." His face was difficult to read in such limited light. He was a white guy with glasses, but that was about all Jerome could make out in detail, the rest of his face obscured by darkness and a low-brimmed ball cap.

"Willy was a good man," Paradis said. "I have to admit, though, at first I was only interested in helping him pursue Harrow because of the money. I thought half the shit Willy said about him was crazy talk, but regardless, it's time to punch this guy's ticket."

"Whatever Willy told you, believe it," Jerome said quietly. "The shit we seen…" and he allowed his words to run dry, knowing these men would likely bail if he revealed the truth.

"All right, let's get ourselves acquainted, shall we?" Paradis said, then introduced Jerome to his men. Both were former Green Berets, just like Paradis, but that didn't necessarily give them an advantage, not when Harrow was constantly changing the dynamic of the war. At this rate, Jerome wouldn't feel safe in a tank, and he dared not even imagine what was coming for them next.

"I've got more people on standby – all we need is a location, and it's go-time." Paradis glanced down the road, predawn darkness prevailing in both directions. The air was refreshingly cool. Crickets chirped in the high grass, and new colors were born in the eastern sky. Nothing warned of an impending storm.

But soon the devastation would ravage, Jerome sensed, unless they could somehow find a way to preempt it.

Thinking briefly back to the first time he saw Harrow at Canal Nine – the odor of death overwhelming – Jerome called Sky and Ki out from hiding. They stepped forth tentatively, holding hands.

"These are the only two people left from Willy's group," Jerome said.

They all shook hands, though Jerome detected the same incredulity in the men's eyes that he, himself, had felt upon first meeting Willy's group.

"You got flamethrower?" Ki asked J.S. Paradis.

Paradis nodded. "Yes, sir. Willy told me the only way to kill this guy is fire. I didn't believe him, of course, but there was no arguing with Willy once he got his mind set to something." A wistful smile formed and quickly departed. "Anyway, with the money Willy put down for this guy's head, I had the boys hook up five propane-fueled flamethrowers. We've also got two antitank rocket launchers, just in case we need some extra pop."

"And grenade launchers, too," added one of his men. "You guys tell us where to go, and we'll light it up."

"Speaking of, any leads?" Paradis said.

"We're working on it." Sky spat against a tree. "Meanwhile, get your maps of Ohio ready. And get me some goddamn food."

Jerome felt the lift of hope tugging at his heart, but thoughts of Willy and Rosa and Bu chased it off. Paradis and his men offered an opportunity for vengeance, but at what price? Would Sky and Ki be the next victims? As the others talked, Jerome remembered his nights in Nam, remembered the stark, suffocating fears of when and how the men around him would perish, each sunrise a blessing because they were alive but also a curse because now there would be more fighting, more death. Oddly, the down time and R&R allowances had been the worst, better to just push straight through than come back overthinking everything, Jerome had discovered. At least during missions he'd been ruled by an ultra-focused sense of purpose, but periods of inactivity had spawned the darkest thoughts – times like this, everyone standing around and talking about Harrow and waiting to die.

Come on now, stay positive. Didn't come all this way to lose.

"We should get movin," Jerome said, growing impatient. "We can talk on the way. Right now we're just sittin ducks, you hear?"

Paradis nodded firmly. "Where to?"

Jerome exchanged uncertain glances with Ki and Sky. "North, toward Ohio," Jerome finally said. "I'm tired of waitin around for this guy to bring it to us. Time to take the offense to his end."

Chapter 4

Cole received the call shortly after dinner Monday night. That afternoon he'd visited Brandon in the ICU, looking down upon his cousin and fearing that he would never break free of the prison that held him. His face had been so peacefully bland, as if he'd slipped far below the surface into a deep dreamworld where there was nothing but beautiful women and fast cars and endless glove saves. The nurse had said Brandon might be able to hear him, but Cole had been sure his words hadn't penetrated that unreachable place, a void as dark and inaccessible as a black hole. Yet it wasn't nearly that magnificent – no, Brandon was only trapped within himself, a captive of his own body, but there was no way to ram down the doors and free him. Only Brandon could find a path out of the maze.

Cole was in the driveway when the call came, about to light a cigarette. The stars seemed unusually bright tonight, glittering down on him like a million little eyes, not only watchful but anticipatory. Cole didn't like looking at the stars tonight; something about them just wasn't right.

"Brady, what's going on?" Cole said, his cousin's name on the screen of his buzzing cell phone. "Is everything okay with Brandon?"

"No change," Brady answered.

Cole felt a rush of disappointment. He was staring through the thin woods at his neighbor's driveway, forcing himself not to look skyward again.

"But there's something really weird going on at the institution," Brady continued. "I just got a call from the kid who went there with Brandon last night. He told me they met a guy who said all this weird shit. I guess he told them his name's Harrow, claimed to be a magician."

By the time Brady finished the twisting story, Cole was briskly pacing the driveway. "So you seriously think this Harrow guy had something to do with the accident?"

"I don't know what to think." Brady sounded flustered and tired, but mostly he sounded desperate. "Vinny said Brandon first saw this guy when we came Saturday night. Did he say anything to you?"

"No, but he said something about seeing a girl in Harrow Hall, remember? I thought he was bullshitting us."

"Me too. Me and Angie thought he just made her up. Jesus, what the hell is going on, Cole? Who are these people?"

Cole thought back to the bus and the lights inside Harrow Hall. The noises. The smell of popcorn. "It's like they're living inside the building," he said. "Ever since that bus came, things have been way off."

"We need to go there and figure this out. After everything Vinny said about Eddy Englehart…what if this guy really is some kind of magician? I know it sounds crazy, but…"

His words ran out of track and derailed, a momentary silence hanging between them.

"Do you think this is a horrible idea?" Brady said.

Cole was looking up at the stars again, and not liking what he saw. Never before had the night sky disquieted him this way, but tonight was different, a night he knew he wouldn't soon forget. Squeezing the phone between his cheek and shoulder, he lit up a cigarette. "It's a good idea, but you have to let me do this on my own," Cole insisted. "I'm not scheduled to work again till Thursday, but the guards won't mind if I drop by. I'm really not supposed to have visitors, though."

"I know, I know, it's just…I want to find this guy. He probably has nothing to do with the accident, but I just want to talk to him." There was a defeated, almost hopeless hollow to his voice.

"I'll find him," Cole assured. "And you can bet your ass I'll grill him for you."

Cole inhaled deeply, letting the nicotine fill his lungs. In fifty years he would probably be in a hospital somewhere, voiceless and dying of lung cancer or COPD, his grandchildren dreading the day their beloved grandpa finally checked out of the hotel. But for now, on a cool summer night in August 2005, the stars blinking down on him, addiction provided a calming relief that justified the guilt.

"Thanks for everything, Cole. I really appreciate it."

"No problem, man. I'm gonna get to the bottom of this – for Brandon. You have my word."

Before heading inside, Cole stamped out his cigarette and took one last look at the stars. A sharp, biting thought came to him then, a thought that Brandon would die – but not just Brandon. It was only an ephemeral, irrational fear – one that lasted a few seconds while he stared up at the sky – but it told him something horrible would happen and thousands would die. But how?

A terrorist attack?

A natural disaster?

The thought didn't endure long enough to be scrutinized. When Cole started toward the house, his fears were gone as if they'd never been there, like a faint line in the sand washed away by an onrushing tide. A slight wind whispered about the yard. Above, the stars glimmered portentously, awaiting the approaching storm.

Chapter 5

Harrow eagerly watched his father's planchette cavort about the Great Board. Livelier than usual tonight, it flipped and hopped indiscriminately across the squares of necromancy like a tumbleweed carried in a dry breeze. Soon it would provide another glimpse into the lives of Jerome Hudson and his band of fools. They were heading stubbornly north, drifting a little closer to the institution with every mile – but the Spirits had advised Harrow to let them come. No sense in dispatching additional forces to track down a handful of pests, the Spirits had said, not when they would eventually stumble upon their own demise.

Harrow disagreed, unable to concentrate fully on his work knowing that these dolts assumed they could invade the darkness. Like ants persistently seeking entry to the kitchen cupboard, they needed to be swiftly destroyed and dismissed from consideration. As such, Harrow was in favor of siccing the Whammy on them again, or at least sending another round of soldiers after them.

Yet the fact remained that those under Harrow's control still possessed limited power away from their master. Like an RC plane, functionality could only be sustained within a certain range, the same to be said for Harrow's own mastery…for now.

"Come closer, children, if you dare," Harrow said when the Great Board revealed the location of his enemies. "Meanwhile, the show must resume. Much work remains."

Long ago, in their bayou cabin, Harrow's father had taught him that among the many purposes of Maleficium is to provide the Spirits with constant tributes of sacrifice. To kill for the Master and to be willing to die for Him – such are the ultimate triumphs in this life, Harrow's father had said that night above the never-still waters. And for their sacrifices the most devoted souls will be given eternal entertainment, their blood exchanged for blood, their suffering repaid with echoing screams, each performance in Harrow Hall a humble offering arranged by the Chosen One to please those who came before him.

And following the Reclamation, what better place to perform endless tributes than this, a little theater to serve as a vestige of its former empire, the followers of the false lord to suffer within its walls?

Following his session with the Great Board, Harrow returned to his Grand Hall. It was finally time for the most troublesome of his soldiers to relinquish their clinging faith and embrace their true callings. Carefully, Harrow would continue to break them down without breaking them, like pushing a muscle as far as it will go without straining it, and he knew exactly how to finish the job.

Twilight was almost over now, darkness just beyond the hills.

Chapter 6

Well fed and hydrated thanks to a diner stop, nestled now between Ki and Sky in the rear seats of the SUV, a pillow supporting his head, Jerome began to drift off when they hit the highway. Unlike Willy, Paradis maintained a fast speed in the express lane, cruising past an occasional eighteen wheeler as the sun crept over the treetops to their right.

Paradis's men didn't talk much, nor did Ki and Sky. Everyone was somber and speculative, privately contemplating their uphill mission and perhaps wondering if this would be their final sunrise.

Jerome's last thoughts before nodding off were of Vietnam, but his first thoughts upon waking were not his own. A woman's voice spoke clearly and slowly to him, each sentence like a message in smoke, briefly lingering before fading away: *"HELP! We are trapped in Harrow Hall, an auditorium on the campus of an abandoned mental institution in Ohio. Please save us before it's too late. My name is Victoria Eldridge…"*

Jerome craved more information, and suddenly there was more, much more, a dreamlike exchange during which Jerome silently communicated with the woman Harrow had taken, learning everything from the town she was being held in to a description of the institution and its buildings.

When there was nothing but silence between his ears again, the strange external spigot going dry as they rolled along, Jerome thought back to that morning on the shore of Lake Pontchartrain. Searching the water for answers, Ki had said he'd seen a theater; he'd also said, "The place starts with O." The others had been convinced about Ohio, and now their various forms of divinity were proving correct.

Jerome smiled dimly, wondering if Harrow was tricking him. Perhaps the necromancer had forced Victoria to say those things.

"I just saw something," Jerome said, unsure and diffident. "I think I know where we need to go."

To his right, Sky stirred from a light sleep, mumbling unintelligible things. To his left, Ki was looking pensively out the window, hands clasped together. In the middle row, Paradis's men were staring into their cell phones.

"What was that?" Paradis said from the driver's seat. It felt weird to see him up there and not Willy. Though they'd only known each other for a short time, two leaves blown together by the fickle winds of the world, Jerome had enjoyed a kindred bond with Willy. He'd not only been an inspirational leader, but he'd maintained faith in Jerome's gift when Jerome, himself, hadn't possessed a hint of confidence in his ability to contribute to their mission.

But now Willy was dead, another man driving them north to Ohio. That's war, Jerome kept telling himself, and they were no doubt entangled in a vicious yet invisible war, free to quit at any moment but unwilling to give up – and not just because they wanted to kill Harrow for Willy and Rosa and Bu. It was becoming increasingly clear that going home now would not preserve their lives but guarantee their deaths, as well as those of countless others.

To resign to Harrow's darkness was surely to forfeit all light.

"I had a vision just now," Jerome whispered, and both Ki and Sky jolted in his direction. Paradis's men exchanged dubious glances; Paradis, himself, glanced in the rearview mirror, frowning at their exclusion.

There were a few seconds of shivery ambivalence, Jerome fearing he would lead them straight to Harrow. He considered keeping his mouth shut, but then Willy's words were emboldening him.

Everyone's got something to offer. You might not know what it is until the chaos arrives, but you'll be able to help us somehow. I can feel it.

Putting an arm on Jerome's shoulders, Ki nodded emphatically. "Trust your gift."

"Harrow Hall," Jerome said after another indecisive moment. "That's the place you and Sky have seen in your visions. He's got all kinds of people trapped there."

"Well, fuck," Sky said, glancing at Ki. "Glad we brought Jerry on board."

Chapter 7

Vicky could feel the connection being made. It was the faintest click imaginable, but a click nonetheless, her words received by (the images were grainy, poorly defined, but he was definitely a man, a tall man)…

…and his name suddenly appeared like a fish rising to the surface: Jerome Hudson.

Very slowly Vicky opened her eyes. *I reached him. Jesus, I reached him!*

With a triumphant double fist pump, Vicky concentrated on sending more information. She had to do it deliberately, focusing on each letter and then the words that followed, Zach and Clay watching suspiciously from the opposite bench.

Brandon was sitting beside Vicky, his hand light and encouraging upon her thigh. It had been his idea to send out a telepathic SOS transmission, and now, miraculously, Vicky was communicating with someone else!

"What's going on? What are you doing?" Zach demanded, but Brandon silenced him with a hand wave.

Vicky and Brandon hadn't actually whispered a word to each other in this room, carefully guarding the secret of their unspoken conversations. It seemed like this was their only advantage over Harrow, and they were quickly becoming more adept at silent speech, forming and sharing messages with less friction and delay, each person's thoughts sliding fluidly into place.

Vicky could also feel Brandon's impulses and emotions with enhanced clarity, his frustration like a pesky itch, his fear a pressing weight, his hope warm and ascendant.

Above all else, Vicky could feel his love, high and all-encompassing, born of chaos and desperation and the impossibility of what had become real for them, dominating the lesser inhabitants of his heart like the sun. Perhaps it wouldn't have been as magnified if Vicky's own heart hadn't dazzled with that same new light...

...a message from Jerome Hudson, his image brightening in Vicky's head. Jerome was an older black man, gray-haired and fear-torn.

We're coming to help you. Do you know the address? Can you tell me how to get there?

His words were watery and distant, but Vicky was able to comprehend them.

Brandon squeezed her arm. His eyes were wide with anticipation.

He wants to know the address, Vicky relayed to Brandon. *Are you sure you can't remember? Come on, you've been here twice!*

As Brandon thought strenuously about it, Vicky felt his mind at work, fascinating albeit invasive, and she wondered if this gift – ?? – operated with such amplification from his end. Could Brandon detect her mental processes, too? Did he know the words she hadn't spoken or even admitted fully to herself? Or was it possible that the ability to initiate wordless interpersonal communications was Vicky's gift, and those she chose to establish such communications with were allowed the benefit?

Regardless, the gift was growing stronger, Vicky sensed. Brandon had already tried to send out an SOS of his own, but it hadn't worked; conversely, Vicky was making rapid progress with a stranger.

Brandon couldn't recall the address, but he was positive about the town and how to get there, even local street names. Good enough.

Vicky conveyed the information accordingly, and Jerome assured her that he and his group were coming. They had weapons, plenty of them – and people who could fight.

Be careful, Vicky warned. *Harrow's dangerous. He can control your mind.*

A better picture of Jerome's group was steadily being painted for Vicky, just as images of Brandon had come to her long before she'd seen him in person. There were four other men and a young woman with blue hair. They were driving in a van or an SUV, something with a lot of seats. They said very little to each other.

Abruptly the picture faded, Vicky distracted by Zach and Clay. "Seriously, what are you two doing?" Zach said. "We have to get out–"

The door swung open, Harrow sauntering inside. The sight of Brandon's sketchbook in his white-gloved hand made Vicky feel sick and shivery.

"Intriguing has it been to witness our young heroes interact," Harrow said with his insufferable anastrophe, a fetid fume trailing him into the room. At once Vicky and Brandon inhaled the horror, Brandon's revulsion coming to her as a sudden spasm.

"Now!" Zach shouted, and both he and Clay were upon Harrow – but immediately they were sent pinwheeling backward like two scraps of paper set down before an industrial fan, tumbling against the back wall with heavy thuds.

You retards! Brandon thought, standing to confront their enemy, his hand finding Vicky's.

Harrow smirked down at them. "Never existed such a power as young love." He reached for Vicky's chin, but Brandon angled between them.

"Stay away from her!" Brandon's voice was level and controlled, hiding the black, roiling currents of fear in his heart as the night hides the sea.

Harrow handed him the book. "Safe she'll remain if you draw their deaths, child." He glanced to the far wall, where Zach and Clay were struggling to their feet. "Remember, I want them hanging from a pair of trees. And don't forget to include the ravens pecking relentlessly at their flesh, the hot sun beating down on them, or perhaps" – he lifted a finger to his chin – "yes, yes, nix the sun altogether. Instead, render a moon of roundest form, would you, sweet Brandon? The audience would cherish such a detail, the Spirits as well." He nodded impatiently at Brandon. "Get to it, child, off you go. Else I'll summon Slaughterhouse Jones to entertain your lover. Isn't he a wonder with the hook and chain?"

Brandon's rage convulsed in Vicky's heart. His fists were shaking, his fingers clenching the book.

"Draw, child, draw! Draw, child, draw!" came Harrow's chant. "Do it, or Jones comes for precious Victoria! How many minutes must I wait for you to finally embrace your gift?"

Brandon, don't do it, Vicky silently protested. *We can survive. We've done it before.*

I have to keep you safe, at least until…

…Vicky could feel Brandon receding, attempting to circumvent. He didn't want to expose another word to a possible interception, and so he opened the book, retrieved his pencil.

"That's it. That a boy," Harrow grinned. "Don't forget the ravens. This will be a good tune-up for you. Later, you're going to draw the levees failing down in New Orleans, a scene for which every detail must be accounted."

With Brandon's very first strokes upon the page, there came a vicious commotion at the back of the room, followed by familiar thuds. Vicky glanced over her shoulder to find Zach and Clay sprawled against the wall, legs entangled, eyes wild with panic.

Vicky was thankful she couldn't feel their pain. Presently, Brandon's heightening desperation alone was sufficient to make her cramp with discomfort.

Please, Brandon, don't do it!

He stole a helpless glance at her as Harrow admired the results of his art. *I have to! I can't let him hurt you!*

Something inside Vicky snapped – it felt like a muscle popping – yet she knew it was a manifestation of Brandon's torments. Her head began to pulse with a sharp, shredding agony. Her stomach felt nauseous. Her legs weakened. It was beyond excruciating for Brandon to do this, Vicky enduring the externalization of his upheaval, yet still he formed the early, torturous traces of his sketch.

"Faster! Faster!" Harrow shouted.

Vicky tried to tear the pencil away from Brandon, but there was an invisible barrier between them now. She was gently conveyed backward, toward the doomed men behind her, as if the floor were sliding beneath her.

"Help!" came a wheezy groan, and Vicky brought both hands to her cheeks when she saw the color draining from Zach's and Clay's faces, fading from a healthy hue to a graying, sickly shade that presaged death's approach. With every line drawn in Brandon's sketchbook, Zach and Clay were wilting away.

Vicky came beside them, touched their faces, tears tracking down her cheeks – but their complexions were suddenly reinvigorated, almost normal again. Vicky turned, saw Brandon on his knees, pounding the invisible wall, the book flapped open facedown on the floor.

I tried to draw Harrow dead, but it's useless. He controls everything.

Vicky went as far as she could and brought a hand to the cold glass of perfect transparency, mirroring his palm. His face was blanched and mostly expressionless, but inside he was crying fiercely; she could feel him wrenching with despair.

*If we die, I want you to know...*his words wavered and broke...*screw it, I love you, Vicky. We've known each other like ten minutes, but I love you.*

His eyes bore pleadingly into hers, shining and misty with self-loathing, for he wasn't strong enough to protect her and he hated himself for it.

I love you, too, Brandon. None of this is your fault. You're the bravest person I've ever met, ten minutes and all.

She smiled weakly, and from the other side he managed a smile of his own – dread-hollowed and desolate – not noticing Harrow opening the door behind him, Slaughterhouse Jones hulking inside, a spiked truncheon in his meaty hand.

Chapter 8

When Jerome finished describing his silent yet detailed discussion with a young woman named Victoria Eldridge, Sky and Ki were understandably suspicious.

"How do we know Harrow didn't put her up to it?" Sky whispered.

Jerome feared she was right. Harrow had infiltrated his mind before – why not now? What if he was luring them straight into a trap?

Jerome, all too familiar with traps from Vietnam, imagined themselves as unwitting soldiers about to fall into a punji pit covered with a bed of grass and leaves. If they went to this place based on information Jerome provided and walked into a massacre, it would be two hundred percent his fault, not only the deaths of his teammates but those of countless oblivious civilians. Harrow's evil would triumph, and the road to his victory would be paved by the deception of a foolish old man.

Jerome remembered his superiors in the Army, specifically the men who'd made decisions for the group and eventually died. They'd been entrusted with soldiers' lives, and in the end they hadn't even been able to ensure their own lives. Such was war, though, and in war you had to make tough decisions and make them quickly. War didn't offer the luxuries of studying at length the combinations and permutations of every strategy. There were personal instincts and external suggestions, and you either went with one or both, plain and simple, no fancy icing on that cake.

Currently, Jerome was taking in all of the suggestions, Sky's advice offered straightforwardly as always. "We should wait until we get more information," she urged, the early morning light accentuating deep rings beneath her eyes. "If we stop by a lake and build a fire, maybe me or Ki will see something that confirms this is the right place."

"I'm sure it's right place. But is it trick?" Ki said quietly.

"Maybe Harrow wanted us to go there all along," Sky suggested. "Maybe he wants us to think it's the right place."

Earlier, when Jerome had mentioned the town and the name of the building where Victoria said she was trapped, one of Paradis's men had entered the information into his phone and produced an address. Upon further review, everything Victoria said had checked out – the place was a defunct psychiatric facility, Harrow Hall one of its newer buildings.

"This all seems too easy," Sky said, even though this new information corroborated both her visions and what Ki had seen at Pontchartrain. "What if there's no girl at all and it's just Harrow doing this?"

"I think she's legit," Jerome guessed. "I got this feelin she's straight. My gut's tellin me to go for it."

Ki agreed, Sky not so much.

"Hey, anyone want to let us in on the development?" Paradis said from the driver's seat. "Are we all on the same team or what?"

Sky shook her head violently. "The same team?!? Where the hell were you people when our friends were killed? Counting your fucking money, that's where!" Jerome tried to stop her, but she was downhill and rolling fast. "You just make sure you're ready. Nothing you've ever seen will prepare you for what's coming."

"And what's that, exactly?" one of the other men challenged. "Lady, you don't even know who you're talking to."

Added the third man, "What the hell are we driving around for, anyway? These people have no clue where to find this guy."

"I just told you where to find him, buddy," Jerome interceded, drawing a collection of snorts and huffs from the men up front. "Call your reinforcements – we're doin surveillance on that address you pulled up. Today. And y'all better be worth the money Willy invested in you."

"Okay, okay, let's all just relax," Paradis said. "Like each other or hate each other, we all want the same guy dead. Can we agree on that?"

After the kettle had simmered a while, Paradis called in his best regional standbys, a group led by a pair of brothers from Ohio who would meet them near the institution in four hours. That meant the ultimate battle with Harrow could happen today, a victor possibly to be determined by sundown.

This realization drove at Jerome like a cold, blustery wind, swirling his thoughts into an inexorable obsession with his own mortality and that of his friends, the same obsession he'd known in war.

He could be killed on this fine, sunny summer day. They could all be killed at the enemy capital. They could all suffer, then die.

Yet the powers of loyalty and determination impelled them forward toward inevitable danger, even Paradis's men, who could have easily taken the money and left them for dead. In a sense, this was biological magic, the mind's way of persuading the body into actions that could potentially be harmful, perhaps deadly. Every living being is programmed to act in the interest of self-preservation, but the magic of selflessness can override, Jerome had learned long ago, a miraculous happening that takes place when bonds of love and friendship and teamwork and patriotism outduel the body's natural impulses to ensure personal safety.

Jerome wasn't sure when he'd reached that threshold with Willy Thunder's mission, but he knew he was willing to die for Sky and Ki, willing to lay down his life for the mission and his new friends, just as Willy and Rosa and Buford had done. In Nam, he hadn't even been sure what he was fighting for beyond his comrades and his own survival. There hadn't seemed to be a definitive endgame in sight, but he'd nonetheless committed himself to his country's cause and fought relentlessly for the men who'd stood beside him, a dutiful pawn supporting the next pawn on the board.

But many years later, on his home soil, with a bunch of people who'd been strangers until only recently, Jerome knew the endgame well. It was simple: destroy Harrow. No elaborations. No obfuscations. Just one mission.

Destroy Harrow before he could destroy countless lives.

Chapter 9

The first blow upon Brandon's back blazed hot, a cutting, glittering pain cascading down his spine, sparks streaming across his eyelids, Vicky's face fading into a nebulous wintry haze beyond the sudden partition that had gone up.

Brandon fell to his stomach, but his eyes – though gleaming with tears – never abandoned what remained of the girl he loved. He couldn't define love, couldn't begin to describe it, but nonetheless he felt it surging through him, felt it muting the pain, felt its seizing rapture for a dreadfully suspended moment as Vicky transformed once more into the girl in the snow globe, a storm of flakes swallowing her in angry gray twilight.

Another strike against Brandon's back sent him down flat. Through the burning cymbal crashes of pain he searched for Vicky, though there was nothing but falling snow beyond the wall now, falling, falling, falling relentlessly, as though Vicky had never been there, only the snow and a dream of her hand in his, a dream destined not for recollection because magic wasn't real.

A third strike spilled agonized tears. Brandon heard a hollow voice above him. "Draw their deaths, child! Draw their deaths!" Harrow repeated, and Brandon's sketchbook drifted down to him like a fallen leaf, hovering briefly before landing atop his outstretched arms, but all he could think was *Why Vicky and me? Why is this happening to us?* Death loomed in his mind like a thundercloud, black and swollen with guarantees of…

…Fight him, Brandon. You have to fight. Vicky's voice was so faint that he could barely register it, his heart echoing with the clatters of his own screaming pain.

"You better draw, kid, or I'll skin ya alive!" came the coarse call of Slaughterhouse Jones. "And that tight little sow as well."

"Don't forget the ravens," Harrow said cheerfully. "And young children to witness the two dead men, yes, yes, little children about seven or eight. Peck out their eyes do the birds of prophecy, the children espying a pair of shadows rocking limply in the windswept grove, bedecked with moonlight and the ornaments of death, and back to their cottage the children go, not to sleep tonight, no, sir, that big moon peeking in on them and bearing cold reminders."

"Skin ya alive, kid, just like the little piggies."

"You're gonna die, Brandon."

"Skin ya alive, boy."

Frayed to the point of breakage, pain erupting from every pore, the black thundercloud creeping closer, Brandon gathered his sketchbook. Opened it. Retrieved the pencil, slippery in his sweating fingers.

Fight him, Brandon! Use your power! It's yours, not his…

…and it came to him, Vicky's faraway words inspiring the final hope of a boy dragged cruelly to the edge…

…Brandon drew furiously, first the moon and then the ravens, appeasing and appeasing, until…

***

…Vicky felt an inward lift upon receiving Brandon's plan, though she tried to divest herself of this knowledge, afraid that Harrow would comb her thoughts.

She turned to face Zach and Clay, who were huddled together and shivering uncontrollably on the concrete floor. They'd all been transported instantaneously to another room – a tiny subterranean nook seemingly at the bottom of a dry well, far away from Brandon and his torments. He'd been beaten down from behind by Jones (Vicky's last sighting of him before the snow had raged), but he was still alive.

And he had a plan.

Vicky studied the men closely, warily, dreading their continued decline toward death. "We'll find a way out of here," she said, but they'd already tried the rusty door. And it would be almost impossible to climb the stone walls to the circle of sunlight at least twenty feet above them, a little portal to freedom that seemed continents away.

"No, we're gonna die," Clay whimpered through his shivers, pallid nearly to a glow. "We're gonna fucking die in here."

"We're not gonna die, Clay. We'll get up there…somehow," Zach managed.

Vicky let out a quick, shaky breath, emboldened by the discovery she'd made within herself. She and Brandon had to be the strong ones, she realized. They possessed the gifts, not Zach and Clay, and as such she felt an obligation to keep them safe.

Don't give in. Don't give up.

She decided to risk an attempt at communication. If Harrow hadn't detected her secret yet, maybe he never would (or maybe he'd already tried and failed, God running interference).

Hurry, Jerome! He's about to kill two people! Call the police! Send them here!

There was brief static crackling in her head, then silence, then crackling again. Finally Jerome's words found their way. *No cops, I'm sorry. They'll never believe us. All they'll do is lock the place down and stop us from gettin there. We'll be there soon. Just hang on.*

Like an eclipse, darkness crept across the circle of light. A stone lid was scraping over the opening, like a cover dragged very slowly over a manhole, shadowing the captives beneath, the sound heavy and anciently baleful. There was a brief stoppage, the lid halfway home, but then the little semicircle of sunlight was whittled down to a grim crescent.

"We're gonna die!" Clay wailed. "He's leaving us down here to die! No one will ever find us!"

In the limited light Vicky saw terror flashing in Clay's eyes, deep and glassy, and it made her think gravely of the jingling bells on Fortunato's cap. Above them the lid was almost fully shut now, just a sliver of light insisting its way down the well, the scrape of stone filling Vicky's head with images of tombs sealed shut and caskets partially loaded with dirt and poor, poor Fortunato.

It lingered that way a while, Harrow surely up there grinning, letting them fear the eventual darkness before it came – and when it did it was infinitely worse than Vicky could have imagined, the black crypt echoing with movement.

There was hectic flapping way up high, quickly descending, something panicking and careening down to them.

"What the hell is that?" Zach said.

"Please God, please God," Clay kept repeating.

Vicky bit her lower lip. The creature was hissing, bashing into the walls, but Vicky was focused inwardly now, eyes closed, for she could feel something rising in her heart…

…Brandon was drawing fast. The plan was…

No, she couldn't think it. She had to let him do it, had to disconnect herself. She began humming "You are my Sunshine," the first song that came to mind, remembering how her mother had always sung it upon waking her on schooldays and before church on Sundays. Sometimes, when Vicky had stubbornly remained beneath the covers, her mother had drifted into "My Favorite Things" or "Over the Rainbow", her voice nothing short of operatic to Vicky's younger version.

Once again the songs of her youth brought comfort. Vicky had often sung them in the weeks and months following her mother's death, singing more than talking in those days, but eventually she'd stopped and hadn't resumed, the songs seemingly buried along with her mother. But now they were back, guiding her through the darkness, helping to distract her from that which she desperately wanted to keep from Harrow.

By the time Vicky finished humming "Over the Rainbow," there was nothing but silence in the tomb. No flapping. Not a sound from Zach and Clay.

A bad feeling dug its claws into her. "Guys?" she said meekly, her voice echoing up the walls, but even as the word breathed life she knew it was useless, a frigid stab having lanced her thoughts, blackest intuition leaking out.

Zach and Clay had been killed.

The stone lid scraped open some time later, revealing the full moon almost directly overhead, yellowish and predatory. Wind stirred the silhouette branches, and a pair of birds brushed across the moon – but Vicky saw none of this, only the visions of what Brandon had done, her heart slamming against the wall of ice that encased it. Zach and Clay were gone from the well, their bodies strung up as Harrow had wanted them.

But how could Brandon have done this? He was supposed to have...

...*I had to, Vicky, I'm so sorry*, came his voice from some distant, dreadful place. *They would have killed you.*

His helplessness stung repeatedly at Vicky like angry wasps, yielding at last to a damp, slithering realization that perhaps their gifts were their curses. What if Harrow had carefully manipulated this entire thing, bringing them together and building their relationship, connecting them inextricably to heighten his leverage?

Characters upon a stage, easing toward our denouement, repeated an unfamiliar voice Vicky had been hearing occasionally these last several hours, not Harrow's voice or even Jones's voice – the voice of an impassive narrator checking his watch often and wondering how much longer this pointlessness would persist. But the words were monstrous with truth. Vicky and Brandon really were a pair of characters stumbling heedlessly about Harrow's stage, confined to the script, it seemed, thinking they were gifted but blind to the shackles, their actions dictated by a malevolent pen.

Yet the stage was not only an isolated chamber of ruination but a microcosm for…

…Oh Jesus, the stage is the world!

That's what Harrow had been doing all this time, Vicky now understood, gathering the tools necessary to deliver unprecedented damage from afar, like a computer whiz constructing a virus with intentions of unleashing it on the masses. His "soldiers" – more specifically, the powers of his soldiers – represented the intricate activation codes of the virus, and once someone was infected there would be no remedies. None of Harrow's soldiers had known how powerful they truly were, not until it was too late and they were enslaved.

Characters upon a stage, easing toward our denouement, she heard again, and buried her face in her hands.

***

WELCOME TO HARROW HALL

Everything was foggy and dreamlike when Brandon awoke. He vaguely remembered drawing Vicky away from Harrow Hall, safe on a distant beach, staring out at the horizon…more memories breaking through the haze…the voracious pain, being forced to draw the deaths of those two men, the awful *CRACKS* that had followed, sounds that had resembled a batted ball from great distance. But these cracks had been firmer, grittier, popping, twisting CRRAAAACKS, as though bones had been briefly wrenched through flesh and then snapped.

Brandon stood, his stomach nauseous. He was in the back row of elevated bleachers, looking down on a glassy swimming pool, each lane delineated by red and white ropes, the smell of chlorine pervading the hot air.

Groggy, Brandon was reminded for a confused moment of PE swimming classes, sitting in the bleachers all wet and uncomfortable after the mandatory lukewarm pre-shower, checking out the girls as they walked over with delicate, self-conscious steps, the fatties trailing the pack, eyes sunken, the teacher sizing them up with her furry arms at her hips, hair short and curly, a whistle around her neck–

Vicky! Where was Vicky? Had it worked? Had his drawing freed her from Harrow's grip? Brandon frantically searched the room, saw no one, but then, impossibly, there was someone sitting at the other end of the bleachers, grinning at him. Wait, was that Howie Mandel? He looked an awful lot like Howie Mandel.

Suddenly there was another person seated to Howie's right, a person who seemed to morph out of the bleachers, a hot young woman in an old-fashioned nurse's dress and white stockings – but the sight of her only sickened Brandon's stomach further. The mental fog was fading, fears for Vicky dominating. He couldn't feel anything from her end, couldn't hear her voice even when he strained to imagine it.

"You're gonna die, Brandon," came the slightest, quickest whisper in his head, like a hallucinated voice immediately following the stoppage of a loud iPod song – so scary at night in a dark room that it might belong to the Devil – and still Howie was grinning at Brandon, the nurse rising to her feet and approaching him.

"Hello, naughty boy." Flicking her tongue at Brandon, she extracted a syringe from her red fanny pack, a white cross at its center.

Brandon grimaced. "Stay away." He sought an exit but found only chain-link fences penning him high above the pool, the nurse uncapping the syringe, slowly moving closer, tongue wagging.

"Looks like someone needs to go back to sleep," she said, drawing to within ten feet. "But maybe you'd like a nice physical examination first, you know" – now she was biting the syringe and snapping on a pair of latex gloves – "just to make sure your vitals are in order."

Backpedaling, Brandon considered climbing the fence and jumping, but it was too high. At the other end of the bleachers, still sitting and grinning, Howie nodded dumbly at Brandon like a bobblehead.

With a lascivious growl the nurse tapped the syringe a few times and dropped to her hands and knees, crawling slowly to Brandon and licking her lips.

"Stay away from me!" he warned, but his voice was shaky. Somehow this lady was even scarier than Slaughterhouse Jones.

Brandon spun around, putting his arms over the railing and looking far down to a floor slicked with bloody puddles. He'd be crippled or dead if he jumped, unless he was already dead.

And why couldn't he hear Vicky anymore?

"Sleepy time, you sexy boy," the woman called from behind him, but when he turned around she and Howie were gone, replaced by two men in gray sweatpants and sweatshirts. They were mumbling something about a garden and pointing at Brandon.

"Guh…gurden…take us to gurden, Dr. Joutel. Want to see flowers," one of them said, clapping limply, a track of drool running lazily down his chin, the other man nodding repeatedly and giggling.

"This is ouuurr home!" the first man hollered. "We weally, weally like it here. Take us to the Balleyboo Gurden, Dr. Joutel. Please don't make us go."

Another morph, and now Coach Goderich was holding hands with one of the idiots, scowling, a whiteboard in hand, meaningless arrows scribbled all over it. "Joutel, you're doing laps after practice!" he pointed. "You better start taking practice more seriously, goddamn it, or I'll give the start to Vinny! I don't care if you're in a coma, Joutel – you better be ready for the game Friday night!"

Morph. Now the crowd was sprouting from the seats by the handful, most of the faces familiar to Brandon. There was Eddy Englehart, yelling at him about getting stronger, then a few teachers bitching at him about homework, and finally his brother ordering him to stop drinking, but it wasn't over yet. Next came that asshole from his bantam travel team, the one who'd held him down and threatened to break his finger. Eyes wide, he was smiling maniacally.

"Call yourself a pussy, Joutel, or I'll break your fucking neck!"

The thug turned and bumped into a few of the others, wobbling and jittering like a wound-up toy, Eddy bumping into one of the teachers on the next level down, Brady bumping into Coach Goderich, until the bleachers resembled a massive bumper car collision, everyone twisted together and rendered immobile, hands flailing and waving like zombies, their collective attention locked on Brandon, who'd climbed atop the fence railing and straddled it, his balls aching sharply from the initial crunch.

In the distance a raucous applause erupted, Harrow's voice proceeding it. "Upon the horizon I spot the denouement rolling in like ba-you fog!" he shouted, his voice adopting the strange inflections of a crazed preacher. "Prepare for a magnificent feat of art, ladies and gentlemen, our young hero to raze the empires with nothing but his bare right hand. In New Orleans the levees shall succumb, the stormwaters to swallow the souls of the damned. In Chicago a new fire will rage. And in Los Angeles, city of farces, you shall witness the ultimate suffering. Then our hero will turn his hand abroad, drawing until he can draw no more, all while our brilliant supporting cast members use their gifts to weaken the hearts and minds of the resistant. Impulses of suicide our sorcerers shall bestow. Raining fire and quaking earth our telekinetics shall precipitate. Sit back, relax, and enjoy the finale, ladies and gentlemen, boys and girls, for darkness is not far off. A new order has come, your leader soon to present himself to you!"

The lights dimmed and fell away. When they returned, Brandon found himself on center stage, blinded by the spotlight, the murmuring crowd shrouded in darkness and fog. Before him was a single object that brought relief but also dread, an object he'd spent his sophomore year filling with images of castles and hallways and, occasionally, naked girls riding motorcycles or skydiving.

But now his sketchbook was a thing of meaning, no longer inane in his hands but a legit game changer. But whose game?

Mostly silent now, unseen, the crowd waited before Brandon, coolly watchful and anticipatory like a tennis crowd, low voices scattered about the dark auditorium as he lifted his sketchbook, retrieved the pencil.

"Label each city you draw, child!" ordered Harrow from somewhere in the blackness, but Brandon raised his left middle finger and waved it in an arc for everyone to see.

"Fuck you all!!!" With that, Brandon drew…

Chapter 10

Cole knew something was very wrong when the shattering thunderbolt echoed down the entry road.

The sky was striated with wispy clouds, none of them formidable. Today's chance of precipitation was ten percent, according to the latest weather report. So what the hell had cracked that whip across the valley?

Cole, who'd been fresh off a needed nap when the eruption came, was now speeding down the entry road toward Center Street, where he assumed the event – explosion? – had taken place. He'd been at the institution all night, questioning the guards and searching for the man who'd said his name was Harrow, his desperate efforts meeting what he'd feared all along would be inevitable failure. It had been a perfectly harmless night, the guards reporting nothing strange, no oddballs claiming to be magicians, no young women near Harrow Hall, nothing.

But now, a few minutes past noon, something was happening, something big. Cole could feel it, and as soon as he rounded the corner and accelerated up Center Street, he could see it. The upper portion of Harrow Hall was afire, flames snarling through the windows and slithering up the walls to the roof, where they swayed and flared triumphantly in the wind, smoke rising up into a black, angry cloud previously blocked from view by the trees.

Cole parked well down the road from Harrow Hall and reported the fire, then stepped out to watch the devastation, the heat licking him even at a distance. For a stunned, awful moment, he thought he heard someone trapped inside, but then reality took hold. There was no one in there, no one to save – yet he kept thinking he registered something above the roaring, proliferating beast. Faint screams.

Impossible. It had to be a trick of the blaze, but suddenly Cole was sure of it, though not because of an external scream but an internal one. A voice was screaming in his head, so loud and shrill he thought his eardrums would burst…and somehow he knew the scream belonged to a person stuck inside, helpless, destined to die unless…

Cole glanced back down the road, hearing sirens in the distance but knowing the firefighters would be too late. The screams were gone from his head now, but the urgency remained.

Cole jogged toward the building, driven reactively by the very reason he'd signed up for the police academy – the desire to keep people safe.

The closer Cole got to the front doors of Harrow Hall, the more intense the waves of heat became, beating on him and warning him to stay away. He frantically searched the windows for the source of the screams, wondering briefly if he was insane. A panic attack? Was he freaking out? No, damn it, there was something more to all of this, something he felt but didn't understand – something he might never understand.

Looking up at Harrow Hall, daunted by the dominating blaze, the sirens growing louder, an image suddenly flashed into Cole's head: a young woman trapped in the basement. Cole immediately recognized the lowest level of Harrow Hall from the fleeting image, and now he was charging around back, down a steep, rugged hill to the rear parking lot, eyeing the door that would take him inside, thanking God this part of the building wasn't on fire…yet.

Shakily, he unlocked the door and released thin swirls of smoke. Heat baked off the walls and the pavement, radiating in surges that stung him. He imagined the inside of a microwave, deathly rotation soon to be had. For a moment he just stood there against the gently outpouring stream of smoke, covering his face with his shirt, a man torn between impulse and fear.

The entirety of the main basement corridor was impossible to see, new phantasms of smoke and shadow curling and creeping upward and outward, nothing but blackness at the farthest depths.

Cole gathered an orphaned brick from the parking lot and propped open the door, still wondering if he would go through with this. The scream that had compelled him now seemed more like a panicked hallucination, but its memory kept echoing in his head, high and piercing, a cornered, desperate scream, a final plea for rescue. Its source was that young woman he'd briefly seen, her face vivid but only for a second – and now Cole *knew* he was part of something greater, the thought of pawns on a chess board springing to mind.

Brandon's girl?

"I'm crazy, absolutely nuts," Cole said, stepping shallowly into the basement. He squinted, tried not to breathe, the smoke seeming to come at him with greater force, as if wind-driven and well aware of the intruder.

He looked behind him, the door like a portal to another dimension, sunlight withering, smoke intensifying. He felt his way along the wall, trying to remember the layout of the basement. He knew there would be an intersecting corridor not far down, which would take him to the heart of the basement, where stacks of boxes and equipment awaited assignment from state officials.

"No," Cole murmured. The rectangle of sunlight was now just a hazy spec behind him, barely visible through the smoke. "I can't do this."

Cole turned, took a few steps toward safety, but then the screams resounded through the basement. This time they weren't in his head.

Chapter 11

Jerome kept expecting something to happen now that they were close to the institution. Something horrible. They would be ambushed again, he feared, their attackers scarcely different than the Viet Cong in their approach yet infinitely more powerful, a possible threat lurking behind every tree, death never far off, trailing them like a persistent dog on a scent.

This was war.

Their recently augmented group was strategizing in the overgrown parking lot of a deserted, dilapidated motel set back from the road, a trio of birds circling them directly overhead in a darkly betokening formation. It seemed like the damn things could sense their imminent deaths and were waiting for lunch to be served.

Jerome shuddered, the August heat suddenly ineffective against the cold of dread.

"We'll set up at each end of the facility. Once we confirm the target, we'll attack from different angles," Paradis said, standing at the center of the huddle.

"Yes, sir," said one of the two brothers Paradis had summoned from elsewhere in Ohio (the leaders of the newly arrived men). Both brothers were former Marines, and they'd brought weapons and tactical gear for everyone, including bulletproof helmets and body armor.

Very little of the gear fit Sky, and even Jerome felt heavy in it. With this much equipment and weaponry, they looked like they belonged on the Gaza Strip, prepared for the next inevitable clash.

"Bordeleau Brothers, I want you moving in from the north, mirroring our approach from the south," Paradis instructed, pointing to a map on the laptop one of his men had given him. "Park off Springer Street and proceed south through the woods." He turned to Jerome. "I want you and two of our reinforcements to come from the west – we'll give you a GPS and a radio. When you get to the North Ridge Street entrance, move east toward Harrow Hall from the entry road. Based on what we can tell from our research, you should come to an intersection. That's where you'll take a right and proceed south toward the building on my call. It'll be on your right, but stay well back of it and find cover that offers a good place to shoot from. We're gonna come in heavy and hit Harrow Hall hard. After the initial strike, you help us take out anyone who tries to assist the target. We have to accept that there may be collateral damage, but if we can finish this guy it'll be well worth it."

Jerome nodded repeatedly as he absorbed the information, occasionally glancing up to the laptop screen. If a mirror had been placed before him, he wouldn't have been surprised to see himself forty years younger, dressed in tiger stripe fatigues, ready for another day in Hell.

Paradis handed Jerome an AR-15. "Fully automatic," he said with a wink. "Fires eight hundred rounds per minute."

"What about us?" Sky demanded.

"Yeah," Ki said with his inscrutable stare. "No bazookas?"

Paradis shook his head. "I'm afraid it's the end of the line for you two. I need people with combat experience on this thing. You stay here and defend the vehicles we leave behind."

"Combat experience?" Sky shouted. "I think getting driven off the road and attacked by a fucking monster qualifies as combat. You think Willy would have brought us on if we couldn't handle things?"

Ki shrugged. "What she said."

"That's not combat – that's running from combat," Jerome heard one of the Bordeleau brothers comment from behind, the other adding, "These people are a waste of space," – and thank Christ Sky hadn't caught any of it, too busy getting in Paradis's face.

"Why did you give us this gear if you're not taking us?" Sky challenged.

Eyes gathering a dark intensity, Paradis stared down at Sky for a few calculated seconds. "They could come at you from the woods and try to disable our vehicles." A moment later, when Sky seemed near ready to punch him: "No offense, miss, but what you've been doing so far is tracking and running. You're very skilled at intelligence, but you don't know war. When the shitstorm comes, there's no room for people who don't know what they're doing. You're not trained for this. You'll freeze up, and then you'll die. Worse, you might get one of us killed trying to protect you."

"He's right," Jerome said, bracing himself. "You and Ki have done enough – let me finish this with these guys. We'll blow his ass out of the water."

Without even glancing away from Paradis, Sky said, "We won't freeze – I can promise you that. Come on, let us do something to help you, even if it's sniping people with Jerome."

Paradis exchanged skeptical looks with his men. Then, shockingly, he relented, telling one of his guys, "Grab two semi-autos. We'll give them a quick instructional and let them have a few more minutes to reconsider their funerals." He pointed firmly at Sky. "But make no mistake, nobody's taking any bullets for you two, except maybe Jerome. If you're coming, you better not bring anything you aren't prepared to lose, and that includes your heads. Stay behind Jerome, do what he says, and pray like hell you don't get shot."

Jerome assumed Paradis's tough talk would scare them off, but after getting familiarized with the rifles, Sky and Ki seemed even more emboldened, like fresh soldiers amped up and ready for battle. But Jerome had learned that no one is ever ready for war – it pulls you down and steals your mind and reshapes your existence with unforgiving hammers of violence, each fallen comrade or foe blasting out another chunk of the person you once were, the cavities slathered with oozing black pus.

Behind Sky and Ki, the Bordeleau brothers and Paradis's men were examining their weapons. Jerome wondered what Paradis had told all of these people about Harrow; and who were these guys, anyway, a motley bunch of mercenaries who waited for the call to kill someone, traveling throughout the country upon request and taking out specific targets?

Whoever they were, they operated with the promise of big money; that much Jerome could tell simply by observing their stockpile of weapons. And as long as they succeeded in retiring their targets, it didn't seem like they cared who died in the process. Jerome wished Paradis had shut down Sky's petition to fight, but instead he'd conceded and handed her and Ki a pair of Remington sniper rifles. To Paradis, Sky and Ki were as expendable as the rounds soon to be fired.

That meant it was up to Jerome to keep his new friends out of war. They were fearless and unfailingly loyal, but they weren't soldiers.

Above them the birds soared lazily, waiting. The once azure sky had softened to a milky blue, laced with watchful, somehow conspiratorial clouds, the universe itself feeling like it was stacked against them.

Looking skyward, Jerome wondered what messages Bu would have gleaned if he were still alive. How would he and Willy and Rosa have proceeded if they were here? Would Willy have actually let those without experience in combat fight Harrow?

"Let's get moving. Remember, we stay in constant radio communication," Paradis said, and piled into the SUV with his men.

The Bordeleau brothers, who'd each driven a vehicle here, split their men among white industrial vans, leaving Jerome, Sky, Ki, and two of the Bordeleaus' reinforcements with a silver Ford Expedition. Jerome eyed the SUV severely, then glanced up to the birds, which had dipped off to the west to attend to more pressing matters. (*They'll be dead soon enough, guys. We can come back then, swoop down and have ourselves a snack.*)

Jerome tried to clear his mind of awful thoughts, for he needed to focus on keeping Sky and Ki safe. They were desperate to avenge their friends' deaths and finish Willy's mission, but they didn't know war, plain and simple. They didn't know what an existence of killing was like, their hearts never bent irreparably. They'd been shot at and run off the road and attacked by Harrow's multi-headed monstrosity, but they'd never taken a life. They'd never seen the depth of fear in a man's eyes who knows his remaining minutes are few–

"You ready or what, Jerome?"

Jerome blinked a few times and returned, taking in Sky's youthful face, but for a split-second the blue hair was gone, her face replaced by Jennie's face, and it was like he was about to drive his own daughter to her death. Memories came dashing back – accompanying Jennie to her cancer treatments; doctors eventually saying there was nothing they could do (THE CANCER HAS SPREAD); Jennie smiling bravely through her tears and wiping his own tears away, telling him, *It'll be okay, Dad. We both know this isn't the end*; praying endlessly with Jennie's fiancé during the months of palliative care; cursing God when it was all over, the same God that had taken Elise a year earlier.

Jennie had lost her battle with cancer, and there'd been nothing Jerome could do about it. Elise had been hit by a drunk driver on her way home from the grocery store, and there'd been nothing Jerome could do about it. His comrades had been killed in Nam, killed over and over and over, and there'd been nothing Jerome could do about it.

But now there was something he could do about it. He could stop death from taking, everyone he loved always taken away – but today he would thwart the greedy hand of death.

"Jerome, what are you waiting for?" Sky said.

"You're not goin," Jerome answered calmly, and it was like a terrific weight had been lifted from him, up and away, rising toward the milky sky.

Paradis and his men were pulling out of the parking lot, bound for the institution, the Bordeleau brothers right behind them in their vans. But Jerome remained where he was, the two men Paradis had assigned to Jerome's mission nodding in support. "Good call, bud – leave 'em here," one of them said. "Don't need 'em shooting *us* by accident."

"I'm so sorry," Jerome told Sky, "but I had a daughter once, and if she were standin where you're standin and some other guy was in my place, I'd want him to keep you away from this."

Ki stepped forward beside Sky, his ancient eyes narrowing in betrayal. "We team, yes? We do this together."

"No, no, we don't do this together," Jerome insisted, stepping back and rubbing traces of moisture from his eyes, Jennie's image still lingering in his head. "I've got enough blood on my hands, man, and I ain't watchin no more of my friends get killed. My wife and daughter are gone. Willy's gone, Bu and Rosa are gone, all them boys from the war are gone. Don't put me through this again. You're not ready for war – no one's ready for war. It's gonna surround yo asses and swallow you up! You won't freeze like that dude said – there won't be time for you to freeze. You'll just die!"

Jerome didn't realize he was shouting and waving his arms wildly until their stunned, frightened faces finally registered in his head, Ki's eyes fixed horribly like those of a child who's just learned there is no Santa Claus in traumatizing fashion. Sky's mouth had fallen open, her eyes blinking repeatedly.

Above them the birds drifted a little closer.

Chapter 12

Harrow was instructing the most advanced of his telekinetics when the explosion gutted half of the backstage room, consuming dozens of his soldiers and – far more devastatingly – the Great Board in a fiery chasm. The ceiling collapsed, the walls bowing and crumbling inward, but the Spirits were there just in time to rescue Harrow's remaining soldiers.

Furious, Harrow invented himself upon the stage, but the flames were far too intense there as well, and so he did not remain long, transporting himself up to the balcony. Only in his home could he achieve such feats, but now his home was burning.

"The boy!" he shouted, but how could this have happened? Each drawing required Harrow's approval before taking effect, each and every one.

Unless…no, the magic of a boy could never best that of his master.

***

Sickened by what came into his head, Brandon jerked his pencil away from the sketchbook as if it were a lit match about to contact a lake of gasoline. Its once sharpened point having dulled with each sketch closer to the verge of uselessness, the pencil now felt like a grenade in his right hand.

Brandon's chest had gone cold with the premonition, his forehead sweating thinly. His breaths kept sticking in his throat, stifled by fear-induced blockages.

Vicky – she was still in Harrow Hall, the shards of realization jagging through him. He could even see her now, trapped in…

…the image was briefly gone, then back again, rising and fading, Brandon desperate to see something more, anything…

…Yes, yes, there she was, in a dark tunnel somewhere – it must be in the basement, he figured, or an underground passage beneath one of the other buildings. It didn't matter, as long as he drew quickly. He had to draw her out of this place, had to DRAW NOW AND MAKE IT WORK THIS TIME, his hand shaking with panicked urgency, scribbling furiously, but there was a crisp snap, shavings falling loose, hardly any graphite left.

"NOOOO!" he screamed, scraping every last available modicum of gray onto the page, a caustic voice suddenly in his head, ordering him to stop.

"It's no use, child. Sweet Victoria shall perish. Return to your task before death turns its gaze upon *you*! There are still so many cities to draw."

***

Forced into the most desperate of tactics, Vicky had attempted to somehow jam the signals of Harrow's army, to cross up the wires just long enough to allow Brandon to…

…and she'd done it! She could feel his triumph, but with it came a cold, hectic, confused fear. Suddenly she knew what he'd done, attempting to draw her in a safe place, but it hadn't worked. She was still in the tomb, birds flapping above her, the cool wind whispering down to her.

"Very, very bad your boyfriend has been, Victoria!" Harrow shouted inwardly.

For a while Vicky kept thinking she saw flitting shadows amidst the blackness, but soon she was preoccupied not with something seen but instead something inhaled. Smoke.

The odor quickly strengthened, forcing Vicky to cover her face with the fleece jacket Harrow had given her. But now she felt smothered, not merely by the jacket but the thought of looming death, its presence betrayed by a burst of dull crackles behind Vicky.

She spun around to see flickering orange beyond a curving wall, steadily advancing. She was no longer in a pit but a tunnel, it seemed, the cramped enclosure having transformed into a thin corridor.

And there was only one way to run with the fire coming at her.

Achy with fear, Vicky was able to sprint a short distance before the fire threatened from both directions. Still pressing the jacket over her nose and mouth, she frantically searched for a recess in the stone walls, any staircase or hallway that might lead her to safety.

But there was nothing, only the converging flames. Behind her the relentless fire was maybe thirty feet away, the onrushing blaze ahead of her even closer. She tried to think reasonably, but the smoke made her feel lightheaded and panicky, the taste of it peeling her throat.

Knowing she couldn't help herself, drowning in her fear, Vicky begged for a rescuer – *Someone find me! Brandon, please, I'm trapped, draw something, anything!*

Scorched by the heat, she removed the jacket from her face and screamed until her voice faltered, the flames roaring even closer, the stone ceiling crawling orange with shadows.

I'm gonna burn, just like in my nightmares!!

Vicky collapsed to her knees, tried to broadcast another…

…but suddenly there was a shouting voice and a rush of water behind her. Vicky whirled around and saw the fire slowly being suppressed, a few flames attempting to caper away but ultimately falling to defeat, a broadening shadow with a hose breaking through the smoke.

WELCOME TO HARROW HALL

***

Cole couldn't believe his luck, though he knew this was more than mere luck.

Two gray water tanks were waiting for him on a cart in the middle of the next corridor, each unit equipped with a hose and valve that made his task dramatically easier. Pushing the cart wound up offering a greater challenge than extinguishing the blaze, for the tanks were fully loaded.

Though the fire survived the first tank's contents, it was no match for the reinforcement. After the flames were quashed, Cole hurried to the source of the screams, a young woman who leaped into his arms. *The young woman from his vision!*

Another fire was rushing in from behind her, and Cole took her hand and led her away, thinking his job was done but never imagining what would come next. When they were outside again, panting and coughing and staring up at the burning building, the woman's first words nearly brought Cole to his knees.

"Brandon, I think he's still inside!"

Chapter 13

Jerome was about to leave Sky and Ki behind when he was jolted by a vision, brief but unmistakable, a vision of Sky's and Ki's bodies in this very parking lot, the birds that currently circled above them feasting on their bloody corpses.

The other men were waiting for Jerome in the SUV, but he turned briskly away from the vehicle and faced his friends. "If you guys are sure you want to go, then who am I to stop you?" he said, prepared for Sky's wrath.

She stormed up to him and slapped his shoulder hard, though Jerome barely felt it with the protective gear on. "Have you lost your mind, Jerome? You're our teammate, not our fucking parent! You don't get to make decisions for us."

Behind her, Ki was staring up at the birds. "We should go. Right now," he murmured, the others protesting briefly upon seeing the change of plans.

"Your funerals," the driver said.

Sky waved a hand. "Just drive."

Sandwiched between Sky and Ki in the back, Jerome braced for one of them to ask about his wife and daughter; he'd opened himself up with his terrified rant, and now surely they would ask.

Surprisingly, though, they stayed silent and focused and scared. They tried to hide it, but Jerome knew far too well the creeping shadow of fear.

When they made it to North Ridge Street, the GPS device estimating two minutes till arrival, an update was sent over the radio. But this time there was no reply from Paradis or anyone else.

"We're on North Ridge," the man in the passenger seat repeated. "You copy?"

Silence, the inchoate traces of a vision gathering at the edges of Jerome's mind, destined to amount to something helpful if they kept accruing. He knew he had to be patient, but the desire for communication and knowledge tugged at him, pulling him in a direction he didn't want to go, outward when he should have been focusing inward.

"J.S., you copy?" the driver shouted into the radio when a red SUV came up quickly in the mirrors. "Hey, anyone copy? We might have company here on North Ridge."

Ki glanced behind them at the SUV. "Old lady driving. She look mean but not killer."

Nonetheless, the driver brought the Expedition to a stop in the shoulder, his friend readying his weapon, but the red SUV charged past them.

They all let out sighs of varying intensity. Again they tried the radio, receiving nothing from Paradis or the others.

"I don't like this, not at all. Harrow got to them, I think," Jerome said, scanning the road ahead, which swept around a shadowy, tree-lined curve toward the edge of town, where Harrow's institution was waiting for them. "Somethin ain't right. They would have responded by now."

"What next?" Ki asked the group, but the two men in the front were arguing with each other now.

"Come on, people, get it together!" Jerome shouted.

Even amidst his dread and confusion, Jerome recognized the completion of life's circle. In Nam, he'd received orders and obeyed superiors, some of whom had been killed, never to issue another order, never again to kiss their wives or hold their children, never to see another sunrise, dying in the chaos of their missions. They'd made their moves and paid the ultimate price for them, sacrificing themselves for comrades and country – and now command had fallen to Jerome in a new war, this one on home soil, unseen and unfelt but soon to unleash unprecedented ruin if it wasn't won.

A new mission, Jerome at the helm. Willy was gone, his thirst for vengeance unquenched, and now Ki and Sky were looking expectantly to Jerome, just as he, himself, had once looked to his superiors. In spite of what Sky had said a few minutes ago in the parking lot, Jerome was apparently in charge, their leader, the man who would give the instructions, life or death awaiting his decisions.

But he held a major advantage his superiors in Nam hadn't enjoyed. In his late, seemingly worthless years, God had bestowed upon him a gift of untold potential.

Jerome strained his mind, desperate to force the embryonic vision that had nearly arrived before, grains of sand that might have piled up into something understandable. But the grains were gone now, only useless vestiges remaining.

"We should wait here a few minutes and try to keep the plan together," Jerome said at last, Ki and Sky nodding in agreement, the newcomers offering no protest. "The others are supposed to strike first."

"What if they're under attack? How long should we wait?" Sky said. "What if they need our help?"

"If they need *our* help, we screwed," Ki murmured. "They got heaviest weapons."

"Two minutes," Jerome said. "Maybe Harrow messed up their radios and the plan's still a go. If there's no response in two minutes, we're going in."

An assenting silence ruled. Then Sky released the floodgates Jerome had hoped to keep sealed.

Yet he'd somehow known it would be Sky to open them wide – any other reaction simply wouldn't have been consistent with the personality of the young woman Jerome had come to love. She was like a brazen, rowdy niece you couldn't help but adore, a rebel with spirit and sass and charm, that person in every group who isn't afraid to swear at the dinner table or stray from the boundaries of expectation. Sky swore without shame and tossed politically incorrect comments around without apology, but she cared more deeply about her friends than any of them. She cared so much that, even now, with Paradis and the others MIA and Harrow's army quite possibly advancing on them – with their combined life expectancy perhaps five minutes – she wanted to know Jerome's story, wanted to identify with him in a way that surpassed the bond of soldiers/teammates. They were fighting a war together, but they were more than comrades, he realized – they were family.

"What happened to your wife and daughter?" Sky said quietly, her hand on Jerome's wrist as the others tried the radio again up front.

Even though Sky's words made Jerome wince, a smile played at the corners of his lips because he was glad she cared, glad this person he'd met only a few days ago cared enough to ask about Elise and Jennie, glad his life had intersected with those of Sky and Ki and the others, people who'd brought light to him on a very dark journey, people who'd made him laugh and delivered joy back into his existence. Being with them was like emerging from a dank, black cellar and feeling the sun on his face; gone were the lonely nights in Canal Nine, no one there but McGreevy and the bottle to provide relief. Even his friends hadn't found a way through to him, unable to pull him back into the sun – though Calvin had tried his damnedest – but now, finally, his life had meaning again, brilliant in its intrinsic value, simple yet profound.

Miraculously, a group of strangers had given Jerome what he'd so desperately craved over the last decade, a sense of being a part of something again, something important and impactful where the people cared about him and the other way around, something he could take to the Big Guy upstairs as proof his life was consequential all the way to the stormy end. A family.

And Jerome had found his new place among five strangers in a slow-moving van, rediscovering himself and also awakening to a gift he'd never known he possessed. It had come at a steep cost, though. They'd gone through Hell these last few days, but now they were stronger for it, their bond forged in steel, somehow as sacred as the bonds Jerome had shared with his very best friends from the Army and the Lower Ninth Ward. He'd initially entered the circle with Sky and Ki out of obligation, dutifully accommodating the group ritual, but now they were in *his* circle, entrenched comfortably enough in his heart that he knew he could trust them with his opened scars.

Back in the parking lot, Jerome had been willing to let Sky and Ki hate him in order to keep them safe. But suddenly he couldn't envision proceeding without them.

"Hell, if we might die today, I guess I'll tell you guys," Jerome chuckled, and then, like a tide finding its way in, the words were flowing forth, a natural thing that seemed not only right but fitting. Maybe this was how he would have felt if he'd gone to those grief counselors Calvin recommended, but this felt inestimably better than confiding in a stranger. Sky and Ki weren't paid to care about him – they simply cared because they considered him family.

When Jerome finally confessed his greatest sin, he felt not merely unburdened but unchained, freed from the fetters he'd thought would always hold him. Before long Sky's hand had found its way into Jerome's – and there was Ki's faint but somehow firm grip on his shoulder. They weren't scoffing at him or gasping in horror but doing their best to understand, their continued support from both sides nearly choking Jerome with tears midsentence. But he kept going, forcing himself all the way to the end, and when the tide had finally climbed as far as it would go up the shore, Sky said, "I would have punched that asshole, too." And Ki's reply: "Why you punch him?" he said sternly, then came his hint of a smile. "Why not shoot him? Would have been easier."

Above them those three black birds were circling. In the distance, beyond the trees, smoke was rising from Harrow Hall.

And the two strangers – they had disappeared, Jerome not even realizing it until the windows shattered.

Chapter 14

The woman's words were pouring into Cole's head, but he knew they couldn't be true. Of course they couldn't be true!

Brandon was in a hospital many miles away, lying comatose, as safe as one could possibly be in his untenable state. There, death might insist upon him quietly, like a night wind whispering against the darkened windows of a house – but he wasn't facing a violent, blazing death, trapped in a building as the flames drew nearer.

Yet that was precisely what this woman – she'd identified herself as Vicky Eldridge – was adamantly telling Cole. She even knew Brandon's last name, and she could describe him as well as Cole could, claiming they had both been imprisoned.

"By who?" Cole demanded, the back of Harrow Hall burning before them, and when she said Harrow's name Cole knew the impossible had menaced its way to the institution, a place where nothing of importance had ever interrupted his overnight shift...until Friday night.

And now it was all coming together. The bus, the people on board, the strange lights and smells and sounds in Harrow Hall – all of it pieced rapidly together by Vicky Eldridge, who was begging Cole to save Brandon.

But the building was completely engulfed now, glass and brick exploding and raining down on the back parking lot, forcing them even further away. Fire engines were blaring down Center Street toward the inferno, blue flashes of police units trailing them.

"Come on, follow me," Cole said, and led Vicky up the hill to the street, where they met the firemen scrambling down from the first truck.

Cole wondered why the on-duty guards still weren't here – surely they would have driven down to Center Street to at least witness the chaos.

"Is there anyone inside?" one of the firemen shouted above the blaze, but then he collapsed, as did all of the others, a collective loss of consciousness.

Hands glued to his head, Cole was scarcely able to trust the surreal scene before him – but Vicky seemed to know what was happening.

"Harrow's doing this," she said, a half-terrified, half-determined glow to her blue eyes. "It's up to us to save Brandon. We have to go in."

***

The fire of his own creation was coming for Brandon, that which he'd engendered with his art now crawling up every stairwell and rushing through every hallway until it found him.

An evil herald, smoke invaded with gathering strength beneath the locked door. Heat oppressed and penetrated the walls. Brandon knew he was going to die in this room, knew he would burn, yet even though his horror seized him firmly, his primary focus was Vicky's safety. He tried to reach out to her as smoke filled the room, as the oven walls grew steadily hotter, but with his panic came thoughts that they'd never met at all, Vicky's image a fabrication that had been planted in his mind by Harrow.

"You tried to betray me, boy!" the magician's voice called from great distance of mind and moment. It sounded like it was originating from everywhere, echoing and cascading simultaneously from years past and days not yet had, the voice of the building and the man who controlled it.

Slowly, a few of the people from the pool room came shimmering through the walls, first the Howie Mandel doppelganger in a black tuxedo and next the young woman in the nurse's dress and stockings, her tongue wagging back and forth as she crawled to Brandon.

Then, all at once, Coach Goderich and Eddy Englehart and the others flashed through the walls, even Brady, but this fake, Harrow-inspired Brady was a mean one who scowled and shook his head reproachfully.

Soon the room was filled with other people from Brandon's life, the nurse clinging to his arm and whispering, "Let me show you how to use your equipment, sexy boy. It's nice and steamy in here – how about we lose some clothes?" Behind her, a whiteboard in hand, Coach Goderich was frenetically drawing up a play: "This is how to find the five-hole, kid!" he shouted, tracing his black marker along two faceoff circles on the board, then rendering a long cylinder down the center. "You're gonna rip her clothes off…", but Brandon wasn't hearing him anymore, searching the madness for Vicky, praying he wouldn't see her among the throng of psychosis.

Smoke clouded the room, heat pounding inward from the blaze just outside, a foggy orange glow brightening beneath the door.

"This is where it ends, boy!" Harrow taunted as Brandon tore free of the woman, kicking and shoving himself into the door. "Perhaps I'll provide you a pencil so you can make one final drawing – that of a poor lost boy who thought he could outsmart the magician, a boy who thought the great show could be his. And do you know how this image appears? Melted is his flesh, incinerated are his bones, child, and in the end there will only live ashes and whispers about a boy who died unfulfilled, leaving nothing for the world to ponder but useless scribbles and scratches, not even a drip in the memory of a woman's well. And do include in your drawing a peek of sweet Victoria, her purest heart burning beside that of the boy who dared to trespass, a pair of young magicians who refused their callings, instead seeking the pursuits of greed and light. But those who refuse their callings – only the wrath of flame will find them, boy, only the wrath of flame!"

Chapter 15

"Down! Get down!" Jerome shouted, lunging past Sky and firing through the blown out back window.

Their attacker was unleashing a heavy bombardment from the woods to their left, the SUV sinking on sudden flats, Jerome vaguely aware as he exchanged fire of new enemy shots coming from the other side of the vehicle.

Scrambling to the floor, where Ki and Sky were facedown, Jerome removed the automatic AR-15 from its case, glass and debris raining down on them. The SUV rang and clanked like railroad tracks in a hailstorm, musical and deathly.

"I'll take 'em out, just stay down!" Jerome urged, springing up and leveling the muzzle against the base of the window frame, his words barely audible above the barrage. He knew he should have been hit by now, but, as in war, the miracle of survival hardly broke the surface of understanding, pushed quickly below again by the need to keep shooting, keep surviving.

With the relentless storm of the automatic weapon, Jerome splintered trees and by sheer probability caught the shooter hiding among them. Military instincts taking over, he exited the vehicle and used it as a shield, ready for the next–

But the other gunman to the right of the SUV was no longer shooting but screaming, afire from the waist up, less than twenty feet from the road and zagging toward Jerome. As if the man's lower body had been doused with an accelerant, it became fully engulfed within seconds, inexplicable, but suddenly Jerome knew.

For he had turned to find Sky standing in the middle of the road, well back of the SUV, stone-still and staring at the man whose death wails drowned any whispers Jerome might have heard from his soul being dragged away.

The man collapsed onto his stomach, dead and burning.

"Sky, Sky, what are you…?"

But Sky wasn't hearing him, her stare vacant and seemingly lost to hypnotism. At last, with Jerome shaking her gently, she came out of it.

Jesus, she doesn't just see things in fire – she can create fire!

When Jerome got Sky back to the SUV, Ki alerted them to the distant smoke. Through the trees it was visible to the northeast, billowing up into an angry black cloud that overspread the approximate location of the institution.

"You think they blew it up already?" Ki said, smiling hopefully. He winked at Jerome. "You great shot, by the way."

"What's happening? Harrow! Did we get him?" Groaning, Sky rubbed her temples and winced.

"We'll sneak in, just like Paradis instructed," Jerome said. "But we'll need new wheels – this thing is shot. Sky, how you doin? Can you count to ten for me?"

She did so, then said her full name, which was good enough for Jerome. He took her by the shoulders. "Whatever you did back there – if you can do it again when we fight Harrow, this war's ours! Ours, you hear? Just let it fly, girl!"

"That's the thing," she murmured. "I don't even know what happened."

There was no time to discuss it. In a few moments Jerome had a blue Subaru Outback pulled over at gunpoint, the driver begging not to be killed. "Just take it, please! It's yours!"

"So sorry, ma'am, but this is a matter of national security," Jerome said, sliding into the driver's seat.

Sky having bustled into the passenger seat, Ki in the back, Jerome sped away and followed a series of wooded curves until they came to a straightaway and the institution was sprawling off to their right, the black cloud swelling beyond a cluster of buildings and a thin patch of woods.

"A building over there is absolutely torched," Sky said. "I can see fire engines and cop cars – that must be Harrow Hall! Paradis must have already lit them up."

Ki leaned up front. "You think Harrow dead?"

"No, definitely not," Jerome said, a new vision arriving. Harrow had survived the fire, his glare directed not upon a nearer target but Jerome, challenging him to the final battle.

Taken absolutely by the vision, Jerome almost passed the entrance to the road that would bring them into the institution, a pair of gates already swung open to allow the emergency vehicles in.

Jerome took a hard right, the car's back end slewing violently left before regaining stability, his unbelted passengers thrown from their seats, Sky shouldering into Jerome.

"Jesus, Jerry!" she shouted. "Don't get us killed before we even find Harrow."

Jerome wasn't receiving her words, though, a fresh series of visions nearly causing him to stop the car. He saw Paradis and his men turning their weapons upon each other, then the Bordeleau brothers doing the same, everyone riven with bullets and felled, a few of them dead instantly, others gasping and writhing and clutching mortal wounds, their souls soon to be whisked away with muted whisper-screams, desperate to stay but compelled to leave.

And the two men who'd been assigned to Jerome, Sky, and Ki – those had been the very two men who'd tried to kill them back on the road, these latest visions revealed, Jerome having finished one man and Sky cooking the other.

Harrow. He controlled them. What if he does the same to us?

Now Harrow's voice was rasping in Jerome's head, a different sounding voice. Instantly – violently – realization slammed into Jerome's heart and he knew what Harrow was, dispatched by…"Yes, Jerome, that's precisely who sent me here, and now you will know my Master, but not before you watch them suffer!"

Another vision, this one clattering against Jerome's skull – there was water everywhere, the whole damn city flooded, and it was New Orleans, unmistakable, the Superdome and skyline in the distance, and oh Jesus Christ, no, a new vision, this one of people floating in the water, people screaming and begging from their rooftops, people left stranded on highway overpasses, a child swept away from her mother, carried off by the floodwaters, and there were close-up images of buildings now, this was the Lower Ninth Ward! Calvin's ruined shop, Mrs. Dawson up on her roof and bloody, her dog in her arms, and across the street was Jerome's house, his little place in the world, where so many Christmases and birthday parties and weekend breakfasts had brought him joy, where his little girl had grown up, where he and Elise had spent long nights talking, never knowing it would all end so soon, that their family would shatter and the storm would come to claim what little remained. And all Jerome could see now of his house peeking out above the water was the roof, just the goddamn roof, and the screams wouldn't stop, the screams of soldiers long dead and Lower Ninth residents soon to perish.

"The storm is coming, Jerome. It's coming for you and the place you hold dear, fool. You should have chosen immortality, but now the man who wanted war shall finally die in its grand theater."

A slap to the face. At first Jerome had no idea where he was, images of flooding and mayhem and jungles still haunting. But then he forced his eyes to see outward – never inward again, for that was how Harrow would take control – and reality came slowly back to him, Sky in his face, Ki leaning forward. Somehow Jerome had safely pulled over, his hands sweating and trembling.

"What the hell is happening to us, Jerrry?" Sky said. "It's him, Harrow. He's making us lose it."

"The visions," Jerome panted, feeling like he'd just sprinted a mile. "They were insane. Harrow, he put them in my head. He's controllin me – all of us!"

Sky grabbed his arm, held it firm. "Look at me! No, seriously, look into my eyes!" Jerome did so, the intensity of Sky's stare like a life raft amidst the psychological drowning. "We're gonna get through this, Jerry! We're gonna kill this bastard, but we need to keep it together."

"You our only shot," Ki murmured. "No time for loony now."

Jerome nodded resolutely. "Damn straight. No more loony. Gonna kill this fucker." Yet he still felt afraid, direly afraid, as if his mind might succumb to Harrow's darkness at any moment unless he constantly supplied it with purposeful messages. "Gonna kill this sumbitch. Take out the enemy, just like Nam."

Sky smiled hesitantly, wishfully. "There you go. That's more like it, buddy. Now let's do this!"

"Time for win!" Ki added.

Even though Jerome's mind felt like a house of cards in a windstorm, he vowed to keep the foundation solid and never allow Harrow to regain control.

Chapter 16

Vicky and Cole (he was Brandon's cousin, she'd sensed right away) were staring at the flaming entrance of Harrow Hall from the sidewalk when the magician's voice echoed from behind them.

Vicky was sure the new heat upon the back of her neck had not emanated from the flames but instead Harrow's words.

"Brandon is dead, sweet Victoria."

They whirled around, and what they saw brought a surge of explosive dread into Vicky's heart, seizing all of her muscles at once and paralyzing her. The people from the bus – Harrow's soldiers – formed a circle around their master in the middle of the road. The rest of the road, for as far as they could see, was filled with legions of fleshless creatures that had once been human, their clothes tattered and faces mashed, their eyes lolling and tongues drooping, their hair charred and smoking as if they'd just stepped off a pyre.

Shoving his way through the rows of the undead was a familiar foe, a gleaming pitchfork in hand.

"Is this not a fitting encore, ladies and gentlemen, to our wonderful show?" Harrow shouted. "How apropos that Slaughterhouse Jones, the master of once prosperous Piggery Lane, should gut his final little piggy on the road of death, her squeals to resound long after his curtain call!"

Jones staggered onto the sidewalk toward Vicky and Cole, waving his pitchfork and sending them reeling backward. His overalls were bloody, fresh red streaking his face and beard.

"Run!" Vicky screamed, but Cole held his ground on the sidewalk, seemingly ready to fight.

"We can't go – they have Brandon," he said, and Vicky could feel the inner darkness overtaking him, Harrow filling him with false confidence.

"No, Cole, please don't be stupid," she begged as Jones inched toward them, whistling a tuneless tune and thrusting his pitchfork.

"Gonna gut ya little piggies. Gonna gut ya real good, then take myself a little taste-a-that sow's brain. Bet it tastes like cake."

"Oh what a terrific bit this shall be!" Harrow exclaimed, tipping his hat. "A celebration of the coronation!"

Vicky, taking a few small steps backward, stopped abruptly upon receiving a strong signal from Jerome Hudson: *Hang on, we're almost there.*

But it was too late now, for Slaughterhouse Jones lunged at Cole with the pitchfork. Cole managed to dive out of the way, but Jones recovered quickly, pivoting and hurling the weapon into Cole's thigh, pain ripping through him with such velocity that fragments of it transferred to Vicky.

She screamed. Harrow applauded. The dead looked on with vacuous faces of blood and ruin.

Cole fell to the sidewalk, Jones moving in and laughing, but a voice rose high and commanding from somewhere down the road. "Get the fuck back!" echoed the scream, and a young woman with blue hair rushed through the curtain of smoke, followed by an old man with long white hair.

They were holding assault rifles, pointing them at Jones.

"Stay away from him!" the blue-haired woman ordered Jones, but the villain only laughed at her, then hulked over to Cole to finish–

The rapid gunfire at close range crashed in Vicky's head like mangled railroad cars, one after another after another, both the blue-haired woman and the white-haired man struggling to control the recoil.

Vicky dove onto the grass to elude the wild, fanning shots, landing hard on her chest as the fusillade persisted. When it was finally over, Cole was shouting and cursing and shaking, his hands pressed against his temples, but he was alive. Somehow he was alive.

Jones, however – there was nothing left of him but trails of black sand disappearing within the sidewalk, slithering like snakes into the cracks and whispering away.

"A most surprising appearance," Harrow pondered, pacing toward Jones's killers.

More gunfire, this time directed at Harrow, but the magician didn't melt away like Jones. The shots didn't even slow his progress.

Harrow snapped twice, and now the rifles were rising away from their keepers, lifting toward the building and disappearing within the flames, the man and woman looking bewilderedly at each other.

Vicky came to Cole's side. "Are you all right? Were you shot?"

He shook his head. "Don't worry about me – just go, get out!"

Cole was silenced by Harrow's booming shouts, his voice taking on a thunderous rattle Vicky had never heard before. "It is time now for one last display of magic!" He made a slow circle, closely regarding his zombie battalion. Somewhere up high on the building, a window exploded as if to herald the chaos. "One final show for the Spirits, and then the world shall be ours to claim!"

Chapter 17

Jerome stared through the doorless frame into the fiery realm within, wondering if his latest vision would guide him or mislead him all the way to the gates of Hell.

Waiting there for a few moments that glistened with terror, he knew this would be the end. Either way, Heaven or Hell, this was it for a life that had begun in the Lower Ninth Ward, a life that had survived Vietnam, a life that had been incomplete until Elise and Jennie came into it. His life.

Now he was ready to sacrifice his life, to lay it down for a cause found late and embraced.

Back on the entry road, as they'd approached the intersection, the vision had come to Jerome. A vision of Jennie. He'd only been able to see her face, but she'd looked peaceful and happy and healthy; gone was the pallid face that had marked her dying months, its vigor and color restored.

"He's too powerful, Daddy," Jennie had said. "He controls the living and the dead."

"So how do I beat him, baby?" Jerome had asked, ignoring Sky's urges to disregard his visions, ignoring even his own fears that Harrow was outdueling him again.

Yet he hadn't been able to ignore Jennie, his confidence that their connection was real growing steadily.

"You won't be able to kill him if you're alive," Jennie had informed, "and you can't kill him if you're dead, either. But there's a place between life and death, a powerful place."

Jerome squeezed his fists tight, forced his eyes shut, took a few steps toward the flames, but then he stopped. He couldn't do it, couldn't kill himself unless he was absolutely positive Harrow wasn't tricking him.

Smoke filled his lungs. Heat charged away from the building, fanning outward and singeing his skin.

Jerome was moving backward now, fearing for Sky's and Ki's lives. He'd told them what to do, promising them he'd received a vision from his daughter that explained how to defeat Harrow, maintaining his faith in the vision even after Sky insisted it was another deception.

Luckily, while Jerome had hijacked the car earlier, Sky and Ki had possessed the wherewithal to grab a pair of assault rifles from the SUV. And Jerome had been confident in sending them to war, fully convinced for the first time that their combined forces would destroy Harrow's army (especially considering Sky's previously latent gift).

And if Ki and Sky could provide just enough distraction, Jerome could access that place of which Jennie had spoken.

"I need to do this. Trust me to do this. And once you get over there, tell the firefighters to look for a girl inside Harrow Hall – they need to get her out," Jerome had told Sky and Ki in their final moment together. Then he'd shouted at them to go, get on with it, get moving, hold nothing back, and they'd hurried around the corner and up the street toward Harrow Hall, rifles in hand, looking back often at Jerome. They'd been his friends, his family, and he'd sent them into war.

Now he could only pray he'd made the right decision. Harrow had never tried to fool him with a vision of Jennie or Elise speaking to him before, but Jerome, aching with a new wave of dread, kept wondering if the necromancer had gotten the better of him again, just as he'd gotten the better of Willy and Rosa and Bu, just as he'd gotten the better of Vicky Eldridge and all the others he'd taken, just as he'd gotten the better of people like Willy's father for centuries.

"Time for you to die, bastard," Jerome murmured, taking a single step toward the flames, then another, the heat warning him to stay away, but he risked another step and another, his skin sizzling with pre-burn pain, a pain known to anyone who's ever lowered a hand too close to a candle.

Jerome put an arm over his face, took another step, and now the pain was too much to keep creeping up to it. He had to do this, make a decision, now or never, and he was running, sprinting toward the flames, into the building, this was it, he'd made up his mind and now he would die, *fuck, this is the big one*, he thought, but it was a thin, mindless consideration as the pain tore into him, assaulting every pore, overwhelming, the flames enveloping him, smoke pouring down his throat.

He was fully submerged in the fire now, but remarkably he wasn't on fire – or at least it didn't feel like he was on fire anymore – the pain lessening, yes, yes, miraculously it was diminishing, his body going blissfully cold.

This was it, the in-between place Jennie had described.

It's real. It's really real.

Jerome imagined himself in a giant stove, a piece of meat about to be cooked up and served on somebody's dinner table, the smell of his smoking flesh mouth-watering to a family of hungry cannibals. There was also another smell, a stronger one, the stench of death. It followed Jerome as he navigated a massive room, persisting through the flames of a burning theater, until finally Jennie spoke to him again.

"You have to take the fire, Dad! Hurry! You don't have much time!" she urged, and Jerome noticed a blue flaming ball up on the stage, a vicious butane-torch-looking flame with three orange rings spinning around it. Hovering above a glass pedestal, it seemed to be waiting for someone to lay claim, a rightful owner.

Jerome rushed up to the stage and reached for the talisman, bracing for the summit of agony, but the flaming mass was frigid, almost untouchable. Gritting through the new burn, Jerome lifted it up, surprised by its heaviness, wondering when the miracle window would close and he'd finally drop dead.

Behind him, the curtains had collapsed and were burning to ashes like scraps of newspaper in a hearth. From the balcony came a chorus of whispers and hisses. In the front row, a two-masked theater performance sign rested upon the only seat that had been momentarily spared, the remainder of the seating section afire, flames closing in around the briefly surviving chair, and then the sign was curled up like a scroll and taken under.

As Jerome climbed down the stage, Jennie was in his head again with more instructions. "Go back out, get to the front, find Harrow."

"Time to end this war!" Jerome screamed, a maniacal sound that bore no resemblance to his voice, scaring him but also emboldening him. The possibility of imminent hellfire stood boldly at the forefront of his mind, but he pushed past it, thinking of Sky and Ki, then of Willy and the others who hadn't made it.

He would finish their quest. He would win their war.

Chapter 18

"A contest!" Harrow exclaimed, pacing before his circle of soldiers, many of whom Vicky recognized from the bus, including the old woman who'd sat beside her, the one who'd called Harrow the master and told Vicky she would learn all kinds of magic. Now she was glaring at Vicky, her eyes biting like a winter wind.

"Whoever sets the Indian ablaze first shall be named my chief emissary in the new order. Go on now, my soldiers. Use the talents with which you were born – first one to ignite the poor old Indian wins the prize." He turned to Vicky, shot her an acid smile. "Watch closely, Victoria, and behold those who were committed to magic."

"You evil son of a bitch!" the blue-haired woman shrieked, charging at Harrow, but with two snaps of the magician's fingers she was repelled, driven backward as if smacked by an invisible vehicle.

Several of Harrow's soldiers stepped toward the old Native American man, pointing at him and uttering incantations and attempting to ensnare him in their crosshairs. One of them recited a deep demonic sounding chant, and infant flames sprouted at the ankles of the old man's pants. The undead, meanwhile, blinked emptily, awaiting the next command.

With useless desperation, Vicky tried to send confusing signals into the minds of Harrow's minions, but they were too strong, their wills rooted firmly in the darkness.

"Run. Get out of here while you have a chance," Cole groaned from the sidewalk, the pitchfork still embedded in his thigh, but Vicky couldn't leave these people. They'd risked their lives to save the prisoners trapped here, and now Vicky would do the same, even as more of Harrow's soldiers came forth, pointing and chanting.

A new voice broke through the psychotic din, abrupt and…familiar.

Vicky searched the road through the smoke. A man was running up from the intersection, carrying something that glowed brightly blue, about the size of a softball.

"Stop! Leave them alone!" the man shouted, and Vicky knew who he was, knew it by his voice.

Jerome had finally made it.

At the sight of Jerome rushing toward them, Harrow stalked past his soldiers and the old man, who had kicked the flames at his pant legs dead.

"Arrived has the time of your death, fool!" Harrow snapped his fingers and produced a flaming sword, brandishing it at Jerome like a medieval fiend. "You should have chosen immortality!"

"Get away from him, Jerome!" Vicky screamed, hardly able to watch, for she had brought him here and would be solely responsible for his death.

Jerome stopped just before he reached Harrow. "You're the fool," he glared. "You can't kill someone who's already dead."

Harrow's soldiers released a collective gasp.

"Time to die, Hudson!" Harrow shouted, grinning, and the necromancer swung his sword at Jerome's head, Vicky screaming, collapsing…but the sword went straight through Jerome, not a drop of blood spilled.

"War's over!" Jerome declared, glancing skyward before hurling his final possession, which now glowed red, into Harrow's chest.

Vicky did not see the terrified realization in the magician's eyes, but she felt it swirling and roiling in his blackened heart, felt it lashing out and shrieking hideously, a dying cancer, the necromancer erupting in blue flames. He fell to his knees, the sword clanking against the pavement, flames yielding to black curls of smoke that drifted up and away, the sky echoing with strident screams.

Jerome dropped to his knees as well, and simultaneously the men fell forward, good and evil lying side by side, facedown, dead. Then Harrow disappeared, not instantly but a slow fade into nothingness, Jerome's body remaining sprawled on the road.

Vicky came to Jerome, rolled him over, tried to revive him, but there was no pulse, an eerie feeling trumpeting into her heart that he really had been already dead when he'd raced up the road to take Harrow with him.

The Native American man was at Vicky's side now. He placed a hand upon Jerome's neck and shook his head. "Jerome died hero," he murmured. "Finally war over."

With shaking hands Vicky clutched her cheeks, unable to believe the nightmare was really over. She glanced behind her and down the road, expecting Harrow's soldiers to avenge their master, but they were gone, all of them, even the undead, defleshed multitudes, only his burning namesake of a building remaining – and soon that would be gone, too, the grand theater reduced to a pile of rubble.

Vicky smiled through her tears at the realization of freedom, but it was a short-lived smile, the boy she loved dominating all thoughts.

Chapter 19

Choking on the thick smoke, Brandon closed his eyes as the tidal flames neared. He thought of Vicky – Snow Globe Girl – who he'd first seen sitting in Harrow's auditorium, looking serene, angelic, perfect, a girl he hadn't wanted to disturb.

Brandon prayed she would get out somehow. He was going to die – he'd accepted that with panicked resignation – but if there was still a way out for Vicky, he prayed she would find it. His prayer wasn't long or elaborate, nothing crazy or churchy, just a few *Please-God-let-her-lives* rising from his heart, hopefully not to be ignored.

By the time the flames crawled and crackled their way to his ankles, Brandon was already unconscious, passed out from smoke inhalation.

***

Vicky introduced herself to the two people who'd come with Jerome, Sky the blue-haired woman and Ki the elderly man. They were kneeling beside their deceased friend, each squeezing one of Jerome Hudson's hands.

Tears fell down Sky's cheeks. Ki's lips quivered.

Vicky hadn't wanted to disrupt them, but she sensed the battle wasn't over, that Harrow's disappearance had only been a trick. Or maybe he'd required time to regenerate himself and would return for them. Soon. Could evil that absolute ever die, or would it manifest in some other town?

"We need to go," Vicky told them. "He could come back."

Ki shook his head solemnly. "Harrow's gone. Jerry made sure." And as he spoke Jerome's body faded just as Harrow's had, Sky flooding with tears when she realized there was nothing left of her friend.

"Hello? A little help? Still alive over here," Cole called from the sidewalk. He'd managed to drag himself a few feet closer to the road.

Vicky came over and slid her hands beneath Cole's arms, then, with help from Sky and Ki, got him to the road, no one daring to remove the pitchfork jammed in his thigh. Instead, Sky stabilized the handle as they walked to prevent additional damage.

But even as Vicky helped Cole she was thinking of Brandon, her chest tight with anguish, each drift of smoke that filled her lungs strengthening her nausea.

She prayed for Brandon's survival, but her prayers were dim and uninspired, seemingly useless. For she couldn't feel Brandon's terror or hope for her own survival anymore – only a devastating quiet from his end – so what was the point of praying? It was over for him.

He was gone.

***

Just as inexplicably as the hoards of mutilated demon-people (that's the only way Cole could describe them) had disappeared, the firemen sprang up from their brief spells of unconsciousness. They grabbed their hoses and got to work as if nothing had happened, one of them yelling at Cole and the others to, "Get back! Get back! It's not safe!"

Then the police officer came to, returning to his cruiser and shouting something into his radio.

Cole looked down at his leg. The pitchfork no longer protruded from it like a slanted dart in a board. The pain was suddenly nonexistent, the injury and weapon vanished.

With cautious relief Cole stood, bracing for a resurgence of pain, unable to accept that the nightmare was really over. Trying to grasp everything that had happened was impossible – *Just get out*, Cole told himself. *Get away from this place.*

But he couldn't leave, not without Brandon.

Eyes roaming the conflagration of Harrow Hall, Cole was overcome with dizzying dread, fear for his cousin twisting a vicious vortex in his heart. He wasn't even aware that his cell phone was ringing until Vicky alerted him (he wouldn't know until much later that she hadn't heard it but *sensed* it).

"Hel…hello?" Cole said in a flat, stupefied voice.

"Cole, I'm so glad I reached you!" Brady exclaimed. "Brandon just woke up!"

***

As Cole talked on the phone, it took Vicky a few seconds to process what her heart already knew. Then the words came, she could hear them in her head, triumphant words that rang like bells, confirmed a moment later by what Cole was saying – "He's really okay? He's talking? That's amazing!" – and now Vicky felt lightheaded with elation. She dropped to the pavement, leveling a hand against her chest.

"Thank God," she kept murmuring, the tears unpreventable as she watched firemen attacking the flames with arcs of water.

When Cole pocketed his phone and relayed the news to Vicky, she leaped into his arms and clung to him. Later she would marvel at the absence of his injury, the damage caused by Slaughterhouse Jones miraculously undone.

Still embracing Cole, Vicky glanced over her shoulder at Harrow Hall, a theater where she and Brandon had been tormented by darkness and its near infinite magic. But even in the depths of the dark – seemingly unreachable voids of misery and agony ruled by the coldest, most ruthless monsters – light can always penetrate the desolation.

Soon Harrow Hall would be razed, another realm of darkness defeated by the light. The victory hadn't been without sacrifices, as in any war, but in the end darkness had fallen.

"You guys should get out of here," Cole instructed Vicky, Sky, and Ki. "If the cops ask, I'll tell them you were residents who saw the fire and came to see what was happening. But if you stay any longer, they'll think you had something to do with it."

"Yeah, let's split," Sky said, and the three of them were off, leaving Harrow Hall to burn behind them.

On her way down the road toward the intersection, Vicky discovered a single item waiting for her on the sidewalk, an object she would keep forever as a symbol that, with a little luck, the right people joining forces, and a guiding hand from above, good magic always trumps dark magic.

Lying flat on that crumbling sidewalk was Victoria Eldridge's childhood wand.

Epilogue

The thunder was rolling a little closer, weather warnings scrolling across the bottom of the television screen. Listening to the gentle patter of rain against the roof, Vicky stood before the living room mirror in her blue prom dress, anxious flutters coursing through her. If someone had told her this time last year that she would go to prom with a boy from Ohio, she might have assumed that person to be wrecked on drugs.

But fate had seemingly intervened last summer, her future rerouted and set upon a new course, one she sensed would fulfill her in ways that wouldn't have been possible on her former path.

The doorbell rang moments later, and even though Vicky knew who she'd find waiting for her, thoughts of Harrow were always evoked by the sound of that bell. Irrationally, Vicky swallowed hard as she peered through the living room window, her mind imprinted with the cold expectancy that had lurked in Harrow's eyes less than a year earlier.

But this time Brandon was waiting for her on the porch, settled snugly into a crisp blue suit, flowers in hand. His hair was cut short for the occasion upon special request, accentuating the vibrant green of his eyes, and Vicky stood there for a few moments in the foyer, smiling at the thought of how much she loved him, remembering last night and how close they'd come to…but they'd both agreed to wait. It was better to wait, she'd said, breathless, the stars blinking down on them. Gathering his T-shirt, Brandon had promised he'd wait for her as long as she wanted. Just being with her was all that mattered to him – he didn't care what they did as long as they did it together, though he sometimes asked if he could draw her naked and see if her clothes magically fell off, just Brad being Brad, she'd come to learn.

Vicky pulled open the door to the scent of rain, Brandon's face lighting with a smile. "You look amazing," he said.

She framed his face with her hands, taking him in, wishing times like these wouldn't end. "You, too, Brad, even without the hockey hair."

They kissed, thunder rumbling across the sky, and then he offered her the bouquet. "Bad luck to make a goalie cut his hair," he grinned, producing a blue-white corsage and slipping it onto her wrist. "You took away my mojo. Now I'm just a dumbass with too many flowers."

They shared in momentary laughter and oddly nervous talk, a jag of lightning dancing along the western clouds. A rising wind played warmly upon their faces; the rain intensified. It seemed to Vicky as if some happening of great importance would transpire, as if the clouds would clear to reveal a message. But that was how being with Brandon always made her feel, lifted and anticipatory of magic, not the stunning/flourishing kind but the intrinsic magic of love. To have found him in the world, a coin in the endless sands – was it not magic?

Glancing behind him, Brandon regarded the umbrella he'd brought from his car and leaned against the porch railing. "How about I just get my sketchbook and draw a sunny day?"

"Only in emergencies," she reminded him, and they kissed for a long while on the porch as the storm moved in, eventually ducking inside to avoid the wind-slanted rain.

In the foyer they held each other silently, listening to the storm and savoring a familiar intimacy which obviated words and allowed for moments of absolute inseparability, even when they weren't together. Vicky hoped they would never lose this connection, for it inspired her in the darkest moments, the ones where memories of Harrow threatened to dominate. Whenever she found herself listening too closely on sleepless nights, whenever she feared Harrow's return in the quietude of an empty house, she needed only to reach out to Brandon and take comfort in his unfaltering embrace, regardless of how many miles separated them. Sometimes she would fall asleep to the warmth of his whispered assurances, telling her she was safe and that he would always be there, describing to her the night he'd first seen her in Harrow Hall and thought she looked like a girl in a snow globe.

Harrow hadn't brought only miseries, it turned out. He really had given Vicky's father five hundred thousand dollars in lottery money, or maybe he'd simply taken credit for Pete Eldridge's fortunes. Regardless, her father had replenished her college fund and invested the remaining money wisely, swearing off gambling forever. After Vicky had come back to him last August, he'd promised he would never hurt her again. Now he was back to teaching full-time, his current position bringing him to a college over an hour away.

That meant a lot of driving and time apart from his daughter, but it also meant much alone time for Vicky and Brandon, time they spent watching movies and playing video games and just talking (some occasions conventionally and others silently). Vicky had taught him to cook a few meals, and Brandon had taught her how to skate, but the most enjoyable of all their activities was magic shows (the light ones, of course, with cards and quarters, never any drawings of real-life stuff or attempts to initiate silent communication with others).

Tonight would be their latest memory, another chapter in what Vicky hoped would be a very long story featuring the adventures of Victoria Eldridge and Brandon Joutel, two kids who hadn't known their strengths until they were thrown together amidst darkness and tested by its evils.

Still holding her in the foyer, Brandon was at it again, dispatching new offers to her: *Are you sure you don't want me to draw a nice sunset for you? It's not too late. I can kick this storm's ass for you.*

Save your strength, she shot back. *You're gonna need it tonight.*

***

At the conclusion of his first solo shift with a smalltown police department, Cole searched back through his night and recalled a largely uneventful shift – an animal complaint that had amounted to nothing; his first traffic stop (he'd let the guy off with a warning); a few suspicious vehicle reports – nothing compared to guarding an abandoned mental institution invaded by a necromancer set on killing and chaos.

Cole sometimes wished he could share his story with the world, but he, Vicky, and Brandon had agreed that no one would believe them. Even as the fire had roared that August day, Cole had found himself unable to accurately report what had happened, stifled by the fear of being ridiculed and then terminated, never again to be considered for an authority position.

The fire marshal had determined the blaze to have been caused by an electrical malfunction, cased closed. No one beyond a handful of survivors knew what had really happened, and Cole had submitted his resignation via email that night, shortly after visiting Brandon in the hospital and learning things that would keep him mystified for the rest of his life.

On his way out of the police station, Cole walked with a confident bounce to his step. Things were good, he thought, really good. He'd finally earned a badge. His girlfriend had become his fiancée. Brady had gotten into Ohio State. And Brad had been like a different person since emerging from the coma and meeting Vicky for the first time in "real life", no longer a partying, immature little creep but a transformed young man who had endured horrors that made him appreciate life. Now he and Vicky were an item (Brad had begun throwing the "L" word around, for which Cole always ribbed him). But they shared an undeniable connection, and Cole could see the big L in their eyes, especially when they held hands and talked with Cole about their ordeal. Even Brady didn't know the full truth, but it would remain that way, at least for now.

Maybe one day they would give up the story, but not yet. As Brad had so cleverly put it once, when life gives you a few minutes of cruise control, don't hit the brake, dude.

***

A handful of years before his death inside the burning coffin of Harrow Hall, Jerome Hudson had dictated in his will that his remaining money be distributed among four organizations dedicated to serving the people of the Lower Ninth Ward. He'd assumed then that he would die quietly, unhappily, most likely in his lonely bed on a dreary night – or perhaps slumped over at the end of the Canal Nine Tavern bar, his fingers wrapped around a farewell glass of whiskey. A sentinel dead at his dismal post, old McGreevy wiping the bar around him.

But Jerome hadn't died quietly. Looking through the windows separating his new and old homes, he saw what he'd fought two wars for, saw the people and the places of his former life on the other side. Some of those people were happy and healthy, Sky and Ki among them, enjoying prosperity and achieving positive daily momentum. But in the Lower Ninth Ward things were bad, really bad, the storm named Kat to which Harrow had alluded that late night in the alley having devastated the city from end to end. The loss of life was unimaginable, and many people were still unaccounted for, probably never to be accounted for. Much of the LNW was leveled and forgotten, including Jerome's old house, his friends and neighbors (the ones who'd survived) abandoned but not forsaken.

Because as hopeless as life seemed for the survivors, people who'd lost everything, people who couldn't see beyond the ruins of their city, Jerome prayed they could somehow know this wasn't the end. It was a miserable, wretched thing, it was life at its cruelest, but it wasn't the end. On the other side of the windows were people praying for them to persevere, to look past the perpetually bleak sky and glimpse the stars that always shined for them.

Jerome knew too well the pain of loss. He could remember it vividly, but like a memory of physical pain, it had faded since his reunification with his girls, Elise and Jennie, who'd been shining all along for him in the night sky. They'd watched him through the windows to the other side and hoped to guide him with their light and prayed for his soul, just as Jerome now prayed for those ensnared in darkness.

Feeling Elise's hand on his shoulder, Jerome turned from the windows and eased into her embrace. Elsewhere in the house that was the city, Jennie was with her man, soulmates reconnected.

"You don't need to keep looking – you'll be there soon enough," Elise whispered, sensing Jerome being drawn back to the windows. For many in this place it was easier to never look through the windows at their former homes, but Jerome felt an eternal obligation to New Orleans – an obligation that had led to a recent request for him to return, temporarily, and guide as many as he could reach.

Lingering in Elise's arms, thinking deeply about his imminent mission, Jerome wondered if perhaps someone had journeyed down from the Great City during his most desperate hours, someone who'd brought Willy to him that momentous night at Canal Nine.

Probably not, but maybe. All that really mattered was that Jerome had helped spare the rest of the world from the darkness ravaging New Orleans, darkness caged like an animal, waiting to be released upon humanity.

But light had won the battle – this battle – light triumphing over darkness, good over evil, both on a grand scale and a personal level as well, at least for Jerome. Since the deaths of his girls he'd searched without success for meaning in his life, but with a group of strangers-turned-family he'd not only found purpose but salvation.

KEVIN FLANDERS

MEET THE AUTHOR

A lifelong resident of Massachusetts, Kevin Flanders has written over
ten novels and multiple short stories. In 2010, he graduated from
Franklin Pierce University with a degree in mass communications, then
served as a reporter for several newspapers.

When he isn't writing, Flanders enjoys spending time with his family
and two dogs, playing ice hockey, and traveling to a new baseball
stadium with his father each summer. He also takes part in several
functions and mentors student writers, currently serving as a guest
instructor at David Prouty High School in Spencer, MA.

But no matter where Flanders travels or who he meets along the way,
he's always searching for inspiration for the next project.

The author resides in Monson, MA.

For more information about upcoming works, visit
www.kmflanders.wordpress.com.

UP NEXT

INSIDE THE ORANGE GLOW
Feb. 2016

… He had to get inside, had to find a way to keep from crumbling. But as he started toward the house, a presentiment whisked a deep chill through his bones. He thought of the groaning tree and the fleeing birds, and somehow – impossibly yet unmistakably – he sensed the evil that was coming for him.

LASER TAG
Feb. 2016

…I once again find it important to remind myself that I arrange the game not because I enjoy it. Laser Tag is a process that must be completed, as basic a necessity as inhalation and exhalation.

I have been robbed, lied to, deprived of my only friend, subjected to the darkness – and so I offer these miseries to a world that has so carelessly visited them upon me.

PREVIOUSLY

BURN, DO NOT READ!
Jan. 2016

…Many hours later, when morning finally came around with its welcoming light, the grandfather clock's chiming song heralded the

arrival of a new day. Children would sit restlessly in churches. Travelers would begin their journeys. The expected and the unexpected would accept their assignments without question.

And a new family would move into a little house in the middle of the big woods, its story not yet told.